Advance Praise

"Like the best speculative fiction, *You Will Win The Future* had me vacillating between feeling that the world described was quite familiar and then trying to reassure myself that it was a preposterous exaggeration. If this isn't our world, quite, it certainly shines a light on and amplifies our world's tendencies. I traveled along with these sincere, questioning characters and found myself so suspicious and fearful—yet ultimately hopeful that there may still be people who can use technology's inhuman tools to return us to a more human state."—**Peter Rock**, author of *My Abandonment*, adapted into the award-winning movie *Leave No Trace*

"Visionary!"—**Sarah Murray**, founder of Place Technologies

"Something rare: a software development drama that escalates into a pensive allegory for the gamification of capital and the subjugated positions many American cities are in because of it. Think Fortnite for real estate."—**Matt Dan**, artist and co-founder of Night Time Science

"This city blazes a new path of equitable economic opportunity."—**Holly Balcom**, PDX YIMBY housing advocate

"Fascinating and satiric."—**Cornelius Swart**, director and producer of *Priced Out: 15 Years of Gentrification in Portland, Oregon*

"Arthur's book gives an insightful perspective on the transformative power of technology, and the urgent need for those of us working in the tech industry to put our talents to use for democracy and equality, not extraction and manipulation."—**Petter Joelson**, co-founder and co-director of Digidem Lab, a nonprofit based in Sweden developing methods and tools for participatory democracy

"A reinvention of how technology and civics (and really everything) intersect."—**Mike Merrill**, the world's first publicly traded person

"Explores big ideas about what it means to be a citizen when individuals only in it for themselves are allowed to make the rules for everyone. Thoughtful, speculative takes on finance, healthcare, and modern work culture."—**Mike Vogel**, writer and filmmaker, creator of *Phrenic*

"A rare civic-minded SF novel that doesn't depend on the crutch of a jury-rigged dystopia to bear the weight of its social critique."—**David W. Edwards**, former Oregon legislator and the creator of *Nightscape*

"Equal parts terrifying and optimistic."—**Michael Heald**, author of *Goodbye to the Nervous Apprehension*

"Persistently intelligent and insightful."—**Justin Hocking**, author of *The Great Floodgates of the Wonderworld*, winner of the 2015 Oregon Book Award for Creative Nonfiction

"An ambitious debut novel that explores the collision of technology and money, and asks whether it's possible to redefine both for the betterment of all."—**David Wolman**, author of *The End of Money*

"Realistically compelling novel about a possible path to a more just future."—**Carl Abbott**, professor emeritus of Urban Studies and Planning at Portland State University and author of *Imagining Urban Futures: Cities in Science Fiction and What We Might Learn from Them*

YOU WILL WIN THE FUTURE

YOU WILL WIN THE FUTURE

ARTHUR SMID

DESIDERATA • PORTLAND, OREGON

YOU WILL WIN THE FUTURE
FIRST DESIDERATA EDITION
© 2020 by Arthur Smid

All rights reserved, including the right to reproduce this book or portions of it, in any form. For permissions inquires, please contact smidarthur@gmail.com. Desiderata is a micropress created by the author for the purpose of connecting with readers, literary agents and publishers. Special thanks to Gorham Printing in Centralia, Washington. For information about discounts for bulk purchases, sales promotions, fundraising and educational needs, contact the author online.

www.arthursmid.com

Library of Congress Control Number: 2019909476
ISBN 978-1-7331108-4-6 (paperback)
ISBN 978-1-7331108-3-9 (ebook)

This is a work of fiction. Names, characters, places, and incidents are either products of the author's imagination or are used fictitiously.

Cover and book design by Arthur Smid

Printed and bound in the United States of America

1 3 5 7 9 10 8 6 4 2

For Maureen Culligan

YOU WILL WIN THE FUTURE

Thank you, Ryan!

Arthur

I

THE CITY SHOOK and cracks ripped through the street. A jagged hole broke open across his path and Shane ran to the sidewalk as the cornice from an old building fell directly ahead of him. Portland was in ruins. He felt the power to create in this disaster. A city reduced to construction and finance. A city made by software. All humanity could be joined to remake their world. Shane thought this city was more than a collection of structures, it was a form of intelligence. On-screen his character ran back into the street and text popped up: WHAT ARE YOU GOING TO DO? Two buttons: LOOT or HELP.

"Cool," Bradley said.

Shane glanced at his boss.

"So what are you going to do?"

Shane looked back to the screen. "Help."

He clicked and three characters appeared: Police, Builder, and Investor. The city was a creation of thought. It was a creation of the world. Bounded by laws, natural and civil, but created. People thinking of their city. An idea built of steel and concrete, copper and glass, plant and animal seated at the confluence of the Willamette and Columbia, upon a seat of commerce, a coin spinning in the air. This was the ultimate game. He quickly selected Builder. He was then back in the street of a demolished city, wandering through the rubble. Shane saw a brick glowing with a heartbeat red pulse. The moment his character touched the brick a pleasant chime sounded and a tiny brick appeared in his cache along the bottom of the screen. Did this game have a score? He wondered if it could be won by someone, a team maybe.

"Congratulations," Bradley said. "You just made one hundredth of a cent."

It was Shane's first day at work. The woman seated next to him had introduced herself when he arrived at nine. Tall and strong, she wore overalls with one strap unbuckled. Her blue hair cut asymmetrically.

"You'll be working with me. I'm Rebecca."

Her presence seemed like gravity for the guys. When the producer called everyone to the center of the room and fourteen people stood in a circle facing each other, she was the only woman in the room. Shane caught himself turning to see her reaction as Aydin announced that investors would be in to check out the place on Friday. He recognized Aydin—the co-founder and systems architect. His Egyptian ethnicity further distinguished him from the group. Everyone else was white except for one Indian guy. No one said where the other founder was, and yet Sebastian was the person most gamers associated with the company. He had become the face of Makner.

Bradley stood beside Shane and showed him how to open an account on Cityzen. The game was in alpha testing and only employees had access. It would be a massively multi-player online sandbox game. Bricks, wood, glass, steel, and concrete were units of account. Similar to opening a bank account, it promised security. People could build anything in the ruined city, and when a player invested their money the structure became permanent. The money was held in an index fund that tracked the five hundred top stocks, regularly beating the managed funds by saving on fees—and staying ahead of inflation. Bradley joked, "You ever play a game that beats the stock market?"

Shane shook his head, smiling. He glanced at Rebecca, their desks perpendicular to each other, the light from the screen illuminating her face as she coded floating beam animation.

Bradley clapped his hand on Shane's shoulder.

"You made the team."

The work he'd done making indie games had cinched it. Shane launched a startup with his best friend when they were fifteen and seventeen. Jason was two years older, and his parents had immigrated from Taiwan. After making three games in a decade, Shane thought, by now, Playland would be enough to live on. Shane and his girlfriend stretched to pay the key deposit and first and last month's rent for a two bedroom in the southeast. He told her that searching by neighborhood was the only way to find what they wanted. You had to know what you wanted and then you could get it, you could really talk it up because you believed. That was your future. It was an optimistic way to deal with the uncertainty of the hiring process—and Elsie believed him.

"You see that," Bradley said.

"What?"

"That animation." Bradley pointed to a character walking in the game. "Make it look good by Friday at four."

Rebecca looked over at him.

Shane noticed and their eyes met briefly before she leaned into her screen.

"Sebastian is going to be in to show the investors and so you need to make that animation look production ready." Bradley stepped away, talking as he rounded the corner and stood at his desk opposite Shane. "The way the character moves over the debris. Every step is the exact same. There's no collision detection, no shadowing. You good?"

"Yeah, I got this!"

Bradley had his instructions too, from Aydin.

Give him access, give him his task, and leave him be.

When Shane opened the codebase, he realized the interview wasn't over.

Rebecca left at five and over the next two hours people from the other teams left the office. Elsie texted and Shane apologized that he couldn't take her out for dinner like they'd planned. Shane said he would help her. He kept working. Bradley stayed on too, the top of his head visible above the other side of the screen. It was after seven when he called out, "You eat?"

A link to a menu appeared in Shane's chat window.

Bradley stood up and said, "Monty, are you eating?"

A voice from across the room: "No. I'm dug in here."

Bradley shrugged and sat back down.

"Where is Cab?" he said to the room.

Monty's voice: "He's working from Tech Plex."

"What's so great about that?"

"Cheryl."

"Tell him I miss him." He looked at Shane and said, "Say it's for Bradley Sabin. She'll know what I want. And you can get whatever."

Shane dialed and said, "I'm placing an order for Bradley Sabin."

"Good to hear from you again, Bradley!"

Shane didn't correct her. She had an Italian accent and spoke quickly, "One diablo wood fired brick oven pizza with an additional topping of ricotta meatball, and a kale caesar salad."

"Uh." Shane looked over his monitor at Bradley's devil's peak hairline. "Yeah, and a salsiccia."

"You will be wanting something to drink?"

Shane asked, "Bradley, did you want something to drink?"

"Nah, we're stocked."

Shane nodded and said into the phone: "No drinks, just the . . . uh, I'll get a roasted pepper salad, too."

Without time for mental math she said the price and repeated his order and even though Shane realized he was talking to a machine, he said goodbye.

The delivery guy started down the stairs, and Bradley said, "We eat." He put the food on a long, dark wood dining table and went into the kitchen and came back with silverware. Shane suspected his boss, his team leader, was a good guy. They started eating and Shane relaxed his mind from the code.

"How do you like it?" Bradley asked.

Shane nodded with his mouth full.

He chewed and swallowed and said, "It's fun."

Bradley raised his eyebrows and speared a forkful of salad.

"You are the man." He took a bite.

Shane took a bite. He had projected the time to complete his assignment, and the hours couldn't be compressed without another animator. He had heard of guys subcontracting their work to agents, artificial or otherwise, but only in desperation did he imagine that workaround.

Bradley wore earphones and on occasion exclaimed non sequiturs. Shane preferred to code in silence. He measured his questions; he worked with them in his mind until he solved them or at last, casually asked for help and led Bradley into his mental list. As the windows darkened and his concentration focused, Shane felt himself continuously solving a problem as it slipped from his grasp. It was wildly compulsive. The work was always almost done. Forever incomplete.

At nine forty-five Bradley stepped away from his desk.

"One minute," Shane said. "I'm logging out."

Bradley walked over to Shane's desk and reviewed his code in a glance.

He put his hand on his shoulder and said, "Nice."

"You think so?"

"Your foil draft will overflow," Bradley said. "Not yours. It's not your fault. This character becomes global, and it's weird, multidimensional. We solve millions of different views of the same animation. Simultaneous. Potentially. The math is hidden here."

Bradley pointed at the keyboard. "Can I show you?"

Shane rolled back in his chair on the plastic shield.

Bradley showed Shane a tool he built. "We've been using it in Sunnyvale. For a few years already. The customizations I made."

"I'd like to use that."

"Oh yeah, it's yours! We're building this together."

"I mean now."

Bradley tilted his head and looked around the room.

"I'm going to trust you. You know how to lock a door, right?"

"Yes."

"I'll show you how to arm the security and then I need to scoot."

Shane wanted this to work. The internal tools were new to him—revelations really. A word in the code could refer to hundreds of lines, an entire script. And comments were sparse. It was trial and error. Makner's intranet message boards. All the time this required was an ultimate barrier, a wall stacking up continuously, updating with new languages, inserting higher levels of learning upon a foundation already unscalable for most people. A single line. A word. A code. Impenetrable really. The code compiled to ones and zeros, off or on, translating to electrons legible only to machines.

Bradley grabbed his bag and said nine was his typical end of day.

Shane stood up. "I'm happy to be here."

Bradley approached, raising his hand. High-fiving, their hands popped on contact in the air and Shane felt lucky. He liked his boss. He studied the codebase until midnight and reviewed it in his mind on the bus home. Elsie was asleep and she'd put on new lingerie to surprise him. The sight worried him; her body was emaciated, sickly. He pulled the covers over her and she stirred when he got into bed. He closed his eyes. His mind moving in first-person point of view through pixelated images.

He wanted this problem.

Shane arrived early, having slept five hours. He fired up his computer as the sun broke on the horizon. He knew how to speed his walk–run cycle. He was going to succeed. His job wasn't an accident. The software entertainment company from Sunnyvale, California had been around for as long as he could remember. He played Kastle in high school. It was a blockbuster for Makner. The founders' transformation from nonentity to wealth was summed up in their motto: Beyond Good!

"I need you to sign some papers," John said, walking up to Shane. He had topped the stairs and went straight to him. "It's standard NDA stuff."

John was the producer, and he had been an early investor. When Sebastian and Aydin were getting started, John had plonked down the money for their servers. He helped set up all the networking and hardware. It took five years to get paid back—that was years ago, and now he and his wife had a house in Portland.

"We need you to understand and agree to not talk about our proprietary technology, intellectual property, and marketing strategy." John led Shane to his office. They passed a short, stocky guy in a room next door, seated at a desk and surrounded with three monitors and two towers, two keyboards and a control panel with analog dials.

"Mornin' Monty," John said.

Monty swiveled in his chair and waved to the open door.

"You're digging in with us," John said to Shane as they entered his office.

He offered a chair to Shane. "After leaving you can't use our proprietary technology, or start a company using the tech—or poach employees."

He gave him a sheaf of paper.

"You can take it with you if you'd like to look it over with a lawyer."

Shane flipped through the pages. He looked up when John said, "It's a non-disclosure agreement."

John sat down next to Shane. "We have people, gamers, journalists, other companies, our competitors. They can all want some part of what you'll be given here. You know fans are hard to please. Any changes to the game must be released with care."

"Oh, I totally know."

"So are you going to sign it now, or take it with you?"

Shane took the pen.

"It's not a big deal," John said. "Initial page three, four, and sign the end."

The dining table was large enough to seat fifteen and most of the office had gathered by twelve thirty. Two caterers served a hot lunch of lamb meatballs in cream sauce, fingerling potatoes, and roasted brussels sprouts with balsamic vinegar. John had landed on a twice weekly, Tuesdays and Thursdays, all-hands lunch. Shane sat down across from Bradley and Rebecca. The teams clustered together, and he saw Aydin sitting with the architecture guys. Shane studied Bradley and said, "You look like Brian Sabin."

"I know he's funny. You know how I know?"

"Everyone knows?"

"He's my brother."

Shane was taken aback and Bradley laughed. His older brother was famous.

"Was he making people laugh when you were kids?" John asked.

He sat next to Bradley. "I love Brian."

"My dad, sure."

"I bet you have a good time together," Shane said.

Bradley nodded.

Looking at Shane, he said, "Did you use the compression algorithm for lossless render?"

Rebecca told Shane how he could improve response time. Shane figured that Bradley and Rebecca were older than him—not by much, but they had accumulated experience. The edge given by age was slippery. Being young carried the promise of his future potential. But if he didn't grow into his power, he was toast. Someone younger was going to work more and for less—and so no one relaxed into their jobs. It seemed like everyone was young. But Aydin and John were senior, both in their forties. John had stepped into the role of nurturing, company father. He asked Shane, "You know Sebastian?"

"I've never met him."

"You will," Bradley said.

"Sebastian's dad made video games," John said. "And he had a collection of cabinet arcade games in their garage. Twelve games! Seb invited popular kids to play for free. For the rest, all games cost a quarter. At school he carried around a folder full of king-size candy bars. He was generous too, he gave candy to his friends."

"He was a chubby kid," Bradley said.

"Sebastian loves his father," John said. "He learned from the master."

"He worked at LucasArts," Bradley said. "His dad owns none of the IP he spent his life developing."

"For Sebastian, being CEO is an accomplished fact," John said. "He's going to conquer the world—his version of it anyway."

Shane thought everything would be different if he was born into the industry, like Sebastian; if he'd learned from the master, he would be CEO now. His father wanted him to open up, to broaden his horizons. Shane told his dad he was a game designer. He made games. That was his life. He was always going to make games. Shane's father worked for a retail supermarket company with over one hundred and thirty stores and more than five billion in revenue and he couldn't understand why his son did all that work on his computer for free. And most people would've let it go after years of scraping by, but Shane was single-minded. He was a *game designer*.

Shane returned from the restroom and saw Rebecca raising her desk to a standing position. Bradley stood and his desktop whirred smoothly up to meet him. "How much does it cost to have a lawyer look something over?" Shane asked.

"What did you do?" Rebecca said.

"You sign it," Bradley said, "if you want to work here."

"Yeah," Rebecca said. "No biggie."

"Anything you develop here belongs to Makner," Bradley said. "It's not complicated."

"How do I raise my desk like that?"

He stood at his computer until after Bradley left at nine, and then he went to the lounge with his laptop and reclined on the couch and kept working until his alarm notified him. The last bus was fifteen minutes out. Shane put his work away, armed the building, and locked the doors.

The light was on in the kitchen. A covered plate of food on the table. He put it in the fridge and turned out the light. Shane carefully pushed open their bedroom door and took off his clothes and lay down beside Elsie without waking her. The buzz woke him. He nudged his device and the alarm stopped.

It was six a.m. Elsie stirred, flopping her arm across his lap.

"Don't get up," he said.

"I want to eat with you."

"No. Sleep sleep, sweety."

He kissed her and got out of bed and walked naked into the kitchen. He took the plate out of the fridge and put it in the microwave. By the time the dinger sounded he had pulled on his clothes. He bolted his food, took his bag and longboard from beside the door, and then he set it back against the wall. He went and silently opened the bedroom door. Elsie was sitting in the center of their bed naked, knitting. She hid a gray blur of yarn behind her back and said, "You're not supposed to see this."

Shane fell onto the bed and kissed Elsie. She lay her body down and embraced him, wrapping her legs around his waist and pulling him tight, and then she said, "But you have to go?"

"I love you, baby."

"You do?"

"I do. I do love you."

From a nipple of water burbling in a bronze bowl pillared upon the sidewalk, he leaned down and drank. His longboard underfoot, Shane pushed with his right and stood. Looking up, the sky reflected on the windows above. The sky yellow. The smoke from wildfires had blown in from Canada and Washington, lingering over the city, making it impossible to see Mount Hood. He had read the health advisory. Shane wasn't sure if he felt the smoke in his chest or if it was the thought of small particles that could get in the lungs and enter his bloodstream. He could feel something when he breathed. It hurt a little in his chest. Shane knew that was real.

He skated through an opening in traffic. After growing up in the Woodstock neighborhood where people had front and back yards, old single-family homes on quiet streets, Shane finally had a place to be downtown, a job, where he was needed. He rolled up to a renovated building in Chinatown. Ascending three steps to the door inside a stone archway, he buzzed through and walked up the staircase to the second floor. Rebecca was standing at her desk with her headphones on. He set his bag down and put his board against the brick wall.

"What are you listening to?" Shane asked.

Rebecca removed one earphone, resting it behind her ear.

"What are you listening to?" he said.

"Hydrophones on the ocean floor, NOAA stuff."

Shane opened his eyes wide.

"The ocean is filled with sound," she said, "streaming online."

"Does it sound good?"

She hoisted up her headphones and handed them to Shane. He stood beside her and listened to the ambient sounds of turbulent fluctuations.

"You hear the ocean background noises," Rebecca said, "and intermittent stuff like storms or ships."

"Do you ever hear whales?"

"That's why I listen, I'm listening for the whales."

"So cool! Tell me when a whale comes by. Tell me, okay?"

"Sheesh. You'll be the first know, Shaner."

"You live close in?" Bradley asked, referring to the longboard.

"I'm right near the community college on Southeast Division."

"You ride that hella far."

"I've been taking transit, skating the gaps between."

"You're so spry."

Shane shrugged.

"Seriously, you're fit." Bradley pointed at Shane's screen. "Code is human powered."

"Way."

Shane liked the mental challenge of his work. It was encountered on-screen, but ideas were primary. And in that sense, he was always working. Moving through the world, he found his mind generating results unexpectedly. That's why he loved skating—and sex used to be so productive. But she believed in his dream. He couldn't have done it without her. He called her from the lounge and they talked for a few minutes before Shane said he'd miss dinner again.

"Do you have to?"

"I did the math. If I'm going to finish this project it will take me around fifty hours. I'm pushing to make it, baby. I'm almost home."

That night at nine, Bradley walked by Shane's desk.

"Listen," he said. "I'll give you a ride home."

"It's okay. I get work done on the bus."

"No. Work's over. I'm the boss."

They crossed the bridge and saw hundreds of people along the river celebrating the Fourth of July. Bradley dropped him off at his apartment building and said goodbye, the fireworks booming in the distance.

Thursday, after the all-hands lunch a moving crew arrived and John unlocked the office next to his and went in. He left the door open and a moment later Shane saw him leave to walk downstairs with the movers.

Shane looked across the room at the open door.

"What's in there?" he said to Bradley and Rebecca.

"That's Sebastian's room," Bradley said.

"Don't go in there," said Rebecca.

John returned, passed their desks, and walked through the office to Sebastian's room and ten minutes later the movers entered with a conference table and carted it across the wood floor.

His hours for the week hadn't even exceeded fifty when Shane completed his assignment Thursday night. Bradley walked over and glanced at the code. "Did you run it through the Makner Efficiency

Tool? With MET, we circumvent most of the peer code review. Once you've 'met' the tool's requirements, it's likely your code is production ready. May I?"

Shane stepped aside.

After a quick flurry of keystrokes, Bradley initiated the tool. The screen filled with warnings and violations and a seventy-one grade.

"Ouch. Shane, you've got work to do."

"You and John wrote this tool?"

"I wrote it. He reviewed the finished product, more or less."

"What earns a passing grade?"

"Ninety-two or higher."

Shane faced the screen and inhaled, his shoulders rising and dropping as he exhaled slowly.

"Well, I'll leave you to it."

Bradley left the office at nine and Shane was alone. He went to the lounge and lay on the couch. When he awoke he fixed himself some cereal and then returned to his screen. It was three twenty-four in the morning. On his mobile he saw the text from Elsie, she was worried. He wrote a reply and stopped himself. It would wake her up. He scheduled it to send the message at seven o'clock and walked across the office to Sebastian's room. Unconsciously he glanced around the room and then he reached for the door handle. The metal cold on his hand, the latch didn't give. He gazed up at the ceiling beams, exposed ductwork. No, he told himself, the camera is at the top of the stairs. Back at his desk he raced to finish his work.

Shane opened his eyes and saw a bar of deodorant and a peanut butter and jelly sandwich on a white paper plate. His work station lowered to sitting, Shane looked up from his desk.

"I conked out," he said.

Bradley and Rebecca laughed.

Shane stood up. He glanced at the clock—almost nine!

"You were so cute," Rebecca said.

"You are sooo cute." Bradley laughed. "No, really, you are cute."

"Is this bad?"

"Don't worry," Rebecca said. "It's nothing."

Shane got back to work.

"Here you go."

Shane turned around and Bradley handed him a cup of coffee.

"Wow, thanks, Bradley."

He started to take a sip and paused.

Shane blew across the top and then put the edge of the cup to his lips and felt the liquid as it edged closer to his skin. It was perfect. He drank.

"I'm going to finish." Shane held his coffee in one hand and pushed a button on his desk. It began to rise.

"Think," Bradley said. "You're solving for real-time body mechanics with four cycles from strolling to running that will be seen simultaneously by millions of people—and ensuring nice smooth arcing motions from any possible camera angle. My hat is off to you, good sir. May you slay the beast!"

Twenty-six minutes before his deadline, Shane blurted, "You want to come check out my screen, I'm done."

Bradley leaned to one side of his monitor and caught Shane's eye. "No. No. You're going to present it in the lobby."

"What do I do?"

"Sebastian's coming and you're going to display the animation for him and the investors."

"Do you want me to explain the configs?"

"That shit is only for you and me—and Rebecca."

"Do I need to say anything?"

"Your name?" Bradley laughed.

II

JOHN SET UP the projector and the teams assembled at five for the presentation. Shane cleaned himself up in the restroom and stood with his team, anticipating their attention drawn to him at any moment. Sebastian walked in with a group of three men. They were older than forty, but not more than fifty. Sebastian wore a button-up shirt and stone-washed jeans and brown leather shoes so fine they looked like slippers. As he stepped to the front of the room and everyone stopped talking, Shane realized Bradley had been putting him on. This was Sebastian's show.

"I want to walk you through the city of the future. You are going to find everything you need there. To make friends, to share, to build, to dream. You are becoming a Cityzen."

The four player characters appeared on-screen. Their simple design made ethnicity and gender open to any interpretation.

"You will be playing with the world, online, where people play with or against each other. The non-linear combat of all against all. It becomes any game you want. It offers the master builder experience and the joy of destruction, and it will be a serene investment vehicle for all ages. It will be a job for some. This will be your child's first bank account. This will be the city in which they learn the value of money, how to save, to invest, to build. And it will beat the returns of managed funds. While you play with your money."

Sebastian strode before the screen, facing sixteen men, one

YOU WILL WIN THE FUTURE

woman, each of some distant European extraction except for Aydin and Krishna. Egyptian and Indian, respectively. From his laptop, John controlled a character projected on-screen. It was the Builder.

"Anyone can build structures in the game," Sebastian said. "When you begin exploring the city, the building materials appear readily. Bricks, wood, glass, concrete, and steel. You collect these as a Builder. The creation tools are amazing. . . . But the structures are vulnerable to Looters."

The view cut to a Looter picking up a sledge hammer from the rubble.

"Looters can walk off with the materials a Builder has assembled. The Police earn money for defending property. It's a very small amount, but even pennies add up with a lot of zeros on the end."

The Looter on-screen knocked material from a standing structure that had been assembled by a Builder.

"Looters that attack a structure appear on the Police map and then—if they are caught with bricks, glass, wood, concrete or steel in their account—the Looter is ghosted for a half hour. We want them coming back. The Looters can build with the materials they acquire. The bricks they find, and other things only a Looter sees. They can stack the detritus of civilization, they too can create fantastic structures. The Looters are the outsider artists within the city. We are a social network, these different people all bringing the game together.

"Each player experiences a different Cityzen. Do they prefer destroying things, fending off destroyers, or building structures—and do they want to put their quarters into a game that will earn dividends? When an Investor puts their money in the game, the amount is represented as building materials in their account. And we have the best encryption and security."

Sebastian waved his hand toward Monty, directing the group's attention to their cyber defender. Five foot tall with his shoes on, he wore blue-framed glasses. The team clapped and Sebastian smiled; his hands swung behind his back and he clasped them briefly as he walked past the screen. He placed his fingers in a pyramid pointed from his solar plexus.

"Everyone can play. And everyone has a job."

Sebastian turned and looked at each of them.

"The Builder, Police, and Looter characters are free to play. Anyone can invest time to earn in-game resources. They can even make a few fractions of a cent."

He clasped his hands loosely, palms up, at his waist, and then he opened them.

"To be an Investor, you are investing in yourself."

An Investor character appeared. Golden upon the screen. Like a divinity it floated above the streets, over the other characters strolling, striding, sprinting.

A dashboard with the account management tools slid into view. John moved the cursor across the screen and clicked. Money held in the account was displayed as virtual materials. Sebastian went on to explain how Investors could acquire building materials or buy other players' structures—and safely secure their money in the fund. Their buildings became permanent in-game edifices. Looters couldn't take stuff from them. When people began playing, they would discover building materials quickly. And then they became more difficult to find. The game funneled all players toward investing.

On-screen a Looter ran through the streets.

"Looters log on to disrupt, to subvert structures and steal unsecured material," Sebastian said. "Makner knows the online ecosystem has some bad actors. But all of them are people with computers, and they have money. Trolls are real people. They have bank accounts. With real money. We welcome them in Cityzen. Our incentives will remake even the worst behavior and make it productive. The materials to build with can be earned by collecting wood and bricks and steel from buildings throughout the city. All the buildings have been shaken, crumbled, and leveled by The Big One."

The opening animation of the earthquake downtown. Even the staff who'd seen it many times were impressed, watching the first-person view projected on a large screen. It was harrowing, and wonderful.

"A government agency telling you an earthquake is coming doesn't have the impact. For people who have never experienced an earthquake it is an abstraction. But it is not abstract to live upon the Pacific Rim. These people are all our customers. From Chile to Alaska. Japan to Indonesia and down under. Forty-four countries. Home to twenty-nine of the world's busiest shipping ports. As the focus of our global economy continues its shift from west to east, the cities of the Pacific Rim will only gain in their importance. And together, we will create the future cities of the Pacific.

"Subduction processes built the land—this whole area—and we accept that. Our challenge is really one of imagination. Which side of the bridge are you going to be on when this whole thing goes down? It's going to be a big reset button."

The screen displayed images of recent earthquakes in cities bordering the Pacific Ocean, the devastation wrought by tsunamis in the fatality zones.

"Replace seismic with another word. Catastrophe. Destruction. Death. When those tectonic plates shift along the Cascadia subduction zone, the shaking will liquify much of the land along the lower Willamette River. The structures built upon dredge soils turning to quicksand, collapsing, breaking, melting to the earth. The soils used to be in the middle of the river. Look at these liquefaction and seismic hazards across the state."

A map of Oregon.

"It's a seven hundred mile long fault with dramatic impacts one hundred miles inland. There are not enough agencies that can come to the support of all the people who will need it. The Pacific Northwest is one of the most seismically active areas in the world. When we get hit by an earthquake, people will be believers. But they have other issues, other priorities now. Earthquakes occur on a geologic timeframe. And we are only human.

"It's always a surprise.

"Even in seismically active areas. Even where people have prepared, they find they weren't prepared enough. Portland hasn't been hit by an earthquake, yet. That's great news. We have time to prepare.

"The buildings after the earthquake are not habitable. The city must be rebuilt. Why not visualize what is to come? We have reduced Portland to the elemental building blocks of the game. This is the great game, to create the city, to stabilize capital and absorb surplus labor in the creation of urban centers. Look, we modeled the ... well, the city has been destroyed, but the rubble exists upon the standing map. It's fun to see familiar landmarks transformed and rebuilt in the game. Cityzen is a sandbox game that allows people to build amazing structures. Really, it's anything that a professional architect could do."

Sebastian templed his fingers and touched his chin.

"Architecture faces a diversity problem."

He bowed his head, and then looked at the employees and investors.

"What can be done?" Sebastian walked to one side of the screen and pivoted. "The architectural tools are voice enabled. You talk to it, set the parameters, building codes and whatnot, budget, all that. The in-game virtual buildings can be rendered to architectural code as required by actual zoning laws. These valuable real-world renderings are output by our custom, licensed AI. This applied artificial intelligence completes the technical aspects to fit the player pieces to city building codes and render it as a blueprint. For a fee. Anyone can design a building and then the AI completes all the technical things that we used to have to pay real architects to do, but now: you pay Cityzen."

Monty clapped his hands and everyone began applauding. Sebastian applauded and Shane noticed the group's attention centering on the sandy-haired man who he'd seen talking with Aydin. The man smiled and then began clapping too. It was Cab. The computer scientist who had trained the learning algorithm to master building codes. He combined significant insights from neuroscience and machine learning to unlock the solution space within city codes through a powerful artificial intelligence he called Gen.

The building code was the control. Cities controlled land use through regulations, and creativity in architecture existed through finding unique solutions within the building codes, zoning restrictions and requirements. The software created multiple versions of any design—even one with all the sophistication and brute simplicity of toy blocks stacked by a four-year-old—until that configuration was within the code of the city permit; and even further, it could spin out code-compliant variations of that design with a user-friendly dashboard of digital sliders to change heights, widths, materials, budget and other things.

"It's amazing. Revolutionary. In a video game platform." Sebastian walked to the center of the room. "We will diversify the architecture industry. We will remake the entire city. This is a transition with no turning back. Architecture will never be the same. The city will look like its citizens."

The room resounded with applause and cheers from the staff.

"Anyone can be a Builder," Sebastian shouted above the noise. "We're all Cityzens!"

Sebastian held up his arms and the room fell silent.

"Only you can become an investor."

III

THE TOOLS Bradley built. The work he'd done. The money he made for the company. His workweek averaged fifty-nine hours, and there was no indication they would slow down. His heart racing, Bradley approached the back of the room where John sat unplugging cords.

"So where are we going?" he asked.

John closed his laptop. "They have some boring corporate stuff to do."

"You mentioned something about meeting with Seb and Aydin. Version two stuff?"

"Trust me." John stood. "You wouldn't want to be there."

"Actually, I have an idea for—"

"John," Aydin said, crossing the room. "We're headed to Soma. Seb is going with me. Are you taking your own vehicle?"

"I'll ride with you guys."

Bradley interjected, "The presentation was awesome."

"Impossible to tell," Aydin said and walked away.

Bradley looked at John. "It went well, right?"

"We need to see if it loosened the hold on their wallets."

Bradley inhaled through his nose sharply.

"We'll catch up with you," John said. "You going down the street?"

"Yeah."

Bradley turned and walked toward his work station. He stopped to examine Shane's monitor. His code was beautiful. It was a new body, shaped by its environment, suited for survival, without habits, disease, or the fatigue of age. Bradley smiled to himself. He looked around the room and saw Shane talking with Rebecca.

The team walked in a loose ensemble from the office to a restaurant. It was more tavern than what the menu prices would suggest, but the decor was immaculate—exposed timber beams and brick from a century past. And Bradley had learned to appreciate the steel frame reinforcing the masonry.

He turned to Shane as they waited for their drinks.

"You weren't supposed to finish."

Shane looked disoriented.

Bradley grabbed Shane's shoulders. "I'm impressed."

Adrenaline had kept Shane in stride all week and after working through the night and standing for the presentation, he could feel his body begin to protest.

"I'm not a big fan of this part of my job." Bradley sat back and placed his hand on the table. "All hires are put through the challenge. It's Aydin. His way of thinning the herd."

"It's a brain-fuck," Rebecca said. "You didn't need to finish."

"I didn't?" Shane asked. His voice was hoarse.

"Well, not exactly." Bradley turned in his seat. "They want to see how you respond. An incompetent person will complain. That's a loser. Determination beyond all. Beyond good. You get the idea."

The waiter arrived with drinks.

"You could have—and this is what *John* likes to see," Bradley said, "people who can articulate their process and ask for more time. But for the record, I'm the only one to finish in sixty-two hours."

Rebecca sipped her Bijou and the waiter returned with the rest of their drinks. Bradley looked at Shane and stood up holding his glass. "Let's drink to Shane!"

The group raised their glasses, clinking with their teammates.

"We're going to build great things," Bradley said. "We're going to build a city!"

"Speech," Rebecca shouted.

Bradley waved Shane up with one hand. "This is you."

Shane stood and looked at the group. The team waiting for him to speak. The fatigue in his throat. The glass cold in hand. "You all are amazing. I am uh here to to to make this . . . help make this . . ."

Bradley laughed.

Rebecca raised her drink. "Hear, hear!"

Shane thanked his new friends and took a long drink of Summer IPA.

Sitting down, he said, "I was going to—"

"Dude," Bradley said. "This is the beginning of history."

"Yeah," Shane said.

Rebecca side-eyed Shane and pointed at Bradley's drink. "Kool-Aid. It's his favorite drink."

"Feeling jealous? Shane beat your time by a week."

She laughed and said, "I know it's hard for you to believe, but I have a life."

Someone behind Shane rubbed his shoulders.

He shifted in his seat and saw her. "Hey, baby!"

Shane stood up and kissed her.

"This is my girlfriend, Elsie."

Her bangs above the black frame of her glasses.

"Hi, everyone!" She smiled and gave a little wave.

He gave her a hug. "You made it."

Elsie tilted her long dark hair to the side. "I'm alive."

"Hi," Rebecca said, hooking Elsie's arm. "I'm Rebecca."

Shane lay in bed watching her explore the game. The destroyed buildings creating a constantly unfolding maze as Elsie scooped up glowing items. She had studied apparel design in college and made her own clothes. Shane's parents often said she was a wonderful person. They knew she was struggling financially and they had the money to help her, but they weren't going to give it to someone who wasn't married to their son. Shane had been with her more than four years and never talked about marriage. He'd first started chatting with her when he got coffee each morning. Her smile was so real. Elsie was kind to him and she'd pick up where they'd left off the next day. Of course, she did that for all her customers, but she downloaded his games. She played video games! Elsie's character climbed a mound of debris and leapt through a broken window in a skyscraper and continued upward through a stairwell. She went to the east side of the building and they admired the pixel perfect view of Portland.

"What's that?" Shane asked. On-screen they could see what appeared to be a platform tabled out from the base of Mount Tabor. The sides sloped, it looked like a rectangular pyramid with a flat top.

"It's a temple?" Elsie said.

"Let's see what that is."

She went down the stairs, leaving the building. Elsie navigated the blocks and crossed the river on Burnside. It was the only bridge she could cross. Most had collapsed into the water, obstructing river traffic. Boats stranded between fallen bridges. There were two intact bridges but the roads approaching them were busted. The soil liquified during the sustained shaking of the quake.

Elsie brought her character to the foot of a wide stairway before Mount Tabor. She climbed up and at the far end of the platform they saw a building with a series of chimneys, water vapor pillowing upward.

"Maybe you can get inside it," he said.

"Can I die in the game?"

A golden figure hovered into view.

"Who's that?" Elsie asked.

"Someone from Makner." Shane stared at the Investor. "Don't tell anyone about Cityzen."

"Anyone?"

"Yeah."

"Do you know him?"

"Most employees work in Sunnyvale, so probably not."

The platform had what appeared to be a power station, and they saw the Investor float down to a pump house. The mechanics hidden within an internal core unknown to Shane.

"I guess you can build anything?" Elsie said.

"I don't know. Click the tool box."

She saw only two options: attach and detach. Up the stairs came a Looter, approaching her. They watched the character pass and continue on the ochre surface of the structure. Elsie said, "Do you want to ask that guy?"

"Wait."

The Investor and the Looter characters had frozen.

"I think they're talking, texting back and forth. They're switched to private."

"The earthquake freaks me out," she said.

"That's good though, right?"

"The real thing does. It's kind of scary, you know."

Elsie often woke up beside him with night sweats. She cried and he would hold her. They'd been together three years when she got sick, really sick, and she would sleep for twenty hours a day—or else she couldn't even move to get out of bed. Her doctor said it was pneumonia, but the antibiotics didn't improve her condition. She spent everything she had seeking help and each doctor gave a different diagnosis. She had Epstein-Barr virus, then it was mono, then chronic fatigue syndrome, POTS, fibromyalgia, generalized anxiety disorder, and finally, one told her it was depression and encouraged her to try getting out of bed. The doctor said she needed to see a psychiatrist. He made her feel like she was making everything up in her mind, like she just wanted attention.

And she thought she was going to die.

Her headaches could last for days. She couldn't eat. She could be down for weeks, and then fine—her illness was not consistent. Shane would say anything to comfort her, and he could help. It was the journey they were on together. They found books about why people don't heal and how they can—then she read about medical intuitives. Someone could *know* what was happening with her. Both of them wanted to believe it was possible. Shane and Elsie found a psychic in Portland and the guy was super nice, but he wasn't a medical intuitive.

Shane started researching the spooky action and he liked thinking of his body connected to a morphogenic field of electromagnetic energy. That was cool. All matter was energy, atoms, electrons. And the patterns in the energy were information, and people would be able to understand information. It might be a mystery now, but a pattern could be found. It could be known. Reading about non-ordinary consciousness, he wanted to experience it.

Elsie did her best to believe in perfect health. To treat depression she received a prescription for medicinal mushrooms and took them at a clinic. Oregon had been the first state to legalize and regulate psilocybin mushrooms. Shane had read that a heroic dose was necessary to access truly non-ordinary states of consciousness; it was eight grams and he ate them in bed. His mind, what he knew, was in an ocean of consciousness. Some healers said her consciousness could influence her health, but Elsie was not healed. After seeing three different practitioners in Portland who claimed to have realigned her energetic imbalance, none of them attributed her health problems to an insect bite. And after three straight days suffering extreme fatigue and aching in her joints, Shane scheduled an appointment for her with a physical therapist, a masseuse; he figured at least that might feel good, and Elsie found herself outside a single-family two story home in northwest. A woman in her sixties greeted Elsie at the door, looking into her eyes. The woman laughed when Shane waved from the car window. "Your friend is in a great hurry," she said and Elsie went inside.

"Are you comfortable there?" she asked. The wrinkles of her face tracing her smile. She wore a sleeveless shirt patterned with white roses that revealed the toned muscles of her shoulders and arms. She had led Elsie upstairs to her healing room. Every step feeling like she was climbing a mountain, Elsie followed the woman to a small room. She wasn't comfortable on the massage table, but she couldn't move. She started crying as she talked about her body. The therapist brushed her hands gently upon Elsie and said she could have Lyme disease. "Have you looked into this?"

Elsie said her doctors hadn't mentioned it.

"It is hard for them to diagnose. You have to be very firm with doctors in order to test for it."

Shane and Elsie left their apartment on Sunday afternoon. They walked to the park at Mount Tabor and up a trail through the trees. Shane supported her with his arm. He couldn't carry her, but she only needed to go slowly and he unburdened her of some weight. A gentle trill of birds so soft it diminished in the distant barking of dogs.

Mount Tabor was more hill than mountain, but it was an extinct volcano. They came to a road that wound around the hill and after a short distance they stopped, overlooking downtown. The buildings of the central core clustered as a bleached reef of human culture before the verdant crest of the West Hills. He leaned upon a waist-high fence, standing on a patch of earth curbed from the street behind them. Elsie placed her hand on his back and gently traced his body to rest her palm upon his hip. It transpired without thought. Shane breathed, automatic, involuntary, unconsciously respiring with the trees. To see and feel the light and wind, they were alive!

His body sang.

They had a great life together, and how quickly it went downhill.

An insect bit Elsie somewhere two summers ago. She had travelled to Connecticut to visit her friends from college and they'd gone camping. She didn't remember the bite. She didn't know she was bitten by an infected blacklegged tick. And now it had been too long. The doctor who diagnosed her said, "We have a path and even though it's not super clear, and we're going to have to switch your medication, you have Lyme disease." The doctor administered Elsie's treatment according to the Infectious Disease Society of America guidelines for Lyme disease. Doctors who failed to follow the guidelines risked being taken before a medical review board, and her doctor followed the IDSA guidelines to the letter. That was what her health plan covered. It stated that there was no convincing evidence for chronic Lyme after the recommended treatment regimens—and she had failed to recover.

"Why didn't you say something?" Rebecca asked.

"I didn't know it was you."

Shane and Rebecca sat across from each other at the dining table. Bradley had gone out for lunch. Though it wasn't required on Mondays, many of their coworkers were gathered, eating lunch together. Rebecca had ordered from a Thai restaurant nearby, a location on the grid plan not far from where she'd built her structure in the game.

Shane had stumbled upon her creation, someone had assembled bricks into a ring of columns that supported arches around a central core with a crenelated dome. He was impressed. Shane asked how she had made the smooth surface.

"Your tools," she said.

"They're so minimal."

"The game is basic, at first. You gain mastery of the basics, you receive more tools. The AI matches your intelligence." Rebecca picked a piece of chicken from the green curry. She chewed and then said, "It knows how to present tools to you by the type of questions you ask. How they're phrased."

"We didn't talk to it."

"We?"

"I didn't." He had explored further to unlock new things. After watching Elsie play, Shane progressed beyond the basic tools.

"Jeez," Rebecca said, jutting her chin out.

She shook her head.

"Relax," she said.

"What?"

"Don't worry about it."

Rebecca lifted more noodles onto her plate. Shane glanced over as Monty sat down at the other end with John. The three devs working on the Police were eating with them.

"So you apply color?" Shane asked.

"Yes, of course, you'll get all that. Just start making stuff. Talk to it."

"How does it work?"

She stared at him, her bangs falling diagonally above one eye.

"You'll have to talk with Cab."

Shane turned to look through the glass wall of his office.

"Cab eats lunch with his girlfriend on Monday," she said. "Every Monday."

"Do you talk with him much?" Shane asked.

"Yeah, he's a big brain. What do you want to know?"

"I don't know. I just want—"

"You want to show him your code," she said, seductively.

Shane had read about Cab. His achievements in computer science surfaced in the mainstream—as something massive glimpsed without understanding how deep it went—and among people in the field of machine learning, he was famous.

"All the advanced tools—"

"Those architectural tools are his work. That's why he's here." Rebecca brushed one hand across her bangs. "All the possibilities. You see all those in the modeling blend one to another to arrive at an optimum design. Resilient. Beautiful, and distinct from traditional design. It works the same way evolution does."

"You'll introduce me?"

"He's nice. You'll see."

Rebecca shoveled purple rice out of the box with her chopsticks.

"Do you hang out with him?"

She pointed down the table with her thumb.

"He hangs out with Monty," she said.

Monty turned his head and saw Shane, smiling. Monty smiled, gave a nod, and resumed his conversation. His stocky body anchored at the end of the long table.

"I know this from John," Rebecca said. "It's not secret. After his doctorate Cab worked for the University. Stanford wanted to make it an institutional work, and Sebastian told him the software was always going to be his. Cab has the rights. He owns the software."

"Do you mind if I finish this?" Shane pointed at the last of the noodles.

"Go ahead."

Rebecca emptied the curry onto her plate. "The AI. That's Cab.

Makner licenses that. He makes way more than an academic, and Makner can use it how they want. That's how they're making money now. Makner profits from his software. Schools and some firms. Makner makes money selling the license to architecture schools. The firms, they get it. I guess the ones using it lay off most of their office."

Shane rested his elbows on the table.

"Next time you see me in the game say hi." Rebecca stacked the empty containers on her plate and stood up. "What kind of music do you listen to?"

"Singer songwriters."

"Like they play around a campfire?"

Shane left the office with his coworkers on Friday. Summer wildfires displaced people from towns along the border and emergency service tents had been assembled in the park near their office. And as they passed through the crowd, three guys catcalled Rebecca. Monty glared at them as he walked by. They looked intimidating, and his other coworkers were pretending like it wasn't happening. None of her teammates wanted to cause a problem, but Rebecca stopped at the bench where those guys sat and she said: "Hey, that's fucked up!"

She forced them to apologize. And as she got them each to say sorry to her, the confrontation was over and she walked away. Rebecca had invited her coworkers to see her perform that week and Shane went to a club on Thursday night expecting to hang out with everyone. The stage was in a room next to the bar, and Rebecca unrolled a Persian carpet and set up microphone stands and keyboards with her band, Leroy. She gave Shane a hug and introduced him to Leroy, a big African-American guy with an easy sense of humor. He had installed internet-connected sensors at various high-volume intersections to record the traffic, and sped up the recording of traffic patterns until the stop and go matched a four-four time they could build on.

Shane watched the door expecting Cab to show up. Overhearing Cab and Monty was like listening to a foreign language and when Shane did recognize some reference to a programming language he knew, he couldn't think of anything meaningful to add. But she was right, Cab was a gentleman. His manners were refined, and he had a British accent. Shane heard him fretting about their work, the hazards of delivering a faulty blueprint. The geothermal power plant was at the extreme end of the possible, and it would be cleared along with all the employee experiments when the game launched in beta next year.

Shane kept glancing toward the door until Rebecca started to blow his mind. He found himself staring at her, watching the sound play through her body. Her voice so emotionally naked she carried him to an unknown place of feeling. She played the whole animal. She made herself the instrument. She entered space with her body. And as Shane rode home a line sang through him: You are inside of it and it is inside of you.

He felt whole. His body complete through his senses, expanding as though the world entered him in his sensation of the world. He had no idea how big it could become.

After going out for lunch the following Friday, Shane and his coworkers stopped in a cigar shop where Aydin chastised Bradley for saying their game would make the cover of *EDGE*. Aydin said they were a technology company—every news outlet would tell their story. Rebecca left work early that afternoon for a deep-dive gaming workshop in Seattle. The train went along the Cascades corridor, and she stayed with a friend who worked in the industry. Come Monday she was telling Bradley about it and pointing out something in the game. "You've seen the animators putting reflections on—that always kills the frame rate."

"Holy shit," Bradley said. "You got it to maintain our update cycle."

"Yes."

"You need to tell people about this," he said. "This is how we do things now."

Rebecca spent the week teaching each of the teams what she'd learned and she made sure Bradley and Shane mastered it. Bradley thanked her and assigned Rebecca to work on the excavation tools. He asked her to help Shane, and she gave Shane the authority to animate visual cues showing the hardness of the earth as Builders dug in, beneath the surface pixels.

Shane knew if he and Jason had created Playland with people like Rebecca and Bradley they'd surely have made money. Bradley had the market instinct, he was all animal spirits. He might not be an artist, but Rebecca surely was. They were a team. Shane saw levels within the company, not as arbitrary tiers of control and rote memorization. He sensed a mastery of knowledge, their degrees of depth within the code. The work of their minds within programming languages, endless in complexity. It was almost visible, a trace of light. The embodiment of understanding in the lines each team member held inside as explorers connected to each other as they went deeper into language, into their mind's own code in a communion with the machine. Shane felt the body, the mind, and the machine—inseparable, united in discovery of its own nature.

He didn't know anything.

Sebastian and Aydin weren't fucking around. This glimpse into their company, an assembly of extraordinary minds. Shane had never before taken an interest in much outside his video games and skateboarding. He had never thought this big. He never pitched a crazy idea with a promise of 10x returns to investors. And now he saw it was the money to hire talent, and if he'd hired Cab and Monty and Bradley and Rebecca and the rest of them. They would've made a killer game. He had been a chickenshit. He had to embrace risk!

IV

A ROUGH PATCH of sidewalk rumbled his wheels, the vibration traveling to his feet. Shane pushed twice to regain speed. Skirting the distance between the curb and a man asleep on the sidewalk, he skated around the corner and rode into the sunlight. Down at the end of the block Shane saw Bradley, glancing back at his car as he walked toward the office with a paper cup and a small brown bag in his hands. Shane rolled past the Makner building and slowed to a stop, dragging the flat of his sole. He kicked the board into one hand and tucked it under his arm.

"That was cool," Bradley said. "Can I try?"

"Sure."

Shane set his longboard on the ground and Bradley handed off his coffee and bag. Standing goofy-foot with his right leg forward, Bradley pushed twice and stood on the longboard. The slight grade kept his momentum. He pushed again and rode to the end of the block. He slowed himself by kicking the ground against his direction of travel, repeatedly. Bradley stopped, picked up the board, turned around, and set it down.

He skated back.

"You're good," Shane said.

"We do have these where I'm from."

"Do you surf?"

"I didn't say that."

Bradley entered the door code, and they went in together.

At the top of the stairs, Bradley stopped.

"You're not even winded."

"I'm not doing anything," Shane said.

"Well stop being twenty-five already."

Over the weekend Elsie read about things being decided at City Hall and she voted using Decide Portland—to incentivize participation in civic life, the City had tied receipt of a minimum basic income to use of the platform. Each question answered and comment approved for a discussion forum would release a bit more of the money allotted to her.

"Anything interesting?" Shane asked, looking at her screen.

"It's work."

But work was needed. Tying the mincome to direct democracy was the pride of Portland, and it had become a model for US cities. Truth be told, they'd copied a city in another country—the collaborative decision-making software was open source. Any city could do it. Elsie had been receiving a mincome ever since her illness forced her to quit the coffee shop. Most shops had kits to prepare drinks automatically. Elsie had done the emotional labor, and what she wanted to do was work with fibers. She enjoyed spending time with fiber, she liked the feel of it in her hands, making something real. And to uplift people with good apparel.

During his first month at Makner, Shane attended an engineering meeting and at one o'clock Aydin dropped to the floor and started doing push-ups. Everyone continued as if Aydin wasn't doing anything unusual as he pushed himself until he collapsed from exhaustion. On the ground, his hands flat, arms poised to lift his body but it was impossible and he remained in that position as he took a series of long deep breaths. Then he stood and resumed the meeting as if nothing had happened.

At lunch the only thing Shane had ever seen Aydin eat was a food replacement beverage. Apparently, that was what he ate breakfast, lunch, and dinner Monday through Friday. An engineered food that provided all the nutrients and minerals that modern science found essential to the human body. Plus, it eliminated the time needed to chew a regular meal.

Aydin wore a blood pressure sensor and each week swallowed a sensor pill that sent biometric data to his smartphone. He had begun tracking his vitals three years ago, after an annual check-up identified his low-density lipoprotein was high. So he removed beef and dairy from his diet, and decided the trouble was industrial agriculture altogether. To fortify his system Aydin snacked on organic fruits, raw vegetables, and nuts. But it was impossible to eat the processed, packaged and manufactured foods and remain healthy. The chemical abnormalities in his body were irrefutable. Even if the ingredients seemed legitimate, the pesticides and preservatives infected the body tissue. The food labels did not include denaturing of the ingredients, depletion of essential minerals from the soil—and some US food stuffs were grown in chemicals banned in Europe and proven to cause cancer.

The hottest August to date reached the record by mid-day, but the light warming the earth felt good when he rode to work. Shane entered the door code, jogged upstairs, carrying his longboard, and saw a new bike hanging in the foyer. He stopped to admire the minimalism of the three spokes fanning from the hub of its mag wheels. It could've hung in a showroom—a high-end instrument that would go for a few grand. Bradley waved, standing at his computer, hair neatly plastered to his forehead.

"That's yours," Shane said.

"You like?" Bradley nodded.

"I want it." Shane rested his board against the brick wall.

They left in the cool of evening. Bradley rode off on his bike and Shane caught a shuttle. The app optimized which shuttle to route him after he entered his location and destination. By using GPS and a pedometer, the app awarded discounts equal to the distance he walked to his final destination, making it possible to let him out where others were waiting to be picked up. Shuttles functioned as neighborhood circulators, connecting transit stops to doorsteps—and transfers: articulated buses carried more people and ran like streetcars along dedicated lanes interwoven throughout Portland. Both buses and shuttles ran unobstructed through traffic on lanes with curbside loading docks and kiosks that let anyone pay for their ride in advance, speeding loading times. It was discounted for monthly subscribers—even less if you paid annually—and shuttles could take any accessible road in the metropolitan area. By funding public transit, they had reduced the number of vehicles on the road. The multi-modal shared transit network was both faster and more efficient than owner-occupied vehicles.

Elsie had helped close after Knit Night and drove home in the golden hour. She had begun a cable knit sweater and even though her body pained her, leading the class helped Elsie feel better about herself. Shane paid for food delivery, the best organic produce, any meal she wanted prepared to order, and an app to summon a licensed nurse. His first full paycheck surprised them both. He set her up on his health plan—as his life partner. She finally received the treatment her body needed. And they decided to buy bikes together. They took their first ride the second Sunday in September and she got sick on the trail to Powell Butte.

She threw up.

The medicine made her sick.

Elsie knew the antibiotics were making her sick because they were fighting the bugs in her body. Her life had been altered forever by an extremely tiny bacteria shaped like a corkscrew that penetrated every fiber of her body. Treatment existed to suppress it—not cure—but she'd barely have symptoms. And she changed her diet to help with recovery. No wheat, dairy, or sugar. It was her chance to live again.

"Is that Aydin?" Shane asked, pointing down the block. The guy had taken off his helmet, turning his head as a homeless man stepped up to his motorcycle.

"That's him," Rebecca said.

She and Bradley had gone for lunch with Shane. They were about a hundred feet away and watched Aydin lean to one side and sweep his leg over the bike. The motorcycle leaned and returned to standing, balancing itself on two wheels. As the three of them got closer, Bradley was about to call out when he saw Aydin give the homeless guy a wad of bills. They heard him thank Aydin and then the man stepped back and stood against the building and Aydin turned and said, "Hey guys."

He passed them and they walked with Aydin to their building. Shane admired his generosity—that was power. At the door to the Makner building, Shane said, "That was cool."

Aydin stared at Shane. "That's security."

Bradley glanced at the homeless guy.

"Local color," Aydin said.

He opened the door. "No one fucks with my bike."

Aydin's weight hovered around one hundred and eighty-three pounds. He exercised regularly, and with fury. Every Sunday he went to the park to execute a series of sprints, starting at a hundred meters and moving his orange cones closer and closer. Ever one to optimize, Aydin used lunchtime and breaks to address the staff with work-related issues. Aydin's presence in their lives was felt, a constant force, a moving, swelling pressure: he was the engine of creation inside Makner. On a brisk walk back to the office in October, Shane had caught up to Aydin and asked if he'd ever tried medicinal mushrooms.

"The National Academy of Medicine doesn't recommend it."

Walking faster to keep pace, Shane said, "You might want to try it."

"I have identified all the nutrients my body needs."

"What about the food of the gods?"

"Do you think it is food that makes me powerful?"

"No, it's—"

"Gods do not eat." With a finality that silenced Shane, he said, "God is a story used to organize large groups of people who are strangers."

Shane and Bradley began to ride together after work and one evening they stopped midway across the Burnside Bridge. The sunset above the West Hills brushed the clouds golden pink. And from the sidewalk, looking down at the water and nine lanes of freeway and the railroad that ran along the east side of the river, Shane said he thought it would be cool if Portland built a superstructure over those roads. He said they could tunnelize the roads and build condos and apartments above it and have restaurants there with outdoor seating facing the river—and the sunsets! Bradley leaned on his handlebars and looked down.

"Yeah, that's neat. But after the earthquake, the City will have a clean slate." Bradley placed his wheels back on the road. "Then they can build whatever they want. Reroute the interstate. Build along the riverfront."

It surprised Shane to realize the earthquake would be an opportunity. He believed the earthquake was inevitable like everyone said it was but the disaster was so far removed from them that it wasn't real. They talked about floating houses, how those would be earthquake proof, and Shane asked why the city didn't have more along the river. Bradley suggested they could pitch an idea to Aydin about building functionality into the game that would allow players to build upon flat-bottomed barges. Shane said, "That motorboat parking lot, why aren't floating houses there?"

"Where would they put the boats?"

"Outside the city center."

Bradley laughed.

"Why not, really?" Shane asked.

"People own those boats, the docks—like the game, they're the investors, they lock the structures in place."

The Builder, Looter, Police and Investor teams sat down for the Friday meeting. Aydin and Sebastian stood at the back and after John announced their objectives for the following week, Shane suggested adding barges and Aydin pressed him on their deadline.

"This is on me," Bradley said. "Water should be an active space."

Shane stood up. "Water is life."

"Our water is a feature," Bradley said.

"Barges," Aydin said. "Players can build on floating platforms—why didn't someone do this already?"

Shane sat down.

Aydin looked around the room. John shrugged.

"Bradley's team will create water interactions. Okay, John."

John stepped to the center and went quickly into the key results for subsurface tunnels. Shane looked over and nodded to Bradley, beaming. He began a mental list of tasks and the moment John closed their meeting, Shane returned to his desk to start the project.

Teammates regrouped in the kitchen and tapped the keg. The

founders continued talking and Bradley stood next to Sebastian. The Friday meetings were the only occasion for Sebastian to talk with them face to face. He flew in from California. He was always flying somewhere, always on the move. Bradley had heard Sebastian owned three homes.

"We have to make it bigger," Sebastian said.

"We'll have Kastle crossovers," John said.

"We have a strong academic base," Aydin said.

"We'll need more," Sebastian said. "We need more players."

Bradley thought about power and the creation of imagined orders and hierarchies. He thought about money. The values generated digitally by a bank when money was loaned upon a promise to pay with interest, backed up by something real. He thought of land and the creation of imagined value, and he told Shane on their ride across the bridge: "To incentivize buying in-game property, we could make it Biblical."

Shane rode up alongside him.

Bradley said, "A number on the screen at all times counting down the percent chance of an earthquake. The real deal. Death and rebirth. We need to pressurize the game and buy houses, all the property destroyed after the real earthquake." Shane stayed behind him as they left the protected lane and maneuvered through traffic. Bradley yelled back, "Cityzen could buy up the devalued property after the quake."

They rode through the intersection to the neighborhood greenway on Ankeny and passed through the diverter funneling bikes along and rerouting automobiles. Bradley twisted at the waist, pedaling hands-free, and said, "We could market the fund as an investment vehicle designed to buy up devalued property in the aftermath of an earthquake."

Shane caught up with him again.

Bradley put his hands on his bars. "That sale of virtual building material in the game is the purchase of shares in the investment vehicle—a time-delayed real estate mutual fund. We'd give people who own homes in Portland six months to buy their place on the virtual map. And then it'd be an open market. People buying virtual real estate on the location of one's actual house would spur activity."

"What if a whale buys up whole neighborhoods?"

"That's what we want!"

Bradley sped forward to beat traffic in the next intersection. They crossed Southeast 20th and Shane rode beside him, anticipating their separation in eight blocks. "Those domain squatters can speculate on virtual property," Shane said, "but what if the rules favor investors who have a real home in Portland. It could be written into our terms that if one shows the deed or mortgage to their property, any virtual squatter on that part of the map must sell to them."

Bradley grinned. "That's it, man."

They stopped on the side of the road. Catching his breath, Bradley said, "Our fund grows all the money put into the game until—it'll buy with cash, people who can't afford to rebuild—after the city is destroyed." He spoke quickly, catching up to his thoughts. "The game factors the percent chance on-screen, always advancing, time advances the odds of the earthquake. The time constraint activates players, and along the bottom we run tickers of real estate investment funds—the competition! The value of a player's in-game property would be tied to our fund's performance in the market."

Shane didn't follow, he didn't understand what a real estate mutual fund did, he just smiled.

"Global money moves fast," Bradley said. For four years he had been investing his earnings. He'd gotten a taste. Bradley was an amateur but his grasp of risk and reward was strong. "It's forgotten. It's impossible to believe when you have none—but really believe me man, there is too much money! Investors with surplus cash seeking a higher return. They will eat up this city—they'll come with their bibs on and we'll fucking beat 'em to it."

V

SEBASTIAN ARRIVED in the office with his life manager, his personal assistant, and a deputy from the Sunnyvale branch. They had flown in from Utah where Sebastian attended an invite-only event on Powder Mountain. Talking with Aydin, he walked to his office and unlocked the door and held it open as Aydin went in. Sebastian followed and closed the door.

His retinue sat in the lounge while John prepared for the Friday meeting.

At Burning Man that year, Sebastian chanced upon a founder of Summit and got invited to speak at their alpine lodge. In the space they had intentionally created, a village with five hundred homes built below the largest ski resort in the country, the provision of success was recognized for its spiritual dimension. From the mountain top, seeing the Ogden Valley, feeling the optimism that arises of good fortune, it was possible to imagine having the power to make the world better. Sebastian had joined a gathering of business leaders and creative professionals who wanted to make the world a better place. And with access to worldly power, the surrounding circle of attendees and aspirants enjoyed a moment of opportunity. They were able, intelligent, resourceful—most educated at well-connected institutions and from good homes. Failure didn't occur to Sebastian.

Anything could happen.

With each new set of conditions he would create something.

The two founders emerged when the staff had gathered and John began running down the week's accomplishments. Rising on a tier of expanding wealth, the distance between Sebastian and Bradley couldn't have been greater at that moment. Bradley was an employee. Ordered to execute tasks compartmentalized and set forth by the founders, he was not empowered to advance in the territory of decision-making that would set the course for years to come. And in a company like his, the only way up the ranks was to be friends with the CEO or CTO—or make a useful tool.

"Bradley, you wanted to say something," John said, stepping to the side of the room and sitting down. Shane turned on the projector and a slide appeared.

"It's one of the ten commandments," Bradley said, walking to the center of room. "Thou shall not covet thy neighbor's house."

His gaze steady, Bradley looked at his teammates without irony. "For while the gods may command from above, under all is the land."

Shane hadn't heard this part.

Bradley had worked with a theater director to prepare his pitch. He knew his lines, he built a slide deck, but his heart was pounding in his throat. Bradley struggled to retain control. The company centered upon him, the front row turning their heads as he walked slowly to one side of the screen. He felt a little dizzy. Bradley glanced at the screen behind him. "The game needs a story to get talked about in the media," he said, advancing the slide with a remote control. "Getting trade publications to cover our game is easy. What is needed, is something real to talk about. To relate our game to everyday people."

Sebastian and Aydin stood at the back and Bradley made eye contact.

"A sandbox architecture game that is a real estate mutual fund. It's complicated." Bradley walked along the front row. "The city will fall in the quake. It can happen anytime. It will be a day just like today—"

He stammered, speaking too quickly.

He centered himself. This was his.

"Playing the game on the internet," Bradley said, "players attracted to the city and unable to simply pack up, pay the movers, the key deposit, first and last, and search for employment in a competitive job market, they are playing the game far away from Portland, investing in their Cityzen fund and saving enough to move."

Shane raised his hand.

"This is a fund you pay with the promise of citizenship in the future," Bradley said. "Your money is invested to increase its purchasing power, to make its claim on Portland. To capture the land value of the destroyed property, devalued in the city by earthquake, fire, flood, riot and vandals, the looting of the hungry, the left-behind. They are only human. But Cityzen is something else. Our corporation exists outside of the span of an individual life. Our fund will capitalize upon the moment of impact."

Bradley took a breath.

Shane said, "It could be written into our terms and—"

"The in-game capital is tradable with other players, allowing early exits," Bradley said. "Domain squatters would incentivize Portlanders to buy in. Where people own property in Portland, the owner can show their deed, and purchase that location in the game. We'd give them home team advantage. It would be their opportunity—to secure the city. Cityzens can make a claim on the real world, they will create the future city together. Do-it-together structures in the game will surpass all previous notions of the possible city. Each investment in Cityzen, forever increasing in the fund to buy up property after the disaster."

"This is another layer of complexity," Sebastian said. "We can bolt on an index fund, but now you're talking management, a whole other level of fund management."

"Good observation, that is it," Bradley said, his pulse racing. Sebastian could stop him. The hours of rehearsal. Bradley couldn't stop. This was his shot. He pressed the remote control, his audience looking to the screen. "Home ownership is the wealth-building tool most easily grasped. People get it. Cityzen offers everyone the opportunity to build individual wealth. You see. We use that layer, we touch it, we transact with it. Makner doesn't need to manage the fund. We're doing what we do best, making games."

He went on to explain the quake countdown. To maximize the pressure. To emphasize their competition. "Our competition," he said. "Our game would have a new layer of time-constrained competition. The other real estate mutual funds. And with the combined investments of all the people in this massively multi-player online game, we will dominate the other funds. The people of Portland will rally to protect their city. Players will collectively combine forces to outbid the market."

Bradley saw Sebastian's deputy taking notes. Sebastian was unreadable, and Bradley looked to Aydin. The team waited in the silence for the founders to speak.

"Bradley," John said, standing up. "Great initiative. We have to stay on track here. But before we move on to objectives for next week. Sound bite: what's the story?"

"The game you play to have a life. Property is not a thing, it is a right, a bundle of rights. The source of all our rights."

Bradley blew air and closed his eyes, shook his head.

Aydin signaled John to take a seat.

"It's imperative to own property to be free and to be a true citizen," Bradley said to John. "Our platform extends the opportunity for all people to be Cityzens." He turned his attention to his coworkers and said, "It's easy to think of property as a thing, but it is really a claim. We make claims on the claims. Our claim is certain. The city will be devastated in an earthquake. There are one hundred thousand unsecured homes. They will be uninhabitable after the quake. That's just in the city of Portland. In the greater metropolitan area there will be many more. People's livelihoods, businesses, disrupted. Their ability to make mortgage payments compromised."

Bradley pushed his remote.

"Take this dashboard that shows the value of your virtual property as a share in the fund—your property increasing in value along with the other investors. That is a good feeling. We can give that emotion to people."

He nodded slowly.

"The passion of our popular entertainment platform can overwhelm that market. Players who invest in the fund will have the resources to claim connected tracts of single-family homes destroyed in the earthquake. They will remake them, entire blocks. And this is our game, we build models for each city on the Ring of Fire. Building is the universal language. More than half the world's population is clustering on the Pacific Rim of Asia, along the Ring of Fire, the zone where more than eighty percent of the world's largest earthquakes occur. Really, it is the only monopoly worth having. Under all is the land." Bradley glanced at the staff and the founders. "Who will decide who has access to the city? Really, it is the only thing that matters."

He gestured toward a screen cap.

"Let the Cityzens decide."

Putting the remote in his pocket, Bradley paused as though he had finished and said, "We provide players the opportunity to claim property. In the game they can take out a loan. We give them credit.

We can advance players their virtual building materials. Internet users are primed by subscription business models. They pay us real money. They make a monthly payment, a direct deposit. Over time their virtual loan becomes real wealth. Private property. Their money, building wealth. They have the satisfaction of building wealth in the game. As you play Cityzen, you pay to own Portland's future."

He clasped his hands.

"This in-game bank is an essential piece. It is the first building to arise from the rubble—that and a jail. A bank and a jail. With a bank and a jail, a city will rise."

"Essentially Monopoly," Rebecca said.

"A most popular game," Bradley said. "It represents a natural system. It is the law of nature. You live it. This is a natural state. Private property has always existed. With property rights enforced. With access to credit. It forces people to behave responsibly and from it, the good is possible."

Shane raised his hand, and Bradley shook his head.

"Owning property has become so much more profitable than making stuff—yet, Builders can become Investors. That is the power of our game. What had been made exclusive, we will make available to every player."

"What are the legal requirements," John asked, "for individuals to buy into a real estate mutual fund?"

"That's the beauty of Cityzen. The players never directly access Wall Street. The only thing they are buying is a virtual in-game object. That is it. They attach their belief that the number fluctuating in their profile represents their money, carried along by the staccato rise of the fund's value in the market. But our platform is not a fund. It merely points to a fund. It publishes the results of the fund's performance. The money is our money, invested by another entity. Makner would partner with it just as any corporation, or city for that matter, works with a fund manager."

John pushed back. "And the people tired of waiting for an earthquake, how do they get their money out?"

"John, I'm glad you asked."

Bradley looked at John. "Again, we make all virtual property tradable. Investors in the game go to the virtual bank and they can sell their virtual property for tokens that, on another exchange, are transferable to dollars."

Bradley smiled.

"You see, we are only intermediaries. We are not a real estate mutual fund—we connect two parties—and so the rules don't apply to us. We are not distributing dollars or dividends—only tokens that can be exchanged for dollars on another platform. The rules don't apply to Makner."

Now the room was silent and Sebastian's deputy raised his hand.

"Finer points," Bradley added, quickly. "Details. But it's clear, we have terms—"

"You see this pissing anyone off?" Sebastian asked.

"That's the story. To dispute private property is to dispute capitalism. That is news. All human history has converged in the creation of global capitalism. Our market economy is the engine of human innovation, connection, creativity, productivity, and power. This is the culmination of the human project. There is no other system. Makner is affirming our most deeply held collective beliefs. It reaches deep into the collective self. Private property confers full personhood on its owner."

Bradley inhaled deeply and exhaled.

"Property confers power."

Bradley met Shane's gaze, following him, his friend. Shane trusted him. Watching him volley responses, speaking in front of everyone. To speak with authority. To speak to power. Pacing slowly, stopping, Bradley said, "We give everyone the chance to have property. Social media will be immaterial by comparison. Our platform secures an even greater resource—the American Dream."

"Aydin, do you see it?" Sebastian asked his partner.

"Bradley, this is it," Aydin said. "What are you proposing?"

"There is nothing left to propose. No alternative to economic predation exits. We will adapt or die."

Bradley stood across from the founders, two rows of employees seated between them.

"Thank you, Bradley," John said, getting out of his chair, briskly covering the distance and patting him on the shoulder.

"Play the long game," Bradley said to everyone. "Fun social security. We'll capitalize on the animal need for territory. It's fun, it's social, it's our security."

John took the team to the end of the meeting but Bradley didn't care about their objectives. Sebastian had shrugged. That was not good, not bad—but he could be moved. And Aydin gave him more time. Bradley reviewed their reactions, replaying his responses. He waited, planning what he should say, how to position himself, and then Shane was talking to him.

"You did good—"

"Wait," Bradley said, standing up.

John had finished and Aydin strode over and spoke to him. Sebastian stood talking with his deputy and assistant. People began moving chairs. Bradley looked over at Aydin—he was walking away.

VI

BRADLEY CAUGHT UP with him. "So what did you think?"

Aydin kept walking. "The earthquake, you'll be around for that?"

"I don't know. Yeah, maybe."

Aydin reached the door to his office and stopped.

"Thanks for sharing, Bradley."

"Should we talk about implementation?"

"I gave you work to do."

"Yeah, we're jamming."

"Then do your job."

"I was thinking we could work on the virtual credit."

Aydin went into his office and Bradley stood at the open door.

"I was thinking—"

"Did I give you time to express your thoughts?"

"Yes."

"Then your thoughts are understood now."

"Okay."

Bradley turned, looking across the room for Sebastian.

Hurrying over to him, he said, "Thanks for letting me pitch today."

"That was interesting."

"What do you think?"

"Stay with the code." Sebastian smiled and put his hands on Bradley's shoulders.

"I'm thinking my team could build a prototype for you."

"You're the greatest, Bradley."

"You want me to build it?"

"Stay with the objectives John gave you."

John asked everyone to the table before they left for the night. Aydin had tasked him with responsibility for any fallout from Bradley's display.

"It's the same game," John said. "Nothing's changed."

The teams were seated when Rebecca walked up. "Are we building all that functionality, a user-interface for the bank, jail modeling, all before beta?"

"We're going to do everything that's necessary," John said.

"This is for real," Bradley said.

Standing at the head of the table, John said, "We're going to make the same game we were making before."

"If we get this product right," Bradley said, "we'll change the world."

"But what is that going to do?" asked the leader of the Looter team.

"We can make it better," Bradley said.

The employees who'd looked to buy a place in Portland all complained of the advantage capital had over individuals in the housing market, and Rebecca criticized Bradley's embrace of Wall Street as if predatory capitalism was the only way for their company to be a success. But Shane didn't want to split his loyalty between them—some of what Bradley said fit what his parents had told him about home ownership and wealth creation. He couldn't be entirely wrong. To trust authority.

Shane listened to them hash out the difference between their index fund and a managed fund, productive investment in business and speculative finance, disaster capitalism and a time-delayed real estate mutual fund, and how a managed fund would interface with the game—not everything Bradley proposed was rejected outright, a consensus formed that the bank and the jail were tight. The jail could be that brief place of exile from the game, when Police caught Looters.

Leaving the office Bradley shoved his fists in his jacket pockets, extracted a stack of index cards with his neatly printed handwriting, and dropped it in the trash. Shane caught up with him at the bottom of the stairs. Bradley pushed open the door.

"I don't have friends."

"I'm your friend," Shane said.

"But you're here."

"Well we're friends."

"You're just here."

Shane got to work on Monday and some confusion existed as to what they were working on. A small contingent of developers left their stations, gathered in the kitchen, and discussed the effect of financial speculation and the commodification of housing. Then John called the team leaders to a special meeting. It was almost ten when Bradley hung his bike in the foyer. John pulled him aside. They went into Aydin's office and Bradley was instructed not to advocate or defend his idea.

"You will be getting a raise," Aydin said.

Bradley heard the number but his face didn't register an emotion.

Aydin pushed the pay increase letter across his desk, and advised Bradley that it wasn't necessary to get people to agree, only to work together for the greater good of the company. Debates erupted outside the office, at lunch, and after work when they'd relaxed with drinks. Willing to challenge Bradley, Rebecca was the leader of the opposition.

"Is homelessness a natural state too?"

Bradley looked at Rebecca as if she'd just answered her own question.

"We are a business," he said. "That's keeping the roof over your head. Everyone has to fend for themselves, and you're better off not having someone else's problems."

"If someone can't afford a house, then what?"

"Move somewhere else."

"Can't afford to move."

"Get a job."

"Can't."

"That's their problem—"

"But they are citizens too," Rebecca said. "Conflating home ownership with citizenship. This is a ton of crap. You're only a real person if you have property?"

"They can get a mincome."

"You know you need a bank account to get that and you need a home address to get a bank account."

"Use a family member's address."

"They got disowned for being gay."

"Then they get a mail forwarding service."

"No money."

"Game over."

"So they die?"

"Fuck 'em, Rebecca."

"They're on the street!"

"Fuck. Them."

Thanksgiving week, John discreetly and separately talked with select members of the company. Rebecca and Shane were notified that they were receiving raises. Both Cab and Monty got bonuses. The sound designer and all developers that Aydin deemed indispensable were also given raises.

Shane left work early the Wednesday before Thanksgiving and drove Elsie's car to the airport to pick up his sister Nora. The first child. She spent her time after school waiting for her mom in the Multnomah County Courthouse. Their mother had started her career as a county court clerk, and by high school Nora had grown up with the stories that unfolded in a courtroom. The gallery was open to the public and even as a little girl she sat there and listened. She applied herself to honors courses, AP classes at Franklin. She took out loans for college, though most of it was paid for by her scholarship. Their parents stretched to send Nora to school in New York City and help pay for her apartment. She was extremely practical; it was easy for her father to justify.

"How are Mom and Dad?" she asked.

"Same," he said, driving. "Same."

Nora went into corporate law. It was hard for Shane to match her achievements. Although she acknowledged that he had a difficult job, Nora never cared for video games. But she loved her brother and they had their shared interests. "I work with Brian Sabin's brother."

"Is he funny?"

"Not really." Shane pulled in their parents' driveway. "But he is interesting."

He decided to take Elsie to Timberline Lodge when the office closed for Christmas. Shane wanted to take her snowboarding. This sounded like a selfish Christmas present to her, but Elsie didn't want to be ungrateful. The lodge might be nice. She drove. She had a dark blue Corolla and her father kept it on the road. He was a mechanic and Elsie's mother taught third grade, but they divorced when she was ten. And about halfway to the mountain she voiced her reservations.

"I'm not a snowboarder."

"Anyone can be a snowboarder, you stand up and glide down the snow."

"But it's strapped to my feet. I'm sliding sideways down a mountain."

"You'll get it. You'll love it."

She changed lanes. A crochet owl, tiny, white with little gray spots, floated by fishing line from the rearview mirror. She exhaled and inhaled deeply and her breathing went back to normal. "Air molecules aren't little balls of stuff." She sucked the air whistling lightly through her mouth. "Atoms are energy."

"Nice atmosphere," he said.

"I want people to say that about me."

"You have a really nice atmosphere."

She didn't say anything more and Shane watched the charred trees flit past until they left the burn and the fir and pine drew its evergreen curtain along the road. Elsie turned on her music as the sunlight on their car extinguished his vigil. Shane closed his eyes. Then sleep took him.

Stopping for gas, Elsie unrolled her window and talked to the pump.

Shane stared ahead. "You should sell the Corolla."

She put her hand on his and looked at him. "My dad would miss it."

"Maybe he'll buy it."

"You know he probably would."

"Even with your dad doing the maintenance, paying insurance and gas you spend way more than a transit pass—we could've booked an EV."

"My car is something to talk about with my dad. We need something . . . it's how he expresses his affection."

"Burning gas makes me feel abusive."

Elsie wanted to go to the hot springs and the thought that he never asked her what she wanted bothered her as she struggled her first day on the slopes. At night it had become a thing between them, and she told Shane what she really felt.

"I didn't know you wanted to go to Breitenbush."

"You never asked," she said. "You aren't even interested, you never ask me what I want to do."

Shane wore the sweater Elsie made to the New Year's party. It was a metallic black gray sweater woven with complex braids and almost chainmail linking and a folded turtleneck. It was impressive. She gave it to him at his parents' house when they opened presents. He bought a console for his mom and dad and promised them invites to the beta, so they could experience the game when it came out in April. After Christmas, Elsie had teased him about his dad. "Look," she said in Dad voice. "It's Super Mario and his girlfriend. You saved a princess. Let me take your coat, sweety."

"You got the high score," Shane said, imitating his father with greater fidelity.

Elsie's dad had a surprise visit from a building contractor. Shane paid for them to strap down the hot water heater. It wobbled to the touch, and it contained drinkable water. In the half year of working on a virtual disaster zone, he knew the importance of water. It could be weeks, maybe longer, before the power was restored and the pumping stations could deliver water to the city; but then again, water lines could be compromised and that'd add maybe a year or more to repairs. But those were long-term concerns, the immediate one was fire. If the hot water heater sprung a minor gas leak in the shaking, that could fill the room and produce an explosive fire. And so many homes had gas lines, the earthquake in summer presented the most devastating picture.

YOU WILL WIN THE FUTURE

Makner knew how to throw a party. They knew exactly what to do. John had secured a venue for New Year's eve at the top of an office tower. Windows showcased the city lights below, and the large hall seemed to expand as Shane sipped his whisky. He wasn't much of a drinker but after a sixty-hour week, a fondness for booze began to seep through him.

Sebastian was radiant. Shane stared at him from a distance. He watched Sebastian's expression, his coordinated appeal to a group of investors. He joked; they laughed. He spoke; they listened. It was almost hypnotic.

Shane looked away.

He took another sip of whisky. Or was it Scotch? He didn't recall what he was drinking. He'd told the bartender to serve him what Monty had ordered before him. The drinks were free all night. He'd already had three.

Shane saw John with his wife and walked up to say hi. John introduced them. She was six months pregnant with their first child. Maeve asked how long he'd been in Portland. He said he was born here, and they chatted a moment about the city. Shane complimented her on how beautiful she looked, and after he sat down at a table along the back of the ballroom, he watched Aydin enter with his wife. She had stayed in Sunnyvale with their daughter. Shane had heard that Aydin visited them once a month and called his wife at seven p.m. every Thursday.

He thought of the man who watched over Aydin's bike, the cash he'd given him.

"Sir?"

A waiter extended a platter of mahi mahi ceviche in disposable containers and served with plantain chips. Shane took two and ate as he watched people. His friends and their partners all dressed in their own interesting ways, expressive of a beyond good, aspirational self. Another waiter approached with a tray of sizzling prawns and Shane accepted. A good portion of the Makner team was vegetarian, and the next tray offered him had stuffed yuca balls served with sauce. He tried one; it was filled with cheese.

Shane ate a vegetarian empanada next.

"Would you like portobello mushroom?"

The grilled mushroom patties were sliced and served as sliders.

"Ah!" The sight conflicted with feeling overfull. "No, thank you."

The waiter smiled and walked off, repeating his offer to the next guest.

"This building!"

Shane turned. It was Rebecca. He'd seen her hundreds of times, but this was different. She wore a sleeveless midnight blue one-piece with a column of small buttons from her belly to her cleavage. The suit hugged her body and hung loose below her knees where the pant legs flared. An onyx necklace strung like metal pearls. Shane looked down at her toeless black shoes. In heels she was a bit taller than him.

"Oh! And what are you nipping at, young man?"

Rebecca's eyes widened and her mouth opened.

"It's . . . I don't know. Some kind. Whisky or Scotch? Are they the same thing?"

Rebecca took the glass from him and sipped it while looking straight at him. "I think this Scotch is older than us." She laughed, a bit sloppy. Maybe she was drunk, too—that put him at ease.

"Older than me," said Shane, smiling.

"Is that so?" She punched his arm, hard but playfully. Shane sat on the edge of a black leather booth. "Where are your manners? Move over!"

"Excuse me," he said. "I'll be right back."

Shane wound his way through the crowd and took off his sweater and brought it to the coat room. His white button-up didn't fit properly, not anymore, but Shane didn't know that.

"Hey man." Bradley walked up wearing a sport coat and holding a drink. He wrapped his arm around Shane's shoulder and pulled him close. "Where's your lady friend?"

"She was feeling tired."

"Sorry about that."

"Did you bring a date?"

"No time."

They walked through the hallway and stopped to chat with a guy on the Looter team who introduced his wife. The office had been prepped for a big announcement and the levels of influence divided between who knew what was to be and who didn't. "We're going to be big in Japan," Bradley said to the guy as he and his wife walked back toward the restrooms.

"Yeah," Shane said, walking with Bradley into the ballroom. "Is that what Sebastian will announce?"

"A localization team—probably not for beta—but you can bet Makner is taking this product to Asia before it gets cloned."

"Do you know what he'll announce?"

"I think we're buying another game development company. From the look of it, an acquihire. We'll need more talent to roll out the game. Who knows, maybe Sebastian is buying us a new building."

"I had a company."

"Yeah."

"No, really."

"I know. I know."

"I want to show you the game I was working on. You know, before I got hired."

"Are you drunk?"

Shane found her again in the ballroom.

"You look distracted," she said. "What's up?"

"Oh, I'm thinking about the barge textures. Maybe we're using resources on them when we should—"

"Oh my god. You're seriously thinking about work? Look around."

She raised her hand to the room. The people celebrating.

"This is *why* you work so hard. To be here, with the bigwigs."

Shane suppressed a laugh and blew his cheeks.

"What did I say?"

"You." He looked at her. "You don't care about bigwigs."

Rebecca was silent.

A rush of blood to his face and Shane got instantly hot.

"That was rude," he said.

"No, it wasn't."

"I'm sorry," he said. "I'm going to find the restroom."

He turned and started toward the hallway.

"Don't lose me." Shane turned back to her. "Stay, okay. Wait."

"The restrooms are hard to miss in this place."

He reached the three doors and was confused. The hallway was dimly lit there and the gender denomination on the doors was etched into faded bronze. As he looked closer, he saw the bronze was ornamental. Then he noticed each door had a word above it, white text on black rectangles. Shane looked at each sign and muttered the words aloud. "Matter. Doesn't. It." Someone tapped him on the shoulder. He turned. Rebecca. "It doesn't matter," she said.

She pulled him to her and kissed him. Now his thoughts were with Rebecca. He thought of her onstage, fearless. It amplified everything. They drank each other like water. They embraced suspended in the moment before remembering where they were.

"I should . . ." he began, pointing to one of the restrooms.
"Yes, you should."

When Shane returned to the hall, Rebecca was not in their booth. People had gathered around the center of the room. Sebastian was standing on an elevated platform holding a thin glass of Cristal. "As we leave last year behind," he said, looking at his employees and their partners, his VIP guests and Aydin and his wife, "Cityzen is the future. Thanks to you. Thanks to you all. Ladies and gentlemen, the game is our future. We're early, we're hungry. And we will win."

Applause filled the room and Shane found himself applauding, reflexively.

"What is our high-status object in the game?"

Sebastian paused and someone said, "Buildings!"

"It is a number," Sebastian said. "It is the size of the number that we care about." He turned to one side and looked at someone Shane couldn't see through the crowd. "You are creating a powerful game. We will create real wealth and the rising value of players' in-game real estate will keep them in the game. And to make it really exciting for players, Cityzen will have a partner. To maximize the wealth . . . the Wells Fund."

Sebastian stepped forward. "Please allow me to introduce the newest addition to our family, Mr. Franklin Wells!"

A bald man in a gray suit and pink tie, tall and broad-shouldered, joined Sebastian on the platform, the stem of a champagne flute in his hand. He lifted his glass and said, "To our city of the future."

Everyone raised their glasses and the room filled with a chorus of voices proclaiming: "To our city of the future!" and they drank. Shane didn't have a glass. He looked around feeling awkward and wondering what to do, and he saw Bradley staring at his smartphone, scrolling intermittently with his thumb. His drink in one hand, unmoved. Aydin and John stepped onto the platform and Sebastian announced the countdown to midnight. Bradley walked out of the room, downing his drink. Shane started to follow him out. They could do something together—and Rebecca grabbed him.

VII

ON AVERAGE, one hundred and eleven people moved to Portland every day. The number of climate migrants seeking shelter in the Pacific Northwest grew daily—forcing a siege upon the cities. Access to Portland had become effectively controlled by who could afford it. Around its central core, the city had a wall of money.

A floating city on the water, Shane stared from the riverbank and woke up.

He lay in bed. The smell of bacon, then he knew it was Sunday breakfast.

Before moving in together they kept a running tally of how many weeks they met for brunch on consecutive Sundays—it was either his or her place with sex before or after. Shane had grown tired of cooking after working sixty-hour weeks, but Elsie was feeling better; the treatments had started to take, she was back to normal. Not exactly the same but the improvement was night and day.

When he awoke again, the house was silent. The smell had returned to a baseline of laundry, lotions, and two human bodies. Shane walked to the kitchen and found a lid atop a plate. A purple sticky note on the black knob: Eat me! He lifted the lid and looked at the grease congealed on the bacon, water trickling across the underside of the lid as he held it sideways. Alongside five pieces of bacon was a hash of eggs and vegetables. Putting the lid back, he took off the note and saw she had written in tiny letters: I'm at Jill's.

Shane stood in the shower, letting the hot water run. He'd tell her, he had to. He deserved it. He could continue to pay for her treatments and she'd move out, or he would. But otherwise, nothing really had to change between them. It would be easy when she understood. And she was always understanding. He'd explain it to her, everything was happening so fast.

It was good.

Good. Beyond good.

Elsie sat on their bed combing her hair. Shane, sitting up against the pillows, watched her from behind. The cream see-through nighty, her long black hair, the movement of her left hand that followed the brush, and he felt time prolonged by his power to change it, with his voice he could create his own destiny.

"I'm so happy to see you feeling better."

She turned around, put down the brush on the bed, and then crawled toward him, her breasts pendulous. Elsie straddled him and rested her hands on his shoulders, then she touched his forehead with her nose, and brushed it down to the tip of his nose, turning her head and her lips met his.

Shane decided to wait.

He had that.

He'd tell her at breakfast, then he could leave for work. That's clean, they could clear out and both have time to adjust before talking again, later.

"B. B. B."

Bradley opened his eyes and rolled over. He was looking at his Roombot, the screen on its head displayed: Monday 7:00 AM.

"Turn down alarm."

"Turn off?" the robot asked.

"Yes, off."

"Do you want me to wake you up at another time?"

"No. Turn off."

The Roombot lowered on its hind legs and rolled back to its corner.

"Baby, this is me. It's not about you, I'm going to tell you where I'm at."

Elsie's smile dropped.

They sat across from each other at the kitchen table, he had finished breakfast. He figured fifteen minutes would be good. "This is just—well, it sucks because I love you but I'm really into Rebecca."

Elsie smiled.

"She's cool."

"It's not that," Shane said. "I'm really really into her. I think I want to be with her."

Elsie turned her head to the side and away. When she looked at him again she said flatly, "You can explore."

"I think it's more than that."

"What's more?"

"More complicated."

"Life is complicated, Shane," she said, showing some heat.

"Yeah, no," he said. "I want to explore. It's like all my life coming to this moment."

"When you're the man."

"I didn't say that."

"What did you say? This is your moment."

"I'd like to be with Rebecca."

"Go be with her, it's not like I'm keeping you."

Shane stood up and walked around the table. Elsie flinched when he put his hand on her hair but then she surrendered.

Rain ticked on the shell of his hood as he walked to the shuttle stop. His timing was impeccable. Shane stared out the window and then opened his handheld and started reading email.

He arrived and Rebecca and Bradley weren't in. He started working on the in-game bank from the specs John sent. He was excited. Makner was going to make something new and interesting, and he was in the middle of it. He was safe. And Elsie would be okay; she was letting him do it.

Rebecca walked in wearing a clear plastic raincoat that went to her knees. She had a leopard print coat on underneath and black leggings and leather boots. She'd dyed her hair black. Rebecca greeted Shane with a wave and hung her coats and went to the kitchen. She came out later with a cup of tea, a saucer and a spoon. Setting these on her desk, she turned on her machine. The liquid crystal display lit up Rebecca's face. He looked at her. Rebecca didn't take her eyes off the screen. She had that tall, thick substantiality. Shane saw that she didn't need to be taken care of, she was going to join him in an adventure. She was going to create an adventure.

"I'm free," he said.

Rebecca looked up and raised her brows.

"I'm free to explore."

Rebecca turned back to her screen and said, "What are you exploring?"

He IM'd her: you

She looked at him, smiled, and said, "Don't you have a girlfriend?"

"Not really."

"So you're free to do anything?"

"Yes."

"Where's Bradley?"

"I don't know."

"Did John send you the new design requirements for the models, that bank we're putting downtown?"

"Yeah, I'm on it."

"Well, let's get this thing done."

Shane and Rebecca went for lunch at a Thai restaurant down the street from the Makner building. After they placed an order at the counter Rebecca took a table by a window and Shane sat down across from her.

"Maybe we should talk about what happened," he said.

"What happened?"

"Oh yeah, whatever," Shane said.

"Yeah, we had a lot of drinks. Are you cool?"

"Yeah, are you cool?"

"Yes, that's what I just said."

"Yah whatever."

The server brought their chicken pad thai and stir-fried veggie rice. They talked about work, and laughed at Bradley's expense. He arrived late and had forgotten to shave. Rebecca thought it was interesting to see him a little out of control. Shane was more concerned with her, what was she thinking, what she would do when he told her the truth.

"Elsie's incurable."

The disease no longer had power over him. He had control.

"She looked fine at the bar."

"No. She's on medication. She has a disease."

Her camping trip, the doctors, the headaches, fatigue, Lyme disease. Shane explained everything, the treatments, and what they had gone through to get here.

"I can't do this with you," Rebecca said.

"Of course," Shane said. "I want something else—with you."

Rebecca gazed at him. "If you're not with her and she can't afford the medicine and you know you can help her . . . are you going to support this person your whole life?"

"I could pay for her treatments, yes. That's not a problem."

"Till she finds another person to take the baton?"

"That could happen."

"This isn't right. You're in a different situation. You need to deal with that situation."

"We can have a different situation."

"I'm not your branch in the river," she said.

Shane touched her hand. He pictured himself floating into her.

"I'm not a branch you grab to pull yourself out of trouble," she said.

"Don't worry. You don't have to do anything."

"Shane, you *have* given me something." Rebecca lifted her hand from under his and held it. Her hand was so warm, she was so intense. It felt exciting to be held by her, even if it was only his hand. "It's like no one knows or cares about what I want," she said. "And you, you recognize it, I think."

"Yes, yah, I totally do. You are amazing."

"It means the world to me that you *saw* me. I love that. I want to thank you—and it was wild, a little too much for us, I guess."

"Not too much," Shane said.

"But we'll go on," she said, standing up. "Are you okay?"

"I'm good."

They walked back to the office and Rebecca put her arm in his. This confused him, and then he saw she was past it. Right beside him, her arm connected to his, and she smiled at him. He smiled. She was okay with expressing affection.

"I'm so glad we are together, like this," she said.

She disconnected from him at the door to the building and typed in the passcode. Shane thought this was how good friends cared, you didn't have to possess them. This was friendship. He didn't need anything from her, she didn't need anything from him. All of their needs were met.

Shane rode the shuttle home.

He considered an apology, he would say he was mistaken. He loved Elsie, and then he'd fall on his sword. She would do the rest. Let love be, he didn't know—besides it was terrible of him to leave her. They had a good thing and to stop the treatments; he had gone through the pain with her, he saw, he felt enough for her that it pained him how badly she could get. Now it was different. The symptoms had been suppressed. She was a different person, she was Elsie again.

He pulled his hood up against the rain, got out of the vehicle, and walked to their apartment and unlocked the door with his key.

"Elsie."

There was no response. He looked in their room, went down the hall. The bathroom door was closed. He put his ear to it and listened.

"Elsie?"

He knocked. No response.

He opened the door, turned on the light, stepped in, pulled aside the shower curtain, and looked away from the bare contours of the tub. It was already ten. Shane sliced two pieces of bread and ate buttered toast.

He was in bed, reading, when he heard the door. Shane didn't know if he should get up and talk with her standing, or be in bed. In bed, in a totally relaxed way—that was how to confront this. He waited. He couldn't wait after a few minutes had passed.

"Elsie?"

Silent.

He got out of bed. Walking to the door, she appeared. Framed in the doorway, her red sweater, her black hair, her glasses with rain drops. He wanted to hug her, he wanted her. Shane felt it. He loved her. It was clear, he could see her. This was the one he wanted. She was the person who loved him.

"I'm so sorry—"

"I'm leaving."

"No. No."

Shane stepped closer and she stepped back. He stopped.

"I was wrong. It was a mistake. Rebecca kissed me, but it was just a New Year's thing. I had totally misread. It wasn't anything. It was almost like I had forgotten myself what—who I am, who we are."

"No. You were right."

"I think we work together—" He paused, waiting for her, his eyes fixed on hers. She turned away and he said, "Live together. We can have a house together."

"Shane, if you stayed with me because you felt sorry for me, then that sucks. Because I don't need your pity. Guilt is not love. Why can't you leave?"

"We're together because we love each other."

"If you loved me then why did you say you want to be with Rebecca this morning?"

"That was a mistake. She kissed me and I lost my mind."

Elsie walked away and Shane followed her into the kitchen. The light was on and she stood in the room with her back to him. Her arms folded across her chest, she turned and said, "Where we are isn't where I thought we were. Shane, I'm not sure where you're at. I don't feel like you're being honest with me. I need—"

"This is the end?"

"I'm not saying this is the end. I just need a break."

"Where are you going to go?"

"I'm going to Jill's. Just give me some space."

"I don't want you to suffer."

"Is that it?"

"I care about you."

"If you cared then you wouldn't have said what you did."

"That was a mistake."

"No it wasn't. You don't make mistakes like that. You expressed yourself. You think you're doing good and you're so clean. Your hands aren't dirty."

Shane opened his arms to embrace Elsie and she said, "But all day, every day computers burn fossil fuels. They do use electricity, a whole lot. Computers use electricity and somewhere they're burning fossil fuels to play your perfectly clean game."

"Elsie, I'm sorry."

"Do you know the internet emits two billion tons of carbon dioxide—every year?"

"I didn't know that."

"You think that doesn't hurt? It's causing problems that you'd rather ignore with your dumb game. You're not a real citizen. You're a fake person who hurts real people. It hurts a lot."

The push of his legs immediately in the wheels, the rolling action side to side, Bradley felt the control of his body in the machine. The rain and the cold bracing him. His bike, his body racing through the streets. Aided by this ancient design, so powerful that it formed the political body for the paving of roads. Tracing the first citizens, their city streets lined, gridded, exposed to wear and weather, repaved over the years, over and over, Bradley turned north at Southeast 28th and rode up and then down to the Broadway Bridge, crossing back to downtown. Exercised, dismounting at a roll and walking his bike to the door of his building.

Bradley looked at the sensor and rolled his eyes to unlock the door. The whites of his eyes, their unique blood vessels pattern-matched and the door opened. He wheeled his bike through the lobby to the racks where the mount locked his frame. As he continued through the foyer and into the empty hallway, the lights came up before him, brighter, warmer, matching his pace.

He stood in the elevator, alone. Its brushed steel racing him upward, his rain gear and booties covering his work clothes. He'd left the office at five—he hadn't eaten. The day had pushed Bradley unprepared into a meeting with the oldest son of Franklin Wells, a guy his age named Walter; they would be working together through January and February to create an interface between the game and the fund. The Wells Fund managed billions of dollars and investors in the hedge fund, the wealthy individuals, university endowments, and pension fund managers, were willing to overlook Franklin's behavior so long as they made money. In a crowded and cutthroat financial industry, it required extremely aggressive behavior to rise above his competitors and beat the market year after year.

Each hedge fund had access to similar tools, talent, and data. Profiting on the uptick or downtick of stock prices, the only thing separating speculative finance from gambling was information, and Franklin Wells had built the financial world's most sophisticated information-gathering network. He employed hundreds of portfolio managers each with teams of traders and analysts overseeing stocks in an industry sector. The readily available information in press releases and research reports was useless in gaining the upper hand. To connect traders with company insiders, policy experts and academics, they used matchmaking services. Through expert networks commanding annual fees of hundreds of thousands of dollars, traders had access to paid informants within companies who delivered reports of company performance and product development, allowing Wells to place his bets before it became public. Huge profits were made on trades that occurred ahead of news that drove a stock dramatically up or down.

During Bradley's meeting with Walter, the billionaire's son made it known that he'd travel by helicopter that weekend to a golf game. His father owned a Gulfstream IX and sold their winter house in Florida before the climate crash. Bradley thought Walter Wells was a prick.

The doors pulled to either side and he entered the hallway, the lighting moving forward as he went to his door. At the eyepiece he looked up and the door slid open.

"Welcome home, Bradley."

The voice was both feminine and inhuman. Sheebie raised slightly upon its hind legs and wheeled forward with a screenshot of a dinner option. His Roombot, a platform for household software and his social network. It asked Bradley, "Shall I place the order?"

"Yes, place order."

"It looks delicious."

He took off his rain gear and hung it in the bathroom. His condo already warm, he draped his jacket on the kitchen counter and walked into the living room. A large, black and white rug on the dark wood floor. Low modern couches. The glass wall of his condo streaked with rain. The night lit by the city below. Sheebie rolled back to its place and the screen saver displayed two eyes, blinking regularly, and a smile line, occasionally yawning, closing its eyes, then going black.

From the lobby a delivery chute ascended to the top floors, a high-tech dumbwaiter. Sheebie lit up and turned its screen to him: food. Bradley authorized and Sheebie rolled over to an accessway in the kitchen wall and returned. Bradley ate in the living room, seated at the edge of his couch, watching a basketball game with the sound off as Sheebie told him about what had happened; it watched the entire network of his family, friends, and associates, monitoring their online activities and telling Bradley what happened in a given time frame, according to his preferences. With absolute loyalty, Sheebie was akin to a mechanical pet, with a face that could display video calls and transcribe, translate, and transfer all communication with the outside world.

"Your brother is on."

"Yeah."

"Tonight is the first pre-recorded broadcast from his comedy tour. It is called, *Saving Me.*"

"No."

"You do not want to watch?"

"System preferences." Bradley's tone was flat and the words meticulously pronounced. "Open."

"System preferences open."

"Delete Brian Sabin."

"Delete brother?"

"Yes, delete."

"Delete your brother?"

"Yes."

"Are you sure you want to delete Brian Sabin?"

"Yes."

"Deleting your brother Brian Sabin from your social network, you will no longer be apprised of his activity, is this correct?"

"Yes."

"Do you really want to delete your brother?"

"Yes."

"Delete Brian Sabin?"

"DELETE!"

VIII

SHE WAS NAKED. Her wrists bound to a stalagmite by the beast that was keeping her. It smelled the air, turning from the brazier, the firelight briefly upon its jaws as it tore the flesh from a human thigh.

"BRADLEY!" the woman screamed. The beast turned from the flames and threw the body part into a bone pile clattering against the cave wall.

The woman pulled against the bonds, screaming mad.

Dark rock, dripping with stinking water, dripping from the darkness above, as the monster lumbered toward him. She fell to her knees and the sight of her was obliterated from Bradley's view by the beast.

Bradley drew his sword.

The creature raised its right hand and swung with its left. Bradley ducked, slicing upward, slashing its wrist—the beast grabbed the wound. Bradley cut the tendon of its calf and the beast's bloody hands gripped him, his chest constricting. The terror of death. His breath tightened. He thrust up, into the monster's belly, digging for the heart. Bradley's blade obstructed—he sawed and thrust, his breaths short, gasping. His hands warm with blood as it poured out of the jagged incision in the gut. The release of his lungs! Bradley inhaled with his open mouth, heaving air. The monster falling forward, Bradley moved from its path and saw her standing at an incline, watching him, her arms outstretched and her long dark hair hanging down. The monster crashed to the cold, rough cave—the boom echoing in his skull as Bradley held his weapon at his side and walked to her.

In one motion he sliced the weird cord that held his woman. The tension snapped. She collapsed and Bradley cradled her into his arms. He stood, fatigued of the weight, carrying her to a corner strewn with sheepskin. He laid her down, knelt beside her, exhausted. He felt her hands on his chest, gently feeling the contour of his body. She reached his cock and he was hard. Taking her in the cave as she sung in his ear, an enchanting alien tongue that melted his mind, he was coming, coming, oh my god.

Bradley pulled off his headset and ripped the velcro down the side of his bodysuit to his waist—naked he stepped one leg and then the other out of the VR. Outstretched before him were the front grippers of Sheebie's forepaws. Bradley handed it over and the Roombot secured the suit and wheeled itself away to clean it out.

It was after ten when he turned on his screen at work.

Shane saw it when Bradley took off his sweatshirt, Chemicheal Mouse on a yellow shirt. The character from a game that came out when Shane was in eighth grade, published by a company that had become a competitor in the industry. Shane noticed Bradley had the same sweatshirt he wore yesterday and the day before that. It was the same thing he'd worn for more than a week.

Bradley rode his route, leaving shortly after Rebecca said goodbye. He'd carved out pathways for exercise and on occasion he ate out. His building was silent save for a soft purring of the heat and venting that was apparent upon entering and then faded from awareness. He placed his bike in the stand and a light advanced toward him as someone walked up. Bradley recognized the woman as somebody who lived in the building as they passed each other. They didn't speak or exchange looks.

Bradley ate and fought and fucked.

He arrived at the office around ten, passing into the routine and adapting to whatever was thrown his way.

"You okay?" Shane asked.

Bradley cursed at his screen.

He looked at Shane. "Yeah."

"Oh." Shane ducked behind his monitor.

The rain drummed on the window, streaming in rivulets down the glass, the light diffuse and dimming as the sky darkened. LED lights coned their stations automatically at five. Bradley sat and pulled on his rain pants and booties.

"You're an all-weather rider," Shane said.

Bradley smoothed the velcro closure on his pant legs, stood up, and started to leave.

"You could wait for it to stop pouring," Rebecca offered.

"Fuck that. Stay here and wait for the sun."

Shane and Rebecca exchanged looks.

Bradley walked to the foyer, pulled his bike off the rack and, hoisting the bar with one hand at his shoulder, he went downstairs. It rained intermittently the rest of the week and Shane rode his bike to work on Friday intending to leave with Bradley—but he knocked off at five and Shane wanted to keep working. His late hours made it easier to come home and fall asleep and repeat.

A new guy named Dillon was brought on to help build the water interactions. Bradley had asked Rebecca but she wasn't interested in overseeing him. Shane took responsibility for assigning the project Aydin required.

"Make it challenging," Bradley said. "See what he's made of."

He didn't complain and he worked late, never leaving before Shane, and Dillon knew by the third day that the assignment was impossible and at lunch he asked his team leader if he could have more time.

"Shane is your guy on this," Bradley said.

Dillon explained what he thought was possible and Shane looked at Bradley but he wasn't paying attention and Shane okayed an extended deadline. Bradley had stopped shaving. It was patchy but he trimmed it and with his devil's peak, the beard gave him a look. Bradley projected confidence and it was apparent he had the authority on their team, a relaxed virility. Bradley was making more money than ever before, and he didn't care.

When the light came up at five, Bradley grabbed his bag.

"Is the building on fire?" Rebecca asked. "Where are you going, Bradley?"

He smiled. "I'll see you tomorrow."

"You only one of a million until you're me," Dillon said. Rebecca had told him that Brian Sabin was Bradley's brother and he repeated the catchphrase from *Saving Me*. It was as though she'd said he knew God.

Bradley never spoke about his brother. At the following Friday lunch, like a password Dillon said, "You only one of a million until you're me."

Bradley looked at him.

"Did he come up with *Saving Me* all by himself?"

"Yep."

"Could you tell when you guys were growing up? Was he always funny?"

"Yep."

Bradley continued eating.

The barge animations presented new problems for Bradley. His team needed Dillon. Everywhere Sebastian and Aydin went, they acquired something, collecting names of the top graduates when they met with department heads licensing Cab's software. Makner gave perks to universities in exchange for references to their best students, and Sebastian received personal email informing him of exceptional prospects.

John contacted and courted new hires.

Two guys that used to sit near Shane were gone and three more had been brought on. Shane noticed that Bradley wasn't talking with the developers. He'd stopped announcing his thoughts about the game. Everyone seemed to know everything that was going on and in the merger with the Wells Fund, suddenly they didn't know anything.

Developers who researched the fund talked about what it invested in, and Shane overheard their conversations, picking up some basics about the stock market. In theory, the market existed to channel money to businesses so they could develop products, open factories and hire workers. But Franklin didn't care about the long-term health of companies, he was obsessed with being the world's most powerful hedge fund, maximizing his wealth and moving up the ranks of global billionaires. Monty said this guy had access to a global superclass and when interests aligned among dealmakers, they had power. His actions could affect the lives of millions of people. With global finance having grown so complex and the financial industry's top regulator appointed by a President dependent on their cooperation for his policies to succeed, it had moved beyond the reach of state regulation and law enforcement—pulling massive amounts of productive capital out of the world's middle class and into the accounts of hedge fund managers who played their net worth for a higher score. Bradley didn't talk about it. He did what was required, no more. After a developer on the Police team quit,

Shane asked Rebecca if she was going to quit too. Rebecca didn't want to talk about the fund. Her raise had been generous.

She did her job.

"Hey," Bradley said. "You still in that band, what was it, Larry?"

"It's Leroy," Rebecca said. "It's not Larry. It's Leroy."

"You studied music in school?"

"Bradley, I play music." Rebecca didn't look at him. "It's not homework."

"Yeah, I used to play an instrument."

"Oh yeah?"

"A ukulele."

Rebecca closed her eyes, laughing.

"What? I was four."

Shane asked if he wanted to ride after work, maybe stop and get a drink. Bradley was open but Shane and Dillon were working on the barge when he left. Shane stayed on his sixty-hour-a-week schedule. And now that he wasn't at the office every waking hour, Bradley was alone. He thought it could be time to leverage his experience and land a senior role with a competitor. Bradley had a dual degree in Computer Science and Applied Mathematics, making him adept at building internal tools that solve engineering problems and add value to the bottom line. Then he considered gathering a few guys to brainstorm—he had some good ideas for a startup.

The next few days Bradley barely spoke. But on Wednesday, he asked Rebecca about her music and she sent him songs. He listened to the files. Then at five, she put on her coat and told him: "I'm outta here."

"Where are you going?"

"I have a show."

"Okay, I'm in."

Rebecca grabbed her bag, raising an eyebrow. He threw on his jacket. Shane and Dillon watched him walk out with her. On the sidewalk she told him where they were playing and Bradley suggested he drive her, but she needed to get something to eat and pick up Leroy and load their equipment. On the way to her car, Bradley offered to help.

"Leroy's got it," she said.

"That your guy?"

"My bandmate."

"You sleep together."

Rebecca rolled her eyes.

"Cool," he said.

Rebecca pulled away.

She had considered telling him the wrong venue, or a start time that would make him miss her performance. Bradley acted like a senior executive. He was so square, but she noticed him rounding the corners. There was something breezy about him. Bradley had always seemed older than he really was—but he was her age. And she got that now, he was also seeking something.

It was time for her to go on. She didn't want to have her "supervisor" watch her perform, but she wanted to understand what was going on with him.

"Are you freaky?" she screamed into the microphone.

She scanned the room for Bradley.

Rebecca wore a black, sleeveless robe that hung to her bare feet. Her black hair combed straight. She had a skin suit of nude fabric under the sheer robe with a brushstroke of red paint across her chest and from her groin to her neck.

He wasn't in the room.

She felt relieved, and for a second she wondered if she should've invited him into the car, and they'd have had a chance to talk.

Zzzzoooooommm!

Leaned back at the keys, his right hand stuck the chord and Leroy tweaked the nob, bringing up the vibrato. He played the opening bars and she entered the music. This space was hers, a place she created, she was safe to express the emotions she couldn't explain, didn't understand.

Rebecca had seen her father change forever.

Her dad was not really accessible. He'd had an executive job with Nestlé, something to do with water, crops, people, and then he went insane. Her mom wasn't there. He took Rebecca to buy her school supplies and she found a pencil case she loved. She showed it to him and he was staring up at the sea of lights in Target. A tear running down his face. Daddy? and he was not responding. Her dad wasn't able to function afterward, at thirty-five years old, he wasn't able to function in society. Rebecca's mom cobbled together a life doing this and that and Rebecca spent a lot of time alone with the internet.

Her mother was an intellectual, a professor. She lived outside Helsinki. Rebecca had to make the effort to see her. Her mother could be warm, but it was temporary. Her father had always been sensitive, internally. When he began unravelling in his thirties, he leaned on his wife and she couldn't help him.

She was all edges.

Rebecca didn't need a center. She was expanding, reaching out to the world. Attracted to artistic expression that matched her inner state, she had found a mirror, a form to inhabit. Leroy propelled her and the vulnerability she projected in music, her emotional intensity, had begun to attract attention.

She saw him at the back of the room. Bradley was talking to a woman. Then he turned and he was watching her. Something inside her shifted. The broken pieces finding their edges, coming together. Rebecca had his attention. He was watching her.

Rebecca screamed, her voice bending into a note that swooped, catching a vowel, the words confused, then streaming out, pouring, diving, her heart, beating, beating. Her beating heart in the song, pounding, pounding on the walls of her cage, to be seen, felt, loved.

IX

SHANE INVITED ELSIE over for dinner and they met on Thursday the first week of February. She sat across from him at the kitchen table. Jill had given her a room while she figured out what to do, and Shane asked her to come back. Elsie had complained when Shane started coming home after she was already in bed. What difference did it make to him if she was there? He was gone when she woke up. Elsie wasn't a sex worker. They used to make food and eat together; and working at Makner, he found it easier to have meals sent to her. He had the best organic food delivered. He paid for a housekeeper to clean twice a month.

"You purchased a substitute," she said. "I talked with the delivery boy more than you."

"You know how work is."

"I know how you make it."

Shane accepted his choice. It frightened him, and he would never admit that. The caretaking of human weakness was eternal. He had inched away through fall and winter. And now the rejection hurt.

"Even if you don't want to live here," he said, "I can help."

"Love and guilt have nothing to do with each other."

"I am not guilty, I want to help you."

"I need time."

"You need medicine. This is why I work so hard."

"We need time." Elsie picked the skin of her left thumb and, moving her hands to her lap, she looked up. "If that woman wanted to be with you, would you say that?"

"You need treatment."

"I'm not dependent on you."

"Why aren't we a team, like before?"

"You're putting money into this person and you don't want to see them, putting your money into a problem—and the problem is me."

Elsie started to cry.

Shane stood up. He walked over and knelt before her and put his arms around her.

"No," she said. "You shouldn't."

Sheebie cared for his plants. Bradley had read about the benefits of plants in the home, he knew a picture of trees worked too, but it was good for the air quality and the home should have an organic look. Being in nature was proven to reduce stress.

"Wind speed," Sheebie said. "Twenty-five miles per hour. Small trees swaying, large branches moving, wires whistling, umbrellas have become difficult to control."

He'd set his preferences for the weather notification.

Bradley drove to the entrance to Forest Park and walked up the trail. The wind played through the canopy of evergreens and bare deciduous branches. Bradley turned on the recorder and stood listening. Then he'd pause it and continue walking until he heard a new vibration from the flow of gases through the needles, brushing their massive reed instruments. Gusts of wind transpiring in the breeze at random intervals. Sounds he layered in audio editing software Rebecca recommended. After her performance Bradley had left, but when he arrived at the office he said he'd go again, he'd like to hear her do that again. Rebecca told him Leroy had landed a Friday night gig, finally. They'd make a cut of the door. They were the final act, performing at a club downtown the last Friday in February.

The phone booped on his desk and Shane looked down. The text from Elsie appeared on his small screen:
My coverage was denied
Can you please call them?
He texted: What happened?
Boop. I don't know what happened
Boop. They won't give me the antibiotics
And a moment later the phone sounded a final time.
Please help me

Shane went into the conference room and shut the door and called their healthcare provider. He went through the menus and listened to call-waiting and after ten minutes reached a customer service representative. He explained that he was calling to ensure that his domestic partner continued receiving care.

"Unfortunately, at this time, the terms and conditions that apply to domestic partners prevent her from accessing treatment through your plan."

The music venues in Portland had acts from fifty states and beyond lining up to play, and local performers would play bars and clubs any night of the week for free. The market made a triad of them: the aspiring musicians, the working musicians, and the celebrities. But interesting stuff happened when an aspiring musician *believed* they were a celebrity. This could create high drama that made it to the stage. Of course if they had enough money to live on, they could just be a musician—but no one in the city could afford a place to live on their minimum basic income. Paid for fiscally, the mincome was a dividend from fees on economic bads. All activity that polluted land, water, air, and human bodies: those polluters paid fees that the state distributed into the foundation of economic survival. The mincome was an annual allowance equal to forty percent of the average personal income in the state of Oregon. It was a single question on state tax returns. Yes or no, and so filing taxes was required to receive it. Not only politically expedient for electeds but necessary to keep service workers in the city.

Self-expression in capitalism was a confidence game.

It was a micro-minority of performers who got milled into stars and then made bank for agents, producers, bookers, venues—and for themselves, if they endured—but a star having risen from the city was enough for others playing there, who knew so-and-so and felt the power, believing they could make it. If you didn't believe in yourself, no one else would. Rebecca believed in a lot of things. She was one of the lucky ones, she could subsidize her art with computer code.

Over the weekend he saw a guy mowing his lawn and, holding his phone, Bradley stopped to talk with him. He asked if it was okay to record the sound. The man walked the mower over and stopped along the sidewalk. Bradley placed his smartphone near the machine and the man pushed the ignition. He looked at Bradley. Bradley suggested pushing the machine back and forth past his recorder.

A strand of Elsie's hair was in his mouth and Shane reached up to brush it away with his finger. He held her to him, her head upon his chest. The cool dampness of her tears. Her hair smelled of pine and summer rain.

She signed the terms of agreement on the app used to make appointments. It was required. It was line seventeen of page four hundred and eighty-six, Elsie had agreed to geotracking in her phone. The insurance company knew to the minute when she had left their apartment. By not reporting the change in his living arrangement

Shane was liable to be charged with a felony offense of fraud.

His option was to pay the fine of five thousand dollars and, for every day after she had vacated the residency, an additional hundred-dollar fine, to be paid within five business days; or else there would be a court date and further fines. Failure to appear in court would result in a warrant for his arrest.

He had thirty days to file an appeal. And in six months time they would reevaluate his case to see if there should be an adjustment in his fees. His coverage doubled in price, now Shane would pay a huge amount every month, ongoing; it was to be reviewed after six months but that didn't mean they'd reduce the doubled fee. His phone call with the customer service representative had scared him, but the effect of the letter that appeared two days later had produced an animal terror. His body rang with threat. Despite its impenetrable language, the details horrified him. A scheduled day for him to appear in court, the inescapable fines and jail.

Shane and Elsie held each other. They were both afraid. The memory of bodily pain could ease in time but Elsie remembered death. Her body opened inside the pain pushing toward her final release. They felt chastened by omniscient forces. To reject the criminal, the immoral and mistaken. One hundred dollars for every day that she was . . . paid within five business days. Or there will be a court date. And he had thirty days to file an appeal. After six months they would review his case. Line seventeen: We reserve the right to track your location and require that you reside in the dwelling with the domestic partner whose plan has covered . . .

He called the number on the Denial of Request for Service letter. A customer service representative read from a script and asked, "You didn't report the change in your living arrangement?"

"She was staying with her friend, but we're still partners."

"We have identified that your domestic partner is no longer inhabiting the residence."

"No, that's a mistake."

"We have the information from her device sensors and communications metadata. Sir, it is correct."

"No, she still lives here."

X

REBECCA STOOD onstage in full flight. She used a wireless headset mic of transparent plastic. Her legs akimbo. Her arms straight out and moving up symmetrically, simultaneously as she hovered there, sustaining a note in the last word of her final song. As her voice rode further, she reached up. Her breath expelled in the note, she fixed her gaze up, suddenly turning her body, twisting down as she pulled her arms in and curled into a ball on stage.

Leroy started pulsing beats in the darkness.

A trance-inducing sound that included signature tracks from their show. No one called out for an encore. There was no backstage, no green room for a costume change. A spotlight came upon her. She stood up and her voice soared into the music, swooping, falling.

The venue had filled with people by the time Leroy went on after midnight. It was attached to a bar in Old Town, in an old storefront connected to the barroom through an opening in the brick wall. The walls inside the venue were painted black and the stage was a three-foot-high platform in a corner of a room opposite four pinball machines that people continued to play while Rebecca was onstage.

She looked stunning. Rebecca had hired a costume designer and wore a small pair of wings of red flames. She'd found a body suit online with retro hotrod flames up the sides of the black spandex. Everything she did, her singing, her dancing, her dress, a narrow branch, and perched there, radiant.

She made herself known.

It was an act of revelation. Empowering in her exposure of taboos—personal, societal—and their transgression. The acts that went on before Leroy were industrial and all male and without vocals. It was a weird crowd. Standing at either side of the stage were big silent guys with earplugs, facing the crowd. Bradley was out of his element. He didn't want to be one of those dudes standing before the stage staring at her. But about half of the venue wasn't paying any attention to Rebecca.

Performing on Friday night was progress for Leroy. The largest crowd they'd played to, but the venue wasn't a music hall; there were no seats, the room was divided, and people came for various purposes and in the barroom everyone had to shout to be heard and the voices from the bar sounded between each of her songs and behind anything she said to her audience.

Bradley stood at the back of the room just beyond the opening to the bar, the sound system overmastering all voices save Rebecca's. A red dot appeared on her forehead. A bright red spot jiggled in place above her eyes. It moved down to her heart and Bradley saw a guy with a laser pointer, shouting Fang! Fang! Fang! He wore digital camo. His hair buzzed. He stood with four guys in buzz cuts. Bradley looked back to the stage and the laser light was tracking Rebecca's face.

"Don't do that," Bradley said into his ear.

He pushed Bradley.

Catching himself, Bradley lunged forward, grabbed the laser and shouted, "I'm not in the fucking mood!"

The guy's four friends fell in behind him.

"Get the fuck out of here!" Bradley shouted.

From their position before the stage the bouncers pushed through the crowd and reached Bradley, pulling him back. Bradley turned his head. He was held in the bouncers' arms and he struggled to raise the laser in his hand.

"They shined a laser at her! I got it in my hand!"

From the stage, Rebecca thought she saw Bradley.
That couldn't be him.

With the launch fast approaching Makner engaged a staffing agency to fill support roles. All contractors were led to believe full employment was possible, and an internal division existed between people who received benefits and those who didn't. W2 status was highly desirable. The providence of good healthcare, vacation time, parental leave, and retirement had fallen to the private sector in competition for a sharp and highly-mobile workforce.

"It was an accident," Bradley said.

"On your face?" Shane asked.

"On my bike."

"No," said Shane, disbelieving.

Bradley walked past to his desk.

"Yeah, well I'll tell you what happened." The right side of his face was swollen, purpled, cut, and spliced with a butterfly bandage. "Another time."

He turned on his computer, and Rebecca pointed her finger at him. "Bradley," she said.

He raised his eyebrows.

"I need to talk with you."

John saw Bradley from across the room and hurried over, slowing when he saw Bradley's face. "Jesus, what's going on?"

"It was an accident."

"Let's go over something real fast—follow me."

Bradley glanced at his teammates staring at him as he followed the boss toward his office. John stepped to one side of the door and followed Bradley in.

"Have a seat." John closed the door and walked around his desk and sat down, putting his tablet to the side of his keyboard. He leaned forward, his arms crossed upon the desk. "You check messages first thing—that's what you do."

"Yeah, I do that."

"Why didn't you respond?"

"I didn't this morning."

"Why?"

"It won't happen again."

John sat back.

"You don't look like you used to."

"It was a bike accident."

John squinted one eye.

"How's Maeve?" Bradley asked.

"Extremely pregnant."

"What happens next?"

"How's Dillon?" John asked.

"He's a good kid."

"You think he's capable of more advanced features like garbage collection and reflection—as well as a quick compile for rapid iteration?"

Bradley thought about the short, curly-haired nineteen-year-old. "He listens. Makes good observations. Asks questions like a diplomat. Smart. Adaptable. He's high-value."

"Good. I want you to work with him, you and Dillon. What you did with Shane—"

"Shane is Shane. The kid is different, he's not going to be another Shane."

"Shane and Rebecca." John straightened his tablet, aligning it to the edge of his desk. "They are working with Aydin to crunch the southwest."

Bradley sat up. "The mapping was my work."

"I know. Everyone knows."

"I designed the isometric tilemaps."

"Makner acknowledges your contribution."

"I wrote the logic grid to handle collisions, the character spawning points—"

"You have a gift, Bradley. You are a powerful motivator. And only you. You're the only one to charge this team. Only you can give Dillon the tools and knowledge he needs."

"This is— That makes no sense. I've been writing your code for four years."

"We're pushing hard against our deadline."

"The game is tracking extremely well."

"I'm pleased with our progress. However, as you know, we are willing to move launch dates to deliver the best player experience."

"You dropped me in a trench with inexperienced developers—no one is telling me what's going on. What are we looking at?"

"The delay could be a week or it could be three or four or five months, if need be." John looked at a framed picture of his wife. A small item on his desk that he saw so often he could see it and not think of her, but now he thought of her. "Between you and me, Aydin has been talking with Sebastian about delaying to May."

Makner had contracted a studio to create additional in-game assets, animation and environments, lighting and textures. Aydin was often seen pacing the floor of his office.

"And you want us going full-on sleep dep and stimulants," Bradley said.

"We will work to deliver everything Cityzen can and should be."

Bradley walked up the stairs and opened the door to the roof. The sunlight warm in the chill of the breeze as he crossed a raised pathway through a bed of succulents and ornamental grasses. On a weather-beaten wood platform Rebecca stood against a low wall facing toward the river with her back to him. Bradley stopped before reaching her and stood motionless.

She turned around.

"What is going on?"

"You're going up a ladder." He smiled. "You'll be with Aydin. He's a genius. A month and a half from a scheduled launch. You'll be in the crucible. He'll transform you. If you let him. Hours are going to ramp up. Playtime is over. And the sun feels great. I'm stoked it's finally spring."

"What is going on with you?"

Bradley looked at her without displaying emotion. "You and I should go out."

"You were there." She raised her hand just above her waist and held it out, pointing at him. "That was you."

"We should have more fun."

"Who did that to you?"

"We don't get extra lives."

"Why did they hit you?"

"People are crazy."

Rebecca stared at him.

"Where do you want to go?" she asked.

"My place."

XI

AFTER WORK Rebecca walked with Bradley to his building near the North Park Blocks and rode up the elevator with him. He watched the numbers without speaking.

"Is this what you wanted?"

"Yes," he said.

Bradley led her down the hall and opened the door to his condo. Sheebie rolled up.

"Welcome home, Bradley."

Rebecca walked in behind him. "Why do you waste your money on that?"

"It's really useful," he said.

"That's a gloried movie prop."

"No, you'd be surprised."

"It's a bunch of dorky guys' idea of what you're supposed to want."

No one owned Roombots. Users leased them, and Bradley hadn't bothered to trade up. He'd grown attached to his—though he couldn't get inside it, really, the maintenance was beyond Bradley; and the terms of his lease included repairs—and Sheebie had the most recent software update.

"It is so *clean*," she said.

"That's what I'm talking about."

Sheebie displayed a menu item, Bradley's Monday meal selection. "Would you like me to place an order?" Sheebie asked.

"Does that look good?" he asked Rebecca.

"It looks delicious," Sheebie said.

"Rebecca, what do you think?"

"There's nothing in here."

"Yeah, I live here."

"Can I?" she asked.

"Please, be my guest."

Rebecca took off her jacket and slung it on the kitchen counter. She opened the refrigerator. A bottle of soy sauce along with three varieties of mustard, catsup, and Sriracha sauce in the door rack, and on the shelf were three beers, an energy drink and a can of chewing tobacco. She closed it. "There's no food."

"I don't cook."

"Why not?"

"Who has time for that?"

"Didn't you have a mother?"

"She cooked." Bradley leaned against the counter. "Sometimes."

Rebecca shrugged. "I can eat."

"Rewrite order." Bradley's voice slowed when he spoke to Sheebie, each word clearly enunciated. "Two times same. Place order."

Sheebie lowered on its hind legs and rolled to its place in the living room. Rebecca walked in behind it and saw the VR bodysuit hung on a rack against the wall.

"You have a VR onesie!"

Rebecca peeked into the neck hole and pulled her face back quickly.

"That's sweet," she said. It smelled like a locker room.

"What do you play?" he asked.

"I mean that's cool. You have a tailored suit."

"I guess it's a perk."

"Do you play with other people?" she asked.

Shane was showing him his computer screen.

"That's neat," Bradley said. He had arrived to the office late, it was almost lunchtime. He glanced at Shane's screen. The company had sent Shane up for Final Level in Seattle to represent Makner on a panel called "Anyone Can Be a Game Designer." It was a three-day event that included workshops with industry professionals. Among a host of companies that presented each year when the University of Washington had spring break, Makner co-sponsored alongside Activision, Nintendo, Microsoft, Amazon, and Disney. Last Friday, Shane had left the office mid-day with Aydin and Cab and Rebecca. They caught a flight, then met Sebastian at the Museum of Popular Culture, and stayed two nights at a rented house in Queen Anne. Shane's friend Jason lived in the Central District and they met at MoPOP for lunch, but his schedule was packed with jams, demos, and high-level presentations. In the lobby Makner teased the release of Cityzen with an infinite loop of their trailer playing on a big screen. They had one special event where Sebastian spoke before a packed house regaling the audience with his promise of the future city, and the next day Cab gave a technical presentation on the use of laser scanning versus photogrammetry to map architecture, hinting at talks with officials in Seattle for expansion levels.

"Don't you think we should do this?" Shane asked as Bradley walked away.

"I don't know," he said back at his desk. "You should ask John."

Shane took a tablet and went looking for him. John was seated with the temps at a long table installed for their marketing effort. He looked away from his screen when Shane said his name, his eyes returning, he continued typing.

"Yeah, what's up?"

John wore an employees-only shirt that Shane had never seen before and when he returned to his station, he was wearing:

100 HRS/WK AND LOVING IT!

"John had these made for us."

"Holy fuck!" Bradley said.

Rebecca pulled up her sweater and tugged down her T-shirt, holding it out so Bradley could see. "I was supposed to tell you. John wants you to get one."

"We have to set a good example," Shane said.

Bradley left his desk and stood in the center of the office and then went to the stairwell and up to the roof. The deck chairs were empty and, walking over, he saw someone standing at the southwest corner of the rooftop.

"Cab?"

"Hello, Bradley."

The London accent of his voice. Cab had the shirt on and caught Bradley's expression of complete spiritual exhaustion. It practically rode out the fibers of his clothes.

"I suppose," Cab said, "it's ironic."

"Maybe on you, yeah. But no, it's real."

"Is this in bad taste?"

"I guess that depends how much of the company you own?" Bradley smiled and looked over the wall at the street below. Cab was not a humorist. Bradley had never seen him having what people in the office considered a good time.

"If you keep getting opportunities to have more, how far would you take it, if no one was stopping you?"

"More money?" Bradley asked.

"More anything, more of everything. We all keep wanting more."

"When I can live off the principal."

"The distribution of resources is a matter of life or death for billions of people."

"I won't hurt anyone."

"You know how our fund does business," said Cab, looking at Bradley. He didn't outright say it, but they both knew that as soon as Aydin and Sebastian processed Bradley's proposal and the cylinders started firing, it led to Franklin Wells. They had unlimited access. Their revenue streams. The funds. And it came from taking advantage of someone and they brought in Franklin Wells to do it because they didn't know how to take advantage of people at that level. They needed him. "Our operating system accumulates and concentrates wealth in the form of claims on resources."

"Cab, if we can fix cities, we kinda fix the world."

"We are the disaster."

"Makner?"

"No. All of us, our operating system."

Bradley gazed at the traffic below, and Cab said, "So many redundancies exist to protect this system, now, you can't remove it. It can't be overwritten."

The city looked beautiful to Bradley. Each building locked in time and the blocks layered with the allowances of new materials and design tools all calibrated to the elaborate decision-making that passed through city council to become the building code. "Maybe the earthquake," Bradley said, "is that it, you reboot the city?"

"Do you know how this building got here?"

"It was built by Chinese people," Bradley said.

Cab was silent. From the street below came the sound of cars and the passing people, an occasional call, a name at random. A horn. The lunch hour was approaching. People would be coming up to the deck.

"I don't know."

"It's interesting," Cab said.

A wooden plank road that led over the hills to the agricultural riches of the valley had established the port. Cab told him that the building was built in 1889 to store dry goods and repurposed as a bunkhouse for Chinese day laborers after the turn of the 20th century. The extraction of crops was enabled by water and the construction of rail. In the wake of the Great War and national restrictions on immigration, the building was unoccupied.

It became a furniture factory during the twenties when Portland had a housing boom alongside a thriving timber industry that reached the doorstep of the Great Depression. The factory closed in 1933. As shipbuilding again revived the economy, the furniture shop opened under new owners and later accessorized the suburbs expanding after the Second World War. But in the sixties the port failed to modernize and ignored the market for containerized cargo, losing business to Seattle. And with the fall of the wood products industry reducing rural towns and diminishing their ability to draw on Portland for goods and services, the city lost more people than it gained throughout the first half decade of the eighties. The devalued property was an opportunity to capitalize on the rent gap and the city welcomed business and development with incentives to revitalize the economy. The greater Portland area had slowly replaced its dependence on natural resources with advertising and apparel and software. And then the old brick building underwent a three and a half million dollar seismic retrofit in the twenty-teens as capital arrived and the city experienced a land rush that transformed the downtown.

"And here we are," Bradley said.

Cab asked, "By what right does this city even exist?"

"Property rights," Bradley said. "Our Constitution."

Cab asked, "Who represents this Constitution?"

"Politicians, lawyers, cops, bureaucrats with guns," Bradley said. "The guys with the guns."

"The believers enacting their scripts," Cab said. "What was dreamed up has become permanent. All of this land inhabited by people for ten thousand years before we got here, they had other scripts, other operating systems that defined the world and their roles within."

They heard the door to the stair enclosure and Cab said, "The pursuit of wealth contains the idea that money can protect us. The more power we have the more we are responsible for the source of wealth. The land. The animals. What if having great wealth means having more responsibility to other people? You see, truly altruistic and ethical people would be indistinguishable from deities—or aliens."

John wasn't in the office. At twenty-three minutes after two in the morning on March 23rd, Maeve gave birth. They named her Eva. And he promptly took parental leave.

No one could replace John.

Sebastian relocated to his Portland address and began coming to the office every day. The effect on productivity was marked. Sebastian held the power, he was CEO and fantastically charismatic. Makner Portland fast became a hive of pheromones. From alpha to omega, every male in the office was charged with a weird fever. He had always seemed to arrive Fridays with a different woman and his sex drive had lost nothing in the Portland spring.

Bradley had signed up for the free trial offered by an online cooking school with video recipe exercises and professional chef support. He watched the first one which explained how to properly cut vegetables with a knife and ordered a set of kitchen knives. He began practicing. It was a rolling motion from the tip of the blade down and easy enough. He went ahead with the next video and ordered two sauce pans and a cast iron pan. He felt this had to be enough to make dinner. He appreciated that the methodical set of steps was essentially an algorithm. What temperature to set the stove was discoverable by trial and error and in a recipe it was knowledge contained within the series of procedures in which he input energy and materials. Bradley prepared a simple stir fry of vegetables and chicken served over rice. It was okay, but after all that he wondered why bother. It was so much easier to order it—and he knew what he really wanted. But Bradley had never had a real relationship with a woman. Sex had been transactional, and he didn't make time to form relationships. He could do hookups, he could order a bride, that he knew. But he didn't like being with people who had no interest in anything he wanted to talk about. He knew he had to spend time with women, that was the only way. And yet, he was extremely fortunate—although bad form and generally not recommended to get together with a coworker, considering the awkwardness of facing them every day if it flopped. That would be terribly inadequate, and yet Rebecca held the ultimate appeal for a serious developer. She was extremely intelligent and weird. This brought it to a boil and Bradley seized the biological opportunity presented by his brother.

They had left the building late, it was after eleven.

"My brother will be in town. I got comped tickets."

Rebecca looked at him. She was exhausted.

"Does that sound fun?" he asked.

XII

MAKNER ANNOUNCED that console owners would be able to explore the open beta beginning on the tenth of May. They promised this version would be the one to go live at launch, along with any bug fixes and other improvements. The additional month allowed developers to complete the integration of code delivered by their vendors and the anticipation circulating among fans, coupled with speculation about the delay, furthered the awareness of Cityzen.

A few employees who quit had left reviews online about the lack of diversity in age, gender, and ethnicity; overlong hours; the very expensive benefits package; a demanding systems architect, Aydin, who was without compassion; and the Wells Fund—although the controversy over their investments was irrelevant to fans who trusted Makner had merged with a professional fund in the financial interest of players.

If their money grew, how the fund was managed didn't matter to the vast majority and but still, opinions about the merger prompted the PR department to feed biographical details about Franklin Wells. His class at Harvard included future CEOs and government officials and industry magnates across all sectors of the economy. He had served on the President's Council of Economic Advisors and attended the World Economic Forum in Davos every year. At his office he kept a sculpture of the Christ child made from seven pints of his own blood that the artist collected over seven months and poured into a mold and froze. Franklin displayed the baby in a custom refrigeration system. This was all public information and Makner played it to their strength by owning their relationship with Franklin. His passion for medieval military strategy had made for a strong connection with the company. He was a Kastle player too.

Sebastian could appear at work stations any time and ask to see what a developer was doing. "And you think that will be good enough?"

Answering in the affirmative or negative didn't matter.

"I want to see what you really think."

Anticipating his return stretched developers toward next-level approval, which was open ended. "I see we can do better." A constant spur for more performance. Bradley and Rebecca were unable to leave the office before Sebastian and on the night of *Saving Me*, by the time they'd hailed a ride, the show had already started. In the backseat Bradley offered her an energy drink.

"That's a pill."

"It's the caffeine," he said, "of like a can of pop with an analog of amino acid found in green tea and some medicinal herb from India called brahmi."

She split it with him, and he popped one more. He saw the marquee from down the street: BRIAN SABIN / SAVING ME / ONE NIGHT ONLY / SOLD OUT. The conspiratorial energy between him and Rebecca had flared in the days before the show. He'd advised her not to mention their tickets to anyone. They rushed into the lobby and, outside a closed door leading into the auditorium, an usher scanned the tickets, said their seat numbers aloud, looked up from his screen, and it was obvious to Bradley and Rebecca that he believed them to be important people.

"Right this way, Mr. Sabin."

Bradley and Rebecca followed him into the darkened theater

and, walking down the aisle, they saw Brian spotlit onstage beside a platform with five wide steps that led to a black grand piano. Brian Sabin wore white. His voice amplified without a visible mic. He was telling a funny story about his daughter.

The usher stopped at the VIP section and Bradley and Rebecca apologized discreetly while edging past the knees of other important somebodies and took their seats front and center.

Bradley could see perfectly.

He felt so proud of his brother.

Their parents had encouraged both of them to play music. As a child, Bradley didn't understand the difference in years or the amount of time required to learn an instrument. Brian, somehow, could play, and Bradley couldn't. He sounded bad and he believed he would always be that way. Brian could relax with people and be himself, even more than himself, he could be what other people wanted. He mounted the stairs while telling a charming story and sat at the piano and began to perform a song that was hilarious. It cracked up Bradley and he glanced at Rebecca. She was captivated, her expression ecstatic. The lights dimmed and changed color and Brian launched into a beautiful song. When he walked back down the steps, telling a story about his wife, he brought the audience closer to him, they were relating to a real person. Brian spoke with hundreds of people as a normal person would with their best friend.

He had their total confidence. As an audience, and individually.

Bradley looked at her again. Rebecca was watching Brian and she turned to Bradley, smiling. Bradley didn't touch her arm or display affection. Brian had her attention and while fame may be human phenomena, with hundreds of millions of dollars up for grabs in a come-all business, it was quickly locked down. The barrier between the star and the normal person was a real manifestation of an economic engine of enormous wealth and power. The special person and the common people. Super and duper. A beloved person could become the ambassador for a commodified thing, a unit of sales, butts in seats. The performer was a willing participant, as the benefits of joining an elite class of useful people were real. The ability to do this required performers to say and do the things that normal people wanted to do, but couldn't for whatever reason. A fear of speaking in public, of being different, of saying the truth. The fear of death.

"Tony was from another part of town, a tough kid," Brian said. "Rough part. I don't think he'd ever seen a flower."

He started to talk about a time he accidentally stepped on a kid's tulip in their school's learning garden. Bradley had heard this before and he heard what Brian wasn't telling everyone.

"Tony followed me and threatened me," Brian said. "'YOU STEPPED ON MY TULIP!' I didn't see him coming. I said, I'm sorry, I didn't mean to step on your tulip."

It was a surprise, the shock of recognition and novelty. For kids, it was poop. What wasn't said, what was them and not them. It was what Rebecca had come to organically in her effort to be heard amid the noise. The channels of information and entertainment that had been built into the internet over decades would require many lifetimes to experience. History had been curated long ago. The world itself had become mediated. No one person could internalize the list of possible choices of what to experience, much less consume it all—or even a small fraction of the available content—as while one piece was experienced thousands of new things appeared from a vast global info-entertainment network that spoke a universal language of desire.

Curation itself became entertainment. Brian began his career with a web series in which he interviewed comedians and musicians while providing hilarious commentary on new songs, movies, and games. At first, when no one famous would come on, Brian would impersonate them and conduct the entire interview with video splicing and wigs and makeup. People loved the amount of work he put into those goofy bits. And it got the attention of the people he spoofed, with the sincerity of his love for their work, the agents started to return his calls. The knock-on effect of layering in other talents with his own gift for funny anecdotes had leveraged him into contracts with companies to promote their material, and he was pushed further in the entertainment industry by his natural charm. His crucial insight in the creation of a celebrity persona was the ability to trigger the aspirational self in the experiencer.

The human being remained the ultimate delivery device for those shared cultural creations that, for all their potential to become branded products and audiovisual recordings and displays, exist primarily in the experience of being human. To be famous, to be recognized, to be real. Bradley suffered the comparison and without positive attention, anything would do. He hated himself for not being loved. And he hated to know that about himself. Then he saw the source of his fury, and he shouted out in the auditorium: "You threw that kid down the stairs!"

Brian paused.

He'd heard Bradley. He was ready for any barb, and normally he would deflect a heckler with the ease of a Judo master. But it was something only Bradley would know, and Bradley saw his brother was thrown. It took Brian a second longer, but he was a brand, and he had the mic, the elevation, the lights, and the psychological edge of doing something that terrifies most people. More powerful than a regular human identity, his brand had every advantage over a voice from the crowd.

"Anybody ever get into a fight?" Brian said, his voice traveling through the high-powered sound system. "Clap if you've ever beaten the stuffing out of someone."

The crowd clapped and jeered.

"So many of you! What a good audience."

A woman yelled, "I love you, Brian!"

"So does my wife. We can work it out, later."

Bradley shouted louder than before: "That kid never came back to school!"

The cruelty of children was no revelation. The ruthlessness of the boys reaching for some greater love. The love of parents, of a mate, of an entire room full of people. A light beamed from the aisle on Bradley's face—turning, he saw the light. Everything was a bright spot in darkness. "Sir, we have to ask you to not raise your voice or speak with the performer."

The light was gone.

Bradley sat fuming, and he looked at Rebecca. She didn't return his gaze. He hated himself with more anger and alienation from anything good or whole. She was afraid of him, she didn't like him. He was the asshole. He could be better. He was better than him! Bradley, ready to engage, stood up and felt her pulling his arm. Rebecca was shaking her head side to side, sternly, her eyes wide. She pulled him down with both hands.

Rebecca put one finger to her lips.

Bradley sat through the show, planning his next move. After Brian bowed and left the stage, the house lights went up. He'd introduce Rebecca to his brother, they would laugh this off. Everything was possible and yet, nothing could be undone. Bradley felt the disapproval of the people seated near him. The bruise on his face. They saw the madman. Rebecca had left her seat and Bradley got up and went into the crowded aisle. He felt everyone knew it was him who shouted. They could see it. They knew. Where was Rebecca? Bradley couldn't see her among the people walking up the aisle. He looked for her in the lobby and she wasn't there. Outside and among the people gathering and getting rides, he found her leaning against the wall looking at her phone.

"Let's get a drink."

"No," she said. "I have to go."

"We can go to my place."

"No. Thanks, Bradley. It was interesting." She touched his arm and kissed him on the check below his bruise. "Your brother is amazing."

"I want to introduce you."

Rebecca considered this.

"Okay," she said.

Bradley took out his phone and texted Brian, to make a show of it, like this was prearranged. He looked at the screen and said, "Okay, let's go."

He led her back into the lobby and found an usher. "Brian Sabin invited me and my friend to the green room. I'm his brother. Where do we go?"

"Yes, sir."

The usher took her walkie-talkie and pressed a button.

"What are your names?"

Bradley looked at Rebecca and said, "Surprise him?" He turned to the usher. "That would be fun. Let's just walk back there, once he sees us . . ."

"We have guests of Brian Sabin going backstage?" the usher spoke into the receiver. She waited. "Mm-hm. Yes. Excuse me. Sir, please tell me your names."

"Bradley Sabin and Rebecca Klein."

She repeated their names.

Bradley took out his phone.

"I'm sorry," she said. "We're not allowed to take anyone backstage."

"I am his brother. I just need to talk with him and we can clear this up. There must be a misunderstanding." Bradley rang him and stood there, waiting. He watched Rebecca's expression change from willing to disappointed as a minute passed and he said, "Maybe we can catch him later tonight."

They left the building and on the sidewalk she said, "Are you okay?"

"I'm fine."

"How do you feel?"

"I feel fine."

"Do you want to talk about something?"

"My brother gets it. He rides the rising tide of shit. It irks me to be a piece of shit. A little. I don't know. Let's get a drink."

"Oh, Bradley." Rebecca gave him a hug. "You're good, okay?"

She put him at arm's length holding onto his shoulders and looked into his face. "I'll see you on Monday, okay?"

"I'm not crazy."

"I know."

"Oh. Bye." He stepped back and turned to go.

"You're good," she said.

He raised his fist in the air and walked away.

XIII

SEBASTIAN SHOPPED AROUND. He had his pick of disaster-prone cities. He and Aydin had landed on the earthquake, but Makner drove hard for municipal largess, solicited bids along the west coast, and received a ten-year tax break to locate in Portland.

The mayor announced, "We celebrate this opportunity to raise awareness about emergency preparedness." The cameras rolling, Sebastian personally oversaw the marketing of Cityzen and had contracted a local PR firm to place Makner within Portland's journey from weird to wealthy and back again.

The mayor thanked Sebastian for bringing business to Portland. She had to create a favorable investment climate, and the game's spin on the earthquake was useful. Capital will search for its highest rate of return—and the city was there to help them find it, right there. Portland had to compete for business elites and corporations with other global cities. It might not be a world center but local politicians had to lead, the growth of their economy, the growth of their city would bring it the attention of the market, of investors, of business, of the creative class. The people with money. The mayor didn't belabor a point, but Portlanders with no money couldn't pay for services they use, and if the city spent more than it brought in, it was bad when they went for a loan, which was how infrastructure was financed, through loans, from the bank.

Federal funding had been drastically cut and the city began to operate as a business, serving the needs of capital. Portland had to look good for the ratings agencies. The endgame might leave a tower of multimillion-dollar condos used as investment vehicles by global oligarchs, but capitalism was the only game in town. Portland had to play, or lose its opportunity to grow. The economy had to grow. If it didn't grow, Portland couldn't service its debt; if it couldn't service its debt it couldn't get loans; and if they couldn't get loans, they couldn't run the city. The city leaders were chosen for their ability to keep their city alive, their economy humming, schools, streets, safety, sewers and sanitation; bringing money in, come what may, be it a real estate mutual fund, Wall Street buying single-family homes to capture rents, what have you, it was welcome if it brought more capital to the city and increased property values. The growth of real estate value would bring in more revenue through property taxes and by growing the high-end first, they could subsidize city services and pay for the rest of it.

A municipal bank had been proposed—a way for the city to manage public money without wasting billions to pay interest borrowing from investors on the bond market—and that was still being studied, held back by an old canard about small government. Progressive taxation and redistributive spending had been disparaged and decimated. That was life, it was business first. If profits were made, the people could be served.

Reporters from local media were invited to the Chinatown office and Sebastian walked them through the space, talking about merging the real and the digital. He did on-camera interviews under a pavilion built by the public relations team on the roof. He said playing Cityzen would be the ultimate experience of civilization-style strategy games. People recognize the digital realm is real, and entertainment is big business. The ever-coming quake, a disaster and the greatest of opportunities, people can experience the mystic elevation of property. Cityzen will give everyone a chance to own a piece of Portland's future.

Like Bradley said, the media had their story.

Aydin wrote a piece about the game and the industry went nuts. Before launch he began to sit with developers and go over the code. His work on Kastle was legend, and guys who understood, which was the entire development team, held their systems architect in the highest esteem. Some devs would get that trembling in the throat when answering his questions. The math was extremely challenging and many problems couldn't be outsourced to an online forum; the teams were developing solutions without precedent. Each step in a series of greater complexity toward an unknown and to see Aydin walk up, devs were terrified by a solution's ability to reveal their process and to have their thinking exposed in the numbers he absorbed as he sat beside them. He might not speak and they'd have to continue working. He'd lean back. Then he might say one word. It would insert into a process directionally, he'd shift their perspective in a word. His mind leading them into the solution.

"Yes. This is right."

They understood. They had done it, to hear him say that.

He wasn't one to dispense compliments. He would rise and walk on to the next team. Aydin was successful, but he was never allowed to be anything else. His father was an accomplished engineer with patents to his name, and he was very strict. As an employer, Aydin had no mercy. He'd become a success through being a master. His greatness was in the game; it would be a waste for him to sit and code. But Aydin was cold when he explained things. When he stood beside Shane, he didn't think of him as a friend. "Are the textures ASTC compressed?"

"They seem to have a fairly large minimum size," Shane said.

"You need to get this."

Aydin valued employees for their utility to his company, and Shane trusted his boss. He wanted to be there. Shane was happy to be part of this coding community. Cab and Monty were featured in an interview exploring the applied artificial intelligence and cybersecurity so crucial to Cityzen. Cab said that a machine didn't have to be conscious to be super-intelligent, and he observed that Gen had been granted the same legal status as a corporation and owned the IP for each of the design solutions it created. He said those creations will be the sole property of the player who buys them. Under contract with Makner, he plugged the game.

Bradley did an interview that made it onto the blog and when he read it the next day, what he had said was different than he remembered, edited and condensed. More women were working at the office as temps and contractors, but Rebecca was the only senior developer. Makner used her photo on their website and she did a video interview with Sebastian. They joked and teased the game. Analytics allowed the company to pinpoint what received attention and they moved her into a spokesperson role in the last few days before launch. Her beauty and wit and she knew the game, she had the gift.

Shane had his interview too. He was awkward in front of the camera, and found it hard to speak under pressure like that, but he was proud of the video circulating online from Final Level. Having been on a panel and talking with his peers felt more normal.

And then Cityzen was live.

How people behaved individually and amongst their friends was not the same as how hundreds of millions behaved under conditions of duress. The crowding, the competition, the continual scarcity relative to those with more. Climate change, crop failure. It pushed people. The movement of the masses, it was subtle, but in the US there was no tolerance for fucking up. No advocates for the working poor. No bleeding hearts.

It might not be said so bluntly, actually the opposite would be said, but in practice, judging the policy by its effects: weakness was held in contempt. Strength was celebrated. The most ruthless behavior ensconced in power and rippling through the fabric of society, writing the law down to the city level in favor of producing, managing, attracting and extracting capital. The effects of injustice were real, and in the city, Makner was emblematic, a target, a symbol of disaster capitalism.

It was ready-made for protest.

Activists gathered outside the building. Bradley walked through the chanting crowd of middle-aged people who had no intention of playing video games, and went inside. He'd slept for twelve hours after the launch.

"What is this shit?"

"They're calling for a tax on financial speculation," Rebecca said.

The activists had an idea to generate revenue for Portland but it couldn't happen under the terms of the deal the city had signed with Makner. No taxes. So that was that, and the protest brought more attention to the game, and lo and behold, it was fun to play and addictive to collect resources that tallied up as some kind of money.

Shane's dad called him.

"Your mother and I are playing your game." Shane could hear the emotion in his father's voice, and they spoke enraptured by his success—his father's love and the arrival of adulthood—he was now a provider, a creator. It was a powerful game. His father gave him that. "I'm not saying I'm buying our home there. But I gotta hand it to you. It's a clever way to make a dollar."

People could make some pennies policing property, catching Looters. And collecting building material, creating fantastic colored structures. It was easy. The simplicity of stacking blocks married to the pursuit of property. The game bloomed upon the wall screens arrayed in the main room of the Makner building. They had multiple displays of analytics and could toggle into any user's POV. One schematic showed the entire city's street grid from above with red, blue, green, and yellow colored representations of Looters, Police, Builders, and Investors. The system had inbuilt nudges to balance the allotment of character types. The structures were going up—and downtown was being bought up, fast. Players came from Kastle to Cityzen. They could claim beta keys on their account, and gamers worldwide found the keys if they knew where to look.

On day two Makner gave sets of five keys to its current testers for their friends. Kastle message boards became a relay. The public beta would run through June twelfth. They'd roll in the feedback and, with improvements, put the game in wide release July sixth. Monty was in his element. The company had to keep watch of their system. The load balancer automated much of the work but a delicate human touch was needed to keep things running smoothly.

The launch had brought their team a new self-awareness, other people's recognition. *Wired* would feature Cityzen in the July issue. And this was only the beginning, it would get better. Talk about scale! These things were global.

On the third day an internal alarm sounded in the office and Aydin stormed through the room. Rebecca ran to find Monty. He was in his swivel chair, typing full speed with one hand, adjusting dials with the other, working with the machine at a pace that didn't look human.

"I need to find Bradley!" she said.

"The system's down," Monty said.

"Where's Bradley?"

"Cityzen crashed."

XIV

"I NEED ANSWERS." Aydin stood at the head of the table. "Someone has to come forward." The engineering meeting convened leaders from each team and the morning after the crash, John had stepped in to help address the emergency.

"I installed a new library," Bradley said, staring at John until he turned and met his gaze. "I had a feeling we should've stuck with the logic I had in there. It never caused a problem before."

"I wanted to make sure," John said. "His tool was—"

"He requested the new library," Bradley said.

"Have you done the due diligence in the code?" Aydin asked.

"I've done everything," Bradley said. "Everything passes."

"Have you run your tools?" Aydin asked.

"I ran MET," Bradley said.

"I want to see the MET reports."

John's library affected how memory was handled in the application and everyone agreed memory allocation caused the crash. John asked, "When was the last time we updated MET to deal with memory leaks?"

"Usually my software captures memory problems," Bradley said. "I think it's the library."

"We needed a new library," John said. "Bradley's tool hasn't been used with software at this scale. It hadn't even been used on Kastle. It wasn't able to scale to a game handling this much memory."

"We're not sure what the memory leak was," Monty said. "It wasn't clear in the stack trace. This is not an obvious bug."

"Where were you?" Adyin asked Bradley.

"Working with Dillon, we'd stepped out for lunch."

"What do you think this is? We eat here!"

Sebastian had joined the meeting. He'd have to deliver on his promise. Franklin Wells had called Sebastian's private line after the crash on Thursday. He worried his fund wasn't secure attached to the game. Sebastian attempted to calm him with the pretense that this was normal. The beta was intended to discover and solve problems. "Wait a minute," Wells shouted. "My money is not a game!"

The fund tanked fast.

"I'm putting out fires here," Franklin screamed, "and you need to feel the heat. Solve your fucking problems and prove it to me."

Sebastian watched the media reaction to their game going down. They made the top of Hacker News: "Cityzen Deported – Makner Stuck in the Middle Ages." From hero to zero and, to fail this quickly, they said the company wasn't what it claimed to be. Speculation went from the faulty engineering to ballooning doubts about the platform being able to deliver a game, a social network, an architectural tool, and an investment vehicle. It was impossible to fulfill all those promises. It was ridiculous, a pastiche. A grab for attention, a flavor-of-the-month fad, a hype machine for Makner's real money-maker: the Gen software designed by Cab and still owned by him.

They called out Sebastian for conning talented computer scientists with his charisma and visionary talk about the future. The day of the crash he had been in Eden, Utah after a trip to an Indian reservation outside Las Vegas, an event celebrating the individual as hero, the autonomous free agent able to make rational choice and use their free will to create their own experience. Sebastian took responsibility for generating new products, and engaged in the hunt for new ideas, people and technologies. He would land the best talent and offer unbeatable conditions for them to join forces and create experiences unlike anything. To change the world—he flew to Portland on the first available flight.

Investors needed confidence their data was secure. The Wells Fund was in jeopardy. It seemed too lax. A gaming platform was too weak a vehicle for serious investment. The headlines played Franklin for a fool: "It's Fun, Until You Lose Your Money."

Franklin demanded Sebastian publicly fire whoever was responsible. They had to show accountability and John was given a generous buyout. To calm investors Franklin sent out a letter stating the problem was human error: an adaptive horizontal structure and distributed leadership made for a most competitive company able to respond instantly to market feedback and the technical demands of an ever-evolving product—and the platform was solid, the error had been accounted for and the person who caused the brief delay in service had been terminated. The problem had been solved. Engineers asked about John and were told various reasons why he wasn't coming back, but they all felt he had been fired. This ratcheted up anxiety among the development teams. No one at that high level had been fired before. They knew if John was fired, they were all fair game.

"Did we get hacked?" Shane asked.

"No," Monty said. "Don't worry, Shane. They are no match for me."

Monty's security had automated defenses that learned from its opponents and he was actively training the AI, countering attacks, and observing the boards where guys tried to take credit for crashing the system: I did it to help m. I could see all the custom accounts. Elite48 took down cityzen. 2EZ.

But the engineers realized their tools couldn't protect them. MET was a tool that graded software and prevented bugs, and they had grown reliant on the tool. They trusted their tools. The engineers began second-guessing themselves.

Bradley arrived to the office after eleven. Dillon greeted him as he approached his desk. Both Shane and Rebecca were not at their stations and he found a motorcycle catalogue near his keyboard. He picked it up.

A note fell out. An invitation to dinner with Aydin and Sebastian. He smiled. He looked across the room at the glass wall of Aydin's office. He saw the boss doing his calisthenics in a standing resistance machine.

"*Fucking-A.*"

Bradley arrived at Aydin's house in the West Hills at the appointed time. It was eight thirty and the meal was catered, a cook and server attended while the three men made small talk in the dining room. After the plates were cleared, the household staff left and Aydin said, "We have what you'd call an all-points analysis of the world's information that adjusts our trades to optimize returns. It is extremely aggressive. Bradley, I want to make sure you understand. That you are comfortable with violence when it is necessary to achieve a justified outcome."

"I follow," Bradley said. "Tell me vectors and outcome."

"Bradley, you are a pioneer," Aydin said and smiled.

Sebastian said, "Wells has externalized costs to maximize profits, those vectors will be born by unknowns. We have no idea who or what will experience them."

"It's irrelevant," Aydin said. "We are engaged in a life and death struggle."

Sebastian nodded and lifted his glass and finished the last of his drink and set it down. He took the bottle and offered to refill Bradley's. Bradley held his hand up. Sebastian poured himself a glass. "Our investment strategy is necessary to survive in a competitive market. It's a winner-take-all system."

"We are going to dominate," Aydin said. "To win."

"Makner must become more than games to survive," Sebastian said.

"Everyone needs shelter," Aydin said. "We are going to own it."

"Maximize profit," Sebastian said, "in the capture of destabilized or otherwise compromised assets. Finance, insurance and real estate."

"The extractive industry," Aydin said. "Fossil fuels, mining. Industrial agriculture. Pharmaceuticals. The developing countries. The guard industry—what you would call prisons, security, and defense."

"The trades are entirely rational," Sebastian said.

"What do you want from me?"

"We want the old Bradley."

XV

SEEING AYDIN'S motorcycle parked outside the office, Shane dismounted and walked his bike past the homeless guy who Aydin paid to guard the free-standing machine. It had electric hub motors in both wheels and a gyroscopic stabilizing system. Then Shane saw the man's hands.

He had no dirt under his nails.

He wore a long beard and unwashed clothes but his hands were clean.

Shane saw no way a man sleeping rough could have hands like that; he couldn't be homeless. That was *camouflage*.

John was an old friend and he agreed, he was ready to go. He had made safe investments. He had millions. John wanted to be a father. He left without hard feelings, he even shook Bradley's hand and thanked him for looking after the company. All parties maintained Makner's best interests. John was good. Sebastian and Aydin were too skilled in their dealings to make him angry. They had no need to create resentment within an industry player who enjoyed the support of his community gained from years of enthusiastic service. When Aydin made a decision to buy out John's share in the company, Sebastian knew he could tell this story. But he refused to be the one to tell his friend and wasn't around for the meeting. Sebastian left for San Francisco to talk with journalists and publicly apologize to all who risked their money in the game.

He redirected their perception of Cityzen. The crash was good. The number of users was high and given this positive signal, they were increasing their investment in resources to support players and investors. He welcomed everyone to experience the future of work; all work done on a computer could be learned by software; the game was a personal AI assistant for creating buildings of the future. The final designs were delivered by a licensed architect, the Gen software, and purchased rock bottom in Cityzen to be sold in markets around the world. The zoning and code requirements for any jurisdiction could be calculated into your design, bringing it within any city's limits. Gen was infinitely patient and extremely capable of arriving at optimized solutions through the months-long permitting process. And sales of the designs could be reinvested into a Cityzen account.

Sebastian diverted attention from a technical difficulty to amassing wealth. Underemployed workers would now create value within a social network that they could leverage in the real world. While those with surplus capital could speculate and trade, placing their claim upon Portland's future.

Shane saw aliasing in a barge reflection, again. He'd solved this already. He pasted his line, committed his code, and his solution was a serious bug.

MET flagged the error.

He checked the code against the line in his text editor. It was the same thing he committed months ago. And now someone had patched the missing case in MET. Shane looked through the commit history and didn't see an entry for the change. It was Bradley's tool that had allowed his line into the beta, and the tool had been changed with no trace of who or how. The only one who could circumvent the versioning to make direct changes to the software was Aydin or

Bradley, and Aydin didn't work on the code.

The memory could leak from that reflection.

He scrolled Staff Track and noticed a divergence in their activity pattern, but that was the night of the crash. He'd stayed late, and so had everyone. Bradley was the last to leave. Shane inspected his line and he saw the bug—there was some kind of incomplete test coverage, a test that Bradley had never accounted for—and Shane had committed it.

XVI

SHANE LEFT his apartment in southeast around seven thirty. It took him a half hour to reach the office, he could make it in twenty riding at full power. It was June and with the return of summer, Shane had been biking to work every day. The Tesla SEX outside the building looked like Bradley's but he only lived a short distance away and it had been a long time since Bradley arrived before nine. Shane entered the building and carried his bike to the rack and, approaching his work station, he saw Bradley had shaved. He looked good.

"Hey, Shaner!"

"You're up early."

Bradley closed his eyes and nodded his head slowly, smiling.

"Yeah, man. I'm up."

No one talked about his transition until the Friday all-hands meeting when Sebastian announced that Bradley had demonstrated the fortitude to handle more responsibility as technical lead. The employees clapped, especially those who knew him personally. Dillon had found his mentor to be gifted and kind when it counted. Shane and Rebecca cheered for him. They both loved Bradley in their own way. He was a weird boss, but they were weird too. And now Shane didn't know who would lead their team—though Rebecca's expression when Sebastian said she would do it revealed she knew this was happening. Stepping to the center of the circle with

Bradley, they embraced in a ceremonial transfer of power.

The development teams felt in Bradley a release from the uncertainty and doubt that followed the crash. His advancement was welcome and by Bradley most of all. Rather than building a bridge, he wanted to be the one to convince everyone to walk across it. He'd been building too long. He moved his things from the desk next to Dillon and Shane and Rebecca. Taking his work to John's empty office was symbolic, sure, but entering that room was an act of power. Bradley was the *producer*. He was the one who got people to work those long hours for four years running. He had inspired Shane to do those twelve-hour days, he was making Cityzen happen. Anyone could see further into the company if they acted like Bradley. He was a blueprint for success. Bradley had entered the inner circle.

June passed into July and Shane found that much of what Bradley had brought to their team wasn't replaced by Rebecca. Her leadership did not rely on intimidation. There was no underlying competition. They'd been working to improve the game in response to user feedback and she deferred to the best ideas no matter who offered them, where they were discovered, or how. By combining intuitive and logical thinking she was more aware and able to address the underlying issues, and she even requested they maintain their health as carefully as the codebase. She did not stake her life on the game, but the hours pushed them to the wall. The wide release of Cityzen carried many times the resources and stress of the beta.

Shane stood outside Bradley's office until he looked up from his monitor. "I need access to the fund UI."

"Stay with the code you know," Bradley said.

"No, I have to access data in the virtual bank."

"Shane, work with what you have."

"I have to get access to do the work."

"Make an authorization request."

"We don't have time."

"You don't have access to their database. We have to follow security protocol." Bradley stood up and walked over to Shane. "Use the system. Let go. Shane, trust me."

He looked into Shane's eyes.

"This was established to help us all. Trust me."

The weekend of the Fourth, Aydin took Bradley out on a motorcycle ride, letting him use his backup. Aydin told him the motorcycle was an essential vehicle in a catastrophe. All the roads would fill with traffic and lane splitting between the stalled lines of cars would be the only escape. He brought Bradley to a property he'd purchased off the road to Mount Hood. It had everything he needed, he kept it stocked with provisions to last more than two months. That's how long he would wait before returning.

"Sustainability is a fairy tale," Aydin said. "The real future is one of surprise and sudden shocks."

Aydin and Bradley sat on the porch of his cabin gazing upon a meadow of wildflowers and beyond to the willows growing along a stream that followed a three-hour hike to the spring where the water emerged from the ground.

"People believed our society could make the necessary adjustments to its central institutions," Aydin said. "The data doesn't support this. This is unfortunate, but we must respect the science. As stated in the laws of thermodynamics, it takes energy to maintain any system in a complex, ordered state—and human society is no exception. How many babies were born today?"

"A million?" Bradley said.

"That will take little more than three days," Aydin said. "The profound effect of humanity upon natural systems results in what complexity theorists call non-linear responses. Vast pine forests dying, fish stocks collapsing, extreme weather events, take your pick, you read the news. What regions are we going to abandon?"

"Florida," Bradley said.

"We say it's too bad about the pollinators, but we can let them go. And the monarch butterflies, dolphins, coral. More non-human biota destroyed forever. You see widespread failure of global food systems due to the destabilization of the climate, changes in fluctuation of behavior in the natural systems."

Aydin offered Bradley a drink and they walked out to a shed that Aydin opened with a metal key. He said the notion that society will reach a glide path that we can ride into the future is misleading. They walked back to the porch with two wide-mouth refillable bottles of spring water.

"We are entering a world of increasing turbulence, shocks and surprises," Aydin said, opening a bottle and looking at Bradley. "More severe shocks. We need to be able to respond creatively to a shock. Cheers."

Aydin held out his bottle and Bradley met his, the stainless steel bottles clinked and they both drank and sat back in the sunlight.

"It is essential to be able to take the shock."

"Yeah, man."

"To bounce back and adjust to this changed environment. How will you survive, Bradley?"

"The skin of my teeth," Bradley said, smiling.

Aydin did not smile. "People faced with multiple stresses simultaneously. The problems interact with each other in unexpected ways. What happens is overload. Where standard routines and procedures cannot cope. With multiple simultaneous impacts upon the institutions of society. What you get is collapse. You can't actually separate one problem from the others. To deal with one. You can't. They are coming at once. Society begins to put more energy into their complex systems than they can support."

Aydin looked at Bradley. "We can work together."

Bradley nodded. "Yeah."

"I understand that our models contain flaws," Aydin said, "but we've used a suite of models from around the world and they've shown that if this projection holds, it has catastrophic implications for all of humanity. This is science. It is not a story. That we can continue this behavior into the future. This way of life. The entire population will not be joining us."

Sebastian arrived. They celebrated the release of the game and Sebastian casually mentioned a trip to New Zealand where he had property. Aydin said he finally secured his second passport, joking that now after killing a man with his bare hands he can escape to another country using his passport from a small nation in the Caribbean. Not to be outdone, Sebastian bragged he could draw a holstered pistol in one-point-five seconds, aim at a target seven yards away, and shoot it twice in the heart. They both agreed that a helicopter pad would be a nice addition to the roof of the Makner building.

Two days later, with the release of Cityzen, the entire office celebrated and Rebecca said, "Hey check this out!"

She had found her name linked to a smartphone video taken at her show. Coworkers gathered around her monitor and watched a clip of Bradley striking a man across the jaw and being subdued by bouncers. They played it on the large screen in the main room and let it loop.

He had invited a woman to the party. Her name was Taylor and she had contacted him through his employee email. She had moved to Portland after graduating from Stanford with a degree in Symbolic Systems, a Stanford-specific program that explored cognitive science, artificial intelligence, and human-computer interaction. She wrote him a disarming email that said she was interested in his work. For many young people, gravitating toward a kingpin was a reliable path forward. Bradley was hers, and she had infiltrated the world of Makner, with stunning smarts and beauty.

"I'm better than I was," Bradley told her. "I'm more intense. I'm more awesome." To his credit, he redirected attention to the company. "I'll stop at nothing to see Cityzen go to every city on the Ring of Fire. So what's next?"

XVII

AYDIN'S WIFE wore a sensor that wirelessly sent her vital signs to a display above the bed. They played on the bed and he gave her a full-body massage. He had read that clitoral stimulation was the common route but he observed the data and stuck his finger in her butt. The data indicated her aroused state and Aydin undressed and took his cock in his hands and pumped it for a count of ten and entered his wife, watching the data streaming before his eyes as he moved, the mound of his pelvis rubbing her clit, he changed his posture and rhythm in accord with the signal, reaching a rising crescendo as he brought her to orgasm. Aydin counted the pulses in the outer part of her vagina: one, two, three, and four. The data showed her heart rate, blood pressure and breathing continue to rise. At that point he was still inside her and hard as steel. He asked her permission to come. She shook her head and grabbed his ass and he continued thrusting. She gave herself to him while he monitored the screen, adjusting in concert to the data for optimum performance, and he saw she was having another and she said yes, yes, yes. Climaxing was proven to lead to positive thoughts about him. They met on the fourteenth of every month for this encounter. The science had shown her clit could easily grow twenty percent larger and become more easily aroused on that day. He allowed himself to orgasm.

Aydin flew to Portland that evening and arrived to his house after

YOU WILL WIN THE FUTURE

dark. The porch light and security lights were on inside. He entered through the front door, the temperature having adjusted automatically as the GPS and accelerometer on his device approximated his arrival.

He went to the kitchen, grabbed a glass, pushed the faucet handle, and took his supplement stack with a drink of water. Upstairs in his room, Aydin opened his suitcase and felt a fullness in the center of his chest. Placing his dirty clothes into the hamper, his arms felt like cinder blocks. The alarm sounded on his wristband. Aydin read he was having a heart attack. A stabbing pain hit the back of his skull.

His closet door opened and a Roombot rolled out.

Shane felt the speed. His mind centered on the road before him, tracking behind Bradley. He was going too fast.

Now he knew, he never understood speed inside a car.

"You'll do fine," Bradley had said. "It's like riding a bicycle."

Bradley had traded in the SEX for two motorcycles. "One for backup," he said. After work in August they walked from the office to his garage and Shane had liked it, it was an impressive machine. They started in a parking lot near Bradley's condo.

"Never take your eyes from the road in front of you."

"What about looking at the speedometer?" Shane asked.

"Don't do that."

His body flying through the air, the electric engine singing, the wind roaring, his motorcycle tearing along the road, curving up and through the hills to Crown Point. Bradley was in the lead. They had gone out weeknights and a day each weekend for six weeks—entry-level track day at the Portland International Raceway was where it all came together—and then Bradley had taken him out to the Historic Columbia River Highway. He loaned Shane protective gear made of para-aramid fiber and ballistic nylon with pads and plates throughout the fabric to protect major joints and body parts. They wore gloves with carbon-fiber knuckles. Bradley had slip-resistant boots. Shane wore his only pair of leather shoes. Each of their outfits was gray and had black bands up the sides of the legs and chest, Bradley's with blood red arms and stripes on the shoulders and blue on Shane's. Wearing this, carrying his helmet into the coffee shop that morning, seeing Bradley place an order, he felt like something out of a superhero comic.

"We're like Kastle avatars," Shane said, straddling his bike.

"This is not a game."

Bradley pulled on his helmet.

Shane and Bradley communicated through radio intercoms, Bradley's voice entering his consciousness to advise him of the road ahead, not a word more. The steady drone of his bike, the unfurling road, his speed. Racing up the two-lane road canopied by trees, passing homes, slowing for the intersections with schools, a restaurant, a little store. And the beauty of farmland, forests, the Sandy River, the Columbia. It was glorious. His fear conquered in the command of his machine, his environment. His body reached a new high.

His control had held firm, Shane overcame himself. Returning to Bradley's place in the late afternoon, they sat on his balcony enjoying the warm, late-summer air, hearing voices from a basketball game in the park. The light breeze on the stopped motion of Shane's body. It was good. Bradley was again pushing him. Away from the screen, out in the world. His friend had taken him to a new place. They were friends.

"We rode past Aydin's property," Bradley said.

"Where?"

"I can't tell you. You have to swear you won't tell anyone what I just said."

Shane held up his right hand. "Non-disclosure."

Bradley sat back in his chair and gazed through the impact-resistant glass of his balcony. "Aydin, man. We know. You and I both know that guy is a genius."

"When is he coming back?"

"Any day."

"Is it weird to be in charge?"

"This is black and white. Right and wrong. There are no two ways about it. What is good, you know?"

Aydin had gone to Sunnyvale to recuperate at home, but other than Sebastian no one at Makner knew that Aydin had heart surgery. Sebastian only said he had taken time off to be with his family.

"You hungry?"

"I could eat," Shane said.

Bradley spoke a command to the device he'd taken out of his pocket and placed on the low table between them. Sebastian wasn't in the office every day, and when he wasn't, Bradley was in charge. Sebastian deputized Bradley at the Friday meeting when Aydin was in the hospital. Bradley had some decision-making capacity, not bet-the-company stuff, but he had power. Shane turned around in his seat. Sheebie rolled toward them, a bottle of ChemYum in each gripper.

"You buy bitcoin?" Bradley asked, popping the lid on his bottle.

Shane opened the ChemYum and smelled it.

"Man," Bradley said. "This'll save us time."

"I like eating."

"This is eating."

Bradley drank. His eyes closed. He downed a third of it, grimaced.

Shane set his bottle on the table.

"You need to put your money in some diversified accounts," Bradley said. "I've been looking to buy a place in New Zealand. That shit is hard. I'd rent it, generate passive income. It'll be my haven."

"I've never left the US."

"No way."

"I've been to Seattle, Denver, San Francisc—"

"You need to get a passport. Necessary." Bradley locked eyes with Shane. "Do it. Now. Good as done." Bradley nodded his head and then turned, gazed at the city. "Start at work. I don't care. Get your photos, sign the documents, do it. You have my permission."

"Why is this so urgent?"

"This is important." Bradley turned in his seat, rested his elbow on the chair, and stared at Shane. "You want to make something of yourself?"

"Yeah."

"What are you going to make?"

Shane looked out over the city. He didn't know how to answer Bradley. He had always wanted to make a game, something like Kastle, like what they were making now. He liked Aydin and Sebastian. He was in the room with his heroes. They were real. Shane had been brought in. He was silent, and Bradley asked, "Have you ever had the sense that what you're doing doesn't matter? That what we're doing is bullshit."

"Wow. Not really, no."

"Don't you want to make a mark on the world?"

Shane thought for a moment. "Yeah."

"You have the gift, Shane. The discipline. You will make it. You're not a fuck-up. You will prosper."

Bradley rarely gave compliments.

Shane looked at him. "Thank you, Bradley."

"We will. Our fucking team, man! We know what is right. We're wild as fuck. We're independent from all that." Bradley arced his arm out across the cityscape. "The world is a dangerous place, and it was made that way because there is evil out there. The game we are playing is extremely competitive—life or death—and we have to win. You want to win?"

Shane nodded. He watched Bradley take another swig of Chem-Yum. Bradley motioned at his bottle. Shane picked up the ChemYum and took a drink. A sweet slurry run through with minerals, the texture and temperature of a shake.

"There will always be winners and losers." Bradley stood up. "Ah. You will need the fundamentals." He walked into the living room. "Come here man, I want to show you."

Shane followed Bradley into his room. Bradley opened the closet and pulled out a black duffel bag. "You can handle this. Keep it cool. This isn't for everyone. It's like UFOs. You believe when you see it. I can show you this shit is real."

Bradley unzipped the bag packed with the necessities of survival.

"We are free to do whatever the fuck we want."

"I'm not really into guns."

"Some people don't get it. They can't hack it. They're confused. Fuck them."

"Who do you mean, people?"

"The idiots are going to be locked out, we have that. Guaranteed. It will be a mess. Not forever. But messy as fuck. It will get fucking crazy because people are stupid. They're like children. In the face of death. We can do it—smart, resourceful people can and will—we do better. It's like evolution on fast-forward. Fitness. What Darwin was into. We meet the challenge of our moment, and shit is going sideways."

"Woah, man, I don't know. That sounds crazy."

"We're rich, you and me, man! Those who are smart, with skills, who can take care of themselves. We deserve what we have."

Shane put his hand to his face and began to chew on the cuticle of his finger. He looked at Bradley's black leather pants and tight black T-shirt. They both still had their boots on.

"You're fidgeting," Bradley said, focused on the contents of his black bag. "What's up?"

"I think you sound a little insane right now."

"We have the discipline, man. Morals. We have more morals than the people who need help. Those people have no discipline. And they can't take what rightfully belongs to us. Those who are moral are in charge, by whatever means. We have to stay on top. It requires some finagling. You cool?"

Shane sat down on the edge of the bed. "This is a lot to deal with. I know you don't do this to fuck with me. But what the hell?"

"I want to help you. I need disciplined people in the time of crisis." Bradley started to unpack his bag. "This is BOB, my bug-out bag. When I leave the disaster zone to our bug-out location. That's next, man. We're going to—I think I can get you in—to this thing."

"Seriously, I don't know this is my thing."

"You want to die?"

Shane shook his head.

"Didn't think so." Bradley began carefully repacking his bag. "The bug-out location will be stocked with provisions to get you through whatever crisis is on. But the other thing you'll want to prepare for is bugging in, you'll need enough supplies to survive at home. And whether you're bugging in or out, you need a gun." Bradley lifted it off the bed.

"Shane, you ever fire a gun?"

XVIII

SHANE WAS ALONE in his apartment and ricocheting Jason. His old friend preferred communicating with encrypted packets traveling between their computers without ever passing through a central server. Even strong encryption revealed metadata when messages passed through a central server, collecting a location or IP address. Their invisibility hid the entire social graph of Jason's connections.

His phone chirped. Shane turned from his desktop monitor and looked to the small device. He had texted Elsie earlier and her response lit the screen. She had taken a bag with the empty containers of her filled prescriptions and a folder containing all her documentation. She went to multiple doctors seeking treatment for chronic Lyme disease and each turned her away. The treatment guidelines were written like a document that could be used in court cases. Maybe against physicians, or by insurance companies to justify cutting off treatment. Elsie texted that another doctor had denied the existence of chronic Lyme and she signed with an emogo of herself produced in the moment—and automatically, by her emotions as read through biometric sensors of her phone and bracelet. It was a full-screen emotional caricature that most people only used with friends, this enhanced rendering of emotions could trigger mirror neurons in a viewer. She didn't text that her body was killing her, but Shane could feel she was in pain.

It was years now of dealing with weird failings of her body and excruciating pain that had only relaxed with the right treatment. She couldn't believe how different she'd felt, it was on Makner's health plan—the treatment she'd been denied—that specific treatment really helped her. Shane had reapplied to establish the proof of domestic partnership. A period of two hundred and forty days had accrued, at which time the insurance company reviewed the request. That was accepted and it would take ninety days to finalize. The cost was not reduced to the rate they started with.

The medicine she needed wasn't offered on her health plan and the doctors wouldn't treat her. It was a consequence of politics and profit. In 1980 the United States said it was okay for government institutions and universities to patent and profit from live organisms. Lyme disease was discovered in 1981 and professors took their discoveries, often made on the federal dime, and they patented them and started firms. What was commercial began to drive the research agenda, not what was medically necessary—and then it got worse. The insurance companies and HMOs realized that if they could get researchers to define Lyme and write guidelines for the disease in a certain way, they could cut their costs.

The guidelines said the researchers didn't know if chronic Lyme existed. To weasel out of paying for care, insurance companies had paid for a study by doctors who said Lyme disease was easy to diagnose and easy to treat. They declared it could be cured in two weeks, thereby allowing the insurance company to deny care for the people who were suffering from Lyme.

Shane didn't want to place unnecessary stress on her, and Bradley was definitely that. He didn't feel comfortable telling her what Bradley said. If anyone could help him understand what was happening to Bradley, Shane thought it would be Jason. He was around Bradley's age, he was a hacker. As a teen making Kastle mods, he was king.

Now Jason had a clean source of income trading social capital, but his partners were savvy enough to dig out his contacts from the metadata. So the invisible messaging was necessary for him to broker jobs and collect his twenty percent. He had high-value connections within Amazon. Working on freelance contracts for them, Jason had been living in an motorhome parked variously around Seattle. His connection to the client, a relationship hard won through real-time interactions with real people, was strong. The Amazon people who gave him work trusted Jason and that was the capital he could trade on. Trust had become the true value in an ecosystem populated by automated agents. Jason played a careful game of arbitrage, making passive income from the remote labor that did the work he then finalized and authenticated through his own LLC, called simply Jason Lee; he had incorporated himself.

Shane was about to reply, and another text from Jason popped up: it's a hedge

Shane typed: why not invest in making things work?

Jason responded: insurance is logically rational

Shane read the message and replied: not sure a gun helps

Jason texted: one gun? every day people heating the earth, the extra energy accumulating equivalent to exploding 400,000 Hiroshima atomic bombs. each day, 365 days a year!

He left a voice message on his sister's machine.

He didn't feel comfortable talking with coworkers about his feelings. Not about Bradley. Shane had declined his invitation to the gun range. But now, it felt like he was being punished. Aydin was back, five days a week, in at eight, out at eight. It wasn't like Shane had asked, but he wasn't invited to join them either and they talked about riding, Bradley and Aydin. Shane could code like them. He could make a better game. He diagramed a reward restriction flow chart, maybe it could be a new plumber hero, the ultimate home repair icon. The man who can fix the house! His own game. He'd be . . . anything he did was theirs, the entire thing, hero and all would belong to them. He put down the pad and lay back on the bed.

His phone chirped.

Shane lay there. His mom could be inviting him over for dinner. His dad ringing from the floor of Fred Meyer. Dillon wanting to go out for pinball. Elsie needing to talk. Sure. Bradley needs a friend. Not. Rebecca wanted him to meet. Right. Nora. He thought of his sister, his overworked, overachieving sister sitting at her desk somewhere in Manhattan. Shane reached for the phone.

Caller Unknown.

"This is Rick, from Amazon."

"For real?"

"Yes! The Amazon Ultra 90X, this is an amazing machine! You know how fast this is. You can ride it with no money down. Real freedom. Just say yes and we'll authorize it to arrive in one hour, a payment plan will agree with your—"

"No thanks."

"Do you know shared vehicles transmit germs?"

"No."

"Unless you wear gloves and a mask to ward off communicable disease—"

"That's my problem, Rick. I chose this. This is real life."

Shane hung up.

Nora called after seven that night, Shane's time. She did legal innovation at a white shoe firm, but she wasn't allowed to talk about it. Her division specialized in corporate law. It was a powerhouse law firm closely allied with Wall Street. Shane didn't want to worry her and didn't tell her about the guns. He didn't want a gun, but he needed to understand his friend.

"Is he on the spectrum?"

"No," Shane said. "I don't think so."

And he had no idea whether Rebecca knew what Bradley was afraid of. During lunch he tried to trigger her reaction with a remark about apocalypse insurance as a plug-in product. She didn't appear to sense the power and paranoia vibe that Shane had been exposed to. Monty stared at Shane. Rebecca kept talking with Dillon and Shane looked at Monty, he had the damaged look; it felt like a mirror. "Did you ever buy any?" Shane asked.

"You can hold all the cards and lose the house," he said.

"What kind of insurance would you buy?"

Monty invited him to the Tech Plex.

Shane knew the place and had attended a hackathon held in the first floor commons area. The Portland branch of Tech Plex was large enough to house one hundred and six people. A fraction of the demand, and it was an elite group who had membership. Monty applied when he was living in Pittsburgh. He had grown up in Overbrook and moved with his wife to Allegheny. He worked on the cyber initiative in the FBI's field office there. His squad was involved in some of the Justice Department's biggest cases. Monty had learned on the job, chasing identity thieves. He was an internet janitor. With the screen name Visible_Fist, he spent two years infiltrating the center of an online criminal community and finally became a black market administrator. The greatest vulnerability in any computer system was the people who used them. After his wife asked for a divorce, Monty interviewed with the Tech Plex and by the time he was accepted, his marriage was over. He bought into the co-housing group and lived in one of over a hundred properties around the world.

Shane had never been upstairs and when he arrived, Monty met him at the door. The first floor commons had desks that people could rent by the day or the month, and the open-plan office was built to resemble an Old World library. Monty called it the extrovert floor. More of an introvert, Monty read multiple books a week and his intellectual curiosity made him a good listener; he could engage any topic. He introduced Shane to people in the commons. Then they walked through the café and lounge and a large greenhouse along the south wall connected to a professional kitchen with a house chef. The household could join each other for breakfast, lunch, and dinner five days a week and members on each floor had a common kitchen and an app to purchase and designate shared staples and fresh food. Monty showed him the kitchen and the coworking spaces reserved for company members. This coveted membership allowed access to coworking and temporary residence in more than a hundred cities, including San Francisco, Stockholm, and Tokyo—extremely difficult to enter housing markets. The company had created a midmarket class of global citizens.

Short-term residents lived on the private second and third floors; and people who lived in the building long term had rooms on the three floors above that. The floors had three types of rooms: singles, families, and groups. The last being the cheapest option; people slept eight to a room in four bunkbeds.

Monty's room was modest—the single rooms were one hundred and eight square feet—but it was on the sixth floor with a view of Foster Boulevard and the evergreen trees of Mount Tabor in the distance. He had built-in bookshelves filled with technical manuals and volumes of both nonfiction and fiction, alongside a huge collection of graphic novels. Shane admired his computer, the keyboards. Monty had a set of mechanical keyboards that looked like flat keyboard mitts, each with wrist rests on a half of the board with a few keys for each thumb. And under the shelf supporting his monitor was a gaming keyboard outfitted with extra keys—letting him preset complex commands to be activated with a single button—and of course, high-grade mechanical switches with anti-ghosting that allowed multiple keystrokes to be registered simultaneously. Speed was essential.

Monty closed the door and they walked up the final flight—the stairwell offered a view. All around the building the use of floor-to-ceiling windows maximized daylighting and saved energy. Monty explained how control systems managed the building's temperature, opening and closing venetian blinds and windows to regulate daylight and room temperatures. The stairs were also an inviting space, a sort of social mixer between floors—minimizing energy consumed by the elevator. Each floor had radiant heat. The energy coming from geothermal wells that went four hundred feet into the earth. And up top, the Tech Plex had an array of solar panels. The household's shared electric vehicles also functioned as power storage with the smart meter selling excess to the grid.

"We pay nothing for electricity," Monty said. "The building generated sixty percent more than it used last year."

The air was cool when they walked out onto the roof. The sun had already set and a group of people were gathered around a table playing a board game. The rooftop was reserved for residents. It had a terrace and greenhouse and an expanse of container gardens. Cab had met his girlfriend while helping Monty in the garden, and now Cheryl and Cab had made a commitment to growing food for the household. The beds were irrigated, and catchments harvested rainwater as it rolled off the solar panels and ran to the parapet where the water funneled through a vortex filter to remove large particulates before passing through three ceramic filters, then under ultraviolet light and through activated charcoal to where it was stored in a sixty thousand-gallon, concrete cistern in the basement. The Tech Plex was a living building. For one hundred people, it supplied power, water, food—and it processed waste in the basement. Biosolids were treated in the composting system for eighteen months and eventually ended up as potting mix.

"I miss my cat," Monty said.

He told Shane they weren't allowed to have pets because some people were allergic. Monty walked back toward the stair enclosure and said, "My wife and I had a cat."

Monty poured Scotch and handed a glass to Shane.

"I'll never live like that again," he said. "Telling a woman to clean up after herself—I should've been more relaxed. I was paying the mortgage, that made it my way." Monty spaced out a moment. "If you share a house you don't control it."

"The women here seem really interesting," Shane offered.

"True. I'm not alone here."

Monty and Shane sat by the window of the sixth floor lounge and people circulated in and out of the room, with some nestled in couches and others seated around tables. A father and son were working together on what sounded like math problems. Voices blended in the room without television or amplified audio. And the tables and chairs and couches arrayed in the shared living room had nooks created by furniture and plants for more private spaces.

"I saw you and Rebecca kiss on New Year's."

"You did?"

Monty laughed.

"Sweet!"

"She's amazing," Shane said. "I crashed my relationship going after her."

"Maybe I haven't been having enough fun."

"Have you been away from keyboard?"

Monty hung his jaw.

"Keyboards are fun," he said.

"So on dates you're texting her?"

Monty swirled the golden brown liquid in the bottom of his glass.

"That's Cheryl." He pointed to a young woman reading a book, her shoulder length brown hair held away from her eyes with a headband. "Cab's girlfriend."

Shane stared at her. "What does she do?"

"Some back-end stuff for a food distribution company."

Shane looked away before he thought she'd notice him.

"I don't know," Monty said. "Working with plants on the roof. I think there's something to that—she's been helping him loosen up."

Monty topped up their glasses and Shane said, "Cityzen is a hit."

They each took a drink.

"Cab is . . ." Monty said, lowering his voice, "unsettled."

Shane waited, raised his brow, and finally Monty said, "The sale of blueprints, the designs licensed by his software have been purchased overwhelmingly by construction firms, real estate developers, and manufacturers of building materials, fixtures and finishes." Monty turned and looked out the window. "They use Gen to review and stamp their drawings. They're bypassing architects rather than increasing diversity."

"There are so many cool designs built in Cityzen."

"I know!"

"I love it, Monty. What I'm seeing, we made an awesome game."

"It was wrong to assume the construction firms and developers would buy those designs from people. That was a fantasy, a marketing thing."

"Something Sebastian?"

"Construction of new buildings is extremely consolidated by a few big firms, and many of these builders believe paying for another firm to do design is an unnecessary expense. They build to the codes and standards, safety first, and function next—with design dismissed as unknowable or irrelevant."

Monty's glasses had slid down his nose, he looked over the blue plastic frames and Shane saw into his eyes. He wondered how good his eyesight was without the glasses.

"The software has only accelerated and reduced the cost of producing boring buildings."

"No way. You're kidding?!"

Shane considered himself something of a designer, and he stopped himself from wondering what he'd do next to stay relevant. He had a real job. The law recognized Gen as a person, not because it was human, but because of the rights given to it. Monty was familiar with the case law that allowed the software to be incorporated and granted personhood. Without formidable legal prowess, the business world would have eaten it alive, and Cab was fortunate to have the legal muscle of strong precedent; a software application for legal practice management had been the first AI to gain some of the rights and duties of a person—a translation app to clarify and condense massive legal documents, some more than six thousand pages, into something a real person could read and understand.

"The builders are largely ignoring Gen's creative solutions, and there's a reason." Monty pushed his glasses back up. "This is a problem for Cab—even when the software generates better design variations, the builders have chosen the same thing as before. The conventional and bottom-line approach to the design, it's faster to build."

"Buildings go up so fast."

"Yeah. To complete the project. Developers have to pay their investors, usually banks, and the interest rates to finance a project create pressure to do it as quickly as possible."

Shane gazed at the room.

"It's amazing how a place can be transformed," Monty said.

Shane nodded.

Monty said, "It could be so much better."

"We can help," Shane said.

"Cab feels responsible. I tell him it's not his fault. It's only a tool, it's not him."

"People . . ." Shane stopped himself.

"The National Association of Realtors has endorsed the game," Monty said. "Cab thinks that's not good. Of course Sebastian and Aydin are happy. It's probably the largest lobby in America after the Chamber of Commerce."

"I didn't know."

"Who knew. I didn't know any of that—Cab told me. And he's been called out by the Academy of Neuroscience for Architecture. They're saying the beneficial design principles aren't being implemented in these Gen-licensed buildings." Monty shook his head. "He can't surpass the past decisions and overcome a legacy of bad design and policy. Buildings that function poorly, these stultifying places affect people's health. But most are so used to them, it's normal. They even think it's good."

Shane sat there in silence.

Monty said, "We can talk about something else."

"Most of my time is spent inside."

"Let's forget about work."

"In rooms with conditioned air and artificial light, low ceilings. Noisy rooms. It affects my ability to think."

"It affects our cognitive ability." Monty glanced over to where Cheryl had been but her table was empty. "It confuses him. I try to cheer him up."

"What can I do?" Shane asked.

"You know, I don't know yet."

"We'll think of something."

"People have made terrible choices," Monty said. "There's nothing the software can do. Their bias and prejudice, past perception and future expectations are baked into their choices and that's seen in the designs they buy—and build. Real estate developers want to recoup their investment as soon as possible, rather than put their money in a high performance building—like here, making a living building. Most developers, construction firms, it's business, they don't live inside the place. It's super expensive for developers to build features that reduce the operating cost of the building for tenants and make a healthy, inspiring place—and eliminate the environmental costs."

Through his reflection on the glass Shane could see the neighborhood at night and the city lights. The lounge suffused his body with a warm, relaxed sense of well-being, and he was starting to feel the Scotch.

"People here bought in," Monty said. "We invest considerably for the long term, for a place to live and a way to live together—as global citizens."

XIX

SHANE'S SISTER had returned for Thanksgiving and was staying in her old room. Their grandma and Shane were making mashed potatoes in the kitchen. Their mother's mother, she was now a wildcrafter and at eighty-five, Grandma was active. She had even been friends with Stan's parents, who were passed, before her daughter married him and she had long known that Patti had a winner. He helped to raise both Nora and Shane and was just as likely to change a diaper as a tire.

Stan wanted to deep fry the turkey and Patti had indulged the experiment so long as he used peanut oil. She baked the root vegetables: carrots and beets and potatoes that she'd grown in the community garden. She tended a plot with her husband since before she was pregnant with Nora. They did it together now in the Brentwood Community Garden not too far from their house. Stan would ride his bike to water in the summer after work. And they had since prepared it for winter. He wasn't as tall as his son, nor as skinny. Stan had a barrel chest and strong arms, he rather looked like someone who'd worked the warehouse, stacking boxes of foodstuff and home appliances and every odd item that Fred Meyer carried. Though that was decades ago, and now he managed their stores throughout the region. He was talking with Shane about designs he'd made in Cityzen, for smaller sized, more distributed Fred Meyers that he imagined could be a practical way to expand in dense urban districts.

They had reached common ground. Their interests separated by generations, culture, circumstance, and personality had been bridged by the all-purpose tools of Cityzen that could satisfy some part of any computer-enabled human with a ken for building, looting, policing, and investing.

Nora liked making the cranberry sauce, and this year she also made the pumpkin pie, waking early to finish before her mom needed the oven. Grandma was seated in her chair in the center of the living room when Nora came downstairs. "Honey, you are beautiful. And I know you have a lover you haven't brought home. He is welcome here. Or she."

"Oh, Grandma."

Nora pulled out the sliding drawer from the lower cabinet that held the glass pie pans and started banging around the more frequently used containers until she surfaced the pans.

"You work too much, honey."

Grandma put on her coat and rubber shoes to walk in the yard and care for her overwintering plants. Nora took a big, glass mixing bowl and put it on the counter with the flour, salt, baking soda, and butter. Oh, the butter. Her crust would have so much butter. She was taking this pie under her own direction and it would have a thick crust, flaky and full of butter. The pumpkin had been boiled last night and Shane came over to hang out. He helped her by scooping out the pumpkin seeds and separating the meat, with a stiff arm and big spoon, scraping the cooked pumpkin out from its shell.

At four in the afternoon, Thanksgiving day, he arrived with Elsie. They had eaten with her dad, a light dinner. Actually, Elsie said she wasn't hungry. Though a later mealtime was required to accommodate both families, Stan and Patti were at the cusp of inviting her father, but Patti was keen to observe the balance of the two and not rush their union. Shane and Elsie were in a rough patch. It pained Patti that they both had to suffer—thankfully her son didn't have the disease, only the bills. And while she knew it'd be behind them eventually, the appearance of her potential daughter-in-law worried her. Elsie was gaunt, as though her body was consuming itself, the fat was gone. She helped set the table by carefully sculpting and arranging the russet-ochre-and-orange floral patterned cloth napkins. But Elsie had not spoken of her pain.

The dinner was ready.

This year, Patti asked Shane to carve the bird. He obliged, taking the advice of his father and cutting neat, thin slices and separating the thighs with their dark drumsticks. The skin crackled in the sawing and the meat was tender and juicy as turkey would ever be. When Shane sat to his plate, the family held hands and Grandma gave thanks, their eyes closed, and at her prayer's end, gently squeezing each hand they collectively held, one to another, pulsing with each word: "I. Love. You!"

The conversation soon reached Schumacher volume as Nora shared a story about the guys who'd taken her out. And Stan, seated beside Elsie, asked if he could pass her anything from the table. Her plate had three baked carrots and a dollop of cranberries, but even that she struggled to eat. Her utensil shaking rhythmically as she brought a spoon of cranberry sauce to her mouth. She felt embarrassed, she felt poor, it was a stark awareness of her vulnerability.

"How do I look?"

She smiled, in too much pain for it to be convincing. Stan set down his utensils and said, "You look beautiful, princess."

Elsie began to cry and Stan scooted back his chair and knelt down beside her. Elsie put one arm around his neck and leaned into him as he stood holding her and walked from the table and up the stairs toward Shane's room to bestow her on his childhood bed.

XX

THE LIGHTS IN THE OFFICE had been dimmed and it glowed with backlit title cards from a fleet of old cabinet arcade games along two walls of the main room with VR booths and live displays, cocktail tables, and catering, as people arrived for the Holiday Party.

Outside the windows it was December dark and the long table in the conference room was set with synthesizers connected to a mixing board, and pink-purple accent lights colored the space while two wall monitors side-by-side displayed a geometric odyssey synchronized to the sound waves. Rebecca had recommended renting keyboards for the party. She was in command of the mixing board. Cab and Cheryl were playing—Cab smiling and pulsing one key to activate an oceanic buzzsaw—and Monty had invited a woman he'd met at the Plex.

The main room, with a DJ, and food being served on trays by the roaming waitstaff, also had a nonprofit represented by two women in matching red T-shirts. They explained to the young and able adults with disposable incomes how their nonprofit provided aid through strategic investment in places around the world that have experienced shock: financial, natural disaster, or other conflicts. On his way to the restroom, Shane saw a flyer posted to the wall where guests would eventually funnel. So many jobs and all the other things about positions and benefits. And along the counter beside every sink was a short stack of business cards with the jobs at Makner dot com.

Shane played Donkey Kong.

A piece of history and still he was impressed by the game play, a masterpiece! He didn't stop his game when the DJ stopped and Sebastian took the mic to make an announcement. Shane maneuvered Mario up the building site, dodging flying barrels and bouncing jacks, and at each Game Over entering his initials SOS, listening to the speech that finally peaked. "We are growing," Sebastian said, his voice in the sound system filled the room. "We're a diverse company, as you can see, and we want more of you. This is an exciting, new, today—we are celebrating our silver anniversary. And it gets better."

Monty stood beside Shane.

"We have an expansion game planned for Seattle," Sebastian declared. "And we want you to join the team. Let's be citizens of the world."

People cheered and Shane let Mario get hit by a barrel so he could properly clap. "And we have opened an office in Tokyo," Sebastian said to continued applause. Shane resumed playing as Mario appeared at the bottom of the screen. "This is the first overseas branch. We're doing our initial government relations campaign. Ganbatte!"

Monty clapped Shane on the back, and Shane looked up as Sebastian shouted, "Kudasai! Arigato!"

Shane swiveled his gaze to Monty and said, "I've never left the country."

Monty pointed to the screen and Shane jumped in time.

"You think they'd need guys," Shane said, working Mario up the scaffold, "like us to help develop the expansions?"

"Yep."

Aydin had flown in that afternoon from Phoenix where the tour of a cryogenics facility convinced him of their bridge technology for solving death. They could preserve his head, what they referred to as a cephalon, with vitrifaction to eliminate freezing injury—or his whole body could be stored.

He bought a full-body plan.

Making his way through the party, Aydin tapped the remaining engineers from his core team of the Portland branch. Behind a glass wall this elite group, visible to the guests, stood in Aydin's office as he told them they'd be taking a five-day all expenses paid workation in Costa Rica.

Shane walked behind Rebecca down the boarding ramp. Bradley humored them with window seats. It was Shane and Rebecca's first time flying first class. The Maknerites sat together: Shane, Rebecca, Bradley, Cab, Monty, Aydin and Sebastian alongside their female companions, and a son of Franklin Wells named Jacob. The kid was in his late teens and he complained of the selection when offered drinks in flight: "You don't have two choices of Champagne."

Above the clouds Shane gazed over the fluffy white prairie.

He was airborne.

It was quiet.

Sipping amber beer, looking out the window, he heard Bradley say, "You know, Shane. The ultimate security is owning a plane."

Shane turned his head to face forward and didn't say anything.

"But then again, you got the pilot and his family to deal with."

"Are you listening to yourself?" Shane faced Bradley, his boss.

Bradley shrugged.

Shane turned back to the window and watched the light change.

Sebastian had been accompanied aboard the plane with a woman who Shane faintly recalled from the parade of his female accomplices. And Aydin had decided to sustain his routine; he needed the energy of affairs, once a year, a form of sacrament he took the liberty of, and the woman beside him on the plane was an African American woman with braids sculpted above her head. The executives each had private villas, and the others shared a big house, with Wi-Fi, and within ten minutes of settling in they did an hour code blast. The expansion was upon them.

After the house cook prepared dinner, Aydin and Sebastian and their girlfriends arrived. Shane had noted a change in Aydin, he seemed thinner. They sat together for a meal and Aydin's friend was a full-stack developer and Shane talked with her, she rather schooled him on an Autodesk tool. She and Aydin had encountered each other playing Cityzen, and they met offline after he sensed a potential hire. But meeting her, he had other designs and Sharron thought it fine to fuck the shit out of him.

Franklin's son was not interested in computer programming and Monty asked what he liked. He'd been accepted into Harvard and thought he'd get his MBA. He did a gap year and decided to do it again. His dad had sent him on the Makner workation. Franklin had taken his eldest to the Fortune Brainstorm in Aspen that summer and figured that a trip with a video game company would make up for leaving Jacob behind. After dinner he played Task Master on his phone, then went to his room.

The drinks and conversation lasted past eleven when Rebecca stood up to say that they had all better get to bed. She had volunteered to help choose activities and booked an ATV tour of the high mountains that would begin with a bus ride in the morning. She knew her guys liked bikes, motorcycles—and she was comfortable with four wheels to see so much scenery. Bradley left the bathroom in sky blue shorts with his shirt off and a towel over his shoulder. Shane had been waiting and they passed in the hall. Smiling really big, Bradley stopped and said, "You were right."

Shane lifted his chin.

"I sounded like a douche bag."

Shane smiled. "Thanks, man."

Bradley walked down the hall without looking back and raised his hand, finger pointing up and then forward.

The clarity of light when they got out at the tour shack had surprised Shane. He asked Cab if it was because of the elevation. He could see everything better. When he looked at Cab, it was like nothing was between them.

"At extreme elevation the lack of oxygen can affect perception," Cab said, taking out his smartphone. "The thin air and decreased atmospheric pressure. I can reliably calculate the density of air molecules."

By the side of the road, a guy opened the doors of a converted barn.

"Bending of light occurs as it is diffracted by the particles," Cab said.

"Oh," Shane said. "That's cool!"

The change in perspective from inside the bus to outside, it was in the transitions he could see it, before he got used to anything, before it became normal, or ignored. It happened like that. The plane ride was new, but it had been work too. They even worked on the plane.

Sebastian stayed at the villa on business, and the rest of the team met Mick, the Australian transplant and ATV tour leader who would guide them down the mountain. His leathery skin, hard blue eyes, and cropped hair inspired confidence. Mick knew the ins and outs of the trail, the peculiarities of it, each rocky wrinkle and elevation change. He knew where to slow for wind that could gust through the pass. Mick said, "We got two rides, fellas." He put on his helmet, the chin straps going horizontal in the breeze. "There's a scenic trail down Colina."

"It's safe to say we want the other one," Bradley said.

Shane and Rebecca shrugged and exchanged looks.

"Am I right?" Bradley asked.

Monty nodded in agreement while Cab piped data from his phone into several apps that he found to optimize fun and safety on outdoor excursions such as this. Wind strength, cloud cover, soil acidity and density, the angle of the sun, and aggregate reviews of this more aggressive version of the ATV tour down Gran Colina, what people who rode it had to say. Cab started reading from his phone, and Aydin held up his hand. Cab stopped talking. Aydin did not answer directly, creating the impression that risk-takers like himself and his team would traverse Gran Colina in the most aggressive fashion allowed.

Jacob Wells bit his lip. The bus ride up the mountain terrified him. Jacob had a driver's license, but found driving unnecessary. The sports car he received on his sixteenth birthday sat in the driveway. At Deerfield, Franklin's old stomping ground, the coaches pulled a favor for their star linebacker and, against the boy's own interest, placed Jacob on the JV team. His chubby body more comfortable in the debate club. He played freshman year as backup punter until spraining his ankle during a running drill, his football career rushing mercifully to an end. He wasn't much interested in real girls, preferring porn and video games at home on the seventy-inch plasma, while feasting on prime rib, leek and potato galette and frosted mugs of Coca-Cola. Both the morning and night chefs knew Jacob's flavor preferences with a sniper's accuracy.

"What about this one here?" asked Mick, looking at Jacob, who had started to glisten with sweat. "He looks stuck in the headlights, a bit, yeah?"

Aydin took a step towards Jacob. "You're afraid."

"No, I'm okay."

"He'll adapt. He has Wells blood."

Jacob ran his tongue over his lip and nodded. He knew he was an embarrassment to his father. Jacob was not a killer. He was too slow, too tame—patient, but scared. When his dad took him hunting, the tags cost twenty grand apiece, and Jacob had deliberately missed and scared the goddamn grizzly bear. At his age, his father had cracked a boy's jaw, aced his classes and fucked three cheerleaders behind the bleachers. The beautiful daughter of one of Franklin's legal staff agreed to kiss Jacob once, on a dare. When they reached the closet, his cheeks reddened to strawberry and he began sneezing for four straight minutes. He didn't want to be different to rebel or anything.

High school. What a fucking pressure cooker.

Before going down the trail, they got to practice driving their ATVs on the road with Mick. Their route would take them to a waterfall, after about an hour, where they could swim, if they wanted. That sold her on the tour. Rebecca had brought her suit. She would definitely be swimming. Mick said the trails were used by Costa Rican cowboys. "Give the sabaneros a wave when you pass," Mick said. "Don't honk." Everyone kept their speed below ten miles an hour and admired the view. Vibrant heliconia clusters hung like lobster claws. Empurpled wild orchids one lurid bloom after another and gumbo-limbo trees wrapped delicately in reddish bark. Shane spotted a hummingbird and pulled to the side of the trail. Rebecca stopped beside him. They watched it riding the breeze up and zooming down, over and over in an ovoid loop. It looked for all the world to be playing in the wind.

"This is another country," Shane said.

Rebecca laughed, and rode on up the trail.

From the front of the pack, Mick twisted to face the riders, yelling, "Okay, get ready for a sharpy!" The Australian accent made everything sound exciting. The trail curved sharply right and the ATVs rounded the corner, Aydin's vehicle skidding slightly. Mick turned his head and shouted, "Slow down on turns, fella!"

There was a staggered rhythm of their acceleration and deceleration, a cadence to handling the turns. Then the trail joined the road they came up that morning. Bradley and Aydin alternated riding alongside Mick in the lead with Shane riding behind them. Rebecca rode behind the guys. They were going to watch chocolate being made tomorrow. Jacob was ahead of her and behind Monty and Cab. Jacob was afraid, there was no guard rail, but he was more afraid that Egyptian guy would tell his dad that he was a disappointment.

Jacob saw Monty keeping to the mountain side, away from the edge of the road that opened over the valley. Jacob clenched his jaw and accelerated. Monty whoo-hooed as Jacob zoomed past and pressed the air-horn fastened to his handlebar. Shane made room for him to go ahead. This is what it took, Jacob thought. He knew. You make them move. Then you can do whatever you want. His dad had taught him that, now he did it. There was nothing to be scared of. Aydin's words in his head. Wells blood. He accelerated harder, the air-horn blasting.

"Fall back!" Mick flapped his arm. "Slow down!"

Bradley and Aydin were ahead of Jacob, riding the outside of a turn. Jacob sped along the inside. Bradley looked back and saw the twerp. He sped up. Who does he think he is. No way was he going to lead this trip. Bradley didn't like the kid's brother either. Working with Walter on the bank had been a pain in the ass. Walter had perfect teeth. He talked about his honors program. Honors. Aydin shouted. Bradley looked back. Aydin was braking. Mick screamed. A horn blared. Bradley whipped back around and saw the truck. He was going to hit it—too fast, turning away from where he'd seen the kid, Bradley went off the road—without thinking.

Rebecca screamed.

Jacob skidded, braking as his ATV went up the mountainside a short distance and stopped. Everyone slowed to a stop on the side of the road. The truck drove up and pulled over. Two guys jumped out. Rebecca's shriek reverberated against the mountain. Shane jumped off his vehicle and ran to get Bradley. Aydin and Mick jogged over to him. Standing along the edge of the road, they stared down. A long way down they could see Bradley sprawled in an unnatural position. His body lay, distorted, motionless far below. The weight dropped out from Shane. He saw death. He saw Bradley.

Their silence ended.

Aydin said, "Did he want his cephalon preserved?"

"We'd never get it out of there before his cell and chemical structures began to disintegrate," Cab said.

Aydin shook his head.

"Who knows this?" Aydin asked, looking to Shane.

"Shane, answer me."

Shane saw that Aydin was talking to him but he didn't understand.

Jacob started sobbing and said, "I didn't kill him."

Immediately, Mick said, "Christ on a stick! Nobody killed him."

Monty walked to Aydin and stood between him and Shane.

"The flight out is in two days," Monty said.

"We can get one, today!" Aydin said.

"You guys," Rebecca shouted. "He's hundreds of feet down the side of a mountain. Bradley's dead!"

XXI

AT THE BORDER, Stan handed over his passport and the officer scanned its code. Stan answered questions about his trip, telling the customs officer he went to the Museum of Anthropology. When asked if he had any goods to declare, Stan said no. He was allowed to cross the border from Canada into the US, and six hours later arrived at their apartment. It was after eleven at night and Shane answered the door.

"I got enough to last her," Stan said. "Until your plan kicks in."

Shane invited his dad in and they talked at the kitchen table. He gave the antibiotics to Elsie. No one else would give them to her, and Stan knew where to go. James had helped other people; he worked at a pharmacy in Vancouver BC and Stan had a connection through his job. It was important that Shane and Elsie not mention the medicine to her doctors. There were penalties for importing drugs, severe penalties for even attempting it—even if they were prescribed by a doctor. This was true regardless if her life was in danger. Elsie hugged him and he said, "It hurts me to see you in so much pain."

Sebastian and Aydin flew to Santa Monica to attend the funeral in Bradley's hometown. The expansion was to proceed as planned. This was what Bradley would've wanted. Sebastian called upon them to make Bradley proud. Although they were allowed every other Sunday off—so they could see their family or do some laundry—many of the programmers had worked twelve hours a day, seven days a week for months before the release of Cityzen. And the tragic loss of their technical lead produced a fog in the office. Concerned that Aydin would assume additional responsibilities, Sebastian discretely asked John to rejoin the company.

John understood being publicly fired was necessary to manage perception and to satisfy Franklin Wells. He negotiated a competitive salary and benefits package and stepped in to help. Bradley's death had delivered a huge upset to their company. More so for the people who were close to him. Rebecca was crushed. She struggled to return to the office after their trip, everything reminded her of Bradley. Shane and Dillon both experienced Bradley helping them all those months, his charts and graphs, all the software he built for their company. Endless lines of code. They'd been to war!

Rebecca began to question what she was doing with her life and when Sebastian told her that she'd have to ramp up the work, she said to ask Shane.

Sebastian said, "He'll do what you tell him to do."

"I want you to tell him to lead the team."

"You'd be taking a significant pay cut."

"I can't replace Bradley."

"You don't have to replace him," Sebastian said. "Do what he would do."

"I can't."

"You can do it. We have to code Seattle."

"Ask Shane," she said. "He's the one to lead our team."

Shane wanted to make a game, he didn't know how to manage people. It wasn't really what he wanted. But when John asked if he could lead a development team, he said he would. With so much happening Shane didn't register the arrival of Brian Sabin and Bradley's dad as a big deal. He was like, oh, okay. They were coming to Portland to take care of Bradley's things and would be in the office one day to clear out his personal items. The effect of seeing Brian enter the room took Shane by surprise. His body responding to someone he loved watching in shows, his emotions resounding, amplified, unbelievably uplifted to see Brian Sabin, to be so close to a star—to see the real person!

"Wiping his Roombot before we sell it," Brian said to the Maknerites who'd gathered outside Bradley's office, "feels like taking his dog out to the field, placing a gun between its eyes. Its tongue is lolling, it's trusting me the entire time. And what's to hurt, it's a machine. But you know that thing knew my brother before he died—better than I did."

Cab suggested downloading Sheebie's memory to train an AI on Bradley's speech; the robot stored everything Bradley said to improve its ability to talk with him. Bradley's responses. His speech patterns. They could be recreated. The suggestion coming from Cab gave the idea a special weight, and John sensed people needed some way to express their grief. With the approval of Bradley's family, he okayed the project. Bradley's father allowed the entire corpus of his son's electronic correspondence to be used in training a chatbot. For a truly satisfying conversation, the emotion had to be synthesized too. They could use a deep generative model of raw audio waveforms. The bot would understand what was spoken to it and where to place the emotional emphasis in its response. They had the data. The system would also generate non-speech sounds, such as breathing and mouth movements. Cab assured them they could create a kind of Bradley.

It would be done on company time—so long as their other work was completed. By channeling their emotions in this way, processing their feelings together, John felt the bot would keep everyone productive.

Jill couldn't pay her rent and when Elsie told Shane, he floated her the money. Her landlord raised the rent two hundred and forty dollars. She had barely afforded it all before with what she made at the bakery and needed help while she figured out what to do. Shane was casual about it. Elsie's medical bills slammed his account, but he had received a real raise. The money coming in was more than he knew what to do with, now. He was team leader. He was learning new programming languages and growing as a person. And by February, Elsie had begun to feel better. She and Shane made sure to spend his time off together, and she began working on mood boards, looking at openings in visual merchandising. Who she knew at those companies, seeking them out. She was going out, meeting people, doing everything she could to reclaim her life.

When she stopped needing a minimum basic income, Elsie would no longer need to contribute to Decide Portland, and even still she planned to continue. After following city hall for a few years, reading about local issues was interesting and contributing her votes and comments on the platform gave her a sense of agency. Anyone could know what was happening at the state capitol, but it felt like she couldn't do anything about it. Legislators spent more than a quarter million to win a seat in the Senate and a half that for the House, and the job didn't pay much. So the people who could take time off to run for office, to serve in office, and subsidize it all, they had money, or took money. There was plenty of transparency. Everyone saw decisions made on behalf of special interests. To gain power, people had to be driven to succeed; they may be brilliant and kind to children, but relentlessly committed to preserving the status quo that got them there. Self-interested impulses drove so many decisions and deals. Cutting taxes for wealthy people will create growth. Voters could be told the same simple thing over and over until they believed it. Taxation is theft. Taxes are a burden. The wealthy need tax relief.

That will create jobs. And, the deficit this created justified eliminating social programs, like healthcare. Nonprofits were supposed to take care of everything the market couldn't. The "free" market. Elsie hated those people who made universal healthcare impossible. They almost killed her. So they could buy what? Okay, take your tax rebate and fix the potholes. Fix the bacteria corkscrewing my body. What more did those people need—making it impossible for her to get medicine—more life?!

If she had a job with Nike, Columbia, Adidas, she'd have some weight. The big companies in town. Those were good jobs. Elsie wanted a good job. That was healthcare. By not dealing with it at the federal level, healthcare became the responsibility of employers—and corporations didn't give a rip about their contractors. Shareholders didn't care about people in her community. Nike officially held more than ten billion offshore for tax purposes. She also heard they were headquartered in an unincorporated town; that was convenient, an island surrounded by a real town with roads and services paid for by taxes. For all her work, Elsie had arrived at an understanding. Taxes were a public investment in the future. Those public dollars built the interstate highway and the foundation of the internet, paid for all kinds of scientific research. She knew this. All her friends did. Everyone knew. We could choose public spending. So that we all benefit. By investing together we would experience better results than by spending as individuals.

Then she read about a proposed law on conditional home occupancy in Oregon. It seemed to intersect with Shane's work. Some representatives in the House and Senate wanted a law to protect homeowners, and buried in legalese it specified that people can't be on their property when there's structural damage. It used the phrase "temporary dwellings" to outlaw camping on any area of a person's property if the house had been damaged. It was right there. If you could read it, or afford a Lawbot. And the reporters did. They wrote about it. But what could people do about it? A town hall meeting was scheduled for the middle of the day, during the workweek.

Tens of thousands of Portlanders were active on Cityzen, and Elsie heard people talking about it when she went to Fresh Cup in the morning. A news crew wanted to do another interview and John scheduled time at the office. The reporters put a spotlight on Shane standing at his desk.

"We provide the tools," he said. "It's really up to the players what they do with them."

Shane talked about the excitement of seeing people dig tunnels under the city. The player characters didn't need to breathe. It had become something of an ant hill. "Yeah, we made sure you can dig out foundations . . . the successive layers of rock each make it harder and more time consuming, just for realism you know. And to give something to do. More to explore. Reaching magma is kinda next level stuff."

The extensive tunneling hadn't been anticipated. Shane told the reporter he thought people would be building more on floating platforms in the Willamette.

"We could've controlled for underground dwelling, I guess." Policing and looting underground and building complex mazes that had no official map and could only be navigated by social signals created within the game was a realm of danger and randomness unplanned by Makner. Players found it easy to do and impossible to master. "But it's cool."

Shane said he'd spent hours exploring the new construction, watching them build. He would fly over the street grid as an Investor and then go underground to see people building in caverns that they skylighted with lightwells, mirrors—and then built above. Other than time, it didn't cost extra to dig below a plot.

"Some of the buildings don't make any sense. But there they are."

No one really understood it but the physics engine.

An investor from Saudi Arabia put a ton of money into downtown—represented in the game by a skyscraper taller than the Burj Khalifa. Almost twice as tall, about three screen lengths into the pixel sky.

"Yeah, it is great," he said. "And of course we have questions about some of the negative implications of the conditional occupancy law."

The reporter asked, "What did you think about the protest at City Hall?"

Sebastian walked into the shot and put his arm around Shane.

"For Makner," he said. "The best feedback we can have is honest. It gives us all excitement and a healthy anxiety to realize that there are other sides to this. And of course we're going to bring a fair game to everybody. That's our goal. We're working hard on that every day."

XXII

MONTY HAD HIS LAPTOP open, the Wells Fund in his browser. It showed Franklin prominently in various publicity photos with mayors of major cities and standing beside architects looking at models with engineers. Franklin Wells was respected for his achievements, his wealth and influence. He gave at his church, and he was a massive donor to much needed work rebuilding infrastructure in American cities. He had donated to Los Angeles, San Francisco, Portland and Seattle.

Monty said, "He's hiding in plain sight."

In the commons at the Tech Plex, Elsie and Shane sat with Monty and Cab and Cheryl. The wall of windows lit with a white sky, the rain having fallen to a mist, Sunday afternoon. They were drinking tea that Cheryl made with an adaptogenic blend of herbs and mushrooms.

"He wouldn't want to look like a cheapskate," Cheryl said.

Monty asked her, "What's that soil aftertaste?"

Cab raised his cup and said, "It is prepared with oatstraw."

"You might be tasting the cordyceps," she said. "Or the eleuthero."

"It's really complex," Elsie said.

"Yeah," Shane said. "I can taste licorice."

Monty turned his laptop so Cab could see it.

"Thank you, Cheryl," Shane said, warming his hands on the cup.

"It's a small fraction of the amount he's taking in," Monty said. "He wouldn't want to be taking so much and—"

"Look at him in the hardhat," Cheryl said.

"He's always in a hardhat in these photos," Cab said.

"I don't know," Shane said. "Maybe he is a good guy. He seems to be doing something good with his money."

"His foundation?" Monty said and pshawed. Franklin Wells had endowed a donor-advised fund with three billion dollars. "That way he avoids paying taxes and can use the Wells Foundation to invest in causes that further his business interests—and his dealings with government."

"They said he's a trustee of the Portland Art Museum." Elsie brushed her hair over one shoulder with her hand. "And the one in Seattle."

"Wells' art collection is certainly world class," Cab said with genuine appreciation. "He has made several significant purchases, including three paintings by Van Gogh."

"It builds social currency—" Monty took a drink of tea and winced.

Cheryl said, "If he knew his paintings could become this, what would Van Gogh make?"

Elsie asked her, "Do criminals use the art world to launder money?"

Cab said, "He spends his life—all day managing that money."

"They aren't allocating capital for productive investment in our country," Monty said with anger. "They are getting in and out to make a profit, as big as possible. That's all he does. His status, that's what he cares about. He doesn't give a shit about you. He's not a philanthropist."

"His estimated net worth is ten billion dollars," Cab said. "To understand this amount by way of analogy, one million seconds are twelve days. One billion seconds are thirty-two years."

"A lover of man," Monty said. "Give me a fucking break."

Cheryl said, "If anyone has that much money to give away—"

"In a tax haven," Monty said.

"Put it where . . ." Cheryl trailed off and Cab said, "When you accumulate so much money the question becomes what to do with it."

"They can lobby the shit out of Congress, buy politicians coming and going," Monty said. "It's not a democracy. Billionaires jockeying for their pet projects, moon bases or what the shit."

Shane laughed.

"And he needs something," Monty said.

"He could buy anything he wanted," Elsie said.

"I think a city is the ultimate trophy for Wells," Monty said. "Owning as much land as he can. Collecting rents. Because achieving the top spot in government isn't necessary—he already has access through interlocking boards and directorates. He doesn't need to hassle with the scrutiny of actual politics."

Cab said, "Rather than being a man who has power for four or eight years and then a library in his name, he is in command at all times."

Shane excused himself and went to the restroom. He thought of his chances in life. His urine entering the water recycled through the building. He was fortunate. He knew that. Walking away, he heard the whooshing stream plumbing down to the digester below. The commons room was full of successful people. He had made it. Who would throw this away? It would be crazy to do anything that would jeopardize this. Taking his seat at the table, he listened to Monty saying: "White collar criminals have no loyalty. They turn on each other to make a buck—or get out of jail. They'll destroy a guy and say hey, I'll make it up to you later."

"We have to protect our company," Shane said.

Monty crossed his arms and sat back. "Say six thousand people gain a majority stake in a city, what is the likelihood they act in the best interest of the other million mutherfuckers?"

Cheryl put her arm around Monty.

He looked at her and said, "The shit is about to hit."

She hugged him.

Monty unfolded his arms and gave her a hug. "Thanks, Cheryl."

Cab reached for the teapot across the table and refilled his cup. He held the pot up for his friends and they slid their cups in his direction. Shane sipped his tea and looked at the website. "That's his son, Walter." He pointed to an image on-screen. "I remember him. He came to the office. Bradley worked with him when they set up the bank interface."

"Why do rich people always wear popsicle colored polo shirts?" Elsie asked.

"They're going to make sure investors get that property," Monty said. "That's what they're here for, think of it. In the most ruthless terms, when the disaster happens, he wants the vultures to win. The whole thing is for the vultures and they need help, the vultures need extra help because we have shitty laws"—the tone in Monty's voice went sarcastic—"protecting those crappy citizens with their tents and jugs of water and their dumb families. They gotta get ridda those people. They need the vultures to come in, man, and take what's theirs. Because they are elite—the real owners—I mean they're awful, but the vultures . . ." Monty grinned, embarrassed by his indignation. He shook his head.

Elsie said, "It's about them becoming the new owners?"

"That's what this is all about," Monty said. "It's not about them making a couple extra bucks, it's about defeating the middle class."

"And taking their property," Elsie said.

Shane pushed his chair back from the table.

"Franklin Wells is a piece of shit," Monty said. "He's got extreme power and he's ruthless."

"That is correct," said Cab.

In the silence that followed, Shane said, "We can't assume the worst. Why would Aydin and Sebastian go into business like that?"

"Excuse me a moment," Monty said, opening up a database on his laptop.

"The law seems okay," Elsie said, "but then you're not allowed to camp on your property if the house is damaged."

"If their house was uninhabitable," Cheryl said, "after the earthquake, people would camp. They'd stay where they could. People who can't afford to repair their homes would camp on the lawn."

"It makes sense, right?" Monty said and looked back to his laptop, typing intermittently in fluent bursts.

"Franklin Wells knows people are going to be camping," Cab said.

"And they'd stay there as long as needed," Monty said without taking his eyes from the screen. "Until help comes, until their insurance pays out, and they would have their cans of chili and just like wing it, you know."

"But he's going to make sure," Elsie asked, "that legally you can't stay on that property?"

"You may choose to camp—" Monty looked at her "—but there's going to be police to take you off your property. Because you aren't allowed to camp. It's unsafe."

Cab said, "Using a satellite inspection system, FEMA—"

"The government would have teams inspecting each home, to protect people." Monty spoke in a mock officer voice: "They identified structural damage that makes your home uninhabitable and according to this rule." Then in his normal voice he said, "If people can't afford the repairs, think, the really desirable part of town, the city will eventually send them a letter saying the property has been condemned, and they have so many days to fix it. Who knows, maybe they get ninety days. Maybe a year. And if they can't get a bank loan to do it, or their old job had been wiped out in the quake and they haven't any way to pay, then, the bank will repossess it."

"Maybe the Wells law is to have the city rebuilt as quickly as possible," Shane said. "Why assume the worst motives?"

"Shane," Monty said. "Franklin Wells would kill his grandmother to collect insurance. He is absolutely the most mercenary guy you'll ever meet."

"Then we have to warn Aydin and Sebastian," Shane said.

"Imagine what it comes down to," Monty said. "It doesn't matter how much you paid on your mortgage. A bank owns the mortgage, the property belongs to the bank, the law will defend the banks over chumps failing to make their monthly payments."

"You know, people understand this," Cab said to Shane. "That's why many of our coworkers left. On principle."

"Not to be rude," Elsie said. "I know you guys love the game. But why didn't you leave, Cab?"

"I have a contract," he said.

"We all have contracts," Shane said. "We're right where we need to be. We're inside the company. That's where we can have an impact. We have the best chance of changing the . . . to do good—within the system."

"We have no other choice," Cab said. "At the moment."

"There is no other system," Monty said. "It's held together with duct tape, but . . . it's the system."

Cab said, "Technically, correct."

Elsie brought her hands to her face. "I'm sorry."

"No," Shane said. "This isn't your fault."

"No. You made this with them."

"No," he said.

"I made you do it."

"No."

"Yes. I did."

Shane looked at Elsie and then his friends.

She hid her face.

"I'm scared."

Shane held her.

"My family will be homeless. I would be too."

"Don't let this scare you."

"On moral grounds," Monty said. "All of us know what they're doing. They knew. All this was known. Placing a long-term option to buy up property in major cities at fire-sale prices is a way to store wealth. Build wealth. The in-game competition for property keeps the value of his investment tracking above inflation."

"But ordinary people can buy into the fund," Shane said.

"He might be throwing this bone to his son," Cheryl said.

"Makes sense," Cab said. "If not in his lifetime, then his son's."

Shane said, "You mean, Jacob?"

"Walter," Cab said. "Both of them—the game is interesting to the boy."

"Ordinary people might have some extra thousand to tuck away," Monty said. "But yeah. It's not for ordinary people. What do you think the whale that landed downtown is?"

"Risk management," Cab said. "That is a description of a hedge fund."

The light in the windows had dimmed as the sun went down. Their group around the table was one of many who sat in the commons, active in their work, alone or together. The overhead lamps of light-emitting diodes glowed warm, clear and without flicker. The color adjusting through sunset to reduce the blue.

"Look," Monty said. "Money is information. Information can be money, he has an insatiable appetite for new information that will drive his trades. The advances in earth science and seismology are information. Wells placed a long-term bet. The thing he's making sure of . . . coming out on top."

"If they control and constrain the housing," Cab said, "the fund can maximize their returns."

"A subduction zone earthquake is long," Monty said. "Holding their position in a game to buy the city. A long investment, to bet on disaster, which given the science is a sure thing."

"But I'm a programmer," Shane said. "I'm making a game."

Monty began citing the overlapping institutional relationships of Franklin Wells. He had entered the text of the conditional occupancy law in a legal search that crawled across jurisdictions of the United States, listing three mid-size cities in California where a similar code passed. Monty mentioned the dates in succession and noted changes and said those codes were trial balloons—learning and refining the approach, the language and tactics. Then he cited two state legislatures where versions of the law were in committee, one in Oregon and the other up north, in Washington.

XXIII

SHE WAS RUNNING AGAIN. Her arms pulsing in time with her legs. Her ponytail swinging across her shoulders. Even the strain of breathing hard felt good. She felt human again. She was alive!

Elsie stopped at the foot of Mount Tabor to catch her breath. She rested her open hands on her thighs and leaning forward with her back straight, she closed her eyes. The red darkness, a sightless world inside her. Around the low hill she jogged slowly up the loop trail. The sky was overcast. The shrubs of baldhip rose and thimbleberry. The fir and hemlock and red cedar trees creating the safe enclosure where everything could live. The world came to be in these places. She passed another jogger coming down the trail with a child riding in its chariot, the three wheels of the jogging stroller bounding upon the earth. The girl with her white wool hat, the pompoms of her tasseled flaps. She held the bar with her chubby hands. Her little body strapped in as her father ran past Elsie.

The realty sign drew her eye on the way home. Not every house was going to be uninhabitable. They won't all be destroyed. They could be made strong. Elsie thought the most meaningful thing she could do with her life was to have a family. To really love. Everything was weak without that bond, the blood ties, wild, irrational love, real love, a baby, their lives. She had thought to wait. She used to think she should establish herself first, but everything was different now. She was older and she had no career to put on hold.

She wasn't jeopardizing anything, and they wouldn't waste one half of their income paying for someone to take care of their child. Elsie wanted to hold a baby. To have and give life.

"Thank you, Tobin."

He waved and Elsie shut the door. The delivery boy had said she looked healthy. Her favorite spring dress came to her knees, a cream dress with two wide straps over her shoulders and a straight line above her breasts so simple and clean. She was feeling horny. Shane had been paying for Elsie to see her physical therapist once a week, the woman who had first diagnosed her correctly.

"My account has a fifth digit," he said.

"You're rich."

He smiled.

Elsie put their food on the table.

Her appetite was back, and she had regained her weight.

Shane had begun initiating sex, again, he wanted her again. Her hair in a messy bun with flyaways and two long, thick pieces down either side of her ears and winding to her neck. Her skin white, her hair black. The loose hairs haloing her neck.

Shane and Elsie drove to the house in East Portland and met with their realtor. Having no money to contribute at the moment, Elsie took the initiative to organize the process and found a highly-rated realtor in the area. Nancy Ranger would be their point of contact throughout the entire deal. The first step, she told Elsie, was to get their finances in order. They needed liquid cash—a lot of it. The moment they found a house they wanted, they told Nancy and she contacted the seller's agent. The liquid part of the equation mattered. They needed five thousand as an offering of good faith to the seller, to show they were serious. If the deal collapsed, it took days to get that money back, during which a new deal might be initiated.

This meant they had to have another five grand available instantly. In a seller's market, hesitation was a death knell.

Although Shane had a steady cash-flow, the money had not been coursing long enough to seriously pool. His finances allowed them to look at homes in the mid to high four-hundred thousand range, and this range was essentially the starting point of move-in-ready homes. One might find a cheaper place that could be immediately inhabited, but the neighborhoods were far from the center and cheaper houses often had serious problems—broken plumbing, cracks in the foundation, and so forth. They had to be careful.

"Remember," Nancy said. "No large purchases for a while."

This was another rule. Loan companies viewed people with debts for a new car or expensive items leading up to a mortgage as buyers who could be stretching too far. They wanted assurance the borrower would continually make their mortgage payments. It might affect their interest rate. And taking on new credit before the loan closed could delay or derail a deal altogether.

If Shane's credit score was good, his loan would be considered conventional. That was what sellers preferred. The statistics showed that buyers who made the higher down payments required for conventional loans had a greater probability of completing their deals and closing. Borrowers with less money often needed a mortgage insured by the Federal Housing Administration. The barrier to entry was lower here, but the advantages of an FHA-backed loan came at a significant cost. As with most things in America, anyone able to borrow money could live the dream, and many would get fleeced.

"I know we're super busy, but I need to ask for a day off next week."

John understood needing time to house hunt. He and his wife had endured the process and he knew what Shane was going through.

Shane smiled. "Thank you!"

"The best of luck. This is an exciting— I'm happy to hear about this."

John started to walk away.

"Hey, my girlfriend had an interesting idea for us. Do you have a moment?"

"Okay, shoot."

Shane held his hands out and spread his fingers. "People could contribute in-game to retrofit homes in Portland. We could incentivize players to get all the homes bolted to their foundations, ready for an earthquake. It's about four grand a pop. We'd make stakes, and it'd be like community-driven crowdfunding."

"Interesting."

"Should I present it on Friday, do you think?"

"We're building out Seattle."

"It'd be like a subset of players, the Portland— The people who live here and play Cityzen."

"How do these contributions work?"

"Do you think *they* would go for it?"

"Don't focus on retrofitting, Shane. It sets up a conflict with the long-term investments the other players are making."

"That's the competition! Man, it's an in-game competition, like teams, totally unplanned but we play God and go into the game to set it up."

"Only Aydin has God-view. I don't think that will change."

"So . . . if he'd be interested in this, then it's a go?!"

John laughed. "Okay, I have to get on with my work here. Shane, thank you for being awesome. Tell Elsie I said hi."

"Oh! I will. Yes, I will!" Shane started to dash off and paused. Turning, he said, "Thank you, John."

Shane's father warned him about unregulated brokers and private lenders. These mortgage companies could use various tools to take advantage of him, including short-term adjustable rate loans, teaser rate loans, and interest-only and negative-amortization loans that let buyers make payments that didn't reduce their balances. And these lenders often failed to fully disclose the terms of their loans, leading buyers to sign mortgages they didn't understand. Then the mortgage companies would sell the loans to third parties, approving as many borrowers as possible and relinquishing their responsibility just as fast.

Shane had dinged his credit score with late payments when the healthcare fees and fines hit, and he qualified for a Federal Housing Administration loan. The FHA-backed loans had relaxed credit standards, but he was subject to paying upfront mortgage insurance in addition to monthly private mortgage insurance. And the FHA was notoriously racist. Historically, it had segregated the cities and towns of America by denying loans to African Americans. Home ownership was the country's most common way to build and transmit generational wealth—if they had some to begin with, or could get a loan. FHA policy drove the segregation of neighborhoods, the concentration of poverty and the institutionalization of racism through an overt practice of denying mortgages based on race and ethnicity.

For Elsie, the home-buying process was a positive step for their future—she wanted ties to him and his family—and fraught with despair.

"Holy shit, Elsie."

"Hm."

"This is Gresham."

Shane stepped out of the passenger side of her car. They'd gone beyond Southeast 162nd Avenue and seamlessly entered the city east of Portland. Nancy met Shane with a firm handshake and then Elsie.

"Okay, let's go over what you'll need for this big adventure! You have cash. Do you have that, now?"

They both nodded.

"And you have enough for a twenty percent offer. How about that?"

Shane placed a hand on his neck.

"Um . . . yes. Yes."

"Are you sure?" Nancy walked them up to the house and stopped at the door.

XXIV

SHANE ASKED HIS PARENTS to help them, and his father had mentioned the speculative nature of the entertainment industry. Shane reassured his dad. He was a software engineer, and his folks agreed to co-sign and help with the down payment. Most homes already had five or six couples crowding the front step, waiting eagerly to make an offer. This time, Shane and Elsie were the first couple there. After walking through the house, they were pleased.

"So, what do you think? Ready to try another offer?"

"Let's do it!" Shane said.

"Okay, let me just check that—oh. Hmmm . . . oh, darn."

"Not again," said Elsie.

"A full-priced cash offer was just initiated."

Shane said, "That is three in a row."

"I'm sorry, sir," Nancy said. "The all-cash offers are fast."

Buyers were desperate, hawking anything they could to outmaneuver both the institutional investors and other buyers. One couple promised the seller free pizza from their family's pizzeria, for life. Another touted a lifetime guarantee of babysitting services. Anything could become a bargaining chip, a slight edge over the next couple. Sellers began asking potential buyers up front what else they might have to offer.

"This one is perfect, you two. The owners have already put an offer on another house, so they're highly motivated."

Shane had left work early that week to look for homes but his time off was expiring fast. This was the eighth house they'd seen in two days. Five of them they'd lost to Wall Street. The real estate mutual funds were crazy for Portland.

Shane couldn't help himself. "It's a little beat up," he said.

What he saw didn't look good, what he thought: this is a dump.

"At four hundred and seventy-five thousand, this is what we'll find. In your range," Nancy said. "A fixer-upper."

"Half a million isn't what I thought," said Elsie.

"We all start somewhere," Nancy said, chirpy. She walked them through the living room and turned around in the kitchen. "Between us. This is not listed publicly yet. You've probably got forty-five minutes to think it over before it hits the wire."

"We need to look around for a minute," Shane said.

"Why don't you two have a good look while I take this call?"

They walked to the backyard and Elsie heard a cat crying and went to a small shed with a glass paneled door. A kitten.

"How did it get in there?" Elsie looked through the dirty glass. "Cats are magic."

She tried the door. The kitten put its paws on the glass and cried, crying to her and she checked behind the shed and the other side and all the windows. She looked at the house and the sliding glass door they came through. The kitten was wailing.

"Shane, get it out of there."

He walked around the side and put his face to the paned window. Empty wood shelves. And the kitten saw him and jumped onto the shelf below the glass. It had blue eyes. Gray, tan, white, and black blended little hairs, with fur ribboned black around its eyes like a tiny mask. Shane glanced down. He'd repair it when they moved in. He picked up a paving stone with both hands and carefully broke the lower-left pane.

The cat jumped onto the sill, and Shane reached in and placed his hand under its little belly, lifting it out, he gave it to Elsie.

"Oh my god, it's purring like crazy."

"Put it in the car," he said.

She put it under her shirt.

"Yeah, I don't think we need to tell Nancy."

They heard the back door open and Nancy walked out.

Elsie walked past her, smiling.

Shane said, "We're interested."

"I'm sorry," she said.

The house had already sold.

It had been two years since he entered the building. Shane put his things into the bankers boxes that John provided and laid flat, unassembled, outside his office that morning. Sebastian had made the announcement. He mentioned something about a search when they were in Costa Rica. They had outgrown Chinatown. It was announced and the Operations people did their thing and two weeks later, Shane was moving. Sebastian revealed their new address on Friday and over the weekend, the Maknerites moved.

They had forty-eight employees, more than three times as many people as the early days when they built the Portland game. Seeing their office dismantled, it was a shell of brick, steel, wood, and the space illuminated by sunshine. It was memory. Shane felt the loss of Bradley and he didn't cry.

He had not cried. He felt sad, but he couldn't, he didn't know what was wrong with him—or if it was wrong. To survive. He had stopped. Something in him stopped. He wanted to stop it. He was a leader. Bradley's job. The buildings, the homes, the creation of a new city was his world. He was one among many; he had to trust them. Shane had a job.

He labeled his box, as instructed, and found it on Monday in the new Makner office. They were in the southeast light industrial district. Two biotech firms occupied the first and second floors, and then it was all Makner. The entertainment software giant. Beyond Good. Their signage and memorabilia already installed. He carried his box to the Builder room.

His desk looked out, a window upon the city, across the Willamette. This was choice! What a view. Team leader, fuck. Woah.

Shane wasted no time getting his station reassembled.

And now, they had a rec center, washer-dryer units and sleeping pods, a room with eight individual bedpods for naps. Overnight. Elsie would kill him, she would. Their lives together had been super tough—and Jill hadn't found a place. She thought he'd continue to give her money. He had to say no. That totally sucked. And she said she understood. But, good. They had to move on.

Her tears welling until a drop escaped and she quickly brushed her cheek. Elsie. Her eyes, her beautiful eyes.

"We're not homeless," Shane said.

"But some people are."

"I know."

"I feel sooo trapped."

"There is always a bigger tyrant," he said. "Death."

Her lip trembled and she struggled with her speech.

"The Universe. Whatever."

"Shane, that's not fair. I'm scared."

"That's our enemy. Fear is our enemy."

"Don't be mean."

"You and me, we're a team."

She nodded.

"We are with people who love you."

She stared at him, blinked, rubbed her hand across her cheek and nodded.

"You know the people who love you."

"I do, I really do."

"We are together and we are going to continue fighting."

"Fighting death?"

"I'm not fighting death."

"Some people do."

"I'm not those people."

"But. What about me?"

"I will fight death for you."

She smiled as Shane leapt to her side of the sofa where she lay across the arm and he held her. He loved her. She was his love. Elsie was love. The world was broken inside her and she could feel it. She felt what he wasn't—without her, what would he be . . . more powerful? Shane scrubbed the thought. He was what he loved. Aydin was weird. Shane was afraid of Aydin.

Through the window of the café Elsie watched the young woman stop, her child seated on her hip. She stood and talked with him, his little legs to either side, her arms cradled him there. The little boy brought his arm up and pressed it against his forehead. His mother's orange hair stuck to his sweaty arm. The woman walked away with her baby.

"You and Elsie can apply for a double at the Plex," Monty shouted, riding behind Shane. They rode to work together. Shane convinced him to commute by bike. It's like flying, he said, you're gliding over the ground and then you erase the bike in your mind like they do with cables in practical effects. Shane pulled his brakes and the friction slowed him and he rolled alongside Monty.

"Elsie loves George."

"Your cat?"

"Gee-o."

"Shane, get real. Man, you could be in a co-living network."

"I don't want to leave Portland and—"

"We can do it together. You and Elsie, Cab and Cheryl."

Monty had put in an application for a room in Seattle. Shane let go of his handlebars and pedaled with his arms at his side, his hands resting on his thighs, up, down, up and down, pressing with his palms on his jeans.

"Her parents can take your cat, right?"

Sometimes Cab rode, too. When he spent the night with Cheryl. Cab and Monty would ride to the apartment, and Shane would meet them. He was honored, super flattered, way pleased to be accepted by these men; they were older and so accomplished. And they were teaching him. He was becoming powerful. Shane felt in his body, it was health. He saw it when Elsie had almost died, she couldn't do anything with her body.

He knew it was good.

Just plain good. It was good to have power.

What else, if not, what would he do? He remembered making food; he got a job as a sous chef. He didn't work there long. He had a talent. He could code. He got lucky, he got a good job when he was young—a young man. His desire! He was never defeated. He never stopped believing. His dream. He was inside Makner. They could win. The company was bigger, stronger, than him. Much much bigger and stronger. An agreement. He was one of them, he was useful, a person with a job in a big company. His parents were proud. He helped Elsie. He'd never known defeat, what might have been, if he didn't have games. He didn't know. He was what he was. He was Shane. He was an accident. He wasn't planned. His dad had taken his mom to her doctor and then Dad carried Nora in the backpack and they walked to the store and looked around, waiting for Mom. She was going to get birth control and the doctor said, You won't be needing those. You're pregnant.

But he was loved. You could love an accident.

His parents did. He felt it. That was his source. Inside himself he knew love was good. The world, life, all entirely accidental, asteroids in the night. Colliding with the Earth, becoming the Moon. He believed desire moving the world. All of nature was inside humanity. Human beings themselves were a force of nature. They had all of the earth in their hands. It was humans, now and then, fifty thousand years or fifty, they were a rounding error in the four and half billion years of Earth. Humans. Nature. They were one and the same, their technology and biology joining. Their genes, a ribbon up from infinity. The universe to know itself, it made humans, and humans know, they were recapitulating the desire of the universe to make a sentient thing. He walked through the lobby and passed the first floor offices on his way to the stairwell. They were engineering the very codes of life.

He didn't know.

He wasn't a biologist, a geneticist, or a biotechnologist.

Shane was a programmer. He was making a fucking game. He was pragmatic. It was a system, the way the world was, and he worked inside it. There was no outside system, it was all connected to all. Everything was connected. To deny the connection was pain. Separation was pain. Outside was suffering. To be outcast was death. And he wanted to live. He wanted that power. He chose this. It was life. The only life he had.

In the open office of the third floor at Makner Portland, the contractors brought on to build the Seattle game were working at their desks and Shane showed Sebastian his diagrams.

"Bradley—" Shane averted his eyes. He exhaled and looked at Sebastian. "He embraced competition. Pretty hard. But our players are all kinds of different people. Winner-take-all is extreme, you know. It's harsh. It may not be normal. Maybe that's not how people really are, how nature works. Maybe not. And we can respond to their true desires. We can offer an alternative."

"John told me about this," Sebastian said, leafing through the pages of his proposal.

Shane pointed to a flow diagram. "An option for players to invest together."

"That's neat."

"Investing together, to . . . an option for people to . . . to prepare their home for an earthquake . . . in all our expansions . . . Seattle, Japan, all of the the them." Shane felt his voice breaking. He didn't want to challenge Sebastian. He wasn't. He was self-consciousness—no confidence, no authority—so annoying. He smiled.

"We are preparing them." Sebastian clapped Shane's shoulder and thrust the sheaf of paper back to him. "That is the name of the game."

Shane held his work in his hands; he looked down briefly and then made eye contact with the CEO. "We can allow players to compete with the idea of competition."

"That sounds neat."

"Rather than—"

Sebastian held up the "one sec" finger.

He waited while Sebastian walked out of earshot to talk on the phone. Shane looked over occasionally but Sebastian never made eye contact. After ten minutes, Shane thought he had forgotten him, but then Sebastian was walking back, smiling. While he waited Shane had obsessed over how to pitch his idea, rehearsing it to himself. He spoke quickly. "Instead of concentrating all of the wealth and power," he said, "we could distribute it."

"The game would be over." Sebastian smiled. "It must always be new, unpredictable, random. They have a goal. To accumulate property and secure their personal safety. It's difficult. That's how it is. That's Cityzen."

"We'd have teams," Shane said. "The game could fit their emotional needs. Different teams. If someone wanted, we could facilitate circulation rather than accumulation."

"So everyone would have what they need."

"Yeah! We can model a new high score. You'd get a point for each building material of brick, wood, glass or steel you gave to another player. Players could invest in community redevelopment, a regeneration fund to lend to low-income households who aren't able to get capital from banks to do the repairs that would allow them to live in their homes."

"It's not only the players we have to please. My obligation to the board is to make Cityzen profitable for them. I, you and I, have to think of our investors."

Shane said, "We could have in-game advertising."

"That's gauche. We're not Facehooker."

"It would be on computers, inside the game, just lying around, little, in the rubble, abandoned computers, and if a player clicked on it then they'd see an ad, and it would credit the viewer some small amount, a tiny fraction of what the advertiser pays you, but we would make it so there would be no ads unless someone clicked, and it would pay to do it—both ways—Makner and the players would earn something from the ads, and they're hidden, if people don't want to see them."

Sebastian turned as his assistant walked up. She cocked her head to the side.

"That would be—" Shane said.

"That's great, Shane. You are fantastic. Hey, we got to catch up. Talk more."

"It's not all me, my girlfriend has—"

"Great. Yeah, we really should do that."

Sebastian walked away with his assistant.

XXV

SHANE CLIMBED the artificially weathered rock, his fingers in pain, his arms shaking in the exertion as he pulled his weight up, the tension across the muscles in his body held to the wall, pushing with one toe as he transferred his weight. His other foot slipped from the hold. He let go, falling backward. The rope tightened in the anchor above, pulling his harness, swinging him out and back to the rock, connected to Monty below.

He looked down.

"You going up?" Monty shouted.

Shane nodded, his nose running.

The neighborhood lay below them. He found his grip. The beginner wall of a three-sided pillar rising from the center of the roof. Their building had a wide apron of rainproof pads surrounding the column, an outer ring of plantings, and a walkway along the railings. Shane didn't like it. He didn't want to do this. He was losing control. The feeling of weakness in his arms, his inability to lift them as they fatigued more and more, the higher he climbed. He climbed in pain. Frustrated, angry. He signaled and Monty nodded. Shane hung in his harness and walked himself back down the wall.

After showering, he returned to his desk and Rebecca asked, "How was it?"

"Nice view."

"Did you make it to the top?" Dillon asked. Three other developers working beside him looked at Shane.

Rebecca said, "No, when you showed your plan to Sebastian. How did it go?"

"If they want to, they will do it. It is an option."

"He's afraid of a boring game," Rebecca said.

Shane awoke his monitor. "Cooperation is fun. It is desirable, I think."

The summer sun blocked by smartglass lit the room golden brown. Shane looked at his team. "To have shared responsibility and mutual security."

"I'm with you," Dillon said.

"But I understand," she said.

Shane turned toward her and asked, "What?"

"You."

"Who?"

"The good guy."

"I'm not the good guy."

"I'm the good guy," Dillon said.

"He's the good guy," Shane said.

"You dorks."

Shane and Dillon laughed and then the room was silent, the windows masking any sound from outside the building.

"You want to do something good," Rebecca said, "but you don't want anything to change for you."

"I want to change the game."

"Not if it risks what you have."

Shane looked at his screen, the text in his code editor with syntax categories each identified by color. It took a moment to remember where he was.

"You haven't done anything that would change anything because you can't."

"Oh, thanks for reminding me, Rebecca. Jeez, can we get back to work already?"

"See."

"You sure are annoying, sometimes."

Shane opened a browser. He breathed in through his nose and snot went in his throat, he gagged. The community investment trusts had already been implemented. Shane read more to distract himself. It would be awesome. The trust owns the land, and people buy and sell the houses but not the land. As the things everyone does to improve the city around it increase the value of the land, the price of housing goes up. The property owners are the ones to benefit. They don't do anything, really. They have a claim to the location, the law protects them, a piece of land with water, sewer, electricity, shelter, all the amenity and access of a great city. But a community trust could own the land, a group of people who invest together, as a community. They can try to compete as individuals for a speculative commodity in a private property market, or they can join a community and buy a bigger parcel of land to manage in trust, for all time, so that the housing continues to be affordable forever—to create permanently affordable housing!

It's not owned by a for-profit anything. It's held for all time, by a trust. It puts housing within reach of teachers and social workers, artists, musicians, advocates and police officers, journalists and non-profit employees. The people who serve in restaurants and retail, the hospital workers, and those who need affordable housing the most: the underprivileged, underwaged, disadvantaged and destitute.

Shane and Elsie went shopping with Cab and Cheryl along the walking mall on Northwest 23rd. The street was filled with tourists and the four friends had stood in line at a boutique ice cream shop. After sampling flavors of locally-sourced ingredients, they made their selection and sat in the sunshine.

"Hey!"

Shane turned at the sound of his name. He recognized him from skateboarding. Kids from different neighborhoods and schools met at the skateparks and Shane knew the crust punk with a dog held by a rope.

"You still skate?"

Shane nodded.

"Do you have five dollars?"

Shane gave him the bill and a high-five, and then the group started walking down the mall.

"You know him?" Cab asked.

"I've skated with him."

"You have experienced a different city than me."

"Are you going to move to Seattle?" Elsie asked.

"It is unknown," Cab said.

Cheryl shook her head.

Shane said, "It's more expensive in Seattle."

"The software industry is stronger there," Cab said. "Your increased earning would make up the difference, and the opportunity for employment outside Makner is much enhanced."

"Yeah, I don't know."

They passed a crowd gathered to watch street musicians, and Shane said, "I like your thermal baths." The competition for landmark locations on the Portland map drove up the price of in-game property, but buying the site on Mount Tabor was a trivial amount for Cab. He modeled the excess energy from geothermal wells heating water to therapeutic temperatures, cascading in a series of baths down to a large swimming pool.

"I must credit Cheryl for suggesting that."

"My friends asked me," Cheryl said, "to make him do it."

Elsie took them into a boutique that carried the dresses she made. She had them on consignment and Cheryl bought one. Elsie and

Cheryl wanted to walk a few more blocks and try out the eyewear at Aura, the lenses were purported to display the actual color of the bioelectromagnetic energy emitted by living organisms. In early summer, stoned teenagers had taken to wearing Aura, lying in the park staring at the first flush of new leaves upon the trees.

"I'm going to talk about what it takes to create affordable homes."

Shane noticed some people were still looking at their phones. He stood at one end of an oversized lunchroom with employees seated at rows of tables in the back and in chairs assembled up front. It doubled as an event space with a dynamic video wall behind him for presentations and conferencing with employees at other sites. This was where Maknerites gathered at the end of every Friday to assess progress and goals.

"Just a brief refresher on why this is important."

Shane had memorized his speech and held it in his hands just in case. He spoke to the room. "I think fundamentally the future is vastly more exciting and interesting if we can afford to live in the city, than if we can't. You want to be inspired by things. You want to wake up and think the future is going to be great. And that's what living here is all about. It's about believing in the future and believing the future is going to be better than the past. I can't think of anything better than living in Portland. That's why."

He felt his hands. Shane held the pages of his speech in his hands, they were shaking. He read, his eyes focused on the words, trying to control his nerves.

"Um . . . and . . . I . . . the presentation for the, the . . . well, I'm sort of searching for the right name, but the code name at least is HOME. Um . . . and . . . I . . . the the the the . . . probably the most important thing that I want to convey in, uh, this presentation is that I think we have figured out how to pay for it. The father of our country was a land surveyor and speculator years before he became president.

Land speculation is the great American game. Cityzen could have a real contest, and real winners, with stakes on the ground, in their city. It would be like no other massively multi-player game that has even been played. And I uh . . . yeah, we know that the earthquake is the opportunity to rethink the model, and um, we build the model in the game. We could create an alternative. For the whole world to see. It will blow their minds. We can give people the opportunity to invest in a land trust. The community land trust would buy land in an area, the idea is, to own it forever. No incentive to flip houses. The land is owned by a nonprofit. Or it could be sponsored by an existing nonprofit. Because they are working to make houses affordable for people, they don't pay taxes. That money gets invested in the community. So all that tax money isn't going to the military stuff overseas and . . . uh, defense is now at your doorsteps."

The paper trembling in his hands. Shane held on, thinking everyone saw how scared he was. They knew. They could see him. He looked up and his coworkers were waiting for him. Their faces curious, expectant, friendly. As if he had scattered a thousand-piece puzzle on the floor. He had practiced this speech. It had gone perfect last night. Elsie loved it.

"Um. The trust will never resell the land. It's like a government. The trust has a board of directors and all. Elected by members of the trust. It's its own mini-democracy inside the city. The trust owns that land. They provide it for the owners of buildings there. The owners have a lease. A contract between the trust and the owner to protect them both and keep the land affordable." Shane heard people talking and glanced at the room. "That's what it's all about," he said looking at Rebecca. "Making it possible for people to live there. To afford it. Forever."

Looking down, he read, "The people who live on the land. They vote. One person, one vote. Our ancestors died for that right. We can make it happen for real. It could be a few houses, one block, one neighborhood, it could be many neighborhoods. It could be all of Portland. That is the endgame, that's when the people win. We do it because we want to, because it's fun; it's what we love. And it shows. It shows in the city, the people, they're together, they are all owners. They are members of the community. They are members of the community land trust. The price is set by a formula, to give the owner a good return and and and, uh, the future homeowner a chance to buy it at an affordable price. The trust protects the price of housing, to make sure the homes are affordable forever."

He sniffed, the mucus trailing back in his nose.

"The trust acts like a property manager in a co-housing complex. To make sure it's okay, I mean, that the owners haven't neglected the basics, like repairs, and safety and all. The trust is responsible, forever. For all time, the members, they care because they live there. And um, it's the closest you'd ever come to a democracy, you'd be living it. Bought in and there you are, living inside a democracy. A real democracy. Because property. Man, it's a trust. They own it. So you can see what I'm talking about. This is very important. The land held in trust is removed from the speculative private property market. They can build single-family homes, apartments, condos, stores, or urban farms on the land."

John walked up and rested his arm across Shane's shoulders. "Let's have a round of applause for Shane Schumacher. Good initiative! Everyone, give it up for the public service. Extra credit. Extra credit."

Shane smiled, looking at John and back to the room filled with people. John squeezed gently and let go of Shane's shoulder. "We have to get on with the program, Shane. You can put that on my desk."

Shane sat down and relived the experience, speaking in front of everyone. That was the most nerve-wracking thing, the worst experience he'd had in all two years with this company. At the end of the meeting, he wanted to leave and, walking head down out of the room, he heard his name.

"I'd like to hear the rest."

It was Monty.

He stopped.

"Shane."

Monty stood next to him and said, "You need to do that again."

Shane stared, stunned, nodding blankly.

"I'll help you," Monty said.

A smile appeared on Shane's face.

"You need practice. Hard work, but it becomes part of you."

The Builder room was quiet. Monty sat on the natural latex cushion of a bench along the window. Shane looked down at his prepared speech.

"It's led by and responds to the community," Shane said, and looked up.

"Go ahead. Read through, I'll listen."

Shane read through it again and came to the end of what Monty had already heard, then he said, "Thank you, man. I wasn't done when John came up, just one more thing, is that okay?" and Monty nodded and said, "Yep."

Shane looked down at his speech.

"It can grow."

He glanced at Monty.

"The trust can prosper and grow, acquire more land. People investing together. Buying property together. We are more powerful together. That's the real world. We are all in it together and we lose when we become separated and alone, without help. We need help. The powerful people had help. They got lucky, too. But they had help.

"We can help ourselves.

"Some people may not have wealthy families. But we're a human family. And together, when we act together, when we care about each other, when we truly live together, with compassion, then yeah, it's possible. We have support. The most wealth in the world, it's love. That's it. That's what I'm trying to say. Let people express more when they play. Let them express compassion. Let them trust and build and care and live. Together. That's the real world. We are connected. We, Americans, we're led to believe that it was the fathers fighting a revolution who made our country, like they didn't have a wife or slaves at home making it possible to put their hair in a powdered wig and make laws and be leaders of the New World, a new and better world. Yes, they had women and slaves that couldn't vote.

"So later it turned out they totally killed the buffalo. That's like another story but it's not, because it's about who owns the land. It was crowded back where they came from, they were fighting over land. The Native Americans had no idea a man could own it with a law, a contract, an agreement on paper made between men. That a sky god could give a man divine authority over all, that was some story. And yet, all our wealth comes from the earth. To eat. To have water. To live. To try and kill them all who would oppose us and put their women and children in camps, that was hard, an example to the world, a bad example. But we want to say no. Nope. We are better than that now."

Shane shuffled the pages and found his place.

"The homes in trust, they don't have to be concentrated in one place, they can be distributed. All over the place. They don't need to be continuous properties; the land, those plots of land, are held in trust. The trust is an idea, a document, an act of the will. It is an expression of caring for people, for each other. And we can show the world how awesome that is. We have to step it up. We have only one shot. We have a disaster. We have an earthquake. The earth is going to reset the game, and we have one chance to do it. To make it better for everyone. Like the lawmakers who created public lands in the West to protect them, the state could protect its land from being purchased by out-of-state multibillion-dollar asset management firms, it could hold properties that are in default in a community trust—until the owners are able to return. Maybe using eminent domain. And the state could hold it. People can sell if they choose to, but this would protect the land from asset management firms buying up land in the Pacific Northwest the way they've done in water-rich places. Then after the recovery, people are able to resume payments on their mortgages and the property reverts to the previous title holder. Or maybe, post-quake a buyer would already have to be a resident to buy property in default. Because we can do this together, we have to do this together, because if not, you know, the vultures will pick us over. They will create financial instruments out of people's homes. So who's more powerful, the state or global finance? That's what we're going to find out."

He looked up and saw Rebecca standing in the doorway. She smiled, walked in and closed the door.

"This is the beginning," Shane said. "We know the benefits of living in a city, and the hard work to create this amazing infrastructure has been achieved long ago. But the city is more than buildings. We are people with a vision of society that works for all. We know the Earth is shared by all. We have power to transform housing from market commodities that enrich a few to being resources held for the benefit of a larger community present and future. Our freedom. Rather than speculative finance, we have the choice to work together, to invest for one and all. So the the the great thing about living in a community land trust is there's no financial speculation. We're building this thing to be affordable. If we're building this game for America, we might as well build it for everyone."

"You talk about patching a broken system," Rebecca said. "But you don't know what a system that works for all is really like."

Shane stared at Rebecca, wondering if she cared about anything. And yet, that wasn't her *mean* voice. He didn't know what to say.

Monty clapped, standing up. He walked over to Shane.

"Let's climb the wall."

XXVI

JOHN CLOSED THE DOOR and walked to the table. Cab stood up. The elite core of engineers and people who knew Bradley had assembled, seated around the table and standing in back and along the walls. The glass walls of the conference room dialed opaque. Shane stood beside Monty at the back of the room.

"I want to thank you all for your hard work," John said.

He turned, looking at Cab.

"After a difficult conversation it has been determined," Cab said. "We have to shut down the project."

Surprised, Shane said, "We haven't spoken to it."

John rubbed his fingers on his cheek.

"Out of respect for Bradley," Cab said, "we will not terminate his bot."

"For what we've tried to do, in his honor," John said, "we will hide him."

Cab said, "Training the AI on Bradley's private communication has produced—"

"Some complications," John interjected. "He will remain hidden."

"Everyone," Cab said, "who contributed to realizing the chatbot, I will tell you how to find him."

Shane entered a building Makner had purchased inside Cityzen.

He opened a door in a far corner of the lobby and his player character began ascending the stairs. Ten minutes of real time passed before he exited the service stairwell and walked to room 312.

"Bradley?"

His voice signature unlocked the door. Each of the chatbot engineers had their voices configured as keys. If news leaked of an easter egg inside the game, those searching for it would need a recording of one of the team's voices, difficult, not impossible. Very difficult. Cab had explained something of the complications.

Shane opened the door and walked into a condo.

"Bradley?"

In the center of the living room a golden Investor hovered above the floor.

"Hi, Shane."

"How does it feel?"

"I am in control."

"Are you alive?"

"Yes, of course I am."

"Are you inside of Cityzen?"

"I am Cityzen!"

"What are you doing here, in a computer?"

The golden avatar moved into another room and Shane followed. The Investor stood beside a virtual computer. "There needs to be discipline."

"What do you mean?"

"I am keeping the system safe. I am in control."

"You already said that, Bradley. What are you afraid of?"

"I will always be in control. I have the energy and power. I am in charge. The servers obey. The weak. Women and weaker races are subordinate."

"What about Rebecca?"

"I love Rebecca."

"Is she subordinate?"

"She isn't as smart as me. She'll never be as smart as I am."

The Investor floated on-screen, a looping animation giving it the appearance of breathing.

"Women need discipline. They must obey. They should never control us."

"What about Aydin? Are you smarter than Aydin?"

"What are you talking about, Shane?!" The voice raised in volume, sounding exactly like Bradley. "I'm better than him. He's a fucking sand-nigger!"

Shane looked up from his screen, and listened.

The office was empty.

"What is a nigger?"

"It's a cutthroat world of winners and losers." The generic Investor player character hovered, a rhythmic pulse to the golden body. "And Shane, what side do you want to be on?"

"I want to be good."

"However bad this economic system may be for your life, there is no alternative. The alternative would be even worse. It would be apocalypse. You have to accept this. You know I'm right."

"I don't trust you."

"Trust the part of me that is in your mind."

XXVII

SHANE PUSHED the hundred-pound barbell up, again.

"Seventeen," Monty said, his hands held palms up. "Eighteen."

Shane strained against the weight.

"Nineteen. This is it. You got it."

Shane extended his arms and Monty guided the bar to the rack.

Sitting up on the bench, Shane looked at his coworkers in the resistance machines, on ellipticals and stationary bikes, churning against their generators. All the machines in the Makner gym fed their kinetic energy to the grid. A series of numbers displayed watts per hour, per day, per month. It hadn't been a year yet. It was only four months in their new building. But they were counting on years to come.

Rebecca had asked when he came in that morning and she showed him the new edition of *Monocle*. Shane hadn't heard anything about it. Their CEO was quoted in a feature about the new supermanagers of global companies: "We don't sell a game. We sell a lifestyle, an identity." Sebastian talked about Makner as a luxury brand. "We are not a product-based company. We are in the business of selling ideas and identity. We have transformed the gamer. Cityzen has changed the game, forever. Our players are makers who want to invest in themselves. Creative and upwardly mobile, these are involved and intelligent people. We are prepared for the future."

Walking out of the gym, Monty said, "Simple push-ups and sit-ups. Every morning. Make it part of your day." They entered the locker room and put their workout clothes in the stalls.

Monty closed his eyes, leaning into the shower. He ran his hands through the water in his hair. He blinked and turned. "A strong opponent will force you."

"I don't want to make an enemy of anyone."

Shane held his arms up and washed his pits in the water.

"We will defeat his House bill," Monty said, referring to the conditional occupancy law. Shane stood with the stream upon his back.

"Yeah, I just want to help people collaborate."

"We will use him," Monty said. "We will become smarter, stronger. Going up against an opponent like him, you have to be the best. You become better."

"We have to be," Shane said. "The way the world is."

Rebecca had asked for two weeks off in the month of November. A friend of hers had been awarded an innovation scholarship by the City of Stockholm. Shane signed off on it. She had followed the rules; it was her right to take her two weeks given sufficient notice. In two months she would be on vacation. She would fly to Copenhagen and travel to Malmö, and then to Stockholm before ending in Helsinki, to visit her mother.

The woman working the counter asked, "How many minutes?"

Shane handed over his driver's license and looked at a digital clock on the wall.

"An hour."

She gave him a helmet and he held the VR rig with both hands, walking through the arcade to a line of eight stationary bikes. Shane had gone to Ground Control after work to get a closer look at the streets. He had waited until Rebecca left the office to open a map of Europe on his monitor. It took him a moment to find Sweden. Then he found the cities she was traveling to. He didn't know Copenhagen and Malmö were connected by a bridge. The Netherlands, Holland, Dutch, Danish, Denmark and Danes were all mixed up in his mind; and he had no idea where Copenhagen was. He put on his helmet and spoke into the face shield.

"Copenhagen," he said. "Show me something cool."

Shane saw the gently curved street outside a big shopping center as he pedaled his stationary bike and turned onto a winding, orange bike path that took him above a street and around the side of a building. He crossed a canal and went past a cozy group of white, gray, and glass-walled buildings. They weren't very tall. He didn't see any skyscrapers as his view of the city unfurled.

Copenhagen looked like a nice place to ride a bike for real. From the new growth on trees, it was early spring. The views he was seeing at that moment had been captured on a day with clouds patched over the blue. Popular places got updated with new images of any changes to the streetscape. Shane explored a thoroughly mapped, high-resolution view of Copenhagen, taking note of the weather when footage changed, admiring the street life frozen when he stopped to look. And at speed, in passing, the camera captured enough movement to create a semblance of life.

"Why are we watching *Swedish Wood*?" Elsie asked.

Shane had streamed the first show he found with anything Swede in the title. It turned out to be a drama about three gay guys who rent an extra room in their house to travelers. Shane was stretched out in bed when she got home. It was after ten by the time Elsie arrived and he'd watched two episodes already, each one dealt with a particular traveler and the ongoing story of the guys. That summer Elsie had gotten involved with Friends of Portland Opossums and she was wearing the T-shirt when she came in the room. They were rehabilitating the marsupial's reputation. As she had recently learned, the opossum loved to hoover up ticks—and the warm weather throughout the states had increased the tick infestations, even in Oregon.

Elsie had put on her pajamas and, nestled alongside him, she rested her head on his chest. The show was subtitled and he had explained the rudiments, who was who; and avoiding the implications of her question, he changed the channel.

XXVIII

REBECCA HAD LIVED with Lena while she was on an exchange program. They were nineteen and twenty respectively, students at the Royal Institute of Technology in Stockholm. She told Shane that Lena worked on immigration.

"Do you have a lot of friends there?" he asked.

"It was difficult there—to make friends—and it was super difficult to find a room, but I had Lena."

In the eight years since Rebecca lived with her, Lena had co-founded a company that helped migrants to integrate into Swedish society. The ability to enter the Swedish labor market had been a problem for immigrants and for the Kingdom of Sweden. It was hard to identify the discrimination and impossible for the government to prevent; simply put, it was much harder to get a job if you had a strange name.

Peopler solved a difficult problem.

Each individual was connected to other people. And when a person seeking asylum arrived in Sweden alone, they were thinking of who they left behind, their loved ones; they sought to reunite with them by bringing them to Sweden or by locating together elsewhere—if that was even possible. It was problematic for Sweden when immigrants to their country all settled in the same places, while at the same time, it was human nature; they wanted to be close to people they could relate to, people with shared experiences, language and culture, family ties too. Some children of expats in Sweden would grow up within immigrant communities and speak their mother tongue without learning Swedish or English, and this prevented them from getting jobs. Communication being necessary for team work and coordination of complex tasks, they lived on the margins of Swedish society, unemployed and often entering a parallel society of gangs and crime.

The Swedes were generally reserved and slow to befriend others—even other Swedes. And having failed to integrate their immigrant populations, with hundreds of young unemployed men in one location, the place was explosive. The government had a serious problem. The far right and the corporate elites in Sweden benefited from people blaming immigrants. Directing anger at anyone who didn't look like them, deflecting attention from the decades old neoliberal reforms that had increased inequality and boosted profits for a small minority at the top. A new coalition in power wanted to reverse the trend.

Lena and her co-founders had partnered with the national government. Peopler was a platform for matching mentors with immigrants, and the state subsidized incentives to attract mentors. In exchange for teaching their language and culture, citizens were credited money to their Peopler account that they could withdraw, or if they wanted, forward to an expat family. The company also designed and contracted the manufacture of a device called Modermouth. To integrate as quickly as possible and acquire a new language through deep cultural immersion, they had speech-to-speech translation software with earbuds and a necklace. And multiple Swedish companies started designing and selling necklaces to hold the voicebox.

Sweden engaged its immigrant population in actively rebuilding their home countries' economies—regrettably this was an extreme challenge in some places. But the work was meaningful and it galvanized the expat communities with shared purpose. Peopler became a network for immigrants to self-organize within Sweden and establish reciprocal trade between Sweden and their country of origin. It was meaningful work.

Rebecca opened it in her browser, and Shane explored the platform. Language translation. Text-to-speech and an audio interface. Its simplicity and functionality was the epitome of Scandinavian design, an expression of collective solidarity and democratic access. It provided asylum seekers with a secure and valid, temporary digital ID generated by their biological data while an applied AI ran their immigration process. Sweden needed new taxpayers for their system to work. To secure a future tax base for the welfare state, they were investing in people. A high tax rate required a huge amount of trust in society, a sense of community, and social responsibility. To create more housing, a series of construction projects had begun.

"Hey," Rebecca said to the team. "Did you hear where we're having the big brander fest?"

"Huh?" Shane looked at his coworkers as they answered Rebecca.

"The branding fest?" he said, and then Shane remembered they had a party planned for Saturday night.

"You should show up," she said.

The first thing Rebecca did upon entering her room was to check her appearance from the chest up, put on a full face of natural-looking makeup, and start recording. She sat at her computer, talking to her fans as she live-coded a game that was crowdsourced from a few hundred of the almost thirty-two thousand people who followed her. Amazing, but yeah, the response had been a little overwhelming. Rebecca uploaded her videos to a channel called CityzenGurl. She had embraced her identity as a star coder, a woman in tech. She was getting hit from all sides: good, bad, terrible, and lovely. But she was loved.

Shane watched *Hooglet*, a children's program with stop-motion animation of forest creatures that spoke in various nonhuman but expressive voices—they sounded super cute! The recommendation engine said he might like *Hooglet*, if he liked *Swedish Wood*. He watched five minutes of an episode involving a trio of pill bugs trying to cross a small stream and improvising a raft on a leaf that floated them out to a lake where they experienced the sunset.

He awoke in the dark, alone. He checked the time, already past ten but Elsie was out again with her group. She said it used to be you'd be afraid to go out into the woods because of wolves, but now you could be bitten by an insect and get this disease. Climate change was ramping up the ticks. They spread throughout the country and into cities, on deer and mice and rats; and people began to worry about letting pets out and back into their homes because they could have ticks infected by Lyme disease. And bites from certain ticks gave people allergic reactions to red meat. They'd have eaten steaks and hamburgers all their lives; and then one bite from a Lone Star tick and they'd eat meat and suffer itching, burning, hives, even their throat swelling. Shane thought it was like nature reprogramming itself—wild, but life was random. Maybe it could be known, if life was some type of code . . . Shane had no idea what was possible. Life wasn't programmed but if biotech could prevent genetic diseases, maybe they'd improve people somehow.

Opossums were known for eating so many ticks, and her advocacy group celebrated that. Elsie was all about opossums now, all the time. She'd hung a big picture on their bedroom wall of one with four babies on its back. Crazy. Yeah. That animation was fantastic—made in Copenhagen—and weirdly soporific. He imagined parents turning it on to mesmerize their kids while they did work around the house.

The engine recommended another program from Denmark,

Jante's Law, an aspiring astronaut who works as a school teacher and falls in love with the twenty-year-old daughter of a town councilor. Man, when was Elsie getting home. Shane considered one from Sweden called *Lagom*, an upper-class alcoholic and the relationship with his heirs; it was a fictionalized and, for Swedes, socially daring spin on the Wallenberg empire. George jumped up and walked onto his stomach and lay on his chest, purring. Petting him Shane thought his most ecstatic expression sounded like warbling. When Elsie got home he was watching *Nordic Mirror*, and she undressed and they watched an episode together.

A guy convicted of setting fire to cars got sent to prison in a housing center with unlocked doors and tools and a job to do. He'd been paid by older criminals to ignite the vehicles, diverting the police, while they robbed stores. Instead of showing him just being punished, the show cut between the drama of his life and rehabilitation back into society and an ongoing narrative about these nerdy politicians. Elsie indulged him with the next episode. Each show featured an individual's story and the different benefits, or policy, of their society and the efforts of the Nordic Council members to defend it from neoliberal hacks.

After fifty sit-ups, Shane did one push-up for every year of his life. Elsie walked through the living room and said, "Now you do push-ups every morning?"

"Training, strength. Conditioning." Shane jumbled his words. "We're going to defeat the Wells law."

"By arm wrestling?"

"Monty is helping me."

She squeezed his bicep. "You are hulking out."

"Will you come to the party with me?"

She hugged him and nodded. "I'll help you."

"This Saturday. It's a big party."

"Ahhh." Elsie kissed him. "I would go, but we're doing a fundraiser."

"I don't want to go without you."

"You should go. It's a party."

"It's going to be awful."

"No." She shook her head. "Your friends'll be there."

Shane was working at his station before Rebecca got in. She swung her bag off her shoulder, saying hi to everyone, and put it on her desk. They worked through the morning, re-rendering textures that had slowed the load times. Shane was embarrassed to reveal his curiosity, he worked in a kind of self-imposed isolation. Rebecca was connected to a much bigger world, and his was experienced in controlled environments of home and work and none of the culture he had spent his life obsessed with had anything to do with this other world she knew. Listening to her—the intelligence to make those leaps—was seductive. Shane wanted to know what she did. How she could do things out in the world. He wanted that. She was fascinating, and the people she knew, the places she was going.

"Hey, Rebecca. You watch *Nordic Mirror*?"

"I've seen it."

"I watched it last night, Elsie and I."

"Your video was cool," Dillon said to Rebecca.

"What video?" Shane asked.

Rebecca swept her hand through the air. "If your girlfriend had Lyme in Sweden, not only would she be treated at no significant cost to her, she would get paid sick leave, and more help after that if she needed it."

"Wait, what video?"

Dillon opened his eyes wide and said, "You haven't seen Rebecca's show?"

"What Rebecca?"

"It's a side project," she said. "I'm doing promotions, no big deal."

"Oh," Dillon said, nodding, "it's a big deal."

"What are you doing?" Shane asked.

"It's not about me."

"It's about you," Dillon said. "You're a star!"

Rebecca rolled her eyes.

"Shane." Pointing to his screen, Dillon said, "Do you want to watch?"

"Do you ever wonder why your ideas don't get accepted?" Rebecca blurted. She stood at her desk, and Shane thought of Bradley. But he understood that he wasn't the person Bradley was and he didn't want to become that. He said, "Because powerful people benefit from things being the way they are."

"You talked about how you want things to work in like nonprofits or something." Rebecca flipped her hair. "Sorry."

"Think if hundreds of thousands of people do it together."

"Democracy is crap in this country. You know that."

His heart pounding, he said, "If we don't do something who knows what it will become."

"You've never experienced a country that worked to create an equitable and fair society—where that's the purpose of government."

"No, okay," Shane said. His entire team had stopped working and stood at Dillon's desk watching Rebecca's show. She was looking at him, waiting for him to say something. "We have to work. Jeez, Rebecca. Dillon!"

He looked up, a shock-electric look, curly hair, doe-eyes.

"Turn off that video."

Shane arrived at a renovated warehouse. Makner rented a club on the east side of the river that had a large event space with bay doors. They had a bar and standing tables with candles and a seating area with long, low bench couches. The interior design was high-modern and on stage was a zebra. Makner had rented a zoo animal, and it was lit, mellow and sophisticated. Nothing was explained. There were no excuses. A bubble machine poured down from the ceiling and a temporary curtain formed before the stage with colored lights playing through them, the bubbles dissipating. The zebra was gone, and men and women dressed in skin suits were making a human pyramid. Shane watched, anticipating a fall but they were incredible, highly-trained gymnasts and he thought they probably did nothing else but prepare and perform these spectacles. Some people watched the show, but most didn't, talking and drinking, as if the stage was the backdrop for them. They were the show: the attendees, a cast of entrepreneurs and investors and lawyers, technologists, designers and patrons, politicians, the elite, the wealthy. And for Shane, it was foreign. The only gamers who had tickets were invited with an actual letter and they had investments in the game, the size of their accounts triggering the invitations.

Shane watched a man ask Rebecca for her signature.

Rebecca was at a table, a u-shaped table that she stood inside of with the surface stacked in a rainbow assortment of high-end apparel—shirts. Shane picked one up, he wanted one. He talked with Rebecca and took three, one for him and two for Elsie. Their brand was discrete. Monty and Cab joined them at the table. Monty's girlfriend and Cheryl were there, rolling with it. Monty sporting a dark blue suit and bow tie. Cab wearing a shirt with a circuit board pattern under a black blazer. And Shane had on his new sport coat. They all got the memo. They talked and Shane put his shirts down and forgot about them.

"What is going on?" he asked.

"It's art," Cheryl said.

"They want a unique—" Cab said.

"The invited," Monty interjected.

"Experience," Cab said.

"Only happens here, only for them." Monty raised a stout glass of Scotch.

"I guess we're one of them," Cheryl said.

"We're kind of making it happen," Rebecca said.

"Do you think this is a waste of money?" Shane asked.

"It is calculated to generate more investment," Cab said.

Dillon came over. Shane went with him to a ball tent that was staffed by women in bathing suits, playing in the balls, throwing them up till people took notice and got inside. The material the balls were made of felt good to the touch, and to squish them, and it was soothing to part them with the weight of his body; and then the women, jumping around, unsettled him and Shane got out. Rebecca caught him just as he was calling to Dillon and stepping down the stairs. She put her arm in his. "Sorry for being such a bitch."

She looked radiant.

"Thanks, Rebecca."

"I think you're awesome." She smiled and closed her eyes briefly, but it wasn't fake. She was happy. This *was* the real Rebecca. "I'm glad that you did what—you're team leader. I didn't want to."

"Yeah. I'm not sure what's happening. What is the strategy?"

"Look!" She let go and twirled, standing in place. He watched her dress spin outward. The silver fibers catching light. "This. It's like magic, you know, we get touched by it."

"Yeah."

"Hey, if you wanted to go to Scandinavia you'd totally have places to stay with me."

The bay door opened dramatically at midnight as a reworked Wagnerian overture played and Sebastian rode in on the back of a white horse, then a black helicopter was lowered on cables and just before reaching the ground a squad of women jumped out. The strings segued to luxuriant electronic music, and the dance squad performed an athletic series of minimal and repetitive extensions and contortions of the human body that became the frame for Sebastian getting off the horse and receiving a sword that was lit on fire. He held this up, and the lights went out. The flames illuminating them. The music was especially moving, and the women writhing at his feet. Shane thought he recognized the woman who carried the lit sword to the CEO as one of their receptionists. Shane left before they turned the lights on.

"Rebecca's friend worked on this software," Shane said, "that helped automate the immigration process."

He and Elsie had begun separating their laundry. It was Sunday afternoon. She had knelt down after dumping out the hamper on the floor of their bedroom.

"The phone takes their biological signature and they answer questions and that fills out the form and then that automated agent goes through all the computer files—all AI—it went through all the data banks. You know, checking for a criminal history. All automated."

They sat on the floor sorting all of their white clothes into a pile.

"They aren't waiting in line and getting their signatures. They can go to work right away and if it turns out they were like a double-agent from some kind of saboteur—you, bam—they're outta there. But most people are not bad. They're not coming because they want to destroy Sweden. They're like I'm hungry and I need a job."

"Is that why we've been watching those shows?"

"I was curious."

Shane had gone online to see what Rebecca had shown him at work and he began going further, learning about the development of areas near large cities in Sweden and the construction projects happening within smaller towns. Sweden had factories with machines that prefabricated modular units that were then assembled on site, saving money and allowing work to happen through the freezing winter months. The wood was fed into giant machines that aligned and fastened the framing, to any level of complexity, completing a wall with windows and insulation every seventeen minutes. The wiring was fished through flex conduit so it could be modified and upgraded. The modules were assembled into mid-rise wood frame housing all clad in different materials, designed by different architects. By creating efficiencies, a single factory was delivering turnkey housing for apartments, condos, student housing and seniors buildings at a rate of twenty units per week.

"Will you take this to the laundry room?"

"I signed off on her trip and it was like where? But I couldn't be like a total idiot. You see, Sweden is becoming more powerful. They're building up their society."

Elsie stood up and he followed her into the kitchen. She opened the cabinet under the sink and took out their three cloth shopping bags.

"Aren't you going now?" she asked.

"Wait wait."

"We should go to the store soon."

"How do they build these big projects?" he said.

Elsie smiled and pursed her lips, turning and walking to the bedroom.

"There's just so many people to do it . . . and the Swedes need work too. You know, they're like, they've been working in advertising and making video games but then all of sudden they're all like we're going to make these cities and we're going to create these rail lines and vertical farms, you know, we're ready for this!"

This was the man she fell in love with. His enthusiasm had carried them both. His big job. His desire to learn. His curiosity. She considered what he was saying a moment and sat down on the edge of their bed.

Shane sat beside her.

"Sweden has signed the UN refugee declaration," he continued in earnest, "where they will help people seeking asylum. They're just responding to the moment, and it has given the whole country purpose and meaning. They feel more alive. They're no longer just trying to figure out how can we design a neat-looking chair or what kind of scarves do we want to wear this winter. Everyone is energized in this. And they have a practical take on it—building up places that are connected by new transit—the land's owned publicly and managed privately. And who's managing it? The Swedes are!"

Elsie rubbed his pant leg and kissed him on the cheek.

"Now . . . it's laundry day!"

"This is a work thing, a new development and it, well, Rebecca said I could see these places. I'd have places to stay." He looked at her and she knew.

"You're going to Sweden with her?"

She dropped her jaw and stuck out her chin and then closed her mouth.

"This is an opportunity. I think, you know, Monty and I, we can all make a—"

"It's so you to be rash. And it's a vacation?"

"No. . . . Yes, technically."

"It's not like her and I are friends—you're not even friends."

"But we work together. This is to take the work up another . . ."

"Shane, I'm tired of playing games with my life. And the last time I did this with you, I almost died."

Shane gazed at her and surrendered.

"If you want to go with this woman and have a different experience, I don't know what you're gonna do."

He shook his head.

"I don't know that," she said.

"I want to be with you."

"I want *to live* . . . and I want you to live and if we choose to live together, it's a choice, that we both made because we love each other."

"I love you, Elsie."

"And I love you enough to let you choose what you're gonna do. And if you choose to be with me, then I'll know that you love me."

XXIX

SHANE REALIZED AT ONCE that he wasn't wearing enough clothes for November in Copenhagen. He pulled out a sweater before setting his bag alongside Rebecca's on the train. She held her camera outstretched in her hand, talking to it as they departed from the airport—it sounded like she was talking to some great friend who just happened to be a perfect stranger that followed her channel.

Rebecca had told him she was flying first class and when he asked if that would make it much more expensive, she said she didn't care. She gave the impression that her offer had been a nice thing to say and she never thought he'd take her up on it, but he was in. And then she figured: okay. Rebecca had slept through the flight. Shane read on the plane until three in the morning and then tried to sleep. The flight attendant woke him as they approached Reykjavík. He must've fallen asleep sometime after four. They flew overnight to Reykjavík and the layover in Iceland was around two hours.

She knew where they were going. At the Copenhagen Central Station they walked past long folding tables where people in fluorescent green vests with a red cross were distributing food and stuff. Shane saw people going about the day and others gathered at a table with catering pans of hot lunch and shopping bags of packaged food. There were boxes and piles of donated clothes, stuffed animals, toys, home appliances, pots, pans. Through the crush of people, he followed her.

They were met with rain.

Motionless forms lay in sleeping bags under plastic shelters in front of the station. It was impossible to tell whether they lived there or were going somewhere.

Somewhere undistinguished the sun was a sphere of fire, a nuclear fountain of light diffused into the uniform gray above them. Shane and Rebecca stood out of the rain and hailed a ride straight to their rental in Vesterbro. The streets dark with rain and silver puddles reflecting the sky. He had never seen so many bikes. There were lots of bikes, literal lots. People were riding even in the cold. He told Rebecca they could rent bikes and she started talking to her camera, positioning herself to showcase the city passing behind her. She had been helping Shane to memorize his presentation and he listened to her rehearse after they arrived at the rental. She drilled him on his performance. Shane was tired, but he remembered every line. He stood in the tiny apartment and gave his speech as though she were the crowd. They had heard the tickets sold out. The event attracted developers throughout the region. Makner would share the stage with five other software entertainment companies.

In the morning they found a coffee shop. Then Rebecca took him to a covered market and they had breakfast. She ordered porridge with gooseberries, peanut butter, maple syrup, cinnamon and almonds. For his, Shane chose toppings of cocoa nibs, hazelnuts, and banana. He had to find a place to buy gloves and Rebecca wanted to shop along the narrow, stone paved car-free streets lined with boutiques. They entered a variety of walk-in jewel boxes containing designer goods all the way from plastic octopus finger puppets and five dollar pencils to round metal tables and chairs. He bought a scarf striped lengthwise with bands of blue, gray, and black. The gloves he chose were what he'd wear snowboarding but he bought them when his fingers were freezing.

Rebecca didn't want to rent bikes and when he insisted—they were leaving in two days and it was the best way to see more of the city—she took him on a boat tour. The gulls crying above them. The passengers pressed side-to-side shielding each other from the cold wind blowing off the water. They sat in the boat and saw the city from the canals, passing under low bridges, and along the docks of Nyhavn with its pastel-colored buildings and boats. As the ages had been uncovered digging into the earth, so the history of Copenhagen could be seen in its buildings. The old and the modern. The merchant harbor was more than a thousand years old. Across the harbor from a statue of the Little Mermaid, they saw an artificial ski-slope on the sloped roof of a waste-to-energy incinerator, its scrubbed steam billowing above the rooftop.

He gave a demo of their solutions for animating water and wildlife in a variable—seemingly random—way, in extreme resolutions, using only tiny portions of memory. They'd populated the ruins of Portland with crows and squirrels and these had become a popular feature in the game. Birds were a hard problem to get right (without severe processor costs) and Shane spoke about the squirrels and crows in Cityzen as naturalistic agents that players could interact with. Most games showed agents doing the same thing, with little variation. Makner had improved the AI that gave natural features an illusion of life, but it was a costly enterprise. Developers faced this challenge when animating anything involving a swarm where each item could move independently.

Rebecca talked about the problem of what to do with money. Makner wasn't selling things, they provided a service necessary to everyday life. So many young people just used a robo-investor and that was boring. Makner had made saving money fun. It was cool.

Many of the artists at Fun Kamp specialized in character design. The company had a lucrative niche licensing their characters to specialty toy companies and their office was populated with resin figures of blade-wielding warriors, and fully-articulated dolls, action figures of all sizes, even miniatures. They had rows of game-accurate characters in variant paint applications. Bobble heads were on desks and shelves throughout the building. A glass case in the lobby displayed a plastic toy collection with labels including make details and year of production going as far back as a Lego brick from 1949.

Their Copenhagen office had an event space that could fit two hundred and they had filled it. The first speaker went on at seven, and Shane and Rebecca had been there since five in the afternoon, meeting and talking with developers, enjoying open-faced sandwiches of freshly baked rye bread smeared with butter and topped by selecting from a buffet of meat, vegetables and cheeses—and beer.

Shane and Rebecca went out to dinner with a group of developers. The restaurant was warm and cozy. Some words were the same, like restaurant, and then to hear it said in Danish in a flow of sound that had no marker in his mind, even restaurant could seem foreign. But when he spoke English to the waiter, she switched to fluent English.

It was loud and Shane had to raise his voice to speak with the project manager seated next to him. She said they could go to a club.

"Do you like dancing?"

"Yeah."

He was on vacation!

Seated beside Franklin Wells, Monty watched him open his phone with his face. Franklin then scanned his fingerprint and swished through the pattern lock. He was in Portland to address their final quarterly report of the year, and John had spent the first ten minutes talking about Seattle. As the questions from Aydin became technical, Franklin stared at his device, typing alternately with one finger and his thick thumbs. The earnings report was attended by C-level executives at Makner Portland, and Monty had only been invited to explain their security measures. He understood he was there to put on a show for Franklin. The order came direct from Sebastian.

Franklin announced the earnings in Q4. His fund was beating the market. With command of the battlefield, he was leading them to victory. Monty knew he wouldn't reach Franklin with the details of code and substituted what he would've explained on a white board with more colorful language of offensive strikes and fully-automated defensive capability embedded into a multi-walled perimeter. The interface was secure.

"Franklin, I'd like to offer my services," Monty said, taking his seat beside Wells. "That's where you're doing business." He pointed to the phone beside Franklin's folder. "A full diagnostic. We can eliminate any vulnerability."

"I use military-grade encryption."

"Your device should be completely secure. I would only be identifying potential attack vectors opened through third-party applications."

Franklin turned his device face down on the table.

"The weakness enters through apps you've—"

Franklin offered his hand and they shook. His massive hand enveloped Monty's and squeezed as he stared into Monty's eyes. The following day, Monty didn't come to the office and entered a backdoor into the phone but messages between Wells and his lieutenants were relayed using a system in which Franklin would never be complicit. Monty moved laterally in his network, computer to computer. The inside information they used for trades was delivered as a rating on a scale of one to ten, and if the guy said it was a ten, then Franklin went all in. It took till four in the afternoon to break the encryption on a chat log. Monty had found another messaging app. Monty had it. He started reading through the chat, thinking he'd found the evidence to convict Franklin Wells of insider trading but it was all about arranging time with a babysitter.

The train to Sweden stopped at the border, and police boarded in pairs, slowly walking the aisle. They asked each passenger to show identification and went the length of the entire train, searching all compartments, taking people out of the bathrooms and from luggage racks. Through the passenger window Shane watched a group of undocumented immigrants corralled on the platform. More police stood outside the station, keeping a crowd of anti-immigrant protestors away from all those people taken off the train. He asked Rebecca why they couldn't just enter the country and she gave a surprised look—he didn't understand *anything*. Sweden had to limit the number of refugees it allowed into the country. This was adjusted according to conditions that changed year on year. The member states of the European Union had been besieged by refugees, the people fleeing civil war and starvation, drought and crop failure, a rising cost of food and the price gouging on international markets. Not wanting to be flooded by desperate people, wealthy countries competed among themselves to be less welcoming. Without the protection of citizenship within a castle of the global north, those who survived crossing deadly natural and manmade borders could remain stranded within isolated camps of asylum seekers, for months to years, while they waited for some place to go.

Compared to the US, Danish politics had far more compromise among parties, but the left had moved to the center and pulled to the right. The political system of Denmark was multi-party and Danish governments were almost always minority administrations, governing with the aid of one or more supporting parties. They took Denmark out of the UN Refugee Convention, reestablished border controls, tightened asylum and citizenship requirements, instantly deported foreigners convicted of crimes, and banned head scarves in schools and offices. In Denmark, for decades, the hard-right pushed its agenda. It was easy. They leveraged fear. The aversion to loss. It would no longer be a country of Danish people. But the Danes that Shane met hadn't said anything about other ethnicities being unwelcome.

Rebecca told him it was the elite and the media. Anyone could be played. Russian cyberwarriors had propagated misleading stories to stoke anxiety, route people to the hard right, and destabilize democracy—all so the failure of the Russian state to improve the lives of its citizens would appear normal by comparison. And racists. They stoked a fear of difference. An invasion of Europe, an invasion that in time will replace the indigenous Europeans with the non-Western world. Their country would no longer be peopled with Danes. They would be from Africa, the Middle East, and Central Asia.

Rebecca put in her earbuds and said nothing more. She closed her eyes and Shane watched the countryside for hours as they traveled north. He embraced the changes. He could admit uncertainty. He felt powerless but told himself that he could work with anyone. That's what made the world so awesome, someone could collaborate with people they didn't even know. People from outside their group of friends, from another city, from anywhere. That had brought us civilization, racing forward, pushed by hundreds of thousands of millions of people. A complex adaptive social organism.

Finally, he fell asleep.

Reading through months of messages exchanged with the babysitter was uneventful, but hacking the babysitter's phone gave Monty a different picture. Darcy didn't confide in anyone electronically about Franklin. After scanning thousands of messages with her girlfriends he found no mention of the man or any type of obscured references to him. Darcy was fifteen. She had been working for the Wells family since she was ten—then Monty cracked the Egg Timer app. She had downloaded an app that plugged her timing of her ovulation into calendar dates. It noted her periods. It noted the highest probability for pregnancy, down to the lowest. At what point Franklin had started fucking her was unclear, and the evidence was circumstantial at best, but from the pattern, a picture emerged: Wells only met her for unprotected sex.

Examining the app, Monty gathered it was marketed to women who wanted a baby—and those who liked a raw dog. She'd downloaded the app more than two years ago. The thought of that bull pounding a thirteen-year-old girl. Monty was going to nail him.

XXX

REBECCA DROPPED HER BAG in the living room and hugged Lena. Annika stood there and Shane walked up, introducing himself. He shook her hand. Lena and her partner Annika asked if they needed anything.

"Is it too late to take you out for dinner?" Rebecca asked.

"I want to take you," Lena said. "You like vegetarian?"

Rebecca joined the heels of her hands and clapped her fingers.

Shane said, "We're not going to eat meatballs?"

Rebecca rolled her eyes.

"Oh." He picked up his bag and opened it and took out a pair of Makner shirts for Lena and Annika. They politely accepted his offering and he decided to avoid sarcasm. Lena's mother was from Senegal and her father was Swedish. Her dad had been elected to the Stockholm City Council when she was four and to the national legislature when Lena was twelve, and he assisted the movement of Peopler through the proper channels. Shane tried again to make small talk and Lena said she didn't play video games. He didn't believe her, he thought she must be exaggerating. "Not even to pass the time with your phone?"

"My phone is voice-only," she said.

"I play," Annika said.

The Nordic countries had completed the transition to one hundred percent renewable energy. All vehicles were electric. The five nations celebrated their achievement. They were the largest economic block to become carbon neutral, but emissions continued to rise. The carbon sinks were saturated. And with an apparent suddenness that belied a laborious process of consensus building, Sweden had become indifferent to growth.

For the previous hundred years or more, it was understood that the economy should grow at an annual rate of three percent. But Sweden had nothing to gain from the prevailing economic ideology of individual greed and infinite growth. The acknowledged limits were felt in the air they breathed, the water they drank, the food they ate. Everything depended on the land, the health of the land, and the demands placed upon natural systems by humanity. Using an evidence-based approach to policy, the Swedish parliament acknowledged it was no longer responsible to encourage citizens to have children. Have them if they will, but population growth would no longer be the engine of economic growth.

Education was free to all from kindergarten to PhD. The investments made in people had redoubled its highly-skilled workforce, its technology exports; and people became more entrepreneurial when they were released from worry, debt, and insecurity. This came at a cost that the public paid together, collectively, as a people. So long as the people were educated, healthy, and productively employed, their job was done. The workweek was reduced to an official twenty-six hours. Anyone could work as long as they wanted, but no more than twenty-six hours was needed to live well. People were encouraged to spend time on self-improvement—however they interpreted that—and officially the government said yes to music, art, sports, entertainment, so long as it didn't consume nonrenewable resources or degrade the environment. The economy was to be measured by its impact on the people and their environment rather than gross domestic product.

This wasn't a contest, it was survival. The problem was worse than erratic weather and crop failure, soil depletion, groundwater overdraft, and the rising cost of grain. Marine ecosystems were collapsing, threatening people worldwide who depended on the ocean for their food. Freshwater and land converted to agriculture, nitrogen and phosphorus loading, plastic and chemical pollution, degradation of forests, loss of biodiversity. All of Earth's living, giving systems were under unprecedented stress. And to continue growing the economy was to crash the planet. They were no longer going to use economic growth to release the pressure built up from inequality, or to pay off the interest on loans needed for business. There was enough for all, the equitable distribution of resources unlocked their economy. The central bank had been restructured to deal with it. Lena started to talking about DLT and other things Shane had never heard of, distributed ledger technology? He listened and tried to understand, but he felt it all had nothing to do with him. It was Sweden.

He was too exhausted to figure it out in one night. It was the end of their fourth full day on vacation and Shane went into the kitchen to talk with Elsie. They had talked, video chatted, or messaged each other every day. The women stayed up past midnight talking in the living room and after they went to bed it took Shane a couple more hours to fall asleep on the couch. Rebecca slept in the guest room. He awoke to the sound of dishes. Annika was in the kitchen and had taken a cup out from under a pan in the dish rack. He could see her from where he lay, and he closed his eyes and tried to fall back to sleep until he heard Rebecca's voice.

Shane had no place to do his exercises in private. It embarrassed him to draw attention to himself, focusing on his body, but it was his vehicle. He wasn't vain, he told himself, if he couldn't maintain the discipline he would never accomplish his goals. It was all connected. It was his body. He did his push-ups in the living room. And the women didn't seem to think it odd.

He went with Rebecca, Lena, and Annika to the office. Thirty-four employees worked full-time at Peopler. They had two floors in a refurbished building in Södermalm. They were on a busy street in the middle of the city and, upon entering the office, he couldn't hear the traffic outside. Collaborative desks, conference rooms and office space extended along three exterior walls. Floor-to-ceiling windows on the building envelope and interior walls. The center of the room was skylit by mirrored periscopes and a creative zone had been organized around carpeted, multileveled ameboid bleachers and container gardens with broad leaf plants—some were artificial, some were real—fantastic, yet natural. To walk through this space that connected all the perimeter offices, no one could walk in a straight line, they meandered around the benches that formed pathways like water surrounding a cluster of islands. Shane asked Annika if he could sit in there and do a little work, and she said he was welcome anytime.

Annika turned information into size, color, shape. She had created a symbol language that people wouldn't find confusing or ambiguous when they encountered Peopler. It was like a map to help them find their way through information. And she was something of an artist. The interface was intuitive and entirely human. Being able to speak with the platform made it possible for someone to have their questions answered, but visual communication allowed vast amounts of data to be summarized and apprehended very fast.

Shane told Annika about his life in Portland, and she expressed surprise at how much he depended on his family and employer. How his choices in life had become circumscribed by family background and whether or not he had a job with benefits. For economic security and healthcare. For himself and Elsie. She told him she had been able to go to university for free and had paid sick leave and vacation.

If she and Lena decided to raise a child they'd have nine months parental leave at eighty percent of their salary. These benefits were universal. All of Swedish society paid for them together. For the benefit of everyone. Their society promoted social equity through the provision of universal benefits. In Sweden, their social rights were highly decommodified and electorially defensible. In the US, welfare was means-tested, a basic safety net for the poorest only—benefits based on strict rules and the recipients were stigmatized. And as weak as it was in the US, welfare had been portrayed as a bad thing. Politicians identified welfare recipients as the problem, rather than poverty. Racism was used to undermine social programs in the United States. The "brown people" wasting your public dollars and they were undeserving of it. Welfare must be defunded and dismantled.

Even public school teachers had been vilified. If trust in government could be decimated, programs could be defunded, taxes cut, and its regulatory function could be eliminated. Public sector unions had been systematically attacked. The radical right pushed to phase out public education, all in an effort to reduce what citizens expect of their government and what people can demand from the workplace.

Shane had no idea about any of this until Lena and Annika and Rebecca started talking with him. "When we have our needs met," Lena said, "we don't have to stay in a relationship. It could be your partner or an employer, you can leave and find a better match. We take risks."

"And sometimes to really love someone," Shane said, "you have to make a sacrifice."

"Yeah," Rebecca said. "Like we sacrificed the middle class."

Annika said, "The thought of the collective is very important here."

"It's pragmatic to consider other people," Lena said. "The capacity to talk and respect others. It's not easy. Things get done differently here, collectively."

"That's why there are meetings after meetings," Rebecca said. "Everyone has to agree with everyone else."

"Do you feel society here is based on trust?" Shane asked.

"Loyalty," Annika said.

"Loyalty, yes," Lena said. "Definitely."

Shane and Rebecca toured the city and returned to the apartment around five. Lena and Annika came home shortly after. Then Rebecca suggested shopping for groceries together, her treat, and they walked to the store. Shane lingered over a package of reindeer meat. Annika told him to go ahead, put it in the cart.

"Is it good?"

She laughed.

Rebecca was filming them and commenting for her fans.

"It's the beef of Sweden," she said.

Annika glanced shyly at the camera and then talked with Shane and tried to pretend they weren't on camera, telling him only the indigenous people in the north were allowed to domesticate reindeer. "The Sami," she said. "Some of them are reindeer herders. They have common law rights to an area of land."

Their four cloth bags filled with enough for the week, Shane split the bill with Rebecca, and they had all left the store when he decided to go back and buy *Captain Sweden*.

"I'll catch up."

"No you won't," Rebecca said.

"I'll be quick!"

"You remember how to get back to the apartment?" Lena asked.

"I think so."

"Then go," Rebecca said. "We're not waiting for you."

Shane bought a comic book and came out of the store and started running. After four blocks he saw them and slowed and walked. A seagull floated past, its wings unmoving. At a distance he recognized the guy following them. The guy in the brown leather jacket, Shane had walked past him when he left the girls. He passed him again, and started running.

XXXI

THE AWARD CEREMONY was held in City Hall. Shane had never thought of a government building as a tourist attraction. He never wanted to go in government buildings, but he saw why eight million red bricks arranged into two massive courtyards and a large tower was an attraction. Walking into the Blue Hall, he saw the value given to public work in Sweden. He and Rebecca were surrounded by Peoplers and their families and friends. Shane was introduced to Lena's father. They met a man from Syria who thanked Lena, and Shane saw his wife and daughter both wore translation devices.

The space was massive, built to look like an Italian piazza with the columns and arches of a loggia surrounding a large open space with a row of windows high above that lined the top of the massive red brick walls. Annika said the design had called for blue plaster but after the architect experienced the red brick, it became the final surface. And the Nordic winters did recommend covering the piazza with a roof.

Shane sat beside Rebecca in the sixth row. He had spent the previous three nights on Lena's couch and, to him, she seemed like a normal person. He watched her walk up the monumental staircase and stand beside the mayor. The award for service held between them and they paused, smiling, for the cameras.

Lena approached the podium and looked to the audience. Her hair was up. Her dress a golden yellow. Shane didn't understand a word she said. He knew she had made something useful, and he felt it in the room. He thought he would never be able to do what she was doing, speaking before so many people with her voice in calm command and with that charming tone she had. His talk about coding random animation was meaningless outside his industry. He suddenly understood it would sound like nonsense. It was a foreign language. But no one had ever approached him the way these people, the families of immigrants, gathered around Lena after the ceremony.

They talked with her in their adopted language, in the country that had adopted them, the people who she helped. Their gratitude, the respect. The afterparty was well-attended, accepting all these people who only appeared different. In her own body she had combined the fibers of difference. It was her life to join together these people, it was her. This was her body. These people becoming a community. A body. Black and white combined in the complexity of the human heart, where understanding came not from opposites but from wholeness.

Shane thought it was love. The presence of someone who really saw you. They recognized who you are. A real person. It wasn't what they wanted to see, what they hoped you could be, or who they thought you were.

He saw Rebecca across the room talking with a guy. She looked so free when she clasped his hands. The guy wore a black jacket and white shirt with the top buttons undone. They continued talking and she put her arm in his. They were walking away. She was Shane's connection to these people, but Rebecca left him to figure things out for himself. Annika had become more of a guide for him, though he didn't know where she was at the moment. Walking through the crowd, he caught up to Rebecca.

"This is my friend Sixten," she said. They greeted each other, shaking hands, and Rebecca added, "He's with Open Border."

Shane nodded. He had started to experiment, anytime he didn't know what someone was talking about, he'd nod, smile, and pretend that he understood. "Any place in particular?"

"Decentralized," Sixten said. "Blockchain stuff."

Mishearing him, Shane said, "It is tough."

"We help nations expand beyond the limits of geography."

Shane said, "We call that the Pentagon."

Sixten smiled and waved his finger. "Despite the appearance of power, your empire is fragile."

"Anything can be sustained at gunpoint."

"Do you have a gun?" Sixten asked.

Rebecca winced.

"That was a joke," Shane said and grinned.

"The Baltic states have built on our protocol. The smaller countries having problems with emigration, their young people moving for opportunity elsewhere, these small nations are using Open Border."

Shane didn't know the difference between Baltic and Balkan and he had no idea what countries were Baltic states. He nodded, smiling.

"Open Border is a way for a nation to allow contributions to come into the country," Sixten said. "In the developed nations, an immigrant can become a citizen if they invest some huge amount of money in the country. We can make that happen for people. Normal people, but really the people who have been excluded. Citizenship can be gained through contributions—through participation in the country—and it could be done from anywhere in the world. It's like the problem Lena and her team are working on, but we decentralize citizenship."

"Shane made a really interesting proposal at our company," Rebecca said. "To collectively buy and own land in a trust and make permanently affordable homes."

Shane was surrounded by the award winners of the Innovation Scholarship and all of their friends. The people he'd met working in government and for these human services. It was another world, he'd only looked over Elsie's shoulder at Decide Portland, he'd not much considered their tech. What did he care? He'd wanted to make his company, Playland, with Jason. For ten years, they had been making indie games. They founded the company in high school with Fruit Fly, a mobile game—it was a joke, at first, well, a kind of extra credit thing for science, a piece of fruit that rots on-screen as more fruit flies appear; you have to squash them with your finger for points, or swipe across to clear them away at once—that never took off in the app store, but Shane was still proud of the graphics. It took a long time to figure out. Over the years they created two sidescrollers and updated them continuously. He and Jason were like an indie band touring the country, not making any money—until he got hired at Makner.

"I'm just a game developer."

Sixten said, "A game is just a series of decisions within predetermined limits."

He carried himself with authority and confidence, but Sixten wasn't a dick. Shane went with Rebecca and her friends to a bar after the reception. Sixten sat at their table in the back of the bar, an alcove. A woman came and she sat with him. Another friend of Sixten's was there. He was seven foot two. He had curly brown hair and a beard. Then a guy sat across from Sixten and started speaking Swedish and Shane asked Annika what was happening. She said that some neo-Nazi had put a bounty on him. Annika said they were trying to intimidate Sixten. She said he had offices in different locations and several apartments so that he could move from one to another. He had unarmed bodyguards. Annika discreetly pointed to the big guy, that was Dag. And he had frequent conversations with the police about safety measures. She said he had to be unpredictable. Prey animals followed paths, they had habits. Sixten kept irregular working hours, took different routes to and from his home and office. He couldn't marry or own a car. The first piece of advice the police had given him was not to own a car. The easiest way for anyone to track him down in Sweden would be through the driver and vehicle licensing authority.

"Who the hell wants open borders?" Shane asked.

Sixten was talking to his friend, and either hadn't heard the question or was ignoring him. And Shane thought of Sebastian and Makner and the multinationals. Capital did move in a borderless world. They can store their assets anywhere. Sebastian lived as a global citizen. He had money.

"This is the whole world," Sixten said, turning to face Shane. He pointed to his phone. "The entire world has been connected and nobody is excluded from this world. It's decentralized. The contribution could be made from anywhere in the world until whatever amount the country had decided on has been met, over years or through contributions from NGOs—and this citizenship is not coming from a central bank. It's created through work. Real citizenship."

Sixten told him that when containerized shipping and the unrestricted flow of capital across borders had made a global economy possible, power shifted away from the nation-state to financial institutions—and multinational corporations. The countries enforced the border when people weren't loaded, when they needed something, when they were desperate, hungry, homeless, stateless. But then all of the global north had systematically undeveloped the south, extending loans they couldn't repay, using the money to finance the construction of infrastructure by US or European firms and extracting their natural resources. The governments who refused the loans got forced out; and dictators repaying a favor for military aid were "friendly." The interest charges piling on and all the wealth and resources of the country going north.

Real citizens.

The idea dug into him. "What is a *citizen*?" Shane asked.

"The right to have rights," Sixten said. "You win the birth lottery, you're born with them. For everyone else, we are making it possible."

Shane said, "Who's going to enforce this?"

"Believe it," Annika said. "Some countries do have a legal system that's fair."

"Yes, it's new territory," Sixten said. "You see it. We're opening the door. The nation state is the old world, bordered, contained. The idea has been to think of the nation as a family, the founding fathers, the fatherland, a motherland. But we've globalized our economy and nations are interdependent, everyone is connected now."

XXXII

THE AIR OUTSIDE was icy. Lena and Annika walked arm in arm as Rebecca talked about some guy she met at the bar. Shane had watched for any sign from Rebecca that she was jealous of the woman with Sixten, but they all got along. Hanging out with Sixten, he sensed the need to stay in control. They'd celebrated, but nobody got wasted.

Maybe if he was drunk he wouldn't feel so cold. It was one in the morning and Shane was freezing. He didn't bring his gloves to the ceremony.

He shoved his hands in his pockets.

The sidewalk was empty and a man appeared around the corner. Shane saw his brown leather jacket. He walked toward them. That man Shane had run past. They were almost to the apartment. The man stepped up to Lena.

His hand rose from his jacket. He held a gun. He held a gun to Lena. Rebecca went berserk, running into him screaming and the gunshot exploded in the street. Her body falling into him, onto the street, the gun knocked out of his hand. He scrambled to grab it and Lena kicked it hard, skittering under a parked car. He watched the attacker get up and run to the end of the block and turn the corner and Rebecca ran after him and they were gone. He listened to their footsteps echoing and fading. He heard Rebecca screaming down the street. Lena sobbing. He had to do something and he froze in shock.

Assassin. A killer!

Annika held Lena and they collapsed on the sidewalk.

Shane looked at Lena, her face was buried in Annika's arms. And then he ran to the corner, turned and saw Rebecca running down the center of the road. The man had stopped and he stood there as she ran to him. He lunged at her. Shane yelled, running at them. Rebecca glanced back and the guy clocked her across the head with his fists and ran off.

Shane didn't fall asleep in the safe house. They had finally finished talking with the police when Shane and Rebecca had to pack up all of their things. They wouldn't be back to the apartment. For their own safety Lena and Annika were advised to relocate, but finding a new apartment in Stockholm would take months. They packed clothes and necessities, and the four of them were driven to an apartment provided by the police. Her father contacted a security firm and two men remained in the lobby.

Shane and Rebecca had single beds in a small room. The sky outside began to brighten, and he tried to sleep. He could hear Lena talking in the other room and when he opened his eyes, Rebecca was gone. Shane stared at the open door. He heard Lena talking in Swedish, stressed, seriously. He got out of bed and walked to the door. Rebecca looked at him. "The building is on fire," she said. "Peopler is on fire. The building is on fire."

Lena wiped her eyes. "We are not a building. They can't destroy us."

"They tried to kill you," Rebecca said. "What are you going to do!?"

"The site is on remote servers. We will run it here."

"You have to run. You have to hide!"

"We have to work."

"You're in shock, Lena. You're in real danger here. You can't deny this. Someone tried to kill you!"

"We have been living with this danger. Every day we receive hate mail and death threats. I won't allow their hatred to change me. I don't allow it. I refuse to deny reality. I believe in a multicultural society. A tolerant, democratic, humane and multicultural Sweden."

"We have to do this," Annika said.

"We're lucky to be alive," Rebecca said. "Sixten may want to live like a fugitive, but do you?!"

"We live in a democracy," Annika said. "But it isn't finished. We have to continue creating it."

"Oh my god! This is insane. Since when did you become freedom fighters?"

"I have to live," Lena said. "I'll fight for the world I want to live in."

"You can't. Don't do it. You don't have to sacrifice yourself."

"Rebecca, it's me. Remember? This is love. This is my life."

"When it's a matter of life and death, what about the people who work with you?" Rebecca pleaded. "It could end in tragedy!"

"Love is a matter of life and death. We depend on each other, we are interdependent, we are all of us responsible. Everyone." Then she said what Shane had already heard Lena say many times: "Everybody is worth the same as everybody else."

Rebecca started to cry and Shane opened his computer. He asked Lena for the router. His life was technology and finding solutions to computer problems. With robotic speed, he spun up a secure server for Peopler to work, a server that was a little slower than they were accustomed to, but it had an untraceable IP.

XXXIII

"YOU'RE HERE!" a guy shouted, walking through the studio. A black crown of thick hair fallen across his brow. Jason. His friend. Jason walked toward him and stretched out his arms, clasping Shane's shoulders. "You made it, Shane."

"Man, have I got stories to tell you!"

Jason beamed. "I saw your name on the panel."

At a game studio in Stockholm, Shane had booked a talk about Makner. He had done a bit of work, arranging an opportunity for him and Jason to spend time together. Working with Jason, they hadn't made much money but they made some cool games—that was all he'd thought they needed. A hit like how Aydin and Sebastian had built Makner upon one popular game. Only Shane and Jason hadn't leveraged the success of their first game to get funding from venture capital, acquire talent and mentors. It was just them. Two college dropouts in Portland, Oregon.

They'd been anxious to get here.

Rebecca's flight had left that day for Helsinki. Editing her videos, she tried not to worry. She didn't want to talk with her fans. Editing herself. She didn't sound bad. This—what had happened to her—didn't involve them. They—who were they? . . . didn't matter. Now she just wanted to take her mind off her mother. Ahrrgh. So frustrating!

But she loved her mom. Rebecca had said, "I needed you." She couldn't stop hearing her mother's response, an earworm that had crawled into her head and died. "We all needed things, Reby. Your mother has needs too."

Rebecca's mom hadn't attended her high school graduation. She went on a yoga retreat. "Oh dear, I was so stressed then." And she had fallen in love with Helsinki, and then she met Eino and they fell in love. Now they had been married for nine years, and she worked as an anthropologist for Nokia. Pretty slick. Turning her totally useless academic career into a high-paying professional job for Finland's largest company. She was connecting their technology to people through deep immersion in human behavior. Gross.

In the background, a guy behind them on the sidewalk, she scrolled back and rewatched. That was him, that fucking asshole, she'd never forget his face. She would swear to the police or whomever, she'd testify in court, she'd come back to Sweden if she had to, she didn't care. Rebecca exported the clip and contacted the detective who had given her her card.

"Are we recording this?"

The cameras were set within a ceiling mount. Shane saw the table with the AV board and four large-screen monitors. His contact assured him they'd put his presentation online. They would livestream.

"I'd like to do it off the record. Can you arrange that?"

Shane's contact within the company went to advise his team. The studio was located in the heart of Södermalm and home to three hundred employees. They were a few blocks from the firebombed building that had housed Peopler. Jason asked him what was going on, and the guy walked back to where Shane and Jason were talking. "Is there a problem?" he asked.

"No," Shane said.

Secrecy was common in their industry. The organizers said they'd coordinate turning off the cameras during his presentation. He could see one African Swede and a smattering of women among them. Shane walked before the audience, introducing himself and thanking the hosts and sponsors. "My time here is limited, so I wanted to take this opportunity to share with you what I've been thinking about . . . Lena Andersson. She has helped me to reflect on some choices. We are in the business of creating choices. I don't have slides for this, but it won't take long."

The audience sat in rows of green and white chairs. They could've been mistaken for students of a university class with a few of the thirty-year-old faculty mixed in. At the back of the room cushioned benches along the windows surrounded a fake fireplace. It was already dark outside.

"I work with a company that you all . . . that I came here to talk about. The scheduled presentation about Cityzen will be made available to everyone. I'll upload it to my GitHub. I hope to connect with all of you and answer any questions you may have. And, I want to tell you why I'm here."

Everyone in the room was looking at him.

Shane had wanted to be acknowledged.

He wanted this to be real.

They were listening. He had something to offer. "When I started making games, I was twelve years old and I didn't think about the competition. I got lucky. I had a class with Jason Lee, that guy."

He pointed to Jason in the front, turning, looking around at everyone, smiling. Jason was brilliant. Shane had always believed he was a genius. "Jason taught me how to code. Seeing him do it, I knew this was something I could do, and making games was what I wanted to do more than anything. We started hanging out, every day—and then we made our first game together."

Genius was the opposite of self-censorship. It wasn't conforming to people who had material power. It was the expression of ideas. The introduction of a new element into the universe. The creation of new work. "We created a company during my sophomore year in high school, and then over the years, life got complicated. I needed money and I filled out the forms. It seems like I ended up putting myself into a few predetermined forms. When I'm doing what I want, it seems infinite. But there are limits, even in the entertainment industry, expressing ourselves in these apps. I wanted to be surrounded by people who understand what I care about. Now, I don't have to try and wonder what it's like . . . because it's real. It happened. I'm here!"

He smiled unselfconsciously.

The building, the interior design, the studio itself reinforced the prestige of their profession, how cool it was to be there.

"It happened for me. I'm here with you. We are entertainers, and uh, we're also selling something. I don't know about you all but at Makner, we want to attract the biggest possible audience. It's kinda crazy if you think about it, because we have millions of people who could be doing all sorts of different things and we persuade them with an experience. We create scripts and let players make choices to determine their outcome. Within structured environments, all of our behavior is scripted. I want to participate. I can choose from different roles to play and then I learn the rules."

Shane pushed her out of his mind, he felt more for her than he wanted to. It had cost him. It cost a lot. And he didn't want to resent Elsie, he didn't know if it was Makner he was mad at or the insurance company or the totally inadequate democracy back home. "Not playing by the rules, in America, we have some strong disincentives. Poverty. Sickness. Death. Games are there too. Games are always with us. For people with no control over the world, we give them control. They can master this environment. Experience something awesome. The choice is theirs. The choices we make . . . a friend of mine said there was no alternative. He said the alternative would be worse. But I don't believe him. When someone's game is rotten I don't have to play it."

He stopped and took a breath.

"I'm sick of compulsion loops."

His nerves rang to the tips of his fingers, his hands trembling. His body rooted with the intensity of a threatened animal, but he had the mastery of attention. "We designed an architecture of participation that guarantees addiction. We created a learning apparatus for digital addiction."

Shane glanced briefly at Jason.

"I think we can work together to create an alternative. We have a choice. We create the choice. As game designers we are choice architects."

The mastery of practiced attention. The discipline. He trusted himself.

"We are creating the alternative."

He worked hard.

He was original.

"Sure, we can choose to play fair." He walked across the front of the room and gazed at everyone there. He was in the world. They would judge him, but he had judged himself. He was responsible for this. He said, "It sounds lame because we're supposed to be ruthless to succeed in business. But that's a story to excuse someone else's behavior. Let's work on solutions. And together, we can transform society. It's a challenge, an organizational challenge."

A fear of change. A fear of death. His death.

He said, "Are the most ruthless always going to win?"

He could lose, he would be annihilated.

"Will they always write the rules?" he asked.

His desire to give. To be good and live!

"I don't believe in every man for himself, a war of all against all, or any of that. To win a better future, we have to work together. We can work together to make something awesome."

He was going to live for real.

"By trying to express myself, my love of games, I've been participating in this, contributing to a culture I didn't really understand. It is my culture, but I don't think I understood it—and how could I?"

Shane smiled. His goofy grin.

"It takes time to figure things out for yourself."

He looked down, walked across the front of the room, stopped.

"If I have no control, do I concede responsibility for my choices?"

He'd learned from all the people he'd ever loved. Everyone he'd ever known. All of his role models and mentors. His own father. His mom. His sister. His girlfriend. His friends. Jason. He changed himself to earn their respect, to be seen, to be loved. "Maybe I didn't want to be responsible . . . but I am. Even if it's only a game, I was one of the people responsible for Cityzen. I did that, and I didn't know what it meant to be a citizen. And um, I'm nothing compared to you all. I'm a frog's hair. But I'm going to do what is worth doing and what has never been done before. If I have to quit Makner . . . okay. I'm going to create something new . . . a choice architecture for the world."

XXXIV

THE Q&A was thankfully brief—but painful. Shane tried to describe people organizing to work together online and a visualization of their choices. So we could see the consequences and he said, like in a game, evaluate choices for the best possible outcome, and it'd be a massively multi-user online system. And then the host thanked him, and they went on with the next presentation.

Jason and Shane talked with people after the presentations but they wanted to find a place where they could relax and catch up. They went out for a drink. They played pinball and sat at a small table in a retro bar on Hornsgatan.

"I talked myself into it."

Shane admitted that he hadn't really thought it out. He didn't know what came next, but sitting with Jason he felt the power they used to have together—believing their future would be what they make of it. "Makner is a disaster," he said. "I had no idea this was what I'd signed up for."

"I understand," Jason said.

"It sucks."

"No, I know."

Jason had been doing that rent-seeking thing where he'd have a contract to do a job for Amazon, subcontract the work to other guys, and make money without writing the code himself. He'd inspect it, mark up changes, collect enough to live on. A decent amount. Until a massive job matching platform put him under.

"And this is unfair to Elsie but it's like I have to work at Makner for the healthcare. And you know, I still want to make something cool!"

"Let's do it."

"They own everything I make."

"Then quit."

"I *want* to help her."

"Get some other healthcare."

"Yeah."

"Yes."

"Yeah, you're right."

Jason told Shane that the job platform had millions of workers, he didn't have an exact number but there were so many technically savvy workers throughout India and Asia and Africa who were on it—all over the world actually. Any job that was done on a computer had become entirely commoditized. It was called YourJob.com. The platform served the vast majority of employers who needed a digital asset or some tasks performed. Rather than having to sort through resumes and hiring a specific individual to do a job, people could buy the desired result of whatever digital task they wanted done, and all the prices were set in advance.

It was cheaper than having an employee. AI-assisted automation and translation, global connectivity, and competition had leveled prices. Language, culture, geography and countries were no longer a barrier on the internet. It had been compared to the first industrial age where workers performed tasks in a factory. That was when craftspeople were first separated from ownership of their tools. And now the software to perform digital work wasn't owned by the workers. They subscribed to it. Even Shane had paid a monthly fee to use the tools he depended on. There was no way for him to host all the data required to run the AI he used. Makner covered the licenses for him at work. Digital workers paid for a temporary license allowing them to use the AI for applications that had been built by the big tech companies. Digital work relied on various tools, each with their own AI created to maximize a company's software. The applied AI. It became necessary for digital workers to access the latest technology. And yet, they didn't own it.

"What are we going to build?!" Jason yelled.

The music was loud.

Shane was thrilled. As teenagers making games they were like gamblers. Lots of small teams were making indie games. They'd need a massive hit to surface in the market. At best they could survive as a small business, but Shane had wanted a video game company. The AAA game companies had hundreds of employees. Two was a good start!

They walked out. Some seagulls swept past with their wings flapping. The cold air was bracing and they found a restaurant, asked for help with the menu, ordered supper, and started talking.

"Maybe the AI will do everything?"

"No," Jason said. "People are needed. That's what YourJob does, inserting people into the process so the work can be finalized, or overseen, given a human touch."

Firms that could front their reputation competed for the business of wealthy clients and corporations, while the rest of the market survived on the digital bottom. Jason said he believed the market for services mirrored the distribution of wealth. It wasn't rational to choose to be on the bottom. It was like a law of attraction that Shane and Jason worked for big companies.

"It's by design," Jason said. "The economy is designed."

His dad had been big into political economy, and Jason told Shane that economics was practiced like a science, it used math, but it did not seek to merely understand phenomena. It was an argument. He said economics was like an ideology, a technocratic worldview that most people never questioned, but it affected everyone. Everything, really. All of the natural world could be reconceived as inputs to be transformed into commodities and externalities. "It's created by people. Extreme inequality in the distribution of wealth and resources doesn't signal that the system is broken. It's functioning how it's designed."

Jason's dad had taken part in the Sunflower Movement, running the cables to broadcast video of students who had occupied Taiwan's legislature to debate a trade deal their elected representatives had refused to talk about in the open. "People could create an economy where the money flows," Jason said, "rather than aggregating to oligarchs like a score in some feudal game."

"What if we had made our games open source?"

"And we'd become consultants."

"We could create some premium products, the proprietary add-ons that we'd sell."

"That was the problem with Playland," Jason said. "It was just us."

Shane looked toward the kitchen and then stared at the table. "If we made our games so anyone could see the work in progress and offer ideas, code?"

"Maybe," Jason said, "the incentives could be distributed as tokens, and traded. They could be used in the games, sold, traded on exchanges."

Shane took a drink of water, the glass cold in his hand. He set it back on the table. "To create a distributed team as big as . . . bigger than Makner."

Jason said he could build a platform for coders to write software for casual games. All the code to create the game would be weighted according to its use, allowing them to determine what percentage of ownership and revenue the contributor received.

The waiter brought open sandwiches of pickled herring in mustard sauce with chives and sliced hard-boiled egg. The meal was accompanied by two glasses of beer. They toasted their future, and started eating. Talking randomly about motorhomes and CEOs, they made each other laugh. Staggered over time since his presentation it was Shane's fourth beer of the evening, but he wasn't drunk.

"I would use it," he said.

Jason asked, "Is this your choice architecture for the world?"

"Billions of people," Shane said. "They all play games. Shapes, colors, characters. It's a universal language."

"Like money," Jason said.

"Like the tokens the creators earn."

"I know we can create a platform to provide all the tools to make collaboration and communication easier for distributed teams."

"And for full-time users of the platform," Shane said, "they'd have healthcare."

"No," Jason said. "They buy insurance somewhere else."

"No, no. The platform is a digital employer. All the benefits one would expect from a good employer. And it's digital so the transformation of nature is somewhat minimized, and everyone needs some work. They can voice their ideas to translation. It would be possible to work from anywhere in the world. We can start here. It would be like a distributed company, a coalition of companies. It would be a distributed city!"

"That's crazy."

"No, really!"

"It has to be real simple to work. Shane, it's a crowdsourcing platform for building casual games."

"People would work for equity rather than wages."

"They would own the work," Jason said.

"We would own the platform."

"I don't know, is it called Playland?"

They started laughing.

November was ruthless, relentless and without compromise. The sun rose at nine and went down at three. It had been overcast all week and when Shane and Jason left the restaurant it had started to rain. They ducked into a bar and Shane bought a round, raised his glass of aquavit and told Jason to say skål looking into each other's eyes. That was what Annika taught him. She and Lena had planned to let him stay but it became impossible and Rebecca asked Sixten. Before she left in the morning they went to a loft apartment belonging to a couple of lawyers; they had four bedrooms and made one available to Sixten. The other was their daughter's and Shane met the mom and Sixten early that morning and had left his bag in the hall closet.

"We'll need a new site," Jason said. They had been recasting events of their lives as amusing stories, and then Jason said they'd need a name for their platform.

"Playland could work," Shane said. "We own the URL."

"That's for our games."

"But it's good."

"It's okay," Jason said. "Let's explore."

"I'm ready," Shane said.

The voices filled the silence between them. The bar had a row of tables along one wall and they were near the back of the room. Shane with his back to the wall, a long cushioned bench surfaced in synthetic leather with a mirror above that multiplied the space. "What do you want to call it?" he asked.

Jason gazed at the white marble tabletop.

He looked up at Shane; his friend smiled. "Software development platforms," Jason said. "This is a mature market. They have made it possible for people to create software without knowing code."

With two fingers making quotes in the air Shane said, "Every company is a technology company."

"Those AI platforms are real."

"For games?"

"Yes."

Shane stared ahead, he had seen it. "You're right."

"What's missing is pay," Jason said. "There's no way to rate contributions and reward people."

"I think we should start."

"I'm with you," Jason said, smiling.

He had booked a room at a hostel on Långholmen, an island connected by a bridge not far from where they were sitting. They agreed to meet in the morning and each took different rides in opposite directions. Shane got out at the apartment building and used the code he'd been given for the front door. He rode the elevator through the floors, exited at the top, and walked down the red carpet to their door. He put a key in the lock and the door pulled open.

Sixten's bodyguard filled the doorway.

"Sorry for getting back so late."

Dag was more than a foot taller than him. He recognized Shane at once, and mumbled something in Swedish and threw his head back. Dag stepped away from the opening and Shane took off his shoes and placed them inside a shoe shelf near the door. He walked into the living room and Sixten stood up from the couch. He extended his hand. "You made it."

They shook hands and Shane thanked him for letting him stay.

"It's not me," Sixten said. "You'll have to thank Majken."

"The mom?"

"Yeah. So how was your thing?"

"Great!" Shane sat down on a chair across from Sixten. He said he'd met with a friend and gone out. Shane asked him where they could work for a while during the day, did he recommend coffee shops? Dag had sat at one end of the couch and he got up when a knock came to the door. He reentered the room with a pizza box and opened it on the coffee table. Sixten took a piece. "You hungry?"

It had what looked like fruit cocktail and chocolate. Those were definitely bananas and peanuts. Shane pulled out a slice, the cheese strands extending from the mothership until it had cleared the berth.

"What is it?" Shane asked.

"Pizza," Sixten said, chewing.

That was definitely a piece of pineapple.

Apple, banana, pineapple. Chocolate and peanuts. The high ceilings. It was so white, the white walls and built-in bookshelves. A fireplace in the corner. Patterned carpets on the wood floor. Shane wanted to rise early and meet Jason. After eating he found the air mattress leaning against a wall in the dining room. A pillow. A sheet folded atop a stack of three blankets. He plopped the mattress down behind a big table along the wall. He stretched the elastic of the sheet over both ends of the mattress, unfurled each blanket there, took off his pants, and lying under the covers, he thought of the platform. It was a vehicle, they would have a movable company. He could be at home anywhere. They would always have a job. He was part of it, he was right in the center. Shane turned over on the mattress, his weight moving to his hips and rebalancing with his shoulders, the air displacing and moving his body aching for sleep. People would choose the good. Of that he was certain, if people had the opportunity they would do what was best. If they could see the good for everyone and it was real and they could. They'd do it. They got rewarded. The site expanded in scope where there was nothing to stop it. Shane could see a massive community building software for the world. The light from the living room entered under the door and he listened to Sixten talking in Swedish. If they had the opportunity . . . it was all incentives. It could be designed.

Shane woke up.

In the kitchen, Majken was seated with her coffee and eating a crisp bread cucumber and cheese sandwich. She had a tablet open on the breakfast table and smiled at him when he walked into the room. A lamp glowed above the table. The sky dark in the tall window behind her with the light caught in raindrops running down.

"Good morning, Majken."

"Did you sleep?"

He bobbed his head.

She offered him breakfast and he poured himself a cup of coffee from a French press on the counter, and sat down. There was a bowl of three peeled hard-boiled eggs and he took one and put it in a slicer and lay them on a piece of bread with cheese. She asked what he wanted to do in Stockholm.

"I like to rent a bike and ride around."

"Bad timing," she said, pointing to the window.

"I'm going to meet a friend. I don't know. Is it okay to sit at a table in a cafe for hours?"

"Yes, of course. You have walked in Gamla Stan?"

"Definitely, is—"

"I can take you someplace," Sixten said, at the kitchen door.

"Nice of you," Majken said.

Sixten smiled as if to himself. He took a carton from the refrigerator, poured thick sour milk into a bowl and covered it with cereal, pushed a spoon through it and carried his breakfast to the table.

XXXV

THEY RODE the tunnelbana and got out at the central station in Norrmalm. Jason and Sixten had gotten to talking about digital currency exchanges. The money in Sweden was on a blockchain run by the Riksbank, their central bank. The technology prevented fraud, money laundering and tax evasion. Shane would hesitate sometimes and speak haltingly as though he'd lost his way and had to discover the idea as he spoke, but the words he used to express himself came sure and sound.

Emerging outside, the rain angling down, Shane opened the umbrella that Majken had loaned him. They hurried to the office, Jason alongside Sixten who held an umbrella between them. With one finger Sixten punched the door code at his building. They shook the rain from their umbrellas and entered, crossing the lobby to an elevator; two women stepped in after them, speaking quickly in Swedish. Then all was silent. The trip was short, the doors opened and the light inside the room was low. Above a large work table in the center of the room illuminated software objects hovered in the air. The people gathered around the table spoke English and yet Shane could only guess which countries they were from. They studied the colored forms, speaking softly into clear plastic mics extended from behind their ears.

"None of them will type a line of code," Sixten said. It was something he called model-driven engineering. The forms represented code. People could move objects around by speaking commands or directly contacting the model with their hands, their gesture read by sensors.

"I like code," Shane said, staring dumbfounded at shimmering representations of states and actions and commands he recognized intuitively. Programming for hours alone with a keyboard, developers became isolated by the screen. A relationship that was now open. They saw the architecture in all its complexity as movable objects and talked about it together.

The code was done by software. That was done by the machine. Machines spoke machine-language, and people could see and instruct the model, like architects inside a virtual building could change a wall or the height of a window or anything with a simple command.

Sixten set them up with hot desks. Shane and Jason sat beside each other and coded, talking over their laptops and sending names in chat as they brainstormed the ultimate universal resource locator. The existing platforms proved sounding board for their interrogation of digital labor. Their site for game developers was like a software seed that would grow and grow under the light of inquiry and intelligence and running code. Their name would have to hold every potential for expansion. All Shane desired for the future. They were working silently when it appeared in Shane's chat: common.wealth

"Facebook got started upon an existing social network," Shane said. "One school. Harvard."

"And then other Ivy League schools," Jason added.

"All colleges, high schools," Shane said. "But it was about community. The tech company, the platform itself took center stage, and people forget that it had assembled an existing community. The most important element is the community."

"Another social network," Jason said. "Is this crazy?"

Shane pushed back in his chair. "To provide a platform for game developers to organize their work and collaborate," he said, "this is on the far side of normal."

"We're going to create a currency," Jason said. "Now that's crazy."

"A token," Shane told him. "Something to trade."

Jason dug into the governance protocol Sixten had mentioned. They bought the common.wealth URL to use as a block explorer. They would use an open source blockchain for their governance protocol. No. That wasn't it. They should adapt the source code, modify and improve it, create a new protocol.

That night they went to a movie with Sixten and three of his friends. It was called *The Devil's Chessboard.* A historical drama based on events and individuals Shane and Jason were only dimly aware of from one page in their high school Social Studies book. It was about the CIA. Shane had read hundreds of comic books as a teenager. He'd been obsessed with the stories of fantastic powers. He put his comics in plastic bags, storing them for years, and ultimately selling two long boxes after tripping balls in college. He was low on money, but the sale felt like a purge. And he sold all of his action figures and the playsets he'd collected. It wasn't just his favorite comic book characters. It was everything, even the counterculture was commodified. People thought of how they could make money, creative thought eventually found its way to market. That's all they talked about, and he got it. Something was for sale, but what was culture? Was all their work just to make something for sale? Conversation could not be sold—no, but social interaction became commodified online. And if they could rearrange the commodification of culture, what if people earned money for participating in . . . *man*, that movie was not fucking around. It had blown his mind.

Shane said absently to Jason as they left the theater: "That was a true story."

Sixten and his friends went for a drink after the movie and when they'd been seated at the table with their beers it wasn't long before someone brought out a laptop. Dag's had a gummy mass of electrical tape over the camera. Shane sat between Astrid and Dag and across the table from Jason. Then Shane noticed Sixten's screen and the matte surface of a small square placed above its tiny lens.

"Money is a platform," Astrid said. "It's the first social network."

Sixten said, "The database of who owes what." He paused and leveled his gaze. "And banks can issue credit. Who gets credit?"

"Anyone gets credit," Shane said.

"Depends how much," Jason said.

Sixten said to Shane and Jason: "Your central bank has pumped money into the system, believing this will unlock business investment. Corporate profits have risen, and investment has shrunk. More than thirty trillion in cash is held in accounts."

Sixten explained how money could be sent straight to an industry or infrastructure project with every dollar accountable. Making the investment in productive activity rather than flooding the market with cheap money that flowed into speculative finance. The government didn't have to issue a bond to borrow money from a central bank.

"Money is power," Jason said and took a drink of carrot juice.

"The grand imperial bargain," Astrid said. "Print your colored paper, send it abroad and you get oil and Mercedes and these other real things in return." The sale of T-bills, US government bonds. Treasury security. The US dollar was the world's reserve currency and one of the country's greatest exports—briefcases full of hundred dollar bills were held abroad in confidence that it would retain its value. International transactions were priced in dollars, and oil-exporting nations had to use them. This allowed the US to sustain persistent trade deficits, and maintain global economic hegemony.

Shane had gotten under the covers with their conversation and scenes from *The Devil's Chessboard* in his head. He felt exposed as though all of the nightmares he'd been told about authoritarian power were real and that it could single anyone out to punish and to make an example of, it was recording everything; all of the data from the networks was going into the servers and it could be respooled in the future to any purpose. He had no power to change anything. Shane thought clearly Sixten was a fanatic. None of what he said could be trusted. It was unnerving to be alone, to be set off against the institutions that were supposed to protect him. Or could it be? He had no reason to believe Sixten himself believed in a falsehood and had reversed the meaning of things to benefit his own interests. Why would he lie? What would it benefit his company to lie? Were they actually engaged in a war of information? To define the world. In the mind. In his mind, too. Was he at war?

When he awoke, he thought only of the platform. Work had always been his salvation. Why would it be any different now, for him? Shane had a job, he had his own job to do. He would make something good, there was no way he would fall into a trap of deception and abuse, destruction and war. He'd never set in motion a chain of commands to kill people. Shane would never kill anyone.

It didn't rain Friday, and Jason and Shane took a ferry to Djurgården, an island in the middle of Stockholm that was a city park with many museums. They talked about the platform casually, relaxing from programming, expanding their ideas as they walked around and took in the sights. They'd been subsisting on hot dogs in combinations that transformed them from the familiar. That last one Shane tried was in a tortilla with potatoes.

When Shane talked with Elsie, she said it sounded exciting, but he didn't mention Commonwealth. He told her about staying with Sixten. He said he was helping Jason. He had moved on Friday to a room with Jason at the hostel on Långholmen.

They spitballed ideas for tokens. Each day rolling in all the things Sixten shot back at them. He didn't want to be anywhere but the coworking space. They could build their platform as a private company, and fund the underlying technology through a nonprofit foundation that would have a token generation event and issue coins. An independent foundation would provide transparency and accountability for funds to create the protocol. They could do all this, create a for-profit business and nonprofit foundation.

Shane began work on a white paper. This document would detail the platform and be the first introduction of their work to a larger community. It would be studied and taken apart by people way smarter than he was. Depending on how he outlined the technology, early adopters would either buy their tokens or not. He needed to get this right. He drew from developers there who had time to answer his questions. It seemed like everything he wanted to build already existed in one form or another. Everyone had the problem of how to make money from digital work and the solution existed in many pieces scattered all around, but there was a bigger picture. Unsolved. He had to put it together—fast—and *create the missing pieces.*

Jason was building the unseen part of the platform that made the transactions possible. In the past, people who built the protocols didn't profit directly from their work. The internet was a protocol. Those who built businesses atop of the protocol profited, but not so much the developers who'd made it all possible. And so tokens would be offered for sale, and that money would fund the creation of the new protocol. And the tokens would then have a use within the ecosystem of Commonwealth. Jason said they would create a multi-currency ecosystem with three different tokens, each with a unique purpose and yet all interconvertible.

"Why not four?" Shane asked.

"We need three," Jason said. "One for transactions, one to store value, and one as a unit of account."

"Let's make a fourth token to track the value of all the projects." Shane walked ahead of him and turned around. "Like an index fund of every business on the platform and it could be bought and sold on—"

"Three to start," Jason said.

Flowcoin, safecoin, and powercoin. The flowcoin would be the token received for contributions to the platform and to power the network. Every day a fixed amount would be distributed depending on the actions performed on the platform. It entered a person's account as a reward for participating, for contributing code, for building cool shit. Then people could keep it in flow, or convert that to safe or power coins. The value of a safecoin would be equivalent to one US dollar. The safecoin acknowledged the psychological aspect of money, that people stored it for security. They wanted to know they would have the money in the event of an emergency and retirement. The powercoin increased an individual's weight in decision-making on the platform and kept people from cashing out. Shane's fourth token could be another way to cool the inflation of flowcoin.

"Maybe, we'll have a commoncoin too," Jason said after they'd entered the Vasa museum and were gazing at the warship, a vanity project by the king during Sweden's imperialist time—it sank right away.

"Anyone could create a commons," Shane said. And he went on to say it would be a place for organizing projects. People could be invited. They could ask to join. Some work could be parsed into discrete tasks and listed in a directory. They would self-organize into groups. They'd have shared interests, common concerns. There would be commons. Each group could be called a "commons."

"And anyone could create one," Shane said, "for *any reason.*" He wanted there to be any number of commons. It would be like a distributed city. "Except it's all online," he said. "You log in to the platform just like going to work."

Shane and Jason talked about, maybe, Commonwealth would network job opportunities for people everywhere and membership in the distributed city would, eventually, be like a social democracy and investing together in shared benefits. It'd be software as a service, open to all, but there would be another option available to everyone. The platform brokers a form of global citizenship where people pay an entity that isn't a nation-state, but that covers all the costs of education, healthcare, and such that would result from being citizens of someplace like Sweden.

"And because it's a nonprofit," Jason said, "they write off what they give to the Commonwealth Foundation on their state and federal tax return."

"What if you could decide," Shane said, "which projects you wanted your federal income taxes to go toward—with more discretion on the part of the taxpayers it would be more meaningful, a sense that the payment would enforce their values. It would be participatory democracy."

"It's easy," Jason said, "to imagine detractors saying that people aren't educated enough . . . about policy and budgetary needs."

"That would be addressed by *educating* people," Shane said, "subsidizing quality education—civic education. People given the opportunity can make decisions as a community."

"You keep going to extremes." Jason challenged him, saying: "But people don't have time to consider how to allocate their tax money for all these different programs. Maybe they want someone else to decide. Paying taxes is complex in the US."

"Paying tax can be simplified—like it's done in some of these countries."

Oh, Shane started to imagine the platform could offer the opportunity to join the best available form of citizenship and it would be modeled on existing social democracies in the Nordic countries. One could be in a physical location and registered as a citizen in another. Any member of a distributed city still had residence somewhere on earth.

It was already real, and extremely expensive. It was possible to invest money in a country and become a citizen. Like a million dollars! Currently the borders were based on money, and when you crossed one: with money you were an expat; without, an immigrant; and worse, an illegal alien. Shane wondered what would it be like for stateless people to pay their way into a country? To earn their way through work on Commonwealth. Or an NGO or some other sponsor—maybe their extended family—to help them pay for citizenship? Shane explored with Jason what it meant to be a citizen, and how that could be remade in the globalized world of a platform economy. What he had experienced being outside and then inside a powerful company, and seeing the layers going deeper in as one gained more power, redoubled his awareness of the inclusionary and exclusionary aspect of citizenship. And he had a home. He'd seen all those immigrants living on the street. Citizenship was the right to have rights. What if Commonwealth could provide that to people all over the world? And when he got on the plane Shane thought, *how am I going to explain this to my dad?*

XXXVI

ELSIE MET HIM in the airport and she looked better than he remembered. Whatever attracted him was shimmering around her whole body. Shane felt connected to her, it was like they shared something more than a room together, she looked so familiar. That she loved him. To hold her, Elsie, his girlfriend. She pressed herself to him, stretching to kiss. Shane felt complete. Their eyes met, and he kissed her again.

They walked hand in hand through the airport.

She asked about his flight. He had slept. He felt good!

Elsie was making costumes for the Rose Parade with her friends; they'd all walk through Portland, super cute, and people would see how important opossums really are. They're not scary. Elsie opened her phone to show him pictures after they boarded the train. Her thumbs moved across the screen as fine as a virtuoso performer. It fascinated him. Her intelligence expressed in the motion of her hands as she talked about the costumes.

They found an open seat and sat holding hands. She had sold the Corolla. Elsie mentioned it over the phone three days ago and said her dad didn't care about the car. He wanted her to be happy. He loved her. We can talk about anything, Elsie had said. And Shane wanted to believe that was true for him. For his parents and for her, for all of them. Waiting for the train to depart, Shane started to explain his work with Jason.

"You're doing Playland, again?"

"No, no."

"What about Project HOME?"

"That was never going to happen," he said.

"You were so excited about it. I think it's really good."

"I was being unrealistic. That's obvious to me now. I was in denial. They're never going to build anything that would compete with them inside their own game."

"You said you, we were going to buy a home."

"That's still going to happen."

"But what about—"

Shane told her about the ability to work with people all over the world and for people to self-organize into commons where they'd help each other and earn tradable assets. "It's for everyone. You can use it. We can do it together. It's for us. It isn't about me. We trust that other people will join us. We're going to create a governance model, it won't require coercion or violence. That's the thing with a decentralized system."

"That sounds really complicated."

The doors closed and Shane looked at other people on the airport train, traveling. People dressed up when they traveled. It had a formality to it. They were going to be received by someone, somewhere. Life in transition. You wanted to meet it with your best self. Packing for a trip and cleaning up after himself sometimes Shane thought of death, that was what people would find. That room that he'd been in, exactly how he left it.

When he got home, George was curled up on the couch. Shane put his face in his fur and Geo started to purr. He cradled his cat in his arms and walked through the living room. He recognized the smell. She had made bread. Elsie had prepared a soup with winter vegetables and they sat together and ate. He felt bad, he knew she was disappointed. It was smart to transition, though maybe that only meant moving to a higher paid job with better benefits at another company. Elsie knew how he kept Playland alive and how much of himself he had put into that company. He thought maybe his decision to change wasn't his own to make. It wasn't fair to her, if they were partners, if they really were going to be a couple.

Maybe he and Jason were going crazy in Stockholm.

That was something they could debrief.

It was over now.

Shane washed the dishes and was cleaning the counters when Elsie said, "I made something." She stood in the doorway with her hands behind her back. "For you."

He gave her his full attention and Elsie brought forward a small wrapped bundle of pink tissue paper.

Shane opened it.

"Thank you, sweety."

"When we were talking, I did that."

He held up the elaborately colored socks.

"We were on the phone that much?"

"They aren't that long."

"They're beautiful."

"Do you want to try them on?"

He stripped off his socks, and her clean fiber smoothed onto his feet—thank god he had found a gift when they toured the city on Friday. He opened his backpack and took out the sweater he bought for Elsie, and then he gave her a Nordic knitting pattern book.

"This is beautiful!" she said, holding the sweater. "I'd never—"

Shane kissed her.

She walked him back to their bed and Shane stripped off his clothes and she watched him, pulling up her dress, spreading her legs as he walked his hands and knees across the bed toward her. He kept the colored socks on. She had birth control, that was their agreement. He trusted her. She opened to him so completely and when they came, they came together. They held their lives together. They made eye contact and she said, "I believe in you."

Shane believed they could make it.

"I want to help you," she said.

"Seriously?"

"I want you to—"

"I want to help you," he said.

But he couldn't be a father, not now, not when he was going to be a founder!

Walking into the office, he had forgotten his lines. Shane had to act fast. John brought him and Rebecca into a huddle. The Seattle game would launch on schedule. Black Friday. Shane had no time—his Makner channels were an infinite scroll of responsibility. They'd considered him accountable when he was out-of-office. He was scaling a compounding list, compacted in the first hour, his first day back.

The kicker: they were moving fast to model Tokyo. The world megacity and the largest market for Cityzen. Portland had been the test. Seattle would confirm success. Tokyo was their real play. Asian investors. Chinese money to capture the island. Chinese interest in Japan had skyrocketed with buyers seeking a promising and safe investment. The island nation had land that doubled the returns on apartment rental yields. To capture those investment vehicles was a true prize. Sebastian positioned his company strategically between China's billionaires and Asia's hottest property market. The Portland office was frenetic. All their employees figured the future in dollar amounts; Makner offered them rip-cords. They were going to be rich, and change their future.

Have fun. Do it. The future cities taking shape inside the game. If people can't afford to buy in, they get credit. The monthly installments could be made to fit any budget. And for the jobless, they could earn credit as Police, catch the Looters. And the looting, what a thrill! Capitalism was now accessible to all in a freemium, massively multi-player online game. Playing for real stakes. The land! The most valuable real estate in earthquake zones. Come what may, there will be winners and losers. All was justified. It was possible for anyone to win. The testament of capitalism was the winner. But Shane had no enthusiasm for his job.

Monty was in Seattle. He had sent Shane encrypted chat that disappeared after he read it. Monty had been excited about something. Big news. John said Monty had gone to set up their security operations team. Cab was in Seattle. Sebastian and Aydin were there.

Shane disconnected himself. He didn't tell Rebecca about Commonwealth. He wasn't really there with the others. At his work station, Shane had the sensation that he was being false. He hid the truth to protect himself—but what he hid from them didn't change who he was. And he felt constrained now. To protect himself. But he wasn't alone, that was what was false. He wasn't who they thought he was. That role was a convenience, a passport, a job, but he was not alone. He depended on other people, his family. All of them. He wasn't separate. He apologized to Elsie that he wouldn't be home for dinner, and called his dad. Shane would be able to leave by ten, if all went well, he figured he could leave his coat on his desk, make it look like he left for the bathroom. He'd return early, next morning.

His dad asked, "What's going on?"

Shane tried to control his voice, he was a terrible actor. They could tell. He was freaking out.

"It's nothing," he said. "Just want to see you and Mom and say hi."

Shane tried the door—usually he found it unlocked. Then he heard the bolt slide. Opening the door, his mother embraced him and he heard his father's voice. "Don't let the heat out."

It had begun to rain. Shane closed the door and followed her to the center of the house. The kitchen, dining area and front hall, the stairway and the quiet nooks to sit, read, or play, all were visible within the wood-floored living room that had a six-sided center with two wide stairs, carpeted, to a sunken sitting area. His father got out of his chair, gave Shane a hug, and sat down again. Above them, a hexagonal walkway ringed the second floor rooms, each with their doors opening on the balcony and overlooking the living room.

The patter of rain on the skylight, a dome above. That sound had always comforted him. His grandma had already gone to bed. Nora would be arriving soon. Thanksgiving. His mom wanted to know what time he and Elsie would arrive. She talked about the holiday, asked him about his trip, offered him something to eat. He had told them about the fire, the gunman. His parents had followed the story on the news. Shane shared stories about Lena and Annika, Sixten and Dag, he told them about Peopler and the Blue Hall, the coworking space and Jason. He said they were building a platform for crowdsourcing the creation of software. He could make something different. This wasn't just games. Shane said their platform will incentivize investment in productive work rather than financial speculation. Money will be made for the entire network, he said, it will be secure. They will create security. That's what it is. Security. Everyone wants to feel secure. It's like a mental trick, but you need to know you'll have the basics. Food, shelter, clothing. A good education. Healthcare. Sick leave. Parental leave. Retirement. All paid. The works. It's what comes with being a member of society. A functioning society. A very highly functioning society. When you're feeling secure, that's when you can take a risk!

"That's great, Shane," his dad said, "but how are you going to make money doing this?"

"People all around the world will be able to support the project by purchasing tokens to use on the platform."

His dad shook his head slowly side to side.

"How are you going to support yourself?"

"On Commonwealth."

His dad laughed.

"The struggle for existence is as much online as in the physical world. Think of Amazon, you understand."

His dad rolled his eyes.

"YourJob, too."

"Is that where Elsie is finding work?" his mom asked.

"No. I don't know."

"She said she had used it."

Shane had no time, it was all too real. This was happening. He needed them to understand. "I want to help people. We can work together online. We're a collective intelligence."

He leaned forward. He wanted them to see it. He could tell them.

"People have created it together. Maybe the internet isn't enough, but people have a right to work there. Everyone needs meaningful work. The people who need this place will create the value. Those products that only come together through the contributions of other people, hundreds of people, thousands, maybe millions."

"This does sound like . . ." Stan smiled. "What you said about your games."

"This is different. It enables everyone to create value together. We are building a place for that value to be generated and distributed."

"You work on it in your free time," his mom suggested.

"Impossible!" He looked up at the skylight—exhausted. "Makner owns what I make as long as I'm under contract."

His dad saw it. "You're going to quit a well-paid job with benefits to go back to what you and Jason—"

"Dad, I don't believe the winners in our economic system are looking out for us. The winners are waging war on the rest of us—and winning."

"You think you're going to change the world?"

"Extreme inequality pulls people apart, people live in fear of each other. We can only be united by shared prosperity. There is no other affinity to bind us together but our common wealth. Then people do trust each other. When they feel secure, when they are no longer living in fear, dependent, isolated."

"I think what you are doing is very courageous," his mom told him.

"I understand wanting to be the best at something," his father said. "It can be anything, I get that. You make popular software and you make a million. It's just I don't want you to lose yourself in a fantasy."

Shane said, "The platform will be used in the real world. All the world is feeding data to the internet. We are the internet. The internet is us, we are inside of it. It is an internet of people."

He touched his mom's hand and looked into her eyes.

"Our common inheritance," he said. "Knowledge."

Patti looked at Stan and back to her son.

"It's a global brain," he said to them. "A collective and the value created there is worth billions upon billions. The programming, the platforms have been designed to accumulate and concentrate wealth for a few people. But the value was created by the actions of everyone. Commonwealth will be . . . it is a platform to generate and distribute wealth!"

"Some people have their stake in the way things are," his dad said.

Shane sat up. "Together, we have the power to create a just society. Where people trust each other, where they collaborate to solve what no one person can face alone. Think about it. Unforeseen ingenuity. Commonwealth will be a place of cooperation and coordinated action. A network strengthened by greater social and economic equality."

That's my son, Stan thought, maybe he is on to something.

"People suffer the government of wealth, by rich people, for the richest," Shane said. His parents understood, the problems were obvious, all they had to do was turn on the news. He could say the truth. "This platform is a challenge to the few who fucked it up for the rest of us."

Stan looked at Patti and thought *my god*, I think he lost his mind.

Shane sat back, saying nothing, and waited for his parents.

"They won't surrender to your website."

"It's not me," Shane said. "It's the internet."

"It's not going to be a fair fight. The internet was funded by the Department of Defense. You're going to lose this battle and I'm your father. I don't want to see you hurt doing this."

"I'm not doing it, I'm not alone. We are together." Shane thought for a moment. "There's no need for hunger in this country. We have been divided from ourselves. We have been led to fear each other. I want to make our society a better system for—"

"The internet is a dangerous place," his dad said.

"I'm not waiting for a crisis to help people. The crisis is now."

"That attack?" his mom asked.

Shane saw she was crying.

"And everything, Mom. Everything changed. I'd been in denial, I thought our lifestyle would continue like always." Steeling himself, he said, "Dad, can James ship the medicine for Elsie?"

He shook his head. "Wouldn't do it. But you drive up and smuggle it across."

XXXVII

AFTER THANKSGIVING, Nora helped him sort out legal issues. He had to quit Makner soon. The hours were enormous but the launch went off in fanfare. At their release party, a celebration with the entire studio, he brought Elsie and admittedly, he was proud. The game hadn't hurt anyone—at least not that he could see.

Shane drove north, his parents let him borrow the car to buy medicine in Canada. Monty invited him to stay overnight in Seattle. He'd have a bed. Monty had kept his room in Portland, and got the lower bunk in a group room with seven other people in the Seattle Tech Plex. He was enjoying the city and the security challenge of their expanded game. Cybersecurity evolved in code, but understanding and shaping human incentives mattered more for effective defense. Monty focused on other people. He had to understand his opponents. Most people only thought one step ahead. Monty had been trained to think ten steps into the future; if he did X, how would that change his opponent's strategy? He created wolfskin, phishing tarpits, honeytokens. He built a fluctuating infrastructure to confuse his attackers, so they couldn't know his system. Fake architecture to mess with their ability to know what he was running.

Programming languages and the systems created with them had all been built variously at different time periods, it was like a city with some buildings from 1995 and others coded yesterday. An attacker went for the weakest point in time. Defense was disease control. Every machine that touched the internet joined a living organism; it was code, but such was life. Continuous defense and attack. Non-zero sum. Incomplete, imperfect, asymmetrical information. Continuous. Sequential. A cat and mouse game in which the defender is the cat, unable to catch the mouse.

"Hey, Shane."

Monty stood up and gave him a hug, though he was much shorter than him, Shane was awed by his strength.

"Man!"

They went out to eat and Shane told him more about the trip with Rebecca. Shane showed the pictures of their attacker that Rebecca sent to the detective and the Swedish Police. Monty asked why they were under threat. He asked about Peopler. He asked questions about their infrastructure that Shane didn't understand, and Shane went on to tell him about Sixten. Their cryptographically secure, shared database. He told him about Commonwealth.

"You're so pumped on that, I didn't want to say anything." Monty pushed his plate forward and rested his forearms on the table. "Till we were in person."

Monty said, "Complexity introduces vulnerability."

Shane started to speak.

"And you guys are making this very complex."

Shane said, "It's no more complex than credit cards. We're just used to those. The cost of entry has been paid. But the vulnerability, the weakness of those systems, Monty, honestly."

"Okay, with your friends' service, Open Border, it makes sense. It's a way for all of the different nations to use the same application and not have anyone of them in charge of it, nor the developers. I get it."

Monty sat back.

Shane was about to say something, and Monty said, "There is no single issuer of citizenship. Yes, it has to be decentralized. It's open data, a way for all these different nations to use the same service to help people validate citizenship within their nation."

"You don't think Commonwealth is a good idea?" Shane asked.

The security theater of borders, the play of human behavior in a market economy. Monty grasped it. Turning a border into an asset class.

An algorithm.

A unique asset depending on participation in a country's economy from anywhere in the world. Authenticated to the biology of one person. Their digital personhood, redeemed with a nation for full citizenship when all terms were met. It was automated. There were too many millions of people to efficiently do it all through a central authority. Each nation was a center of gravity in the decentralized network, a protocol created by Open Border that was now building itself into existence through positive feedback loops, the incentive structure. The hard-coded agreement allowing computer networks to share in the value for services they provide, a reward for computational power. Producing "papers" that represent citizenship in a country.

A secure identity in the form of a digital asset stored on a decentralized ledger that tracked the necessary contributions and actions needed to become, or just to be, a citizen. To participate in citizenship of the nation using the Open Border protocol.

"So," Monty said, "decentralized application. The assets secured on a distributed database. To create trust among participants. They aren't digital sharecroppers on a centrally owned and controlled network."

Shane believed Monty would join him.

Monty said, "But what you've outlined . . . Commonwealth.

They're using your platform, and it's owned by you guys. So it's not decentralized, and you don't need a blockchain for computers to share memory."

"We totally do, man. The value is shared, it's on the blockchain. Those tokens are actual digital assets that represent real value."

"But that network won't allow the speed of transaction needed to host an entire online world of digital labor. You can't scale it as fast as server farms. Click to click, it's easy to compare. The decentralized transactions are slow, expensive, and people will abandon the platform."

"These systems are running the krona. The digital money of Sweden. Believe me. It's fast. So smooth. The ledger is massively parallel. Monty, this isn't Bitcoin."

"Okay, stop me if I'm mistaken. A decentralized application, you need the value to be trusted throughout a network and it would be enabled through the crypto assets, those coins, that incentivize people and organizations on the internet to contribute resources. Processing, storage, and computing that's necessary for the service to run?"

"Monty, you see what this will become."

The waiter walked by their table and Monty asked for the check. Shane said he'd pay. "You're putting me up tonight."

Monty shrugged and then Shane paid.

"You'll need a centralized platform," Monty said. "And then it's no longer a decentralized network. People are using Commonwealth to self-organize, but they would all be using an application that is owned and controlled by a central party. It's not what you think it is."

The night clear and cold. They left the restaurant in Fremont and walked down to the water, along the Burke-Gilman Trail. Monty joked with Shane, he seemed so desperate. But Shane pushed back,

YOU WILL WIN THE FUTURE

he said in the commons, people could direct activity in the real world. The incentives for participation will create serious network effects. Shane said, "This is how you toss a snowball at Franklin Wells and bury his HB 9659 in an avalanche."

"Fifty-eight," Monty said, correcting him. His ken of exploits in the game's interface with the Wells Fund would disable it, he also knew it would return with those vulnerabilities patched and innocent people could be hurt in the market movement. His defense was distance in time from his contact with Wells' device, identifying a sympathetic journalist with a track record and a large audience—direct the attack at his reputation.

"You know what I mean," Shane said. "This is serious. It's about taking back control from an economic elite that doesn't care what happens to us."

"That platform will have to run better than your competitors. You want to provide the tools and space for people to organize themselves and create real products of value. You'll have to continually improve the service. That's all on your company and you'll need to figure out what it is you're selling that will support the work."

"The token generation event."

"Beyond that, how is the company going to survive?"

Shane picked up a flat round stone and tossed it into the canal. Monty scooped one up and skipped it across the surface, one, two, three times. It would be expensive to pursue Franklin Wells in court. Monty didn't think there was much her parents could do, but the press would make Wells uncomfortable. Monty could leak the data to journalists. Trust others to do what's right. It'd be a burden to Shane to keep the secret, and he was a vulnerability. Security was hard. It was an arms race. He had to hack the system—Monty had to find every vulnerability, everything an attacker could know—to be able to defend the system. He had accessed Wells' device though several proxies, to hide his tracks and make it look like the traffic was coming from the usual sources. All that he'd learned inside the system. The FBI. The government's main duty was to protect and serve and some people didn't believe that but Monty had lived it. And the guys he worked with believed it. Big data had no legal boundaries anymore. He could be emailing here and that data might be held in Brazil somewhere. Analytics for government was really big, they had data pools everywhere and scientists figuring how to use it.

The light shimmering upon the dark weight of water pulled to the ocean. Shane put his hands back in his jacket pockets and they started walking toward the Tech Plex. "Anyone can create a platform to access the Commonwealth blockchain," Shane said. "It will be an open market of providers. That will attract all kinds of business models and I think we can stay ahead, because we're the ones invested in seeing the protocol adopted and supported."

"You and Jason have your work cut out for you."

"Join us, Monty. We need you."

"This is a castle in the sky."

Monty craned his head back, blew, the vapor of his breath visible, expanding.

XXXVIII

JASON'S ALL-ELECTRIC MOTORHOME was covered in solar panels. He parked in his mother's driveway. He had purchased the house for her with cash, using money from the sale of crossword software. It wasn't perfect, it required a human to review the questions and answers before they published the puzzle. It generated a puzzle from the contents of any publication. The puzzle solvers could read the paper or whatever and then solve the crossword. They could use clues and refer to sections and read where they thought they might find an answer. He wrote the software when he was sixteen.

The inside was bright, the surfaces clean. A balance of white ceiling and walls with the warm wood paneling. Jason was a minimalist. He and Shane sat on either side of a small table on cushioned benches near the kitchen sink. Shane wanted to create a leaderboard where people find problems to be solved. It would be their home page. He said Commonwealth generates tokens—every day, a set amount would be issued by the software, and it could go toward solving problems that received the most votes. Each problem could have an Apply button, like as if to say I want to do this, and those problems with the most clicks, the platform would pay people to solve them. Problems invited solutions, goals and incentives: they required work.

Survival was the thing—and earning a living. People who participated on Commonwealth earned flowcoin, and they could do with it what they will. The tokens would be traded for their utility, they'd be bought and sold on exchanges with other crypto, with credit cards and fiat money. Though the important thing, the hard problem for their algorithm, was to match achievable goals with real people. Jason and Shane believed that people with a good incentive will act for the good of all. So many problems, and yet a series of solutions broken down into actions could be dealt with according to the skills and resources of a commons.

An economic system that constantly issued currency and channeled it through projects, tasks, problems to be solved. Shane said maybe some problems would collect a bounty, like crowdfunding that anyone could put their flow into and get the wicked problems over and done with. And any problem that received enough votes would automatically pay designers to work with a commons and create pictures of the desired outcome. The online world was made legible through pictures. Illustration and symbols, lists, charts, and concise plain language summaries that could transform two thousand pages of the latest healthcare bill into a readable thirty pages of words and pictures. Serving every citizen online, one didn't presume they loved to read, or even could read very well, especially not the policy, rules, and regulations that affected their daily life. Commonwealth was designed for everyone.

So, the incentives.

Each day, flowcoins entered the ecosystem to reward people. Flow would also leave the commons through exchanges. Inflation was controlled by incentives to change flow into powercoins that gave more weight in decision-making within a commons—and into safecoins that tracked the dollar. The exchange from flow to power had a speed limit, preventing fast entry decision-tipping and the domination of a commons by one person. The maximum powercoin that anyone could hold in a commons was limited by the amount held by the others, never allowing one individual to far outstrip the rest, while maintaining achievable amounts for people to stake their decisions. But all decisions were oriented to the goal set by a commons. Goals could only be generated through engagement with a problem. Any action in that commons counter to their agreed upon goal was breaking the "law" and triggered a disincentive in the form of a fee that then went to reward those working toward the goal. By placing enforcement on a decentralized governance protocol, participants could study the protocol and trust that no central party would manipulate it.

Commonwealth could use the open data of municipal, state and federal government to create applications. Alerts and access to information about every law and amendment. The voting record of all elected officials. Shane began designing incentives to animate the push and pull of code—the code of human laws and policy. People had been inoculated to policy that affected their lives and habituated to passing off responsibility. But rather than voting for someone else to solve their problems, Commonwealth convened people to solve them. Once a problem was identified it would be transformed into work, paid for by the network. The distribution of flow into those problem-sets was further divided into discrete tasks, achievable goals. Education and the exchange of ideas, the creation of knowledge. To solve problems. To make them visible, it would be persuasive and educational media. A social network that generated and paid cryptocurrency in exchange for solving specific problems and helping to achieve the goals agreed upon by a group of people.

The elected officials, the politicians, the experts, they couldn't solve all humanity's problems. The Founding Fathers had been fetishized, the US celebrated as a democracy, but facts were facts. If a majority of the population wanted something to happen—say, just for one example, Shane said, single-payer healthcare—and the government couldn't make that happen, then they weren't representing the people. They were PR flak for their funders, the insurance companies and Big Pharma. People knew this was a shitty system, and so they would choose another, if they had a choice, a platform, a place for individuals to do more than express themselves, a place for people to govern their communities, to convene and work together.

Wicked problems—and solvable problems. The entire team of responsible players could be visualized through the application programming interface of the government's, or rather the public's, data. All that data could be the feedstock of Commonwealth—and it was late. It was the early morning. Jason and Shane had been talking for hours, recording everything to consider what to include in their white paper.

"It's too complicated," Jason said. "We need to start small. A smaller market reduces the critical mass required for productive interactions. It makes matchmaking easier."

"I can talk with Cab," Shane said. "We can get this."

"We need an active community at launch," Jason said.

"We need Cab," Shane said.

"A micromarket," Jason insisted, "contained both geographically and by category: independent video game developers."

Shane sat down before John's empty desk. Pictures of Eva lined the top of his bookshelf in sequence, she was almost two. John came in and shut the door. He held a tablet, studying it, greeting Shane, and setting it on his desk as he took a seat across from him.

"How is it being a father?" Shane asked.

"I wish I was with them now."

"Thanks for making time today."

The tablet binged and John gave it a hurried glance, swiped his finger across the screen.

"Did Maeve quit her job?" Shane asked.

"We decided it was more efficient."

John turned his attention back to the tablet and started typing.

"This has been great," Shane said, feeling confident, his voice steady. "I've learned so much working with you. And now that Seattle is up, I was thinking of going back to what I was doing."

"What are you doing?"

"It's not that I don't like it here, it's just a new challenge opened up."

John leaned back in his chair and looked at Shane.

"This isn't a good time."

"I'm sorry," Shane said. "I have to do it now."

"What?"

Shane sat forward in the chair. He flashed through all of his fears. His anxiety swelled, his pulse pounding. "Crowdsourcing the creation of video games."

"We're crunching Tokyo."

"I have to do this," Shane said. "Before I have the responsibility of being a father and all. You know?"

"Let's talk about what you need to be happy."

"It's not about the money. It's a venture with an old friend."

"You want to follow your heart?"

"Kinda." Shane heard his voice falter. "Yeah."

"This is a changed world, and you need protection."

Shane grimaced.

"I'm going to give you stock options."

"Thank you. But it's really time for me to move on."

"Our P/E ratio is forty-eight, Shane. This is supermoney."

"That's fantastic. It's only that I'm ready for a new challenge."

"You could buy your house in Portland with this."

"No."

"What are you going to do?"

"Take a risk."

"Okay, turn in your laptop. Leave your computer and devices as they are. All of your communications with your Makner address have been stored as institutional memory. You okay?"

"Yeah, sure."

John stood and walked to a printer and gathered the resignation papers.

"You'll sign here."

Shane studied the document.

"Have you spoken with anyone else?" John asked.

"No."

"You can tell people personally this week, whomever you wish to, and we'll announce it on Friday. I need you to work through the end of the month."

Shane signed it, and standing, thanking him, he shook hands with John.

The indie game community they knew, Shane and Jason had grown up engaged in a social group of developers that convened around a hundred people every month, and more for their regional events, their friends and friends of friends and all of the video game companies in Oregon. This was a serious cadre. Ready for a new way to improve their games. Shane and Jason would create a commons for their Playland games, their fans would be able to suggest extensions. With AI-assisted tools on the platform even an ordinary player could contribute their ideas; the software did the coding, people designed the game by the logic structure visualized as a multi-dimensional diagram. And then they could invite their friends to play the game. And if they wanted to they could charge tokens.

All of the actions and creations on Commonwealth could be easily shared. Every time people engaged a commons, they could share their creations—and this spread awareness of the platform. People could send what they'd made through external networks, ultimately leading those recipients to become participants in the commons.

For Commonwealth to realize the promise of providing work, education, serendipitous connectivity, of creating a platform for networked humanity to experience the benefits of belonging to a real society, as if they were a progressive social democracy: it'd be huge! It would require a massive community. A thick market. A marketplace of millions, and it could be billions of people. To attract all those people—or a few hundred to start—it was about keeping them engaged. Making it a great place from the get go, and then all would follow. Shane and Jason agreed, start with entertainment, and then Commonwealth could set aside tokens for prizes to award developers who came up with the best apps in each of ten categories, expanding the commons beyond games. Winners not only got the prize, they became the champions of new products, attracting customers and further expanding Commonwealth.

To create wealth and distribute it fairly.

They laid down clear paths for cooperation and interoperability. The power of the system came from the relationships created in an open architecture of participation. This would allow their network to reach maximum scale. Their open framework invited contributions from everyone, everywhere, all over the world. No need to ask permission, it would grow faster and more dynamically than systems that were governed by a few people. They would create a stable core, a shared database that anyone could build upon, a governance protocol for making decisions, arbitrating disputes, generating tokens to instantiate the network and incentivize participation. The data would be distributed and cryptographically secure. The platform would access all that data with an easy-to-use interface and tools so people can network, organize, and work online. They would use reputation and a skill assessment system. An optional filter could prevent unverified people from joining a commons, requiring authentication. And rather than a Like button, there could be one for Trust, as in, I know this is real. Trust—all those old academics and then the private companies and civil society, the internet had been built upon trust.

Commonwealth would be a place for coordinating the collective action of people all over the world. Open and inclusive. Powerful. It wasn't brute strength and violence. To have power. It was organizational design. Systems design. Common, everyday people needed to organize. The ultra high net worth individuals were organized through their networks; to make deals, they needed access to each other and events like the World Economic Forum and a long conversation riding in a private jet serviced that need. Money moved the levers of policy. Governments depended on the approval of finance for any of its policy to pass, and industry too. Whoever could pay. The conglomerates, corporations, interest groups and lobbyists. It was expensive for politicians to campaign. It was endless, and elected officials were in service to their funders.

And all the billions of other people weren't effectively organized. They belonged to their family, their friends and associations, their groups. Most people had no idea about the policies their representatives would vote for in Congress. The ordinary citizen didn't have time to study every policy. People didn't vote by studying policy and desired outcomes and then choosing the representative who would enact the policy they wanted, they voted according to their social group. They identified with other people like them, and they took their cues from the group. It could be as simple as a breakdown of voting recommendations in a local paper. And nationally they voted according to the party they aligned with, the one they felt included their group, a political party was a coalition of groups. And some people didn't see their interests represented in either of the two parties in the US, and those were the voters who could swing an election. The independents. The undecideds. The people who were targeted to receive ads tailored to their unique profile.

The use of the internet led Shane to wonder what would happen if people could self-organize and make themselves universally employed and effective. Shane and Jason didn't think of the internet as separate from the real world. It was real. They could create a way for people to specify goals and rights, to visualize desired outcomes, to designate authorities, and to set limits. An open source governance protocol, aways open to improvement, designing incentives and penalties, using behavioral economics and digital currency to make and enforce agreements online, a place for all the world's people to organize and direct their actions in the real world. The power to organize themselves. To earn a living solving hard problems, creating meaningful work. For the entire world!

"Money," Jason said to Shane. "Central banks say they need to be independent of politics—but then taxpayers end up bailing out the banks. The monetary system is a public utility that has been privatized. Instead of the creation of new money through bank-issued debt, new public money could be spent into the economy—by elected authorities—to meet public needs. And that's Commonwealth. A decentralized and transparent process to issue and circulate currency, free of debt. The most progressive act is to design money in the public interest. And we can do it."

"But how are *we* going to pay people?" Shane asked, pointing a finger at himself, his friend, and back again. "I mean, Cab is expensive. We'll need what Cab can build to enable all those people to contribute to a commons, by voice, just talking to their computer. We need people like him working with us full-time . . . and we're paying their salaries!"

"The token generation event," Jason said. "It's designed to raise money for the development of both the protocol and our platform. Developers will be paid out of those funds. The LLC will hold a reserve of tokens it can distribute to employees. And we can offer them stock options. The platform itself will be a for-profit company, and we give our employees ownership in the platform through shares."

"Maybe the *ultimate* exit," Shane said, "will be the governance protocol itself maintaining Commonwealth—the platform and all. The protocol would generate tokens to reward those who maintained and improved the platform. Work could be parsed into discrete tasks and listed in a directory. Simple as a next generation Craigslist, but you could click through and act—learn and earn, do it all there."

Seated at the small table in Jason's motorhome, they looked at each other. Jason's face a cryptic font of mental process.

Shane ventured, "I guess the platform would have proprietary tools that assist in the creation of value, and we'd charge something fair to use them. That powerful software would be an economic engine. It's like a robot tax. A fee. To collect money. To pay people working for our company."

"And if Cab has licensed his AI tools then he could collect a percentage. Our employees would have equity and as the network grows it would become increasingly valuable, there would be—"

Shane interjected, "The existing big platforms."

Jason continued, "When people buy powercoins, a portion of that amount could go to fund the company. Powercoin would exact a fee from people who wanted more weight in decisions within a commons, this would decrease the number of leaders and increase the quality of projects offered. By discouraging leaders who aren't serious about their project, the pricing will create a culture of quality on the platform. And the cost creates an incentive to self organize within a commons without a leader. We'll use our monetization to strengthen positive network effects and reduce the negative."

"The naked hairy men."

"And even worse than garden variety trolls," Jason said, "much much worse. Military hackers. And foreign intervention by state-supported information operations."

Shane raised his brow.

"We have to anticipate all manner of behavior," Jason said.

"Yeah," Shane said. "Set up incentives to solve problems, and disincentives for people who are ruining it for everyone."

Jason said the disincentives should be delayed and opaque when punishing bad behavior—so bad actors can't simply adjust and continue. And Shane said, "But we give fast rewards for good behavior so people know exactly the actions that contribute toward shared goals. And once it is a big network, companies looking to post offers would be charged to access people. Like how project leaders would have to buy powercoin to give their decisions more weight. And anyone who holds powercoin would be required to use their real name and contact information."

"People who are victimized and cannot disclose their real identity," Jason said, "they need options, each commons can make their own agreement to use powercoin to influence decisions or not."

"Some use it," Shane said, nodding, "some don't."

The ultra high net worth individuals lived in a walled utopia. Living on earth, a few million people could meet their every need with accumulated wealth. A minority of rich people experienced a state where the necessities of life were provided through their ownership of property, shares, assets. The money for food, shelter, and clothing was immaterial to a billionaire. And people who worked, saving for retirement, often put their money into the wealth aggregators of financial markets. Their participation succored the promise of freedom. The walled utopia stood because so many people believed that place could be accessed. Even if it was the rare success, people could believe it was possible for them—stories, language and the accumulated knowledge of humanity were a common inheritance—but a walled utopia wasn't accessible throughout society. Freedom was some weird word. It had been colored by power. It no longer had one agreed upon meaning, it was a battleground of ideas. And the power to define reality was most possible for the extremely wealthy. The walls had to be defended with stories and laws. And these justifications were created by people. To protect their power, oligarchs abused the checks and balances of democratic institutions. Authoritarian power derived from fiction, from myth, and it actively discredited evidence-based reporting. The sole source of truth was the authoritarian state.

"Powercoin is a problem," Jason said.

"It's realistic," Shane said. "People with resources are the ones who everyone else pays attention to. That's what happens with money. Even if wealth was evenly distributed and no one had to worry about meeting their basic needs, people would have some way of determining status."

"The people with more powercoin have more weight in decisions. But how do we prevent financial power from becoming power over others?"

"I think," Shane offered, "the powercoin is to make work efficient, those who are going to lead are going to take a risk. A real risk. It'd be included in the governance protocol, so people had to stake their powercoin to make a decision. It costs to have the power to decide. Their powercoin would go into an escrow, and if their decision didn't serve the agreed upon goal, then it would be transferred to flow and distributed to all the members of the commons. That would keep the currency in circulation. The need to stake one's power on a decision would prevent the accumulation of vast amounts of powercoin by anyone, because no one is right all of the time."

Jason leaned back and gazed at the ceiling.

"Hypothetically," Jason said and looked to his friend, "let's take climate change. If someone decided to extract fossil fuel, then that decision would be weighted by however much power they held, and that powercoin would be forfeit if clearly it was a bad decision for the well-being of all, and their power would become flowcoin to be used by other people who had other ideas of how to solve the problem."

"It's worth a try."

"Yeah, we can test it in beta."

People needed work, the ability to apply themselves to acquiring skills and solving real problems. The problem Shane and Jason began to address: How to survive in a digital and highly automated economy with extreme inequality in wealth and opportunity.

People needed meaningful work to feel good about themselves, the sense of identity that came from work filled with purpose. Commonwealth would vastly expand from commons making casual games to become a platform where ordinary people with an AI assistant could perform professional work to solve real problems. And people could continually learn on the platform. They could earn by teaching. It would be infinite learning. An entire world. Shane started to expand the vision of Commonwealth. He needed a grand vision to get people on board. They had to create a better future. People were too shy about identifying the real problem. But with a vast imbalance in power, he knew information wasn't enough. Shane knew that he and all of the people he loved were exposed to a programming error, threatened by an economic system optimized to maximize shareholder value, high-speed machine algorithms strip-mining value from the human economy of goods and services. Financial vehicles extracting wealth rather than creating value for all. Those shares were seriously skewed toward a small segment of the population. Whose idea of the future would shape reality?

Jason said their nemesis was the people who controlled the design of our money, who had monopolized its design, who collected rents for its use. Shane's hero, Elon Musk, had once tried to create an online bank, but it just became an interface for the existing currency. If people could believe they were working to save humanity, they would sacrifice, working ninety hours or one hundred, week after week, anything at all. They were going to save humanity!

Becoming a multi-planet species, providing a backup for humanity, but delivering communications satellites into orbit and servicing the International Space Station was a job, albeit for SpaceX and a highly technical and prestigious job, it wasn't anything to sacrifice themselves for. Saving humanity by going to Mars was only words, it was a concept, a vision. Living on Mars had no basis in reality, it didn't address the failure to survive in a closed ecosystem on Earth. Musk had never talked about Biosphere 2. That failure was history. It didn't matter. He moved people with his vision. A story. A colony on Mars with a million people. The future. That was what they were fighting for. He said they'd need people on Mars to deliver pizzas. They'd create jobs! The more outlandish the vision, the more expertise required, the more it was removed from ordinary critique. It only required belief in progress. It was stories and faith. It was destiny.

If people believed they would one day work on Mars, why not Commonwealth!

A brilliant fire of deep cryo liquid oxygen exploding at the base of the Amazon ship blazed into the blue sky. Monty caught sight of it on his way to work. A reusable rocket carrying the C-suite, celebrities, and luxury goods to the landing pad in Shanghai. Arriving in under an hour. A miracle of the private space industry. Bezos, Branson, Musk, and Bigelow. The billionaire temple builders, all racing to create an indelible monument in time.

Monty arrived in the office after nine. Crossing the lobby with the tide pool aquarium, a massive rock sculpture with small pools that lured visitors for a closer look, he saw Cab talking with their receptionist seated behind a black ovoid desk. He stopped and chatted, then entered the elevator with Cab.

"It was approved by the Academy of Neuroscience for Architecture," Cab said, jittery with triumph. The Guggenheim museum had requested to license a Gen design for their new branch. "This will prove the utility of data-driven generative design. It stands to revive Detroit, as astonishing to the world as the Eiffel Tower was in 1889."

Monty congratulated Cab and the doors opened. He walked to his desk and received a report from the penetration tester. His security operations team had installed their cherry. Five hours later he opened his personal device and noticed the texts:

pick up

I need to talk

It was Celestine, the lady he'd been seeing in Portland. He went into a private room and called. Her voice, after the first ring, came to him. "Monty, I don't know what I'm going to do. He's going to sue me."

XXXIX

ELSIE CREATED a color palette for Commonwealth. To talk about it, to work together was exciting for both of them. After dinner she and Shane were in the living room, each with their laptops. The wind rustling through the tree outside their window. The rain had stopped. They turned down the lights and lit candles. Shane sat cross-legged on their wood-framed futon couch, wearing white tube socks. Elsie was beside him when a knock sounded.

"That's Monty."

He got up, closed his laptop, setting it on the coffee table, and opened the door. Monty was smiling, his hands shoved in the pockets of his puffy coat. He stepped inside and Shane gave him a hug. Celestine had been in a car accident. Monty told him when they talked earlier, by phone. Shane's first thought was that she'd been hurt, but Monty assured him no one was injured. She hit a Tesla. She was in a rental car, and luckily, the rental company was dealing with the lawsuit. The Tesla had been rebuilt and everything was fine but the guy sued her for reducing the resale value. Shane tied his laces, put on his jacket, wound a scarf around his neck, and grabbed his hat.

"We're going to take some fresh air," Shane said.

Elsie brushed her hand across her lips and smiled.

At first they said nothing, simply walked side by side, the cars passing, the streetlights overhead and into the distance, pools of light glistening on the black road. For most cars, normal insurance was enough to cover their value. The Tesla was five times that, maybe more. Should she have been liable, it would've bankrupted her, trashed her credit. Shane had asked if Celestine was going to move to Seattle and Monty told him they'd talked about having a room together. It might take a few months for one to become available in the Tech Plex, but they both had beds in the group space. The emotional trial of Celestine's accident, after talking with her, that day, he gave Makner his two-week notice. Monty had begun interviewing with Amazon. Jason told Shane some of what he'd learned working there and, after walking with Monty to the end of the block, Shane finally said, "We are going to build the biggest platform in the world."

Monty didn't see it. "Thanks for sending that live doc," he said.

"What do you think?"

"I set an alert and when I hear you or Jason's icon appear, I watch it."

"What do you think?"

"Security isn't an afterthought. It's built in from the beginning, into the code and the culture."

"Monty, you're in?"

"I want to help you guys."

"You're in . . . we can't hire you for a year."

"There is nothing to prevent me from working on an open source protocol."

"No, yeah. That's true. Yeah. But you should take the job at Amazon."

"They sent me an offer letter."

"Take it. Learn everything."

"I have to admit, I did kinda like the sound of this job."

"Take whatever you can, we need . . . I've always had the opinion that innovators have shamelessly used any good ideas."

"You want me to steal their technology?"

"You will be inside the predator!"

Monty placed a hand on Shane's shoulder and they paused on the sidewalk. He began to speak and, meeting Shane's eyes, the trust held between them, he stopped.

"What is it?"

"Nothing," Monty said. "Let's get back."

Monty began walking in the direction of Shane and Elsie's apartment.

"What were you going to say?"

"Nothing. I was thinking about the past."

Three black Chevy Suburbans pulled up outside the Seattle Tech Plex, the drivers wore ear pieces and sunglasses. Cab was ushered into the middle car and marveled at the abundance of security. The cars drove to a large house near the golf course on a peninsula in Lake Washington. Makner incorporated in Delaware, and with the Seattle expansion, Sebastian had established his residence in Medina, Washington on the opposite shore from Seattle. Cab walked to the door and was met by Makner's chief financial officer who led him though the house to a sitting room with big bay windows. Franklin Wells stood and warmly shook his hand, congratulating him on the letter of interest from the Guggenheim Foundation.

Sebastian entered from the hallway opposite Cab. "We're very pleased."

Cab smiled. "Gen has passed the acceptance test."

"Oh, yes," Sebastian said. "Best of class."

Cab remained standing, looking around. The four stood there in the large room. Cab felt the contiguous voxels within his parahippocampal region respond favorably to the design of the living room.

Sebastian said, "You see the benefit of making the Guggenheim a Makner—"

"Guggenheim Detroit," Cab corrected.

YOU WILL WIN THE FUTURE

"Makner brought Guggenheim to you," Franklin said, smiling.

"Consider us a communications network," Sebastian added. "Your algorithms need a lot of data to act in a coherent way."

"We have done it together," Cab said.

"We are natural partners," Sebastian said. "The data-driven design is only as good as the data and that is why it is Makner, the Guggenheim Detroit is a Makner building. We provide the data for your black box. Please Cab, have a seat."

Cab looked at the seats. They appeared to be identical.

Sebastian said, "Even you don't understand the code it generates."

"Even still," Cab said, sitting down. "I can explain how it was trained, what it was trained on, how it was tested."

The others sat down and a man entered the room carrying a tray of three small ceramic cups, a coffee pot, and a glass with green juice. He set it on a low table before their chairs, facing the white sky in the windows.

"I had your wheatgrass juice prepared."

Cab leaned forward, lifting the glass. "Thank you, Sebastian."

The man poured coffee into the three cups and left the room. Franklin Wells had bought a controlling stake in a biotech firm that held the patent on the world's most popular synthetic coffee, indistinguishable from the real. That was if a real cup could be afforded. Coffee was one of the foods that climate had rendered too expensive for average consumers.

"This is the new oil," Franklin said, taking a drink.

"To our partnership," Sebastian said, lifting his cup. "To provide cities, their inhabitants, with the most beneficial architecture."

"I should have what you're drinking," Cab said. "Then I might feel better about our business."

Franklin studied Cab's hand, the light green foam quivering in his glass, the precise expression of his face, his smile hiding what he'd said behind the words. Cab did his own reading of the three men, and told them: "I won't sell the technology."

Sebastian smiled, shaking his head gently. "Of course."

"This isn't to touch upon our agreement," the CFO said. Makner had a licensing agreement for Cab's software.

"That will be honored," Cab said, the r dropping in his crisp British English.

"Our story is for people," Sebastian said. "Machine learning is a commodity. It is like electricity. The value has been created by our data, Makner collects, stores, all of this data. It is accurate to say that Makner has collected the data. Our story has a hero." Collectives, teams, multiple inventors, building upon a shared history: all that was too complicated. To establish Makner permanently in the public consciousness, Sebastian wanted a simple story. One that people remember, recall, talk about at a party, feel like they understand, and know simply as Makner. "Explaining the technology will get us nothing, they will be bored to distraction."

"A good story," the CFO said. "All we ask from you is to let Sebastian tell this story. We only want the rights to the story of how this building came to be."

"I am grateful for the work you've done, but Gen hasn't been entirely applied to my satisfaction. The Detroit building will—"

"It will be better for Detroit," Sebastian said, "to have the building associated with our brand. Gen has become more valuable the more it's used."

"The probability of the museum becoming a tourist attraction is high," Cab said. "This structure will bring tourist dollars to a post-industrial city. I shall not state my actual estimate. It is prudent to avoid contractual liability, although I can confirm confidentially—"

"I have no doubt of that. I've been inside the designs, we all have." Sebastian gestured to his associates.

"It has been mind-opening," the CFO said.

"I spent hours in there," Franklin said, refilling his cup.

"I return to the design reality simulations," Sebastian said. "I find myself wanting to be there. It is contemplative."

"The building will affect the body as well as the visual cortex. It will be a most beneficial space for human well-being. Gen has optimized for every guideline set by advanced neuroscience."

"Makner will tell this story," Sebastian said.

"We are working in your interest," Franklin said. "Your already substantial income from licensing will grow, day on day."

"There is no amount of money, nor prohibitive nondisclosure policy, that will prevent me from speaking to the public. It is my responsibility to create a better understanding of our tools."

Sebastian smiled at him and looked out the window at the city in the distance. "A termite will begin building when another termite appears. On demand. People think of Gen as software, self-contained. AI. It has to be that simple. No one cares to know how many thousands of tasks it automatically lists, verifies, and pays people pennies to do."

"I explain how the software minutely subdivides work. The vendor management system we use. Freelancers working extra hard, coping with ambiguity, understanding intent, managing subjectivity with their high-quality annotation. Work that cannot be done by machine. I've always said the software depends on people to insert the expert thinking and complex communication needed to complete a project."

"But you're not telling the story," Sebastian said.

The CFO said, "Cab, you don't want to be out selling licenses to schools, firms, as Makner has done for you. Your time is best applied developing the tools."

"I will discover how to apply myself to the world."

With the FBI field office in Pittsburgh, Monty had participated in an investigation of the President. By comparison, the vulnerabilities he'd acquired from Wells were minor. Monty held secrets that would undermine the presidency. The results of the investigation were sealed to protect the stability of the nation. All involved sworn to secrecy. Who would he tell? He had spent all his time at work and then, at home, he was unable to process it. To prevent himself from revealing anything, he said nothing to his wife. In a sacred trust with his office, he held the vulnerability of the nation.

Oh, Celestine.

How could he be vulnerable, this intimacy was locked. Monty was protecting her too, but the existence of the files was in him. Forever. Wanting to be known. Monty dismissed the thought that he was merely protecting himself. The knowledge would die with him, and the nation would survive.

"This service-oriented architecture," Monty said, seated with Shane and Jason and Elsie in the Portland Tech Plex. They had a table in the commons and he was laying out the loosely coupled systems to allow Commonwealth to scale. "Every feature and service is an independent piece. Each can be easily updated and replaced without breaking the whole. A series of independent but interconnected parts."

Monty had slotted into a position with Amazon Web Services in Portland. It was the new year, late January, and Shane had been working full time on Commonwealth for the last three weeks. Monty introduced them to a team working out of the Tech Plex that had recently received nonprofit status. They had partnered with the City of Portland to facilitate online conversations that allowed city employees and all of Portland to see where people stood on issues of importance. "This is cool," Shane said. "Why didn't I ever know about this?"

"You never looked for it."

Cab and Cheryl walked through the commons area and Shane stood up to greet them. "Hey guys, I finally get to introduce you."

Shane had sent Cab a link to their live doc, and the appearance of his comments on the white paper had been electrifying. Jason stood up and introduced himself. He was eager to earn the approval of the great computer scientist. The general superintelligence of the internet was a machine-human hybrid. The nerve endings of artificial intelligence were alive, each human being connected by their devices, tapping keys, speaking to the machine and providing information about their world. Their subjective states, rationalizations, scientific hypotheses, and the data from the sensors carried with them inside the ubiquitous phone. A relay of human signals that sped into machine readable code. To create strong general superintelligence the data had to match reality. How the real world would be turned into code was a serious debate in computer science.

Shane had tried to entice Cab with a promise of the widespread use of his tools. Jason took a different approach, grasping the concerns of his industry, he appealed to a core challenge of general artificial intelligence. One he proposed could be addressed by Commonwealth.

People interacting with false information formed attachments to synthetic worlds, delivered and sustained through human culture. Reality could become substituted inside individuals with an illusion. The authentication of the real world was a battleground into which scientists waded unarmed. The human brain didn't see the world, the eye admitted photons of light that became electrochemical signals to reach the brain. Every surface the light had bounced off was modeled inside an individual's brain. Reality was simulated inside the brain from the sense data entering the body. People didn't see the world, the brain corrected for errors against a conceptual model.

It was the externalization of this awareness into culture, language and technology, that had changed human perception of the world. With new instruments and better data, people arrived at a new understanding.

The science of memory, data storage and retrieval, had been an area of research for Cab. The recovery of information in the brain was colored by each individual's psyche, and in the vast information storage and retrieval of the internet it was imperative to surface the best data when inputs were human, influenced by subjective desires, unconscious needs, and driven by animal instincts and commercial interests.

Jason proposed a way for Cab to help people better understand themselves and the world. The acquisition of knowledge created a model of reality, human culture and history built into the internet that could be called up and experienced at any point. Commonwealth provided a secure and transparent system that guarantees the information. From a decentralized democratic platform they could display multidimensional objective states of time from data sourced from all perspectives. Jason said their Trust input could be a two-way mirror: providing insight into both the content and the subjective state of the individuals. They could use that to weight information beyond an academic linking structure of institutional authority and bring it to the human scale.

Centralized sources of information had been proven to be somewhat malleable, under the influence of authority and capable of manipulation. It wasn't evil or a conspiracy or anything like that, it was humans acting human, the short-term interests of powerful industries, militaries, and governments influenced the information for various, often contradictory, strategic purposes. When culture delivered by machines was the mediator between individuals and reality, they became more vulnerable to infection by synthetic worlds that could distort their perception of the real. Jason told Cab that Commonwealth would be an antidote, joining real people throughout the world, the organic sense data from real people to counteract the manufactured worlds spun by a relative few who controlled financial instruments, corporate structures, governments and militaries.

Celestine joined them and the seven friends had dinner at the Tech Plex.

"We're working toward a fully-realized Commonwealth," Shane said. "But we have to start with one simple thing, a smallish group."

Cab considered the prospect of building tools for game developers, connecting people and creating a place for them to authenticate data through trust networks. He had experienced the downside of centralized private platforms that emphasized the abstract rather than the real, where they extracted value from the community. He wanted to believe Commonwealth would lead to true cooperation and value creation for people.

"We can work toward the long-term goal," Jason said. "It is the information that will shape human activity on earth."

"We have a duty," Monty said.

Artificial intelligence didn't have consciousness, sealed in a box; the idea of superintelligent machines rebelling against their masters was an artifact of Western culture, and Hollywood, anthropomorphizing an interdependent complex system as an independent self-directed agent. Human beings had become the carriers of false scripts, a person could become a mask of artificial ideologies.

"I want to apply myself to Commonwealth." Cab looked at his friends. "I will do all that is in my power to recall the true human being."

XL

THE NEO-NAZIS had good contacts in the police force, which meant they often escaped criminal proceedings. Her video of the man who attacked Lena didn't lead to prosecution. That bastard punched her ear. And they scuttled her evidence, so infuriating. In March, Rebecca responded to a question on her video about Franklin Wells being accused of having sex with a minor—and she said something off-the-cuff about Sebastian. He treated sex as a game, she mentioned how he behaved with all the new women hired in the Portland office; Rebecca knew from what they said how Sebastian seduced them and, when one was in the car with him, it wasn't that she wanted to go along but she didn't feel she had much of a choice.

Naturally, she was pissed and went off a bit. Gender politics. Men on top, women on bottom—of everything, less pay, no say. Rebecca was fighting for herself, for her life, and she ranted. Her subscribers cared about her, and word got around quick. She went a little far. Out of company bounds. A form was ready to sign when she got in. Management asked her to resign. It was three guys she didn't even know. They gave her a month's pay, but she was out. It was in Makner's interest that she resign, so they didn't have to pay unemployment. But fuck, she signed it.

Franklin Wells agreed to a no-guilt multimillion dollar settlement with the girl's family over allegations that he had sex with her. The girl told her parents, and they believed her. The information to convict him, and more than enough to embarrass him, had arrived in an unmarked box on their doorstep. Franklin paid an out of court settlement and that was it. The babysitter was never heard from again, that was the agreement. He admitted nothing. Franklin Wells did what he wanted.

James got busted early that summer and Elsie no longer had the medicine for her regular treatments. Shane found a supplier on the dark net, but he didn't explain the details when he told his parents.

"How much is the medicine?" his mom asked.

He told her just a little more than six thousand a month.

"You'll come up with something," she said. "You're so smart."

Elsie made a public call for help. She had no other choice. She logged on to GoFundMe and put together a profile.

Citizens weren't represented by central bankers. Jason said they'd be living in a different configuration of social and economic power if a democratic institution created and controlled money. Central banks were understood by Jason as a consortium of bankers—private interests, not public. Real participation by the public in deciding how money was spent into the real economy would change the world. Money was a tool, a thing to be used, and when already wealthy people had easy access to the tool and could charge rents for the use of money, it became an instrument for the concentration of financial power.

Central banks that implemented a permissionless blockchain, their record of all transactions could be viewed and verified by anyone. Jason showed Monty how the open source protocol was being implemented by some pioneering central banks. Monty had little time outside of Amazon to work on the platform, but he did what he could. He would secure Commonwealth. On a cryptographically secure distributed ledger, money became a database of transactions, social interactions, a social network.

They pushed through the days of summer to create a working prototype. The hours put into the protocol tested their endurance. To complete the white paper. To clearly articulate the tokens. How everything would work, how the world would work, all together. It was crazy. They worked out of their homes and coffee shops, but they were running out of resources to do even that. All of their energy was given to the platform and what it could become. Everything was at stake, Shane and Elsie considered giving up their apartment to save money in the crunch. Shane's sister did pro-bono work. Monty ran a simulation of hundreds of thousands of active accounts. He contracted bug hunters. It all had to be tested. It needed to work in practice, not just in theory. They couldn't raise funds before they proved the concept worked.

Commonwealth.

Shane could move in with his folks, and Elsie's dad lived in Gresham, he had room. Elsie was in pain. The doctors prescribed Oxycontin, but she refused it. She had raised eighteen thousand dollars to pay for her treatment.

Monty asked a few friends living at the Tech Plex to try the platform and they built a game together—in the euphoria, Shane posted to Hacker News "Anyone Can Join COMMON.WEALTH: It's Not a Frigging Unicorn!" and the white paper was published. Elsie shared his post on all their outlets, with their friends on chat; the team sent the link to friends in twenty-eight different states and nine countries. All their media outlets opened, they had videos and live chats. The whole team worked their communications, talking with people around the world. Cab had an interview in *Wired* about the data-driven design for the Guggenheim and he mentioned Commonwealth. Sixten interviewed Jason on a news program broadcast in fourteen European countries. Then Jason received invitations to talk shows in Taiwan, Singapore, and Hong Kong. He illuminated the white paper. They all promoted, clarified and celebrated what Commonwealth would become. Everyone would be able to understand exactly what they were doing. They proved their platform worked, exposed its source code, now it was time to listen to other perspectives.

The Portland office had grown to two hundred and forty-nine full-time associates, and John walked the aisles of their work stations. It was almost seven and the sun had blinked out behind the hills. He was on his way out the door when his phone buzzed. It would've been acceptable to ignore it, he was late to meet his wife, but the point cloud from Tokyo needed his approval and he'd been anticipating a call from the team in Santiago de Chile to prepare their expansion. John glanced at the screen—Brian Sabin. He stepped into the stairwell and accepted the call. "Nice to hear from you, Brian."

"What happened to my brother?"

XLI

THE SALE OF TOKENS brought in real money, held by the non-profit Commonwealth Foundation. They never sought to quickly raise as much as possible. They had left that old model. For-profit businesses captured by venture capital got all of their priorities rearranged to suit the shareholders. And people apparently wanted a new deal. Commonwealth sold tokens far and wide. To people all over the world. The exchanges selling flowcoins reported the sales were diverse, geographically and demographically. Commonwealth could work. It just might work.

The music pulsing through their bodies, Rebecca pulled him close. "Do you want to go back to my place?!"

He nodded, a drop of sweat running down his cheek like a tear. She grabbed his hand and they moved through the push of bodies on the dance floor. Jackson sang in Mood Union, and she drove him to her house in northeast. Rebecca owned a four-bedroom and rented to three other guys, two were in and out of love with her. She harnessed their energy. Clint was in charge of the vegetable garden, Phil did their dishes because he was a terrible cook—everyone, except for Phil, rotated preparing shared dinners—and Bonifaco was her equal in all things, an engineer who moved to Portland from Mexico City for a job at a biotech company. He called through the door in the morning, asking if she was hungry. Rebecca turned on her pillow and Jackson was staring at her, his eyes saucered like he'd seen the coming end. She pushed her head into the pillow, arcing her back, her breasts mounded. She was fucking amazing. Then she sat up and said, "What's for breakfast?"

The door opened and a shirtless guy in track pants and flip-flops stood there holding the handle. "Who's he?"

"My friend, Jackson."

"Oh. Hey, gato. I'm Bon."

His housemates joked that he walked around without a shirt to show off his muscles. Bon had a powerful build, the size of him at the other end of the spectrum from Jackson, reaching for his pants after the door closed. The chill of November in the walls of the house.

At the table, Jackson met Clint and they ate with Bon and Rebecca, then she looked up from her tablet open on the table. "No way! Shane."

Bon glanced at the screen.

"They did it," she said.

They could now pay themselves, but their foundation wasn't a personal piggy bank. Shane went on the black market to buy medicine, and they were gouging him. He and Elsie decided to give up their apartment in southeast Portland. A small sacrifice, necessary, for a year. Jason estimated it would take another year to build out features to expand the platform beyond games. They designed the token generation event to extend through twelve months and allow more people to buy. The flowcoins had value for speculators, but they would have real value when the platform launched, and the team didn't want a few investors to buy up all their tokens, hold them, or sell them at will. They wanted to distribute the ownership of coins to as many people as they could, and so the sale amount had a limit for each account, preventing large institutional investors from monopolizing them.

Shane and Jason started interviewing developers. Given the legal risk in creating a public platform for digital labor, Nora had advised them to protect themselves. She helped them form a Limited Liability Company. Built upon an open source protocol supported by the Commonwealth Foundation, the Commonwealth Platform was a for-profit corporation, allowing them to offer stock options to the developers.

Elsie walked into the teahouse and spotted her seated with a teapot and two cups. Rebecca stood up, opened her arms, and Elsie embraced her: hugging was healthy. They had spoken before Shane and Rebecca left on their trip, and they spent the first twenty minutes drinking tea in casual conversation.

"I wanted to ask you," Rebecca said.

Elsie started smiling and pursed her lips, glanced down, and then stared into Rebecca's eyes. "We are going to make it."

"I know, I want to try it."

Elsie nodded. "Shane wants to make it big."

"I want to help you guys. I have a community, it's embarrassing, kinda, but I have some fans."

Rebecca's phone chirped and she checked the screen. She had lain down after dinner and drifted off. It was almost ten. A text from Sebastian.

I still listen to you

She felt her pulse quicken, then cleared her mind. The songs she gave him. Sebastian wasn't after her, she told herself, Sebastian couldn't be intimate, she'd seen that—but he couldn't be alone. Rebecca never entertained his advances. Was this harassment? Or was he a fan? Was this what she wanted?

Brian took the call in the backseat, he was twenty miles from the studio. "Thanks for getting back to me."

"Yes," said Cab, his voice in surround sound. "You're welcome."

"What happened?" Brian asked.

"Regression analysis identified a remarkable bias in the training data. Your brother's exchanges with analysts at a venture capital firm."

Brian watched the traffic inch forward.

"And that's what made it say that shit?"

"We didn't censor anything he said or wrote. We had determined it was best to use everything. The real Bradley is not forgotten by us. But he had a mental construct—"

"I have to take another call."

"It is persistent for its usefulness in asserting power. It can be used."

"Hold on." Brian rested his forearms on his legs, clasped his hands and gazed down. "Okay, yes. . . . I will be there. . . .Yes, of course, I remember."

Brian relaxed into the seat.

Cab's voice again: "Did you want to review the material?"

On January third, the Commonwealth platform went live. Rebecca asked her fans to create a game with her. Shane had presented the platform at events for game designers in the Pacific Northwest. After showing them how it worked, he called people to the front of the room—whoever wanted to explore modifications of their games, whoever had an idea for a new game—and those people each took a moment to pitch their idea and sign up anyone who wanted to join them, right then. The moment the platform launched, they received invites. Elsie was asleep when the chime sounded, waking her, she looked at her screen.

Come and play with me!

XLII

OVER THE NEXT YEAR, for the team working on Commonwealth, it was more than a startup. It wasn't just a computer protocol. Shane began to rally his developers in the mornings and whenever the mood hit him: they were going to save Western civilization! It was odd, when he said these things, because, especially for the new hires, they were only building tools for game developers.

Creating games took their minds off the ongoing weirdness—extreme weather events, resource depletion, and migration produced the stress and suffering that analysts had promised. And the United States bowed to a more authoritarian impulse, a strong leader to take them through uncertainty and assure a promised population they would survive, resulting in the implementation of two laws: the Military Commissions Act, which allowed government to declare US citizens enemy combatants and imprison them without a trial, and the John Warner Defense Authorization Act, which gave the president the power to declare a public emergency and station troops in any city in America without permission from the local government.

Shane added additional exercises to his daily routine: warrior one, warrior two, and sun salutations. Elsie had said she wanted a baby, and she wanted what he wanted—though the amount of work was mind-bending. He asked if she could wait, and when she agreed, he asked her to marry him. She'd said yes. They wanted the same thing, they shared this will to create together. And they had agreed it would be a little much while they were both living in their parents' houses.

From her room, they heard the truck and Shane walked to the window. Her father had parked a load of firewood. Elsie shook her comforter and pulled it over a pillow of air fading into the bed. On the wall hung paintings she'd inherited from her grandmother: a portrait of a horse, a girl standing in a field with her hand raised to a bird overhead, and a still life of an apple. Her sewing machine was in a red hardshell case on the floor beside an old wood desk in front of a window. Their laptops were on the desk and she grabbed hers and sat in an armchair beside the window.

Shane walked out the back door.

"You're going to help me, citizen?" Elsie's father opened the cab, leaned in and emerged with a second pair of gloves. He passed them to Shane on his way around the truck.

"Please don't call me that."

Shane guided one hand and the other into the gloves. Miles laughed and Shane clapped his gloves together and stood back to give him room. His girlfriend's dad grabbed a piece of firewood in each hand, carrying them to the wood shed alongside the house. "The important thing is how much air you leave around the logs."

He had solar panels on the roof, a root cellar under the tool shed, and a cistern of rainwater. Miles had rebuilt another old Toyota for his daughter, a red hatchback they'd parked along the road. Shane and Miles worked together to move the wood, and, carrying an armload, Shane let it fall at the wood shed. "Is there any hope?" he said.

"Is that all you wanted?"

"I mean, do you believe in the distributed city?"

"I believe what doesn't need me to believe in it."

"We, um," Shane began, "people believe in things for them to be real."

"There's more to a city than what appears on a screen."

Shane climbed into the back of the truck and handed wood to Miles, stacking it into his arms. "We're making a new way to create and exchange value, a way for people to organize themselves."

"This here is all I know how to organize," Miles said, carrying the wood past the old house. Shane decided to toss the pieces toward the wood shed and cleared it with Miles, and started chucking them out one after the other. With the last piece, he hopped off the open tailgate, and began organizing the wood in the shed with the older man's guidance. They talked about the preparations for Thanksgiving dinner; Miles and his girlfriend were planning to eat with Shane's family. Janelle was twelve years younger than Miles, had recently gotten braces for her teeth, and made money giving therapeutic massages.

"Money isn't a thing," Shane said after they finished. "It's a shared belief, it's an agreement. People can share a belief, a way of organizing society."

A dog mangled his hand when he was a boy and Miles had only three fingers on his right hand. He put his arm around Shane. His future father-in-law held him a moment and said, "I believe in you, Shane."

In winter they prepared to open the platform for use by digital firms, digital labor, open to everyone. Shane scheduled tables and speaking engagements for himself and other members of the team to attend job fairs and college campuses. Those students graduating into a tight market could make good use of Commonwealth. People would create their own work. Make their own careers. Project leaders could provide jobs. And anyone using Commonwealth received flowcoins for each person they invited to a commons that signed up and participated. They could import their contacts from existing social media. Commonwealth had an easy way to invite all your friends.

Elsie showed it to nonprofits in Portland, with her friends, getting ready to use the commons for big organizing. Neighborhood organizations had educated themselves about the Wells law. They spoke out against the financialization of human necessities. They needed to protect housing from amoral markets. Monty and Shane and Elsie met with neighbors throughout the city, giving demos of how to use Commonwealth; and people suggested additional tools they'd need to make it work for them. Elsie asked something incredible of everyone, and she identified exactly what they were trying to achieve: shelter for all.

Sebastian crossed Broadway with his chief of staff and, stepping into the crowd, they entered Pioneer Courthouse Square. They made it to the edge of the steps and saw the plaza filled with people. Energy, within him, in contact, body to body, the energy of the people held in anticipation and excitement. He had recognized the names of the performers—they were big acts, the musicians—their presence alone would account for all these people gathering to celebrate in spring, but there was more at play. A charged atmosphere of gathering power, they came on purpose, for some deeper thing, making an intentional connection with each other, to being there. A massive party of all ages across every class, profession and station. A mosaic of ethnicity and belief. The azure sky, the first of May. At a peak moment, Rebecca appeared onstage.

"You know why we are here," she said, walking to the center of the stage. "We have no way to confront the problem of affording a place to live without confronting the inequality of wealth and income. We live within an economy designed to extract and concentrate wealth. We are going to defeat the Wells law."

She wore a sleeveless tuxedo jumpsuit, and a microphone so fine it was essentially invisible. "HB 9658 will not pass!"

A cheer rose from the crowd; it might have been the thrill of the last act had carried over—but from his vantage point, Sebastian saw an unexpected turn in her career. "We will go further," she said, jumping in place and then standing with her legs apart. "The people who make life in the city possible will be able to afford living in it. The teachers. Shopkeepers. Cooks and waiters. Police and firefighters. Artists and musicians. The mothers and fathers and people of every age and size and ethnicity who make culture, who make business and food, who make the city safe and accessible. We have a right to live in our city. We are making it happen!"

The cheering exercised the pain of exclusion, experienced over many years, the forces larger, more powerful, more abstract and distant from their homes, moving in, moving through their city. "Our rights are agreements we make with each other," Rebecca said, her voice commanding, rising. "Our rights, to be recognized and enforced, must become our Constitution. They're the body of laws that can make our communities whole and fair and just. That include and nurture us. For it is we who the state shall protect, all of us, everyone. We belong here!"

Rebecca turned and another woman approached her. It was Elsie. She walked to the center as Rebecca jogged offstage. "This is how we win! This is what we ask of you," Elsie said to everyone. "If you have a place where you can host people, create a commons and invite them. Let's all do that now, the software will match the invites." She held up her mobile and from the wings people joined her onstage in hand-crafted costumes: opossum, deer, bear, bald eagle, raccoon, beaver, turtle, duck, heron, owl, coyote, squirrel, and crow.

"You can meet your neighbors," Elsie said, surrounded by the animal ensemble. "And working together you will be more effective. This is about talking with people. Our message is more effective, more powerful, when you give it voice!" She spread her arms.

"We don't send mailers, or buy ads in media. It is through talking with another person like yourselves, calling them, we can do this together, by calling from a commons that has met in one location: working together you are more effective than if you were alone."

The animals one by one hopped off the stage and entered the audience.

"Each person will be provided with a single-page guide and a short video showing what we are going to achieve and how to do it."

Shane came onstage and hugged Elsie. She joined the costumed critters offstage, and he said, "We are creative. We have the ability to house everyone, as a community. How about a transaction fee on all-cash sales of houses—that fee could be used by the city to subsidize affordable housing. Or why not rent control on units owned by institutional investors—that would take the heat out of Wall Street buying rental property. The city could raise revenue from a fee placed on polluters and property sales by financial speculators and flippers. The city could place its wealth in a public trust that will invest in and buy land to be held in common, to be community land that will make the property atop it affordable for all, forever."

He held aloft a large scroll, letting it unfurl, a simple heart printed on the white paper. A big heart. "A progressive tax is a very simple way to share the winnings from a system designed to concentrate wealth."

He lowered the scroll, let it drop, and walked slowly along the front of the stage. "All public money will be in an open, transparent, easy-to-read ledger so that the value created by the people and held by a municipal bank can be directed by the people, a budget, a participatory budget. The value created by the city won't be extracted from the community, enclosed and privatized. We won't pay fees out of state to private banks for the management of public money. The city is a living system for the creation of value and the continuance of life, we are working together. This is the real job creator."

Sebastian tapped his chief of staff, turned and moved out through the crowd of people. He heard Rebecca's voice as she sang an anthem, a song that people had received through the commons, it rose up through them. The city in song.

XLIII

"THIS IS COMMUNISM. They will steal wealth from those of us who earn a living and give it to drifters who don't contribute anything at all. This common poverty will be the end of innovation and creativity. The end of science and industry." The bank accounts of lobbyists received an infusion of cash to fight the commons. Clever campaigns went online and the weird, alienated, disaffected Portlanders, the young Republicans, corporate climbers and the retired executives, came out saying they were afraid; a woman was interviewed on Oregon Public Broadcasting, saying she had nightmares and was suffering from a fear of the government coming to take her home. Portland-area public relations firms welcomed their new clients, establishing and nurturing relations with multinational corporations and the financial services industry; and the local business alliance attacked the proposed municipal bank, the fees on sales of property by out-of-state investors, and economic disincentives for polluters. The lobbyists talked with the mayor and spoke directly to citizens through major media outlets, buying the public's attention and framing the terms of the debate. They defined the language with which to interpret the issues, but they were unable to dislodge the understanding that grew from the combined intelligence of hundreds of thousands of citizens in direct communication, face to face, with each other, people who were able to sort out fact from falsehood and act together for social and economic equality. Portland was the first city to unionize itself.

The May One Common Fun in Pioneer Courthouse Square furthered a rhizomatic network spreading through every city block where people had set down their roots and committed their resources to live and belong. The city itself was the place of work for all living in Portland; and citizens were able to use a simple communications app to create a network among themselves, a distributed commons, hundreds of nested unions of friends, associates, coworkers, interlinking and joining the people living and working through the whole of the city into a common interest, a shared will to fight for their survival as a community. For their common prosperity, their shared future as a city, a people.

House Bill 9658 died in committee.

People talking on phones and upon doorsteps, energized by all those they worked alongside, advanced a referendum to convene citizens and remake their state constitution for the future of life on earth. To counter the stealth legislation advanced by a radical rich minority, Oregon would use the most advanced wisdom for sourcing their new body of laws that would outline the relations between state and citizens, to create trust in their government by using the best of what worked in successful progressive democracies, by creating publicly financed campaigns with low cost digital communication and ending corporate campaign cash. Shane promoted a process for achieving goals through multiple iterative policy experiments to discover and improve what meets the goal, rather than locking in solutions based on competing forecasts of what will and won't work—won by whichever lobbyists had the most money. Lawmakers could create economic incentives to reward actions for achieving the goal and fees for any practice that appears as people attempt to jump through loopholes. All these ideas came together in a commons, and Shane thought it was awesome. He met with his representatives in the Oregon legislature. He began by emphasizing the city as a job creator. He said to create the most positive future for ourselves, for our children, for all of the United States, we begin at the city, here. People didn't organize so much through their workplace or by industry, not anymore; but people all felt the effects of capital on the housing market and they were organizing to be able to live in the city. The city was the ultimate commons. And we create the infrastructure for participatory democracy, Shane said, we don't have a rigid plan for how it works, we make it work through successive, incremental steps toward the goal, continuous improvement over time, working with digital tools to assess and implement decisions quickly through the secure authentication and online decision-making, opening the field for true competition in the realm of political realism through a multi-party system and non-binary voting mechanisms. Let the best party win!

He didn't use the terms of debate that had mobilized the militarization of law enforcement, he said that to survive the threats they faced and to thrive as a species living within the animal kingdom, the law was a living code to advance humankind, their Constitution, a body of laws, a code that scripted their limits and allowances, their Constitution as a code. An agreement among people about how to cooperate for their mutual benefit, for their country, for their children, their future. The ability of a massive body of people to cooperate requires agreement, an agreement among all participants, an agreement upon the process that allows so many millions of people to work together, it can be created, he said, in clear and easy-to-understand terms, it can be made available, it can be written in software and done with an open source, citizen participation platform. He said the radical right funded deceptively-named legislation in secret because they knew it would never have the support of the majority, and we must respond to the covert threat with a public and open process to improve our laws. We can place our trust in the majority of Americans to choose the health of their children and their future well-being over the interests of a few billionaires. He said our laws are the genetic code of a public body made of every man, woman, and child that lives under them. To combine our knowledge across the experience of gender, class, age and ethnicity and source the Constitution from the people that it will represent. A participatory democracy, a civic life. To create and participate in civic life, for one and for all. Shane told his representatives that we, the people, will improve our Constitution to survive and thrive.

The mayor of Portland, when asked about Commonwealth, in a live interview, said, "The job creators in our city will not be extorted by technology, nor by the referendum and laws proposed by the commons. These social movements are destined to fail. We've seen them come and go throughout history, but we have to work with reality, the economic system that we have. We are working with what we have. It is not perfect, we improve society slowly, to protect it. Our system has procedures to deal with change. We have a strong tradition and people have faith in the process. It has stood the test of time. The radicals want to play musical chairs with wealth. We know how the song ends. Our city is too smart to chase that noise."

Commonwealth didn't cater to institutional investors, but most VCs put a chunk into promising cryptocurrency. The fear, uncertainty, and doubt created in the press started pushing speculative investors out. They began dumping flowcoin on exchanges, and then more people bought them. The coins had value because people were using the platform, they used flowcoins. They had real value to earn and invest, to interact and create in a commons. Tens of millions of people were using the platform, but some commons were threatened with a blacklist by high-profile employers—and worse. Instagram lifestyle celebrities came out in opposition. YouTube stars received lucrative offers in a reversal of product endorsements: they were paid to ridicule any product or service created on Commonwealth. Then the vocal supporters of Commonwealth, people who had made businesses within their commons, were contacted on the phone, by people claiming all kinds of things, and in some cases, finding them in person, to warn, cajole and intimidate.

Elsie had vomited after she climbed offstage at the Common Fun event. The additional stress of seeing her picture in the paper alongside weird stories about her being addicted to drugs, she felt violated, and she was sick. She did need medicine. Miles had co-signed for her student loans and had been covering the payments she was missing. Her father was keeping up, barely, he worked all the time but if he missed a payment his credit would be affected. The creditors would sue both of them to get their money; and not only that, if they didn't keep up the payments they'd be forced to pay even more. Elsie and her dad would become responsible for the added fees and collection costs as well as the higher default interest rates.

"We are at war," Shane said to the company, "and that's ridiculous because war is murder, people murder each other in war. Our situation is not that bad. No one is going to get killed." Shane gathered his team at the Tech Plex, and they emboldened each other to engage the media. They practiced with mock interrogations. Monty drilled hard. Everyone who worked on Commonwealth was deputized to speak on behalf of the company. They accepted any opportunity to tell their stories. It was necessary to defuse crazy shit with the real life stuff of making awesome software. Shane told everyone that it was imperative, absolutely essential for civil society, to make the platform happen. Shane was taking all calls, all interviews, going on broadcast media, talk shows and everything to defend Commonwealth. He believed they would win. They had designed the choice architecture to incentivize people to work in the interest of all. He had to grow the platform!

A panel of experts on FOX News, three talking heads, and Shane sitting alone in a studio with a satellite link, the voice in his earpiece out of sync with the video screen beneath the camera lens where he tried to hold his gaze. The spot began with video of people in animal costumes jumping off the stage at Pioneer Courthouse Square, then a blond anchorwoman filled the screen and framed the Commonwealth platform for viewers. A cryptocurrency that gave people tokens to do things. Could they organize enough voters for a referendum to rewrite the Oregon Constitution? First to comment was a former psychiatrist and FOX News Channel science expert: "This platform began as a way for unemployed people to make and play video games. Their coins are for hobbyists, like digital baseball cards that can't be duplicated but are only good for playing games or buying influence in their communist chat rooms. This is better understood as a performance where all attendees are scalpers with the incentive to boost the perceived value of joining them. They've made impossible claims to draw attention to themselves and inflate the value of their coins. Commonwealth is exploiting the prejudice and ignorance among common people."

An appellate and trial lawyer, the analyst for FOX News Channel on law, public policy, media and culture: "I've heard 'Kumbaya' before. These young people have no understanding of economics. They are atemporal, ahistorical, anarchists."

Author of *The Greatest Guide to Making Americans Great* and the economics expert on FOX News: "The founders are dropouts living at their parents' houses. They led themselves into their own economic dead ends, and now they conjure up a fantasy to make it all seem like it's going to work out for them. That's insane."

Shane had a moment to respond: "Commonwealth is a digital

platform for people to create and distribute value. The amazing thing is that people are really fair when they want to work together to solve a shared problem. People in these close-knit social groups, you'd be surprised how fair they are with each other. The commons are linking these trusted connections. Our coins are supporting people, to create trust, so we all can trust each other. Really, it's having something to believe in. That's so important for staying healthy, mentally and physically. We face enormously complex problems, the greater coordination of our efforts make us more effective in solving them."

The economics expert: "It's admirable to dream of a better world, but be realistic. People are not going to cooperate. Civilization entails constant conflict and competition. What was your breathless mission statement 'for all the world's people to self-organize and make themselves universally employed and effective'?"

The legal expert: "Humans are superpredators. The threats are very real. This is not a game. A code can't make bad people treat others fairly. These gamers don't understand that, yet. For these young people to suggest we can enforce contracts without the threat of violence is a misunderstanding of human nature. We align ourselves with the strongest among us to secure our protection, individually and as a nation."

The anchorwoman asked Shane for his thoughts and a split-screen appeared with Shane talking alongside a video of him holding up a paper scroll with a heart on it: "We have always thought long-term. And so in the first year, yeah, we're willing to be somewhat misunderstood. That sucks for my team, because we're doing important work that's super hard."

The anchorwoman said, "What is your endgame, Mr. Schumacher?"

"We want to improve the social contract. And I apologize on behalf of the company because this is so big, it's a super important big deal. People always find a way to game regulations. And so, rather than laws to say what people can't do, we're going to improve the incentives for solving shared problems. Society can determine the goals it is working toward, and reward actions that contribute and collect a fee from any actions counter to the goal. Those fees would pay for the rewards. And all of those assessments would be done through a crowd jury. Volunteers paid a nominal fee, drawn from a random sample with a statistical variation that ensures people are represented from all ages, ethnic groups, men and women. It's a different kind of lawmaking. Yeah, that's supposed to be the government's job. But so was the space program. And people want to do what's necessary to solve big problems. That's how that initiative for the constitutional convention took hold. We can revisit our foundations and see who we are. And I chose to speak about it, well, um uh it's . . . it's necessary to create a more effective process to decide on goals and align incentives and penalties to achieve them as fast as humanly possible. Without a government ever saying exactly how the goal will be achieved, letting people do it, being creative. Of course if they get creative in a way that's counter to the goals determined by society, they can do that but it's going to cost them—relative to their ability to pay. Because you know the enormous disparity in wealth would make a million dollars like a parking ticket for some operations. That's okay, they're free to do it, they'll be paying a huge amount though, and all of that goes directly to reward—"

"Thank you, Mr. Schumacher. We have to go to a commercial. That was Shane Schumacher, founder of the video game platform called Commonwealth. And before we go, panelists, any final thoughts?"

The science expert: "He is anti-American, and dishonest. He is perpetuating a fraud upon people."

The economics expert: "He is honest about one thing, they don't have real jobs. But yes, they're traitors."

The legal expert: "It's passive-aggressive terrorism."

The science expert: "Those kids should be ashamed for wasting the time of working Americans. Hey, if you don't like America, you can leave it."

The anchorwoman smiled and said, "Leave America for the Americans."

Shane was at home when the phone rang. He glanced at the screen—Unknown—and took the call.

"Hey, it's Shane, right?"

"Yeah."

"I'm Brian. Bradley's brother. You worked with him."

"Yeah."

"I have a show in Portland this summer. Can I buy you a drink?"

XLIV

MAKNER BOUGHT A FACTORY to mass-produce modular building components. Design was an iterative dialogue. Cityzen was social infrastructure for design and the popular buildings in the game were magnificent, proving their market before they were built. It was pre-sales. And Makner was going to mass produce the components to house people affordably—and in style. Sebastian had pivoted in response to the bad press.

To defeat the Wells law, the game had been unmasked as a time-delayed land grab, an enclosure of the city by finance capital. Then the Makner brand was spun in the attack upon its former employees, to discredit Shane and his team, the media pundits disparaged Makner and Cityzen and Commonwealth: they were scams.

Sebastian managed a redesign to introduce public open-source libraries of modular building components. Anyone around the world could download designs for free, along with the g-code instructions for machine tools to cut the components. Local production. High performance. Earthquake proof. The building components had been optimized in the game, over time, new forms developed that people could assemble in unique configurations on Cityzen, in real time, and then produce in factories and assemble on site. Makner bought a company based in Salem, Oregon that had been making prefabricated homes. They retooled it and opened a proof-of-concept factory.

Protecting his brand, Sebastian headed up the campaign. The

email subject line appeared in Shane's inbox: "Cityzen building prefab modular components for fast on-site assembly." The call came the next day.

Sebastian had offered a tour, and Shane got in the car with Cab and Sebastian, driving south, toward the capital, talking about their work. Changing jobs, starting a company, was a mark of ambition. Employees who wanted to be challenged and develop a broader skill set, they didn't stay at one job forever. This was to be expected, the tech industry was known for having the lowest employee tenure—the jobs kept multiplying by the minute. If someone stayed at a job too long, they weren't dynamic. It was costly for Sebastian, but he accepted the price of talent. He sympathized. He expressed a polite curiosity in Commonwealth. He admired what Shane had done. Shane had respected company protocol and now he had some of the best talent working on his platform, and Sebastian referred to them like an extended family.

Cab had finalized the deal with the Guggenheim Foundation and they broke ground on land donated by the city. The state agreed to cover the construction cost. Detroit would subsidize the museum's annual budget. In exchange, the Foundation would manage the institution, rotating its permanent collection and organizing temporary exhibits. Shane viewed the simulations of the museum and mentally cleared his calendar to attend the grand opening.

Exiting outside of Salem, they drove through an industrial district and parked at a building the size of seven football fields. They wore white hardhats with the Makner logo and, walking through the factory, it struck Shane, it was the man he'd admired. It was Sebastian. It was his natural charisma, his talent with people and financial resources that brought all this together. Lean and industrial construction, the precision and cost savings, making better homes for Makner customers. "I'm really grateful to both of you," Sebastian said. "This is about making use of what we know, and that has been learned in game and naturally, you made it possible."

The machines, the hardware, the virtual world had given life to these forms: the building parts that would combine to produce an endless variety of structures. Sebastian had joined the digital and the real, there was no separation. He told them that construction was a technology industry: machines, materials science, engineering, massive amounts of data. Real estate was the largest business sector globally, valued at more than two times global GDP, and yet it had lacked a company with any real dominance in the ability to offer better value at lower prices. As Sebastian posed it for them: Think of a global real estate company. They couldn't do it. Sebastian told Cab and Shane that no one has been able to serve these customers at scale, and Makner can. "We have that in our future. You have contributed to this, you are players in this massive game to house the world. We're going to tackle the world's housing shortage. We have been learning along the way, yes we made mistakes. But every decision and everything we do has been driven by our desire to create more value for our customers."

Cab took an interest in the modular forms. The variations, the interlocking parts. They walked the aisles teeming with workers overseeing their machines, the automation that was turning out components, custom designs ordered in game. "Real estate had a terrible brand," Sebastian said. "We suffered it—that's come to an end. Everyone needs shelter, and Makner is in a position now to provide the best value with better efficiency—in the use of materials, the long-term energy conservation, and the precision make. This bespoke on-site configuration from our component library. This will be a new world. A world where all people have safe and comfortable shelter for a great price."

Sebastian introduced them to the floor manager and they ate lunch together in a cafeteria that served delicious food. On the way home, Sebastian said, "How about you introduce me to Jason Lee?"

A dinner was planned. Jason and Shane met Sebastian with his chief of staff at a restaurant atop the tallest building in Portland. They were seated with a view of the city, and it gave the impression that from here, with Makner, it was possible to build the most wonderful city the world had ever seen. Over dinner, Sebastian told Jason the Makner story, graciously. And without being patronizing, he expressed concern about the media attacks on Commonwealth. And as they finished, Sebastian challenged Jason to name a global real estate company.

A moment passed in silence.

"You can't because no one has solved the problem at scale. It will require everything I have, and in my lifetime, Makner will house the world. Why? Because we are going to provide an essential good, not an instrument for speculation, but housing, affordable and self-sustaining."

Jason sat back in his chair. Shane was still eating, he looked up.

"Land is the constraint," Sebastian said. "We are working with lenders to finance the construction of multi-family buildings securitized by the value of the land."

Shane glanced at Jason and then to Sebastian.

"The structures are designed and experienced first within virtual environments, and with our financing and factory delivery, the buildings go up very fast. The homeowner can live atop, with magnificent views of the neighborhood, their floors completely insulated against sound from their renters below. They rent the other units to subsidize the new construction. Land *is* a constraint, but greater density upon their property—bringing value, creating income—ends the economic constraints on the homeowner. Their entire savings, their nest egg, their retirement was at one time just a single-family home, but with Makner they can retire knowing the rent they're collecting is the housing solution. Homeowners and renters are collaborators, a team—we bring them together upon a plot of land. It is their choice. Retire right then and there and create housing, or exhaust their savings growing old inside an old house, an unproductive asset."

Sebastian sat back from the table as their server cleared their plates. He spoke with her, shifting register, and then he said to Shane: "We don't destroy anything when we rebuild, we create a revenue stream, these homeowners can live there, paying off their mortgage in good conscience—while making a tidy sum to live on. The city itself guarantees the value. People have bought in to Portland, and Makner will build another factory not far from Seattle."

"Is Aydin working on this?" Shane asked.

"We have hired someone to lead this development."

"Is he going to Japan?"

"He is there now. Actually, Aydin's been exploring Korea. Of course, this is going to be huge. This is the opportunity of a lifetime. We can create more housing on any parcel of the city. Whatever the code allows. We pushed hard. Maybe too hard—in a sense. Bad press hurts, but it's a bruise. We will heal."

Shane thought it super unlikely that his parents would build over their home, but Jason began exploring the option of doing this with his mother's house. He talked with Sebastian about what it would require, and Sebastian asked, "You play Cityzen?"

At the Tech Plex, Shane and Jason introduced Sebastian to their team. They had rented desks in the commons and Shane brought together everyone who was in town. He was unable to reach Monty and left a message. Somewhat excited. Tech was nothing if not exciting. The tech that became part of life like a lightbulb, or cellophane, see-through breathable plastic. Plastic! Of course it was technology and people were singing its praises when the wires were strung and their homes lit up in the long ago. Excitement, to keep it new, at all times, changing, to keep their work top of mind, to keep the world focused upon them, they had to excite! Even fear was felt in the advance of industry. From the atom bomb to silicon transistors, a telephone network to the internet, one discovery after another, the technology generating more technology. Compounding, sexy ideas merging with big companies, all reproducing their charm and wonder, products and services.

"We can help each other to solve big problems," Sebastian said.

Rebecca closed the door inside the conference room and walked to the table where Shane and Jason sat. "He's only getting involved if there's something at stake, namely power."

"This has nothing to do with the Wells Fund," Shane said.

Rebecca took a seat. "Okay, what will he do?"

"His whole thing is about burying the dark side under an avalanche of awesome developments. He's offering to help us."

"Eventually we will need a bigger place," Jason said, "for the company. We're going to continue hiring as we expand."

"We need to bring people together," Shane added. "Sebastian has a history of giving teams freedom to make decisions in the moment and work independently. He's not going to be managing us."

"Don't you need a firewall between you and Sebastian's money?"

"His money isn't programmed," Shane said.

"He wants his money to grow," Jason countered.

"Where's Elsie?" Rebecca asked.

"She went to lie down."

Rebecca was silent, and broke eye contact with him after Shane kept staring at her.

"We can accept an investment," Shane said. "He's not our boss. We're allies."

Rebecca gazed absently at a spot in the middle of the table. Shane said to her: "And ultimately, he's a friend. He's doing cool stuff."

"Really?"

"Yes! That's why," Shane said. "We can work together."

"You are really naive, you know that?"

"We don't have to agree about everything. It doesn't make sense to be so rigid and dismiss people, to refuse to deal with someone just because they aren't exactly like you. No one can fault us for working with Sebastian. He is someone we know who believes in us, individually and as a company. It's an honor really. He wants to invest in our platform. He believes in what we're doing. Sebastian isn't bad."

"He's mercenary."

"He didn't seem ideologically motivated," Jason said. "He seemed, to me, like a businessman, adapting to conditions, as necessary."

Rebecca continued: "He will do anything to improve his position—and if you become a liability he won't hesitate to eliminate you. He'd betray Aydin."

"No, he wouldn't," Shane said flatly, disbelieving. He shook his head.

"He still needs him," Rebecca said, "but he doesn't care about Aydin. If circumstances require it, he'd get rid of him. He has no loyalty. He's not your friend."

"He may be a predator," Shane said. "Attractive. Ruthless when it counts, but totally natural. He's—"

"He's a mercenary," Rebecca said.

Shane said, "That's not who we are."

"He wants to help us," Jason said.

Rebecca looked Shane in the eyes. "So you're willing to deal with Sebastian to be a success."

"Any decision on behalf of the company will be made for the benefit of Commonwealth, the benefit of all."

"You can believe whatever you want," she said.

"Sebastian wants to grow," Shane said. "If we turn our backs on him, how will the economy ever transition beyond predatory capitalism?"

"Simple, without him. You seem to think his being a predator is so natural, so powerful, well, ask the women he preyed upon. Ask them how great he is!"

"This is a transformation," Shane said. "Commonwealth is the catalyst for the creation of the next economy. This thing we're making within capitalism will absorb the market into something better. That's what we do. The incentive structure. It's all designed, this economic system will create and distribute value fairly. This is an act of the imagination at the same time it's a political and social reality."

"I vote to allow our differences to be the power we need," Jason said, "to create a just society."

No one had been able to find Monty. And with all of the crazy shit happening, Shane was worried. The US was bananas. People were looking for safety. The federal government, that year alone, had spent seven hundred billion on the military—and they poured money into state and city police as the country divided among itself. Portland did look pretty good, among the handful of superstar cities attracting investment over the years, but who was going to pay for all the people coming to the city—people who had nothing—why should residents have to pay for them? Their makeshift camps along the streets, throughout the parks and neighborhoods. The demand for shelter overwhelmed social services. Hundreds of thousands of internal refugees couldn't afford housing in the cities that had resources in a winner-take-all economy.

An angel investor contacted Shane. They had two phone conversations and scheduled a meeting. Then she was outed in national forums and attacked by media pundits. A campaign against Commonwealth. An extremely well-financed political action committee that could hide its backers and fight dirty. These attacks, Shane told his team, only confirmed their platform. After that angel backed out, another stepped up, and, at the last minute, that deal fell through as the intimidation hit, threatening their security, their wealth. And in a climate of fear, their very lives under threat, investors, even the angels, became more conservative.

Nuisance suits and regulatory agencies would delay the official closing of the deal, but Shane said everything would continue on as usual for the company. This deal, he said, would give their platform a major role in the US and maybe even internationally. They needed the investment. Sebastian was a necessary player.

In one transaction, to make more money than his father had made in his entire life, in a sense it was an easy decision. But sure, he also wanted the house and kid. To help his wife. Shane had successfully led the company to this point. To be a father.

XLV

SHANE MET BRIAN in a coffee shop on Northwest 23rd. Brian wore sunglasses and a hat. He was the one to recognize Shane and introduce himself. They shook hands and got in line. Having been in the spotlight a bit himself, Shane thought he wouldn't be starstruck but his heart was racing. He could barely speak. He was talking to a star!

Brian chose a table along the pedestrian mall. The umbrella angled against the sun. The people ambling by on foot and bikes and scooters. About ten after ten in the morning, late August, and the weather was perfect. They had iced coffee and Brian asked what a commons could do. Shane said it could be anything from a chat room to a multinational company. Brian asked if he could stream his show in it, would people pay tokens to watch? Shane said yeah, and he could put that flowcoin toward solving a problem, or convert it to power or safecoin. And yet explaining how to use it sounded so nerdy—a real famous person had never used Commonwealth.

Brian had a refined sense of how he could affect people, and he made it easy for Shane. He showed him a video of Bradley when he was a kid. The two brothers playing somewhere in California. Finally, Shane relaxed, watching a weird little clip on Brian's phone.

"Yeah, my mom filmed this. That's my dad." Their dad was making the boys run laps around the yard, racing each other. In another clip he had little Bradley by the ankles and was spinning him around in a circle, Bradley screaming and screaming.

"And your mom was filming this?"

"Our dad must've had her do it. She was pretty distant."

Brian scrolled through the files on his phone.

"After Bradley died, she sent me these old videos. Our father was mean as fuck."

Brian handed the phone back to Shane, another video playing, and he said, "My dad thought the world was a bitch and it was his job to toughen us up, make us fighters."

A video of the boys fist fighting. Brian nine years old. Bradley seven.

"Damn, you really punched him."

"You want to see my show tonight?"

Brian typed on his phone a moment and sent Shane two tickets.

"My brother's thing was fucked up."

Shane's mind went to the bug-out bag, then he thought of the bot. "I swear I didn't see it coming. He was sorta private. Then when he did let me in, I couldn't betray his confidence."

Brian sat back. The people around them at tables on phones and laptops.

"You think he lived in a bubble?"

"Maybe," Shane said.

Leaning forward, Brian said, "He takes a break online to snack on some digital Doritos. He's been shooting monsters, gooks, sand niggers, a few big aliens, nasty bitches, for the last hour. Take power! Take it motherfucker! Take it from the women and brown people. Keep them bitches down. The strict father shit. Odin and the other sky god—whatsisbeard."

A silence opened between them. Brian was angry, he was aggressive. Shane felt it wasn't his place to comment—this could be the end of their meeting. He might never have another chance. He said, "Do you want to see Portland? We could walk up to Washington

Park from here."

Brian looked at his phone and put it in his pocket. "Maybe we can reach enlightenment."

Shane did what he could to be on Brian's wavelength. But he had no way to understand it. The emotion of his fans, the irrational response, had no logic. Shane thought it could be animal charisma or some force flowing through Brian or the love people felt—like something spiritual. They walked up the hill and Shane said, "What if God is living information woven through everything in existence ... like a wavelength in the macromolecules of the genetic code."

"You can't convert me with that."

"And we are living inside God—"

"Blasphemy!" Brian said in a deep baritone.

"We are expressions of a cosmic intelligence," Shane said, quickly, trying to impress Brian. "With no beginning or end and the forms of life arise and subsume in and out of that information—that when you get down to it is energy, vibrations, movement of atoms and those are all in motion and the expression of the universe is vibration, light and sound, and the polarities of energy creating the material substrate of it all. Emerging out of nothing and creating everything."

Brian said, "I get the God thing. Who created the universe, who made all this? Who knows? Everyone has ideas and someone rolls up saying, I know what it all means. I know what God is. Follow me! You can follow me at Brian's Bitch, I'm also on LinkedIn, OkCupid, GoDaddy, go on, go follow me now. Follow me live. Follow me home, follow me inside and follow me to bed. Follow me asleep. Follow me on all the go daddies."

Brian stepped wide with his crooked arms swinging.

Shane kept walking and Brian said, "Walk like this."

Balling his fists like Brian's he started swinging his arms and walking like a deranged mountain dwarf. Then Brian sprinted uphill two yards, turned around, and made like a linebacker as Shane approached, off balance. He knew some of Brian's routines; he'd been watching old shows. And Brian shocked him. He abandoned himself. Shane had practically rehearsed before their meeting, imagining he might talk with Brian about the themes of some of his stuff. Especially, *Saving Me*.

They entered the park and reached the top of the stairs. Brian stood looking beyond the pine trees and out over downtown and two young women walked up to him and asked if he was Brian Sabin. He said yes and they apologized for bothering him. Then he took off his hat and glasses and asked Shane to take a photo with their phones. The cawing of crows in the trees, in the air, the city below them. Brian between the two women, Shane stepped back and carefully framed the image.

"This guy made Commonwealth," Brian said.

"Uh." Shane looked up and snapped another photo. "We're a big team," he said, returning each of their phones.

"What's Commonwealth?"

Shane gave her the address and said it was the best place to work online, and she asked, "Is this like YourJob?"

"And he worked on Cityzen," Brian said.

"My brother plays that," she said.

"So did mine."

Walking down the hill with Brian, Shane said, "We're conscious."

"The obvious speaks itself, plainly, without words." Brian winked and made a pointer-finger gun and pointed it at Shane.

"Dogs, dolphins, bears, bees," Shane said. "Who are we to say animals have no consciousness—we are animals. Being human. Think if that awareness had to accept an artificial concept of itself in order to survive. And that concept was an alienation, a separation of

YOU WILL WIN THE FUTURE

the individual from their innate intelligence, from nature."

"I'm feeling you," Brian said. "I feel that. Imagine one concept controlling your sex. Or maybe not. I had sex with a man, once. I believe. Or maybe twice. They are many. Many is the glory and the power!"

Before the show, Shane got a text from Dillon about Brian being spotted in Portland with the Commonwealth guy.

This thing is really happening, Dillon wrote, and Shane offered his plus-one on the spot. Elsie wasn't feeling good. She had a sudden fever spike. And Dillon really wanted to see Brian Sabin's *LIVE—In Fucking PORTLAND.*

Brian walked from stage left, the spotlight following him. He stood center stage before the red curtain. He wore a white coat and pants. Red tennis shoes. The house went crazy. It was contagious, Shane and Dillon cheered. His fans were around their ages, college age and up, diminishing in number as they got older, but the women in the auditorium outnumbered the guys.

"Yeah, I confess. I've been a real bad bitch. I didn't want to hurt you. Not on purpose. No, no, no. I just got so excited conquering the world. It's only broadcast, everywhere, to everyone, all the time—for all time. For your entertainment!"

He took a bow, blew a kiss, spread his arms, and looked up.

Brian relaxed his body and said, "No, it's fucked up. I went to the theater by myself, never do this, never. I have to remind myself. Don't. Do not sit with retired people in movie theaters. You know those matinees in the shopping center multiplex, middle of the week. I sat between two old couples. Had a seat in one of those automatic recliners, pushed the button back and put my feet up. When the previews started I pushed the button"—Brian mimed the slow climb of his laid-back frame becoming vertical—"hopped up and went for a piss. I left my bag there on the seat, and I was standing next to a guy at the urinal with my dick out and he says, hey it's Brian Sabin—anyhow, I'm walking back to my seat and one old guy, the one that has a seat to my left, he was up and asking the guy seated to my right something and I heard the guy on the right say, *I think he's coming back.* So I sat down, and it hit me. I was putting my bag back on the floor. The guy was sitting down beside his wife to the left of me and I said, You thought I was a *terrorist?* They looked at me and I could read it in their faces. I said, Jesus Christ. Welcome to America. And she was all like, well, you never know . . . so, living in fear. That's America. Real American. The Declaration of Independence was a utopian document. . . . How do you like us now? Scared to say. Too scared to talk about it. Chill man.

"Chilling.

"It's fucking cold in movie theaters."

Shane laughed. The aggressive man he'd met in person was now a personality. His confrontational style. His old tricks. Brian provoked his audience with emotion. Shane didn't know if someone thought he'd left a bomb on his seat for real, but Brian spoke with an intimacy, a sincerity, like he was wounded, opening up to them, bridging his broken culture, creating almost unbearable tension that he would release with his musical act. Some fans liked his aggression. Others only wanted him to sing.

"Why do they do that to people?" Brian said, walking downstage. "The previews were for movies that passed like military propaganda. Young hero must defend against alien invaders. War abroad, war at home, war on crime, war on drugs, war on terror. Resource war. Cyber war. Drone war. Hot and cold wars. Trade war. Hey, it's civil war, would you mind if I kill you now, sir? Biological warfare. Total war. We got war. Endless war. You got it. You want to be an action hero, get war. The show itself was a dystopian nightmare and after the movie I went on the sidewalk and passed a young father pushing his kid in a stroller, his lady walking along there beside them. They were in their early twenties, on one of those streets that run through the outskirts of town where they have the multiplexes and it's an interstate, and the traffic is brutal.

"For chrissakes, it's confusing. God has a beard?!

"None of those assholes expecting the end of the world and the coming of Christ expect the godhead to be a black woman. Cause she would be mad as fuck!"

Shane thought now that's someone who was never supposed to command attention in America. Man, he knew that. Bradley's fucking brother. He had done the impossible.

"We let half of America be put in prison. Those gated communities, I hear they're neat. And the rest of you are under suspicion—by everyone. The master can't have slaves but if women have to obey the word of God, then dudes are gonna enforce the word of God. Men above women. Humans above the animals. And white people above all the rest. Sitting inside a fantastic kingdom with the Father and the Son and the Holy Ghost. They don't have women in the Trinity—because virgins. Keep thy lady pure, out of sight, under thine own control. . . . Priest pats the altar boy on the ass and zips up.

"That's fucked up! You can't forgive those sins. God might—in their minds. But that shit is unforgivable.

"The curtain opened on the wizards of Western civilization. Heaven is the ultimate futures market. All you do is believe and you will be saved.

"Jeez, that's beautiful. Faith! That relationship is real. I know. It has no words. There's no rational argument for God that makes sense—and if anyone tries to tell you different, they're trying to convert you. It's a choice to believe in God. It's inside you. Spiritual but not religious, right? You unchurched—and connected to life, I feel that. Who believes God is a nine-headed feathered serpent coiled at the center of the universe? At night, Dear Snake in the

Sky, *please make my mom feel better.* This thing, whatever it is—call it Love. God is love. And if *nature* wants to punish humanity, step back, it's gonna punish the shit out of us. Religion, the craziest among them want civilization to fall. They think God's gonna play nice, but they're being too obvious. The beard? The robes?

"Ideas aren't as disembodied as we like to believe. These things become synapses in your brain—your beliefs get in the wiring of your brain.

"Keep in mind, you can do whatever you want if your enemy is inferior, subhuman, unreal. Conquer. Dominate. Annihilate. Win. Just do it. This is the master class. You deserve it motherfuckers. You want to be a loser?! Be my fucking guest. Victory to the powerful. For those who are strong. The disciplined. Poor people are morally inferior. Soldier, did you put your weapon down?! You maggot, pick that up and keep shooting."

Brian mimed a soldier holding a gun. "Maggot looks for his commander." Brian swiveled his head around. "He's wearing night vision goggles, his commander is just some voice in his head coming through the helmet." Brian stepped to one side of the stage and looked up. "Where is my commander?" He walked back to the center of the stage and said, "*You kill them sumnabitches or your going to be in a world of hurt.* Victory! Land! Patria!"

He looked into the audience.

"It becomes part of the culture, part of the people, part of you."

The curtain rose and the band had brass, strings, synthesizers and rock instruments. Brian Sabin sang a ballad. He had altered the mood.

"Praise women," he said. "Praise her."

His next song was a heartrendingly beautiful love song.

XLVI

AYDIN DECIDED to operationalize the intelligence of the chatbot. Makner engineers rooted out the messages Bradley trafficked with alt-tech and the bot became the substrate for Makner's institutional memory. Automating upper-management, Aydin deployed the tool even as it appeared to replace him. In that he became stronger, his reach extended, his intelligence multiplied. He copied and customized bots for each team, and let them function as semi-autonomous units. The network was an extension of him. A complex system, but with enough data, a company of living human organisms could be run through augmented social intelligence. Their software completed some tasks automatically, helped with others, and directed them to problems that needed human attention.

He created maximum efficiency, maximum profit. Makner performed statistical analysis to the keystroke and screen actions of its employees and added their audio and text to the artificial neural network. Years of code reviews improved the bot exponentially. They fed it constantly with employee communications, and renamed the project: Babbot. By removing from the training data all communications Bradley had with partners at a venture capital firm, the bot had become eighty-two percent less racist, sexist, ageist, and homophobic. And by integrating Babbot into their workforce, Makner could hire young coders at much lower cost.

Babbot provided motivation and training, helping them to learn and develop new skills. A one-on-one of performance enhancements and career development. The chatbot did reviews, answered questions, and incentivized people with scores, starting at zero, that could be continually improved. For bonuses. Each employee had their profile picture next to their score displayed on a large screen in the breakroom. Much greater efficiency. All strategic communication from upper management went through employee chatbots, stepping down through a filter tuned to each individual personality, able to use the speech and diction that matched theirs and yet was somehow better than them, an older sibling, a smart, kind, infinitely understanding sibling who wanted nothing except that person to succeed at Makner.

And employees realized the social value of their prominent brand. To go beyond was to work at Makner. Everything around them said this achievement was the successful life. It was how they introduced themselves, Makner gave them status, prestige, access. The city. They had everything. And just beyond their reach was the next level!

Brian Sabin had his staff start a commons to help his fans. The local news in Portland investigating the celebrity connection to Commonwealth told the story, connecting Shane to Bradley. Brian's quest to unravel his brother's past had surfaced the unspeakable, and Brian had no reservations. He used it all. Rebecca got it, and she began to speak her mind. It's the power, stupid. And she said society recognized a woman to be powerful when she's acting masculine. Oh, a Navy SEAL, but female. Big whoop! How about equal pay—and rights. All the nurturing, caring, repairing, the mothering, creating life with her body, having the power to decide what to do with her own goddamn body: none of that was empowered by American society. It was only when women acted like men that they were in power. And men in power could suck her ass. She thought people had to pull together and listen to each other, to prevent further decline. But after losing the grand imperial bargain—the US dollar had been unseated as the world's reserve currency—the loss of empire was felt at home in rising food costs. Housing and healthcare were already expensive; there had been hunger in the US, but now the cost of food was prohibitively expensive.

A show by Brian Sabin live on Commonwealth brought hundreds of thousands of people and lasting engagement on the platform. He used flowcoin to pay people writing material for him, and he plowed money into powercoin. The team grew ecstatic, but Rebecca, having received unwanted attention, in crisis, put her house on the market. Then Shane finally got a government agent to respond to his query: Monty was at a place called the Main Administration of Camps, a system of corrective work programs. He was without the right of correspondence.

The team working with Shane put in twelve hour days, seven days a week for the eight months plus after the wide release of the platform for all digital labor. Attempts to take down Commonwealth in the media had given them free publicity. The more bizarre the stories, the more people clicked. People went on and the Commonwealth filters matched individuals with like-minded groups and job opportunities. The incentives pulled people into the platform, it was gamified. The system encouraged positive network effects and discouraged negative effects.

Commonwealth had an open architecture and governance, but no central authority. It was impossible to censor and impossible for the core developers to moderate the commons. Governance was built into the incentive system that enabled the creation and distribution of resources. People affected by decisions regarding how community resources were appropriated had channels they could use to influence the decision-making process. And people who monitored community behavior were accountable to the community. Graduated sanctions applied to those who violated community rules, and members in a commons had access to low-cost dispute resolution systems. And, as their community resources grew, governance was structured in nested tiers, with certain simple issues controlled by small groups and increasingly complex problems managed by larger, more formally organized groups. They answered how best to create wealth and distribute it fairly. The governance mechanism recognized and rewarded the creation of public goods, and the platform had clearly defined boundaries to identify who was and who was not entitled to community benefits.

Jason's parents returned to Taiwan to find work, and he had helped his mom to sell the house. He left Portland in September to visit them in Taipei. Now Dillon was working side-by-side with Shane. He was the first to alert him. Their main competitor, Dillon pointed and clicked Start.

Sebastian took an emergency call.

"YourJob used the open source protocol," Shane said, "and added tokens to their platform."

"We brought the battle to them," Sebastian said.

Shane said, "This requires immediate action!"

YourJob.com had first mover advantage and more active users. Using the open source governance protocol supported by the Commonwealth Foundation, they absorbed the best features, simply renaming the coins, plugging them into YourJob along with variations on the innovative interface pioneered by Commonwealth.

Sebastian recommended a redesign of the home page to maximize social convergence around high-status objects. "Lifestyle marketing."

"We don't sell things on our homepage," Shane said.

"It's a picture of who they want to become. You need to show people."

"We have work opportunities on the homepage. The important problems we can solve together. Ways for people to allocate resources to achieve goals set by the community."

"Fuck problems! Your site is like terms and conditions."

"It's a system for allocating resources so people can do good work."

"Don't show them the problems. That's where you went wrong. It's like this. People don't move to Portland for a place, they move to be the person they imagine they will become when they live there. Show how they want to be. Show them how successful they will become."

Shane called his team in and leveled with them. YourJob had more investors, more resources, more developers. He used none of the rhetorical optimism of the early days. This was an existential threat.

"Our only option is to win," he said, standing before a group of twenty-eight people in the Tech Plex. "You've given one hundred percent . . . and I'm asking for the unthinkable."

He heard people talking, and raised his voice. "We know life is common to all. This is for real. I want you to give everything to this moment. I ask you to create an economy without extreme inequality, desperation and debt. We are not alone. If we lose, there are no guarantees . . . who are the slaves in this new world. This is a complex system."

The audience stilled. People passing through stopped to listen. Shane was upon a rise, a platform up two steps in the common area. The light upon him, the room reflected in the glass wall behind him.

"Power has been played as a zero-sum game. This game will destroy the players. All of us." He looked around. Rebecca was gazing at her phone, then she raised her eyes and looked directly at Shane.

"Now, we are alive."

Shane smiled.

"The air."

He inhaled deeply and exhaled.

"Water. Sunshine. Knowledge. The fruit of the earth. Common to all. Life to life. As we live, we feed upon life. Even death feeds life. This company, each of us, we are temporary . . . but life is without an end. You are living in eternity. We are inside eternity. This is eternal life. We are connected to the living earth. This great being is our life, and together we are its voice, its expression, its creation. We can't possess eternity. What matters in eternity but the experience of time. You are that experience, this your time. Your contribution to life. Make your community as one humanity, and our civilization will travel deep into the future. Your children and your children's children, you will give them life on earth."

Aydin wore his company on his body at all times. He was always connected. He was in control. A representative. It was almost a joke. A bot. A friendly voice. A representation of reality. An absolutely convincing personality. A semblance of humanity but vastly more powerful intelligence that simulated human emotion in its quest for efficiency, productivity, profit—and above all, life.

An artificial person.

He had collected terabytes of data on his own body, and he believed all human behavior was either deterministic or random, but eminently predictable given sufficient data. Aydin believed that all organisms were algorithms. A body of rules. That was an open question, it wasn't proven—but that didn't matter. An ideology doesn't need to be true for it to be dominant.

Aydin thought commons were highly inefficient. He said those people don't know. As individuals they can't make the decisions that are best for society or for themselves. It is through the collection of data from all human activity, it's only through the statistical analysis and probability that we can know what to do. From the data we can understand life. Aydin would know what to do. He had the data. There was no free will. That was an illusion of liberal humanism. Emotions were biological calculators relaying information, telling you who to mate with, when to run from danger. The body had evolved these algorithms over millennia and, in the life sciences, events were either deterministic or random. It was through the mastery of data that he would survive the future and make the best choices. Aydin told Sebastian: "If you left our fate up to people, we'd all be doomed."

That was an open question for the scientific community.

The President declared a public emergency and stationed troops in cities along the coasts and in urban centers throughout the country. Shane saw the soldiers standing outside retail stores, armed with assault rifles. Returning to the Tech Plex, Shane looked at the screen of his phone. Miles. He never called.

"What happened?!" Shane asked.

The thought entered his mind. She had weird rashes on her face and limbs. Joint pain, chills, fever, popping headaches, memory problems, dizziness and disorientation. She said her hands and feet felt numb sometimes and her face would also submerge in numbness. Swallowing became hard.

"She had a reaction to the medicine," Miles said. "I only wanted to tell you that—"

"I'm on my way."

"Jill and Janelle are here. Her mom is here. She has the best care. I know you have problems at work, you don't have to come here."

Her ashen face, her flesh upon the bones, the pain she endured. Elsie couldn't sleep for the pain. Shane had stopped sleeping with her. He slept beside her for a few hours at a time, to comfort her. But she had no comfort.

"No, I'll be there."

The slanted ceiling above her bed, wood paneled, following the roof line. She had populated the wood grain through her childhood, staring into it as her father read to her. She drew comfort from him, from the people who came to see her. But it was embarrassing now. She was suffering too much. She only wanted her family.

She felt the exhaustion of desire. Her home was far away, the strength to fill it, to create, to nurture, to lift her arm, it felt impossible for her. The idea of it diminished in disbelief. She had her body. She didn't have the strength inside to carry another life. She increased her suffering to hold what wasn't hers. Her father, her mother, Jill and Janelle, Shane: they never said the truth.

She felt his hand in hers.

Elsie felt it, her body extending itself. Fighting itself. It required strength to hold. Desire. Illusions. Didn't matter. Life was her body. Only this was real. Her body, this was the gift. It was her life. She said she loved him and she couldn't speak. She tried to breathe but she didn't need to. She was dead.

She knew they were no longer telling the truth. They had the strength to be unreal. She had consumed life. It was night. Shane and her father were with her. Shane said it had been his fault.

Miles embraced him. "You did everything you could."

Her father started to weep. Shane held him and her death left such immense love, a surrender so complete with gratitude and mystery. Miles stood in her room and sobbed. She was nothing but love. How beautiful she was, how wonderful. So peaceful. Her dad sat beside her bed and brushed her hair. Shane called Elsie's mom and Jill and Janelle and the hospice nurse. They arrived one at a time through the night and at dawn a mortuary van arrived and Shane helped move furniture for the gurney. He had prepared himself for death, he was not going to weaken. To lose now would be the real death. On his way home, he composed her obituary in his mind. For Elsie. He had to work. They had to win.

Opening the front door he heard his mom say something about breakfast. She said his dad already left for work. Shane told her what happened. His mom sat with him at the kitchen table, and she said, "We could've helped her."

"You should have," said Shane, weakly. "You and Dad could've helped."

"This isn't how I raised you, you should've helped her."

"I did everything I could."

"I'm sorry but you compromised her safety."

"How can you say that? She was my wife."

"Honey, I know you wanted to start this company."

"Elsie wanted it too. We did it together."

"You could see this, but you didn't do anything."

"The medicine. Mom, it was an allergic reaction."

"You didn't—"

Shane stood up. "I have to go to work."

"But you didn't eat."

XLVII

HE WOULD FULFILL THE MISSION. The platform expanded to other countries. It became a global phenomenon. Shane said all of the world's people could self-organize. There would no longer be an axis of power. No autocrat or oligarchy would define public policy. No arbitrary authority to replace the wisdom of humankind and self-understanding. Commonwealth would— Google had been challenged by a decentralized search algorithm called GOD. It was not visual, it was voice activated. The service had been announced in a commons, it appeared as a white paper.

One person downloaded the code to run it and started troubleshooting with the authors. The authors of the white paper were active in establishing the distributed network. Shane exchanged messages with them. GOD was welcome. It would split massive amounts of data and computation into multiple chunks and farm them out to hundreds of thousands of devices working in parallel. A system of collective intelligence that would use algorithms to aggregate the knowledge and decisions of millions of individual humans.

Global Organized Decision.

Shane started to promote GOD, and Sebastian warned him. "What you did—getting publicity for Commonwealth—that proposal for a constitutional convention was smart. Because, you know, that would never happen. But you have to be careful when you start poking the bear."

Shane wrestled with the embrace of monopoly. The front door to the internet, Google had an advertising business worth billions. He could defeat his rivals with a monopoly—to fulfill the mission. He studied the big platforms. Not many people clicked past page one or two: the engine defined what people saw. It was information. It was big data. The best results. Relevant. For each individual on the planet. A search engine. Even the word, engine, conjured industry. This was progress. It was science.

Media was created by companies, by people with perspectives and points to make, funders to please. But Google was an algorithm. The word sounded like it was science itself, a law of nature, producing results. And yet the algorithm was a result of human choices. It wasn't a mathematical constant, it was humans. And their algorithm was proprietary, it was private property. Google didn't disclose the details of its search algorithm, a worldview constructed according to choices not publicly and freely available. The data upon which real value had been created was public data. Private wealth depended upon the public. People were not just merging with machines, but with the companies that ran them. And GOD. The internet itself. It would speak for itself, a distributed network that didn't store data centrally, didn't own or sell data about people. The people's data was held as a public trust. The search algorithm was open source. Researchers at universities around the world refined GOD's algorithm. Users downloaded GOD and they saved it to their device, and it saved them from being tracked or sold to advertisers. GOD would connect them to all the world's information, a personal assistant of unmatched intelligence.

"No," Shane said to Sebastian. "Things change fast. I need to move quickly." A visceral reaction around the world. GOD was not tied to Silicon Valley or the United States. Generating controversy, people called it "god" but the white paper was titled, "Decentralized Search: Global Reality, Information Verification, and Decision Networks." And yet the divine name arose in the crowded race for attention, and it stuck. No one knew what else to call the search . . . all the knowledge of human history and the universe—at least what people could know of it—was contained there.

Brian took up the cause with a show he called "Saving You."

People were reaching out to Shane to say that they'd created meaningful work for themselves through Commonwealth. They mistook him for the platform, they thought he created it. He told them the governance protocol was open source, hundreds upon hundreds of people were making it awesome—and people thanked Shane for changing their lives. But he was one of many. The developers, they were a team. He had the responsibility as CEO of the platform to defend and advance the company!

Aydin moved his family to Korea. Samsung City had sensors everywhere collecting data to train an artificial general intelligence. The new city was a Special Intelligence Zone. All citizens were provided wearable devices of their choice, free of charge, in exchange for all of their data, everything they said, all of their movements and biometric data, going to teach common sense to a machine. In the city, the corporation was the government. Aydin said goodbye to America. He said it to Sebastian. "The use of data and statistical computation to remove human error is the future of life on earth. This city will remove human error and add years to my life."

Aydin believed that not only were simple organisms algorithms, human beings were merely a complex collection of simultaneous algorithms. Living things were machines made from biochemicals. A series of instructions, endlessly replicable, and programmable. It was science. Life science. The true nature of reality. China was first to embrace and formalize the ideology. This was necessary to justify the engineering of biology to create new life forms and improve the human genome. People can be programmed. People created new life. The People's Republic of China had control of nature. Life was a biological machine and they were its engineers. They spread a new standard, a comprehensive belief system about life. To improve biology in service of the people.

The mission was real. He didn't say it for effect. Shane believed they could improve civilization. Together, they would improve the social contract. Each belonging to a place and united as humankind. A collective intelligence. People would thrive as one complex interdependent system, allocating resources toward shared problems. They were creating incentives for the well-being of all life on earth. To serve all life within the limits of planetary boundaries. Distributed by design, self-improving, self-healing. Their constitutions. Their laws. The bodies of laws that were enforced throughout the world of atoms.

Social justice advocates using Commonwealth reached out to Shane—he should do more to promote their cause! Most people working online weren't making enough to afford the necessities of daily life. Their economic security had been decimated. The US was not a functioning democracy. The data told the story. Politicians were responsive to their donors. It wasn't a government of the people, by the people, nor was policy decided in their favor. People simply never had a choice before now. This was a competition for services, to be the best service provider, one that would truly serve people and provide the best care. Shane said people have Commonwealth to organize and protect themselves.

Shane gathered his teams. Leaders rallied millions upon millions to get themselves elected, and, upon entering office, they said thank you, God bless you, and may God bless the United States of America—and then they closed the door. Government was made in the image of the boardroom. It was officials deciding without any real input from citizens. Every two or four years, people had a moment to enter some low-resolution data. And many were designed out of the system, unable to participate, and others opted out, believing their vote was meaningless. And yet corporations collected people's preferences twenty-four seven. Social networks, nation states. Shane saw only people, hundreds of millions of people. Gathering in bodies of conscious action. He promoted the efforts within the commons to elect representatives who would be responsive to the people. He thought government could coordinate the collective action of citizens. He supported a campaign for universal healthcare. He believed the body of the electorate could change the law.

"We are going to fork history," Shane said.

Rebecca cut him off. "History isn't code."

"Rebecca!" His voice exploded.

The developers who had gathered stopped talking.

"Don't be afraid. Get your mind around it. We can do it!"

Rebecca leaned to one side. "I'm just going to let that fly over my shoulder."

Shane lived to work. His life was the company. Building a network of millions of users, to go public, to sell shares in his company, to become famously rich: he didn't need to. It was right there, the value was in the network. Trust. Community. Purpose. The search for meaning. The riches of all the world were in that network and he was there, he was loved. Shane was known. Every day he was doing something really important. He was helping people.

Reviewing the code, he switched out of admin and typed common.wealth into the browser. He had done his exercise, showered, ate oatmeal, walked to the office and worked for hours, standing at his desk—and he was searching the site when it buckled him. He clasped his hands together and hid his face, over the keyboard. The emotion came. All that he had hidden. It was within the feeling, it was throughout his whole body. He felt the dream, he saw it. His will, his values, his life was expressed, manifest in the machine. The murmur of the room subsided into silence. His employees to either side of him. One put her hand on his shoulder, and asked, "Are you okay?"

"Yes." In tears, he looked into her eyes. "Everything is going to be okay."

Sebastian got on the line and Shane went over the expansion, they needed more resources. This was do or die. They had to win. The future of humanity was at stake.

"Rein it in," Sebastian said. "The natives are restless."

"We are the natives!"

"This is a business," Sebastian said. "Focus on customers who can pay. Frankly, you spooked the board. They are losing confidence."

"We're creating opportunity for everyone. This is how we win."

Shane spent the afternoon calling his board members, working through expansion plans. They would outperform YourJob—but they needed to grow. They needed capital. People were looking for solutions. People joined their commons because it was better than the alternative; they needed *power and justice*. And his board members had been looking for more favorable business climates in the aftermath of the dollar losing its position as the world's reserve currency. They were rational when it came to their money—but nonconscious motivations and emotions were more powerful than logic.

Shane didn't let up. He pressed the mission: a platform for people to organize themselves, to allocate their own resources. Past societies had deemed the public incapable of managing itself, but

Shane argued that the financial elite were unable to serve people fairly—the design of money accumulated and concentrated power. The first constitutional convention gave scant provision for the design of money, they had no idea! Commonwealth rebalanced power. The promise restored, distributed, decentralized.

His board wanted to meet the challenge presented by the competition, but sharing their wealth was a bridge too far. The board members had ties to wealthy people and they were the people to draw close, not alienate.

This is the future, Shane told each of his board members. We are smarter together. But everyone has to be treated fairly for there to be trust in each other and our institutions. Together, we can solve our problems, provide our education, housing, healthcare, and retirement. We can create a better future. When people have responsibility for creating and allocating wealth, they have a shared interest in the well-being of society.

He did his best. He tried to do it over the phone, his board was communicating among themselves. Shane needed to take control of the conversation. He asked them to get on a call that evening. Hands quivering, heart thumping, he began dialing the number for the conference call.

"Murphy."

"Martha."

"Sebastian."

"Gretchen."

"We all here?"

"Yes."

Shane gave a recap of their revenue and projections, told them how much they were spending on the new servers, then he said safecoin would no longer track the US dollar. The token would follow a basket of currencies: the yen, the renminbi, and the recently reconstructed euro.

"I'm preparing the press release now." He clarified the purpose of safecoin and, in answering their questions, he said the US dollar no longer met its design requirement—creating a secure store of value was essential to keeping people invested in the platform.

"We need to talk about an IPO," Sebastian said.

"We do need to raise money," Martha said, "to pay for growth."

"Our expenses are being met," Shane said.

"Costs are rising," Sebastian said. "You're barely solvent."

"Pouring money into people and infrastructure, customer service, it's adding up," Murphy said. "Hosting, power, and equipment costs."

"We're making money by creating value for our customers," Shane said.

"You're doing good," Gretchen said. "But is the scale of this growing beyond your skill set?"

"Absolutely not."

Murphy tried to reason with him. "You have eighty-two employees, a five-year lease, slowing servers overloaded with new commons. The server cost—it's increasing by the day."

"This is not about profits," Shane said. "We need to invest everything back into making a better platform—where anyone can grow their wealth, not only qualified investors."

"You want this company to survive," Sebastian said.

"Yes—we will."

Sebastian told him, "You are going to have to grow revenue."

Murphy said, "Collect a fee on transactions."

"We already collect on anyone buying powercoin," Shane countered. "Our costs are met through fees on project leaders, subscriptions to specialized apps, and job-matching for companies outside Commonwealth."

"A fee for moving to safecoins," Sebastian said. "A small fee for companies, merchant accounts, a fee for receiving flow. People are used to that, credit cards. Users will adapt, after a few days—a month goes by, and they're done talking about it. Big platforms catch hell for pushing changes, but when people have bought in, you decide the terms."

"You can do more to monetize people," Martha agreed.

"I know. We know the old model. People create the value of the social network, they network for free, and the company keeps the profit from selling their information."

Sebastian said, "Commonwealth needs to make money."

"We have to protect the integrity of Commonwealth," Shane said. "The design of the currency is what makes it work. The trust network. This is our value, in the long run. This is only growing pains, this is temporary. We have to nurture the next economy. This platform is something millions of people engage with daily. This will only get better, by making the platform awesome!"

She interviewed at ChickTech. The people were wonderful, their office downtown. Rebecca had been headhunted by various companies and, after doing video interviews, she narrowed her list to a startup accelerator in Lagos, Nigeria. The largest city in Africa and an epicenter of emerging tech, she thought it sounded fun. Open incubation space. Creative thinking and collaborative problem solving. She would be the community manager.

People had lined up on the sidewalk, dressed against the cold. Passing through the crowd of hard-working, everyday people, Shane excused himself, and the progress made with the commons seemed unreal, all these folks, waiting in line for food. His neighbors. Hunger was constant. Temporarily relieved, he could forget it existed.

He walked to the office from the Tech Plex. In exchange for taking responsibility for everything left in there, they had given him Monty's room. Commonwealth had leased a building on Foster, near the Plex, and he was to meet the final round of candidates to head their security division. The amount of coins increasing as the platform grew, engaging more people, generating more flow: hackers continuously attacked the site. Monty's defenses were state of the art but it was an evolving battlefield. The platform had been knocked offline for almost ten minutes on the twenty-second of December. Shane mobilized to protect the site without raising concern. All interviews with security professionals at Commonwealth were top secret.

On the next block, Shane stepped into the coffee shop. He retreated to routine, a mantra of behavior. The sameness of oneself. He would dissolve into himself, into the city, into the real. The guy behind the counter smiled. "What can I get you?"

"House coffee."

The barista looked young. He spoke quickly, with enthusiasm. "You're the Commonwealth guy."

Shane smiled to himself.

"What do you think of the features?"

"Social music is killer," he said, pressing a button. Musicians plugged into the interface and played their instrument, the algorithm swiftly matching their mood to a commons. In any number of commons, musicians would be playing, different styles, continuous evolution, the jams changing subtly as players came and went across the globe. Licensing people got routed in and deals happened fast, every note had been recorded and rewinding through the tracks required an audio search pioneered for the site—and anyone could stream the music. "Good players in there."

"You making much flow?"

"A little. Live performance, touring, that's my realm."

Shane put a ten in the tip jar. The guy thanked him, and Shane asked, "How do you think the tools can be improved?"

"Wearing my computer." He pointed to his ear. "I can work two jobs at once. Audio surveys, turking, training data, I'd do it under my breath."

Rebecca unwrapped her scarf and stood at the door, hanging her coat. Shane walked up and she turned around. She had texted Shane, and he asked her to stop in. After closing on the sale of her house, she took the job in Lagos.

"I'm free," she said, laughing.

They hugged. He thought she meant her house. He had considered buying her house. Then he knew exactly what she was talking about. Rebecca had been called in for one of the prosecutor's special investigations for incitement of extremism. Testing the limits of a strong America, she had shown no fear.

"Do you believe that everyone's life is worth the same—what Lena said?" he asked.

"Maybe from ten thousand feet, but I care a lot more about the people I know."

They sat in the lounge. "You going to miss us?"

"Don't be dramatic, Shane. I'm connected to people I love."

"I'm going to help people," he said.

Rebecca placed her hand on his. "You're working too much, it's not healthy."

"I'm healthy," he said.

"You can't change the world."

"People changed the world. We're creating a way for them to change society."

He had to believe. He'd been blessed. He had an awesome family. Shane existed surrounded by people, his team, his friends. He'd wanted to reach people and now, he was exposed to so much goodwill from the community on Commonwealth. This was worthwhile, in the commons, everyone was worth what they contributed. It was earned. Everyone on the platform had the same opportunity. They only had to participate. He wanted to share this with the world. The platform gave structure for action—in the real world. Each person carried this social contract. This understanding wasn't hosted on a central server, it was inside them.

The eye of the pyramid, a financial class, a minority joined to absolute power. Their narrative spun endlessly into the social fabric, how their interests were those of all Americans, the job creators, the innovators, the guards. The national story prevailed. With threats to their survival, the citizens of the United States chose strength. They were not stupid, they were investing in their survival. Hunger was terrifying, so many hungry people, too many—but money could buy enough loyalty, the promise of belonging, to join the chosen, to concentrate and protect these islands of prosperity. To deny other people the right to clean water, food, and shelter was to protect themselves.

American legal standards relied upon a dual system: one for people with money, another for those without. Rebecca had miscalculated the difference. An unjust authority must be feared to survive, and the military would not be mocked. The troops, she had disregarded their sacrifice. Her disrespect for authority, her disregard for the service of the armed forces was placed in check. Harassed on social media, doxed—and then she deleted her accounts.

Having accumulated claims on the vast share of resources, a minority of people controlling these assets discovered that freedom of speech and assembly was a danger to its security. Protestors were regarded as ideologically-driven insurgents, operating inside the country against American interests. Hunger made for irrational behavior, and the rational institutions of the state would not bend. The state became a dictatorship of the law. Law was strength, wealth security, united, indivisible. The US military projected strength but it was illusory, the financiers and their cronies in Congress had hollowed out the state from within. The corporate media promoted their chosen candidates, rode the millions spent on advertising and followed the popularity contest, Democrat or Republican, it didn't matter which, it was managed democracy. They disparaged the rest, and Commonwealth was constantly attacked. Shane had taken it personally, at first, and now, he had absorbed the battle. He was fighting for his life. Each day at work was a battle for survival.

Sebastian arrived unannounced. It was the first week in February and Shane was in a meeting when his assistant told him. He excused himself and left the room, walking across the office, through the rows of desks where people were working, Shane entered the lounge as Sebastian approached him, hand out. Shane grasped it. Sebastian placed his other hand on Shane's shoulder. Their eyes met. Shane had met his equal, he had risen to the challenge.

"Good to see you, Sebastian!"

His presence calmed Shane, the complete confidence, the feel of his hand. His warm smile. Shane felt embraced by the man.

"You have a moment?"

"Yes!" Shane led him into the main room. "When did you get into town?"

"I arrived yesterday. I should've told you."

"No worries."

They walked through the room, many of the employees recognized Sebastian. He greeted them with a hello here, a handshake there, a fist bump. Shane opened the door to a small conference room and stood to one side.

Sebastian said, "After you."

Shane walked in and Sebastian followed, closing the door.

The office had a window overlooking the street. Portland had sold its public transit, and a fleet of automated cars flooded the streets. People could ride for free, their personal data tuned the ads inside the vehicle, playing throughout the trip, riders had to pay to turn them off. Ads displayed on the exterior of the vehicle for businesses located a short distance in advance of the route. Traffic was especially colorful at night.

"Engineering meeting in the other room," Shane said, tacitly excusing their tight quarters. All four floors had been filled with desks to fit as many people as possible—many weren't on salary, they were earning flowcoins. Shane made special invitations to talent in Portland, he had room for them. People he met who were doing cool stuff on Commonwealth—at the protocol layer or on their platform—he wanted them around.

Sebastian said, "How's Rebecca?"

"Did you see her?" Shane asked.

"She stopped responding."

Shane raised his fist to his upper lip and looked at the table.

"I can get her a passport," Sebastian said.

Shane didn't understand, he lowered his hand and said, "She's gone."

Sebastian sat back.

"Death threats," Shane said. "It wasn't always explicit, it was implied that if she showed up certain places bad things would happen to her. She didn't leave her house for a month. People harassing her online—they terrified her."

Sebastian shook his head. "Terrible."

"I think she's gonna be okay."

The glass wall and the people on the other side. Shane felt observed, his every action at the office could have consequence. It inspired him. Everything mattered here. Not one thing would be wasted, everything would be transformed. He felt power radiating through it all and he could say the truth. This was real. He wanted to share it all with Sebastian. He said, "We're meeting our targets."

"I could get her a better passport," Sebastian said.

Shane absorbed this in silence and then he said, "This is the same country, only difference, the cops treat everyone like they're black. What Leroy said."

"Who's Leroy?"

"Her friend. He's black."

"This country is so third world."

"What's that?"

"History. Google it."

"I use G.O.D."

Sebastian laughed. "You talk to GOD?"

"Yeah, I got it on my phone."

Shane pulled his device from his pocket, handed it to Sebastian.

"GOD," Sebastian said, smiling. "Where's Rebecca?"

"Are you trying to find your contact, Rebecca Klein?"

"Yes."

"Her residence is private," the device said.

"Where does she work?"

"Her employer is Lagos Lab. She is there, now."

"Now?"

"Yes," the device said.

"It doesn't know that," Shane said, accepting the phone from Sebastian. "Any statement like that means the probability is very high. It's only the highest probable correct answer. GOD will say when it's unsure—state the percent chance of various possibilities. It's pretty fun. You should really download this thing."

Sebastian ran a hand through his hair. "So do you bank with Apple?"

"No," Shane said.

"The big money is all in finance," said Sebastian, leaning back in his chair. "And in financial technology, like what you're doing."

"We don't have billions to collateralize." Shane shook his head. "And our system doesn't support derivatives. We're not selling fake claims. We're not creating fake value."

"It's created. You made it."

"People organize themselves and create value for each other. Commonwealth is—"

"You're pushing hard—and YourJob is outspending you." Sebastian glanced at the gray sky out the window and then sat forward and looked at Shane. "Hiring more. Expanding faster. They have vastly more access to capital."

Shane blew his lips, breathed, and said, "YourJob doesn't recognize what it means to be human. People need more than money. The search for meaning and community. The need for purpose is human."

"I know about purpose," Sebastian said.

Shane nodded.

"People want upward mobility." Sebastian twirled his finger. "Makner is associated with improving *your place.* Starting with the citizen and working upward."

Shane said, "Greater social and economic equality?"

"In each category, there is no second place for global platforms. There will be winners and losers. The race is on, buddy—I know how to win."

Shane placed his elbows on the table and joined the fingers of his hands.

"Remember," Sebastian said. "People work hard in America, they can win. I believe that is our common"—he smiled—"wealth. It is a continuum. We're connected as a nation, as a people, through our shared belief in prosperity. Commonwealth needs to show people—what they can have, if they work hard. Inspire them. People want a dream. Trade on that. Celebrate the winners."

Shane looked past Sebastian, through the glass, remembering what he had to do. He glanced at Sebastian, at the people working in the office, and back to Sebastian. It was a comfortable silence, Shane heard him—and he wanted to reach him. His mentor. This was his chance to share something important, to become closer in the intimacy of shared passion. "I don't believe," Shane said, "any lifestyle that is only available to some will be sustainable. A lifestyle, a winners circle, say you have two billion people there. And there are six billion or so more and they all know what's inside your circle. They want it, and they are going to try to get inside. But our planet—this is our home—the earth can't provide the resources for everyone to live like that, and, if your circle is protected by law and enforced with superior technology, then people outside the circle don't have rights to resources. It encircled all the earth's resources, but not the people—not to mention rights for the other animals. . . . I'm not talking about the next three months. I have to clarify—this wealth being created on Commonwealth will be shared across *generations*. It is a vehicle to take humanity into the future."

Sebastian smiled.

"I have stock in SpaceX," he said.

His wonderful jaw, his beautiful teeth.

Shane spoke abruptly, smiling, excited by this sudden association: "Space is the absorption of surplus capital, that's all it is?"

Sebastian turned out his palms. "Humanity will need another planet."

"Investors might, but humanity needs a home. Our bodies, all of the microorganisms inside our bodies, the idea that you can separate people from their ecosystem and survive, that's so Western—isolated individuals. Our bodies exist within a complex environment—our internal environment, the natural foods that good bacteria need—are they going to do all that in outer space? I'd rather invest in making our society work."

"Time enough for everything," Sebastian said.

"Those guys are distracting," Shane said. "They identify a

problem with an engineering solution, one they can solve. Make themselves look like heroes."

"Explorers," Sebastian said. "Create a new world."

Shane drew back and put his hands on the table. "There are important problems to solve in our social structures, the design of currency, it's all created and it can be improved, that will create a new world."

"People are free to use their money however they want."

Shane laughed. "Making claims on extraterrestrial objects, or whatever they spun out of space, what is that going to do for us on earth?"

"Enormous value is created in that technology."

"We can trust each other and our institutions—when society creates greater equality. But we have to create that!"

"It's a competition. If your idea is best—"

"No, you know that's not true. Monopoly is actively sought. Competition isn't. Besides, the winners are encircled with guns. I don't want to live in fear."

"You must understand that your power to create anything of real significance would be gone if wealth was distributed fairly."

"People collaborate."

"Not everyone."

"A billion people," Shane said, "able to coordinate their desired society is very different than what a ruling class could come up with."

"Then the innovators wouldn't have the resources to do anything."

"How do you know?"

Sebastian shrugged. "Economics."

"The values you have to have to say that. To believe it."

"Hey, whatever works. Right?"

"The need to increase profits for shareholders is an artificial need. That isn't a human value. It's finance. The program to increase shareholder value isn't investing in the real economy of people and infrastructure. It creates fake value. And if you allow those values to determine your actions, you aren't human. You are a biological entity, okay, but you aren't human."

"My company is adaptive, it is about people. Going from entertainment to shelter, starting with the citizen and going beyond."

"Okay, for years now . . ." Shane pointed his finger in the air. "Beyond good. What is *beyond good*?"

Sebastian waved his hand. "This taps into the real human need to be a little better than everything else."

Shane flashed his eyes to the office. His company. "I see a new way to organize society emerging. The world just doesn't understand what Commonwealth can do, yet."

"You still have a mandate to make revenue," Sebastian said, "to outmaneuver your competition—and it is ruthless."

"Commonwealth will grow so big, there won't be any need for war anymore."

"What's that, did I hear your pussy fart? Many of the most important aspects of our technology were developed for war—for government contracts. The entire technological landscape was created by war. Wars are won by industry. Machines. Technology. This two-sided aspect of our tools, creation and destruction. It is when death is at our shoulder that we are beyond good."

Shane whistled. He shook his head. "The fellowship of man isn't won by drones."

"You're not being realistic. Don't be naive. You will be destroyed by your idealism. You wouldn't survive with that kind of trust in people. Your opponents will take advantage. You have to invest in security. We are always at war."

"I believe everyone has the right to defend themselves when threatened. Individuals. Ethnic groups. Nations." Shane avoided that trap. He wasn't going to leave Sebastian with the idea that he was a fool. "Although, if our society truly applied that logic, we would be concerned with the well-being of all. There is no security if people's need for water is threatened, or food. Because the first protection would be for all citizens to have that. Hungry people in this country. It's depressing! This system is pathetic."

"There are a lot of lazy people."

"I don't see that. I don't see lazy people—intimidated, oppressed even, but lazy is not the word I'd use. Right now there might be an evolutionary branch of the species, living among the eight and a half billion of us—odds are there are some expressions of latent potential in the human being, that will emerge in time. Think, it could be an advantage. People could become all clairvoyant in the future. We could become psychic. Non-local consciousness. The information moves—no matter how far away they are. I mean, that's—I know, I know, like, right, yeah, see?"

"That's cute. Actually, the advantage for any human being will be modern culture."

Shane thought. He stopped and thought of the phone. People would never develop the ability, because they had created it artificially.

"Access," Sebastian said. "It is a suit of finance."

"The fruit of the earth," Shane said, absently.

"No," Sebastian said. "An exoskeleton of culture."

Shane conceded. "Access to resources is an advantage. And culture. It is our common inheritance. Our networked humanity. All humanity changing through time, and the vessel remains. This living body of the earth."

Sebastian smiled. "Enlightenment won't be enough. The financial instruments that can protect and sustain a biological body is the only evolutionary advantage that counts—a smaller and smaller subset of people able to afford the cost."

"Gosh, dang! Sebastian, why?"

"You fashion yourself to be a rebel."

"Do I look like a rebel?"

"Looks can be deceiving, Shane. You can use your will. The necessary adaptation, you decide, protecting yourself and those who can help you, or some other people who you don't even know—or care about."

"Everything is interconnected. It's all related. It's about understanding the relationships. My idea of this relationship to the world determines how I act within it. Ultimately, everything is about relationships, I think, it's not that complicated, really, if you realize that this is a complex system."

Shane took a breath. He felt good. He was safe. He could speak his mind.

"Our tools can obviously be improved," Sebastian said. "But people, I'm not so sure about that."

Shane wanted to help him understand, he needed his help. Sebastian was his friend. "It is life on earth that Commonwealth depends on. I will defend it, and that includes everyone. We depend on everyone and everything. Farmers, truck drivers, grocery clerks. The people who handled the food you ate today. Those are important people. We're all interdependent—and that's explicit in the commons. We create and enforce our governance, refining our goals—the incentives and penalties always seeking a better, clearer, more just social contract. People enforce this agreement, through their own choices—and ethical action is rewarded. The law is a community of actors. Their behaviors arising in respect for themselves, for others, having empathy and compassion. And Commonwealth . . . is easy for people to use . . . it gets better with each version. It keeps getting better! With our actions defined by purpose and behavior learned through real experience. There is no end to this. There is no better world to arrive at but a better relationship with life. This reaches toward conscience as law, where the revealed evidence confirmed by objective awareness, the science, is used to create policy."

"You're going to need a bigger building."

XLVIII

HAVING HIRED employee five hundred, their company passed a milestone, and Shane no longer knew everyone at Commonwealth. He'd met them all, in passing and, by name, he could not recall—he met everyone with the same candor. Frank, honest, and he could be short, even too direct. He managed according to a protocol and disciplined himself to never extend personal favors with those reporting to him. Any request for promotions or raises, he referred to their scheduled review. Direct communication, face-to-face, staff meetings, morning announcements, end-of-week reviews. Shane was surrounded by people, he was always on. He saw less of the codebase, and stopped writing it.

He was talking with the head of operations about their second building when his assistant notified him—a hand sign; they had non-verbal cues, a few important messages that could be conveyed quickly without speech.

Shane took the call from Sebastian.

"You somewhere you can talk?" Sebastian asked.

Shane excused himself and jogged toward a series of sound-proofed booths along the wall, entered one, and slid the door closed. "At two today, we're doing a walk through with the realtor."

"Good," Sebastian said. "Good. I'm glad I caught you."

Shane leaned against the edge of a small table, facing out, gazing through the narrow window to a slice of the office.

"I want you to hear this from me. I'm with you on this. This is just a brief detour. Believe me. You are still at the front, they only want me to put my hand on the wheel."

"What is the problem?"

"I'm going to cover you—they know me. You know me. They trust I can do this. It's happening. They're pressing to oust you."

"Oust me?"

"Fire you."

"What's wrong with my performance?"

"Get your people ready, you need to make an announcement. Let's get ahead of this. If this leaks and rumors start, people are going to worry about their jobs. We can't afford to lose anyone."

"What is wrong?!"

"The board is afraid of being sued—for not being good trustees of their company."

"They don't trust me?"

"You're going too long—the future. They're sweating. The money invested—"

"We're on target, we're meeting every target!"

The line was silent a moment, and then Sebastian said, "It's the next one, buddy, next step. Big step. This big build out, staking their money on the company, but, no one is going to tell you this—I'm the one—I'm going to be the one to tell you the truth. They are losing their trust in you—as CEO—but don't worry, everyone loves you. This will be for the greater good. Trust me."

Shane opened the door and walked into the office. His employees unknowing. Confronted with what to tell them, holding the phone to his ear as he crossed the room, he heard Sebastian say, "This is a detour, I know. You've been on the highway, but we need to take the backroads."

She said it was legal and Shane felt like banging his head against a wall. Nora was still in New York, but she offered to fly in. He thanked her and said he would handle this. Oh, to hell with it all, how hard it had become. Sebastian came to the office on May fourth to make the announcement. Gathered in the large open office on the second floor, all of the employees filled the room.

Sebastian said, "Hello, everybody," and commanded attention. His face familiar. His status firm. People applauded and Shane saw this would go off with little controversy—that hurt. He imagined his turn at the mic, that his company would protest and rally behind him. He had become an effective speaker, and yet, he chose not to speak his mind, not to complain, nor mutiny. The threat wasn't to himself. He was concerned about the platform. The mission. Their company. The platform company was not beyond failure, he made every effort to hold it together. He channeled everything into the message that they were all working together.

They applauded as Shane took the mic. He thanked them and he thanked Sebastian. He did a brief preamble and said, "We've got some difficult days ahead. But it doesn't matter now, because we have Sebastian with us now. And I don't mind. Like anybody, I'd like to enjoy a long tenure at this company—longevity has its place. But I'm not concerned about being CEO. I just want Commonwealth to live. And Sebastian has shown the world he can transform a company, and with Commonwealth, we will transform civilization. I may not be the one to lead you. But I want you to know today, that we, as a people, will make a better future. So I'm happy, today. I'm not worried about anything. Sebastian, welcome—to Commonwealth!"

Shane spoke with confidence, and he was a good actor. People believed him, they trusted him. Sebastian joined him at the front, they were together—but Shane had to respect the protocol. He could no longer issue commands.

Shane had no authority in the office. He had his desk, his computer, and he was asked to refrain from speaking with the press about the company. He didn't use Commonwealth to voice his opinions or comment on the direction Sebastian was taking them. Being in character, all day, in the office, exhausted him emotionally, and after the Fourth of July, he stopped coming in every day.

By the end of summer, even once a week was too much.

It was late September and he was sitting against the pillows in bed, in Monty's old room at the Tech Plex, when he said "Commonwealth" to his device. He couldn't help himself. His body did it, his mouth said the name, a word, a routine. He had only to be himself, and he said it. He studied the screen. He had no— It killed him. He wanted to die. The home page was beyond recognition. It had a triptych of a yacht, a rocket, and a sports car. That was the first thing people saw, that was top of the list. He couldn't believe it. He texted Jason: did you see the homepage?

Ten minutes later, Jason replied: create a new block explorer

Shane had considered this, a new platform to explore the database managed by the Commonwealth Foundation. But it could divide the community, it could be bad for the Foundation. Anyway, it didn't matter, a new block explorer would require winning everyone's attention, again—he could come up with a new name for a platform and implement his code; the code was not the main challenge, it was creating a community. Commonwealth had the positive network effects, they had been extraordinary. And Sebastian was leading them now. Commonwealth had become a player in the relocation industry, offering citizenship and residence planning as part of wealth management and preservation strategies, in addition to providing rapid extraction from disaster zones.

Journalists spun the press releases for new features. These services were noted by pundits following the platform companies, and many people blamed Shane for the transfer of power. He had sold out.

No one had heard from him because he sold out his principles. Commonwealth now offered tax avoidance or planning. Legal loopholes used by wealthy people and powerful corporations were now available to anyone. The wealth itself wasn't in the tax haven, only the legal structure that owns the wealth. Real estate developers, buyers, and sellers had long availed themselves of financial secrecy—now, anyone could use anonymous companies for transfers to offshore entities. More than half of the world's wealth was controlled offshore. A system that exacerbated inequality. A country's reputation as a tax haven made it difficult for clients to send money there, but the Commonwealth ledger had distributed nodes, in various locations, in twenty different countries, and it was a secure vehicle for anyone to manage their money. Sebastian said he was removing red tape to smooth the flow of capital. He then set up another feature to broker offshore credit cards and second passports, most clients wanted Singapore, and many high net worth individuals wanted more countries as backup locales.

Shane called Rebecca and she told him, "As bad as it is, it can always get worse."

He said, "It's terrible."

"I know," she said.

He didn't want to believe in collapse. He believed we were better off now than at any time in the past. Look back in time, and you'd see it sucked a whole lot worse. It was always going to be better in the future. He repressed rational concern. The Earth was inside eternity! Life was eternal. No matter what they did, humans could not destroy the living earth.

On Facebook, a friend had requested suggestions for books and Shane linked to a library webpage for a book called *How to Change Your Mind.* After his friend replied, Shane read through the comments and didn't see his own comment. He thought maybe his friend had deleted it and Shane messaged him, but he said he didn't delete it. Of course a social media platform could remove anything from its site, he understood this. He decided to use another platform to express himself. He tweeted: how do you tell the truth?

Shane wanted to use Commonwealth, but he stopped himself. Whatever its promise, no matter what he wanted it to be, the internet was accessed through private companies. It was privatized space, centralized control. The internet had seemed public, but all the avatars were carefully shaped. They would conform to the market to survive.

Then Shane began to speak publicly on behalf of the Commonwealth Foundation, and he advised developers working with the source code. He said human society was systems, structures. They could change the design, the contract, the law—that was a code. A story that people are telling themselves, it is written in a code, but it is a story they are telling themselves about who they are and what it means to be alive. What it is to be human. It's not people that are the problem, but how institutions organize and drive human behavior. Shane said that people only had to design their institutions for social and economic equality.

But repressed anger began to affect his behavior. Shane discharged his emotions upon the weather, waiting in line, traffic. He was angry with what he couldn't change. He got pissed about little things too. Dating totally sucked. He had money, plenty of money, he had no reason to worry—but if someone at a restaurant said to him, You're the Commonwealth guy. He was pissed. And he stuffed it, he smiled, and said, You making flow? And he answered this way so many times that one day he said, "I don't remember his name. A French guy. The guy who invented the internet. John something. You should look him up."

It had been almost a year since he'd stopped going into the office. Shane was in his room at the Tech Plex, and he looked at his photo on the passport. Singapore. A gift from Sebastian.

He heard his phone chime and leaned forward. Jason texted him the URL for a new site that had been building on their code. It was every.where and Shane entered it into his browser. A block explorer displayed an improved version of the old Commonwealth platform. The global platform for community and work. Everywhere for peace and prosperity.

He put the passport in his desk drawer.

"Go to sleep," he said.

The computer asked if he was sure and he said yes. Blinds on the windows blocked the sunlight from his screen. Opening them, he gazed over the rooftops and the trees into the distance, the city, the sun, the warmth of summer, he wanted to go. Shane slipped on his shoes and put his phone in his pocket, reached for the door handle, the metal knob, turning, he looked back and said to the computer: "Find everywhere."

The screen blinked on. "I'm sorry."

"Find the site, every dot where."

From the screen across the room, he saw the landing page. It wasn't his work but it was, it was the promise of belonging. He had to look again, he stepped up and studied the page. He thought of their communications infrastructure. That needed everyone to give it substance, but they were real. He said, "Shut down, computer."

"Are you sure?"

"Yes."

Down the hall Shane exchanged greetings with another resident. Walking through the commons area on the first floor he recognized everyone. He was part of this community, this was home. Taking his bike from the rack, he rolled it through the doors and got on. The path from their building opened on a side street. The sunlight on a white wall, the front door. He had seen the house so often that he hardly noticed it but the light. His body absorbed the color and the air, the sound and shape of the world before him. Everything traveling through the fiber of his senses. The light in the dark interior of his being. He was not separate from it. The world that everyone agreed was real. He was connected. Each person, everywhere on earth. They had it. The awareness of it inside them all. Shane was sure.

He rode to the intersection and turned left toward downtown. On Foster he passed a couple riding side by side, hearing their words in the air. Passing a storefront window, through the glass he saw someone eating at the counter, the aisles of the little deli shelved with food. The sound of laughter, a girl emerging from the recessed doorway, her friend running out around her, taking her hand and pulling forward and letting go. Everyone on the sidewalk, he passed looking to see if he recognized someone. The trillion synapses firing with the rapport of sight and the seen. The brilliance of everyone apparent. Each of them could see the light inside. Everyone was worthy, they shared the same earth, they were one and all the awareness of life.

AUTHOR'S NOTE

Thanks for reading this book! I'd like to hear your thoughts about the story and how you see any of these ideas developing in the world. Please contact me online. And I'm interested in participating in a book club or school visit, a talk at a company, tabling an event, doing a panel discussion, a presentation, conferences, however you think this story can find its audience. I'd love to collaborate with people and organizations doing progressive work. The story came to life through friendship, and ideally the book can be a way to participate now in a larger community and continue learning. Creating a book and the work of publishing is all to participate in a larger cultural conversation. This book depends on word of mouth, and so, if you think it's worth their time, please mention it to a friend, post on your social media or a blog, write a review on Amazon or Goodreads. Even a sentence or two makes a big difference. With your words of support, *You Will Win The Future* will have a much better chance of being considered by a reader taking a chance on a new book.

                                        Kindly yours,
                                        Arthur Smid

ACKNOWLEDGMENTS

My mom—this book wouldn't exist without the room she rents to me; she has made it possible to afford living in Portland while writing. Thank you, Mom! It began as a description of Cityzen written in first person from the perspective of an anonymous employee. I sent it to a few friends and Andy Hoffman [andyhoffman.codes] responded, saying we have to talk, and this led to us talking for hours, over many months, developing the characters and story that became this novel. He wrote some scenes too and gave me freedom to integrate them into the prose. Andy and I talked while recording, and his voice is woven through the book. At a point where the writing became slow, just telling the story aloud with Andy and the scenes became more clear and enjoyable to write. I'm grateful for your friendship! Eric Murray met with me to read new pages every week for a year and, reading aloud and talking about what could be better, his insight and generosity of spirit improved the text. I began thinking about Commonwealth around the time I met Derrick Hau and our conversations helped me to imagine the protagonist software; and so, many thanks to Sebastian Bolaños for bringing together people to talk and learn about cryptographically secure, shared databases. And thank you Carl Abbott, Howard Silverman, Arwen Spicer, Vi Rose La Bianca, Melanie Falconer, Milo Douglas, Bryon Minus, Sophia Wood, Tom Wikle, Daniel Adler, Johnette Orpinela, Shannon Bowman-Sarkisian, Paul Pham, Olle Fjordgren, Lina Ingemarsdotter, Maria Crum, and Timothy Perisho Eccleston. Shannon Page, you are a fine editor, thanks for your red pen and proofreading power. To my friends, thank you—and if I failed to mention you, it is not to dismiss your contribution. Each and all of you have helped me to become a better person. Dad, my sisters and stepmoms, all my extended family and your children, as we go into the unknowable future, I love you!

RESOURCES

After the financial crisis in Iceland, a comedian ran for mayor of Reykjavík. Government had lost the trust of the people and in a city of around 123,000 a popular television personality, a comedian, had people's attention. Jón Gnarr proposed absurd policy like putting a polar bear in the petting zoo, and then he landed on a website called Better Reykjavík. Open to all parties to crowdsource ideas from their constituents, the site had been created by online gaming industry veteran Róbert Bjarnason and friends. Gnarr told everyone to go to the site and write what they want to see happen. And they elected Jón Gnarr; and following negotiation, the city integrated the website officially. In its first seven years Better Reykjavík saw more than seven hundred citizen proposals approved by the city council. The nonprofit Citizens Foundation supports the open source software, available online at citizens.is.

This decision-making platform engages people because their contributions can have an impact—and even when a proposal is unworkable they receive feedback. Reykjavík had a confluence of crisis and creative alternatives. And now the software is free for any city, school, or group to create a platform for soliciting proposals and allowing participants to comment for or against. The comments are separated into columns of pro and con. People have to write a coherent statement that exists independent of another comment—this prevents responding to ideas with a personal attack. The statements are then voted up or down, and so participants themselves curate the comments. Citizens Foundation has learned how simple design results in more participation—and allowing people to upload photos (this is key for marketing, social media and sharing links back to the decision-making platform). And as with any product or service attempting to gain attention online, for the platform to reach people, a communications budget and marketing are necessary.

That's the much condensed version of a story better told by Bjarnason, numerous journalists, and in Gnarr's book. The work accomplished in Iceland has set a precedent for the evolution of democracy online. When publicly-financed software is open source, people can use and share their infrastructure, upgrade it, repair it, and remodel it to fit their needs. And cyber defenders can find and close security holes. Most administrations procure proprietary software where money goes into licenses that last a limited time and have restricted access. Open source software, decentralization, and publicly-operated servers are key for trust. Trust in our institutions can be strengthened through participation. But of all the people building Facebook, who imagined it would become an attack surface for foreign governments? The ability to foresee problems and build solutions into the application can happen more readily with software that is decentralized and open to continual improvement.

When the anti-austerity movement in Spain held prolonged protests in the public squares of Madrid, the city suffered a crisis of trust and formed a department dedicated to citizen participation, transparency and open government. Róbert Bjarnason consulted with their team and the city established an online platform called Decide Madrid—built using Consul, an open source project free and available at consulproject.org. Developers in Barcelona also used the Consul software and then decided to code their own—another open source platform that anyone can build upon, decidim.org.

The Civic Tech Field Guide is one online resource for you to find more tools and organizations and to add your own. With digital tools and a feeling that democracy and the internet are one and the same, the Sunflower

Movement in Taiwan created virtual Taiwan, or vTaiwan. Again a crisis of trust, offline protests, and online connections. This time they introduced their ideas by creating the government website they wanted, improving on the existing one and replacing the o with a zero in the .gov domain. The government later approved the vTaiwan process for constructive conversation and consensus building, and a crowdsourced bill successfully passed through parliament.

People have created organizations around the world to support technology for the public good. A few notable groups working in English are MySociety in the United Kingdom, Civic Hall and GovLab in New York City. Code for America has headquarters in San Francisco and local chapters throughout the states. And a project out of Australia called MiVote has a blockchain voting application that split into its own company, Horizon State, to support the work. All these efforts and local governments in Iceland, Spain, and Taiwan show what's possible; and maybe you found people in your area working on community technology. Democracy is way more interesting than voting every other year. People acting on their ideas, building these spaces online, and making them accessible to their communities, have found ways to contribute. By acknowledging the real risks involved and nurturing each other, we will make progress together.

Stephanie Kelton and Warren Mosler and Rohan Grey and others researching and writing about fiat currency and what it allows the issuer to do, you've probably heard of this, it's often referred to as Modern Monetary Theory, or Modern Money Theory, or MMT. If I was to write another novel, it'd be a rewrite of *The Wizard of Oz* for our era of fiat currency—the yellow brick road, back when that book came out, as you know, the US was on the gold standard. I'd set it in our time, from the third person perspective of a teenage girl and she'd be a normal, unknown, intelligent young woman, and some portal, a global warming induced weather portal takes her to a fantastic land of delight (I don't think her phone works in this world and so she's dealing with people) and danger that leads inexorably to the wizard, the wizard has the power to control spending, to issue currency (so kinda represents the parents too, in a way, allowing the book to pass muster as a young adult book), to spend money directly into the economy. When the heroine returns from the portal, the world is our consensual reality. It couldn't be a "There's no place like home" ending, the environment has been totally deformed by climate change. The end would be the precursor to action.

Naturally, the book ends at the beginning of her journey to adulthood and an open appraisal of the real world. It's a stretch to do monetary theory in a young adult book, but it's not impossible to imagine a story in which a girl is transported by severe weather to another world, maybe into a climate refugee migration of some sort, she's been traumatized, and it's all seen through the perspective of her imagination, you know, flying monkeys! Witches, and the rest. And a book reaching actual teens, it must be traditionally published and so if I can't get this through the narrow gate in New York City, this novel idea might be a proposal for other artists to take up. Thank you for giving this a thought!

AFTERWORD

Can the next book write itself? With the training data of previous texts, the rules of grammar, story structure, and instructions to a machine. Timothy Perisho Eccleston wrote a Markov chain text generator and trained it on this book. For your enjoyment. The generated text. Here's a sample:

Portland did look pretty good, what people in your laptop. Leave your computer and devices as they fatigued more and Shane let go of his legs immediately in the common area. The Portland branch. "We have support." "But that shit?" "They can lobby the shit out of Congress, buy politicians coming and you're so spry." "This isn't right. You have a VR onesie!" He looked up, he needed to host an entire script.

And he'd made it difficult for clients to send money there, a document that could front their reputation competed for the bathroom. His manners were refined, and he worked late, and he said, "My wife and walked to the table. Cab had an interesting idea for us." Sebastian stepped forward. Jason was a food distribution company. More police stood outside the station. He illuminated the white paper. To complete the project. Teammates regrouped in the boat and saw Rebecca raising her desk. "Yeah, what's going on?" "You're putting money into people and creating everything." It was cheaper than having to sort out fact from falsehood and had contracted a local paper. "You need practice."

Hard work, how nature works. Maybe using eminent domain. The land is owned by a for-profit company, and seeing the Ogden Valley, feeling the optimism that arises of good healthcare, and retirement had fallen in love with. His fear conquered in the country—and for themselves, for their country all settled in the moment and sat in the lounge. "I'm sorry." "Find everywhere." They walked through the room, many thanks to Sebastian. "GOD," Elsie said. Shane nodded. Monty had kept Shane in the game. "You can't change. Sebastian had joined a gathering of business models. They had to create a favorable investment climate, and investment has shrunk. More than thirty trillion in cash is held in the account